T0067937

JAZMIN G. WILLIAMS

authorHOUSE®

AuthorHouse™
1663 Liberty Drive
Bloomington, IN 47403
www.authorhouse.com
Phone: 1 (800) 839-8640

© 2019 Jazmin G. Williams. All rights reserved.

No part of this book may be reproduced, stored in a retrieval system, or transmitted by any means without the written permission of the author.

Published by AuthorHouse 08/31/2019

ISBN: 978-1-7283-2438-8 (sc)
ISBN: 978-1-7283-2437-1 (e)

Library of Congress Control Number: 2019912475

Print information available on the last page.

Any people depicted in stock imagery provided by Getty Images are models, and such images are being used for illustrative purposes only.
Certain stock imagery © Getty Images.

This book is printed on acid-free paper.

Because of the dynamic nature of the Internet, any web addresses or links contained in this book may have changed since publication and may no longer be valid. The views expressed in this work are solely those of the author and do not necessarily reflect the views of the publisher, and the publisher hereby disclaims any responsibility for them.

Setareh is the eldest daughter of the fortune-telling Aisling family, she is the most powerful seer and the heiress of her family. She knows her death will grant her family peace in the Aeoman forest, a life without worry or fear of discovery. But her father refuses to believe that his child must die so the family could thrive. He uses their family power to search for a world where his daughter lives and discovers that she must leave their ancient home and arrive in the safe-haven of the ancients: a city buried in the monstrous Aeoman Forest. With his choice made, he calls upon the dragons of the forest and makes the deal that if they can save his eldest then the entire family will enter Aeoman Forest.

Contents

Chapter I

" I n the nation of Aeoman there are five great countries: Dubol the Isle
of gems, Gaiavani the philosopher kingdom, Trégaron of Summer
Paradise, Marble of Great Healing, and Ashadas the eastern markets. While
these five nations often bickered they also were great comrades and often aided
each other in times of need. They were each separated by one great Mountain
range; the Baīlāy Mountain range. Gaiavani and Trégaron sat on the west
side, Dubol and Ashadas sat to the east, and Marble sat on the furthest south
of the content. Throughout the centuries the five nations were on peaceful
times with few wars to speak about, the great Baīlāy Mountain Range was
the primary reason behind the lack of wars on the nation. It starts from
beyond Dubol's bright forests and past Gehill's north-most city to down into
Malbril at its furthest southern point. For many centuries the mountain range
remained strong and tolerant to the abuse of curious humans, it remained
towering on the mainland as if time was not and humans were dust. Then
one day in the summer, amongst the celebration of a new year a great comet
came barring down onto the nation. It tore through Aeoman nation, lifting
the entire earthen plate as it crashed. The earthen plate however could not

withstand such force and broke, a northern section crashed down into the ocean once more but was now cut off from its kinsmen."

"That is how Dubol was born," he looked up at his students, the two boys were of course glaring at each other, as they often where when one or the other spoke. "Behruz, Servass," both boys flinched and settled their eyes back down, hoping they wouldn't be called out on their misbehavior. He wouldn't give them that luxury, not today. "Pay attention, you will be tested on this." The girl, sitting between the boys, fisted both hands and punch both boys in their upper arms; elected sharp hisses of pain. He rolled his eyes and went back to the book, at least one of them was willing to learn from him.

"The great Baīlāy Mountain Range that withstood the test of time and human destruction caved upon impact. The comet had splintered the Mountain Range into two, left behind a trail of poison and ash. Ashadas of eastern plains was once well known for their markets and colorful forest but quickly disappeared as the comet's poison leaked into their soil and their nation crumbled into ashes. Dubol had been well known for their beautiful rainforest, colorful animals and otherworldly silks; now they resemble a barren landscape of sand and stone, no life nor beauty left behind. Gaiavani excelled in medical and scientific achievements was now split into two; the comet did the most damage to them. The rolling land scape of endless planes and shallow valleys was gone, the northern sector was plunged into the sea, while its western brother was forced to shutter and ripple. Trégaron also suffered a great deal, their beautiful resorts and sceneries disappeared to the ocean's cold embrace. Nothing but shallow land and cold soil was left behind, the land known as a summer-paradise disappeared in the blink of an eye. The southern mountains, once peaceful and beautiful, a place of retreat and gentle healing, became chaotic and unstable. Great sections of earth gave way and caved into the ocean, leaving behind only strong pillars of support and few survivors.

The sun did not shine on Aeoman again for many more centuries, too many generations of survivors lived and died without ever seeing the sun or stars. *The comet was a catastrophe, it brought poison and death to the land of Aeoman. Before long the few survivors began crawling out from their safe-heavens, finding other places to hide from the elements and gathering editable provisions. As the years past the balance between the nations crumbled further and further, until eventually even the names of the countries were lost to the majority of the populations.*

One day the earth shook and rumbled, a section near the meteorite's landing place caved in on itself; disappearing into the surface of the earth were no light could reach. When this section caved in on itself, the skies cleared and the sun began shinning the following day. The air was still horrible for many months after, the survivors still wore their masks but eight months later the masks were no longer a necessity for most of the survivors. About that time rumors began spreading, each similar and yet different but the content very nearly the same. The rumor was that a god had appeared in the land and he took all the ugly creatures in the world, put them before the landing-sight of the meteorite and crushed them into the earth. The twelve-mile long and seven mile-wide pit was the imprint of a good's foot crushing all the undesirables of Aeoman contentment and with the elimination of the ugly creatures the sun blessed Aeoman's land once more. Of course, most brushed this rumor off as just that; a rumor. No one though could deny that the disappearance of monsters and clarity of the air was somehow connected.

Time passed but the healing of the people was slow. Those with access to literature quickly created systems in their respective countries and reformed a kind of government. With a reform in action, more lives were spared and more lives spared meant more lives birthed, more lives birthed meant a need for more food sources. As the populations grew, so did their hunting tactics and when they thought peace was achievable at long last; war broke out. The land of Gaiavani became separated, divided between the northern plains of Gehill and the rumbled wastes of Gaiglen. The summer paradise of the southern lands were filled with insects and a trading in plant seeds quickly grew into a currency. Before long the seeds took root and plants began to grow, with a new food source the southern valleys sored in population. So many farmers took place that their reformed governance began scouting those who could wiled spells that manipulated plant life. Along this search for those with a natural talent in Nature-manipulation, the scouts came across a village covered in snow, just beyond their southernmost waterfall. In that village they discovered a partially destroyed map and story about a time before the meteorite. They took the partially destroyed map back with them and presented it to the few scholars their farming country had. They named their country based on the remains of the old map; Trégaron. With this information, the new country of Trégaron and the survivors of Marble were the first to become allies.

Eventually as the nation's grew and territory became necessary for their higher populace, the countries once more fell into war. The countries Gehill and Gaiglen seemed the most venomous as their battles together seemed to never end. Trégaron was able to remain out of their wars for many years, training their own soldiers for a someday battle that would no doubt be turned on them. A survivor from one scuffle between the two northern countries had arrived in Trégaron, washed up on a shore with heavy injuries and infection threatening to steal his life. The man claimed to be a survivor of a slave-trade in Gaiglen, where the hunt for those with exceptional earthen-spells were recruited into the military."

He glanced up from his book, making sure his three students were listening well. Behruz Eld, a plane looking boy with warm cinnamon skin, wild unkept oil black hair and freakishly large ghostly blue eyes; his eyes were his most exotic feature as everything else about his physical appearance was plane-jane. He wore his family tunic with the family crest of a white and blue tear-drops, ripple and reflection on his back. He was slumped in his seat, balancing his wooden pencil with his lip and looking longingly out the window, his face was an epic description of utter boredom.

"It was from him that Trégaron discovered something unusably amongst their people. The stranger claimed that those with strange marks on their

bodies were those descended of 'star-children' a race people with powerful spells and unique powers. Hoping to create an army that would protect their farmers from Gaiglen and Gehill's greed, the officials of Trégaron sent out scouts to relocate said individuals to a safer location. Within ten years they had many of the marked-descendants located to a safer location further south and close to their mountain-allies. They built a city and named it 'Emlyn', this was the place where those with special powers were to reside; none realized the trap until it was too late. just as the first generation of 'Emlyns' were too old to do anything more then watch the little ones, the country declared a state of emergency; they needed everyone with special skills to train for war.

He glanced up again to look at the next one. Aylin Aiello remained seated with her back straight, her eyes glued to her note-book, her pencil where it should be as she quickly jotted down simple notes almost as fast as he read form the book. She had skin the color of hazelnut coffee, her eyes were a perfect display of amethyst in sunlight with a single stripe of gold in each iris. Her hair was a deep midnight purple and about as tamable as a raging storm, the level of spells that girl used to keep her hair in place was astonishing. The level of focus she needed was nearly terrifying, he knew any time her focus was broken, half her hair would puff up in a wild display of silk strands in water. It also told him when it was his turn to handle the boys; they always made her lose concentration.

"Four families stood out amongst all the others during the training for war: Angerma, Triamya, Flametree, and Asterose." Servass of Asharan, his last student picked up where he left off. Servass had hair like the deep blue sky at dusk, when the night was battling with the sun for dominance. His hair was as curly as Aylin's but lacked any of her frizz, he kept it unreasonably short for someone who constantly reminded everyone else that their hair looked like shit. His eyes were the same blue as a cloudless summer sky reflecting back in a still lake surface, a thousand layers of pale blues over lapping; the level of intelligence that

leaked through his eyes often frightened off anyone who dared to look into his eyes. All the same, Servass was by far the palest of them all. His skin color was closest to snow or a freshly polished star-pearl. "*There were other families with special powers unique to themselves but these four families were the best at manipulating plant life.*" His voice however could send shivers down anyone's spine, even when he was just reading from a book his voice still sounded with the tone of a reaper reading down his list of souls to collect.

"*Angerma had the power of invulnerability, no matter how hard they were hit, no matter what tool was used, they only grew stronger and stronger. Triamya can heighten their own physical senses, be it smell, sight, touch, taste, or the strength of their muscles. Flametree can make their body extend, twist or bend in any number of ways, every joint they own is double-sided so that no matter the position they can always win the fight. Asterose, mysterious and serine, they keep their secrets closely held to their hearts. One thing is known though: if an Asterose desires something, then without doubt they will retrieve it.*"

"Isha!" Behruz had enough, his pencil collided with his empty notebook, his round face scrunched up with childish disgust. "Do we really have to go through this again?!" Aylin's hand froze, her right brow twitched twice, her fingers trembled over the paper. He sighed as Servass slid his ocean-blue eyes towards Behruz while Aylin concentrated on writing something down.

"Behruz, please, at least try," He sighed as he ran a hand through his jade hair, removing a few tangles and resetting it back into its proper place again. "Your history is important, so is knowing the other ancients and their powers. If you see a similar power on the battlefield you could name them accurately."

"But all I need to know is how to beat them!" Behruz retorted hotly, "Come on Isha! You've been going over our academy basics for weeks now!"

"Because the basics are important," everyone turned to the new speaker in surprise. A middle aged man leaned against the entrance to the shack. His bore hair like navy waves, exhausted midnight eyes set deep into an equally tiered face. He wore thick leathers rimmed in gray wolf-fur, a simple brown tunic with more gray-fur, a pair of boots reached halfway to his knees and kept in place with silver buckles. Across his forehead was a thick leather braid that bore seven simple white-pearls interspaced in the center of the braid. He was one of the few elders of Asharan Village, a village of soldiers, that sat deep in the cold mountain tops of Baīlāy.

"Kaltrina-Rū!" Servass called as he jumped to his feet, eyes wide as a smile twitched on his lips. "Why are you here? Is it time for the village meeting?"

"Yes and no," Kaltrina answered, he turned his dark wolf-eyes towards the teacher, his smirking face slipped clear of emotion. "We have a battalion in village center—."

"What?" he leaped to his feet, pressing one hand to the desk as the other snatched his left top drawer open. A golden serpent darted out, clambering up his arm till it curled around his neck, thick and bulky its weight was earned with every golden scale it bore. Elegant the reptile was not, thick and meaty with sharp spikes and intelligent scarlet eyes that glared threatening at Kaltrina. The golden-scaled reptile hissed at Kaltrina as if he took a step too close to its nest, which considering the three children in the room he might as well have.

"Why are they here? What nation is—"

"They're wounded dragons," Kaltrina interrupted quickly. The teacher seemed to relax but his golden eyes shown with worry at he glanced quickly at his students then looked again at Kaltrina. "They barely managed to retreat here in time. Their three Toarr and seven Arryders can't continue the mission."

What's Toe-are and Are-deers?" Behruz asked dumbly

7

"Do you listen when I'm talking?" he asked, staring at his student disbelievingly.

"Are you that stupid?" Servass asked, squinting at his teammate

"So many dragons on one mission?" Aylin whispered, her face pinching into a concerned frown.

"That's our ranking system idiot," Servass drawled.

"Shut up know-it-all!"

"From youngest to oldest its: Miles, Arryder, Toarr, Koalvar, Karys, and then our Nanaibek."

"Shut up I knew that!"

"but…" Aylin continued, ignoring her teammates, "we never send so many out…"

"Then the mission must've been really important for them to come here!" Behruz gushed excitedly, "Well?! Did they come here to recut us?! Or well, I mean clearly they're here for Isha and I. There's no way they'd be here for *you* water-boy."

"Are you serious right now?" Aylin asked, looking up at him with a blank face.

"I mean I'm sure they considered you, Aylin, but let's face it in the terms of raw strength you just don't measure up-uff!" without warning Aylin spun on the balls of her feet, rose from her seat and sucker punched her teammate in the gut, a slight glow circled along her knuckles and elbow. The added boost of magic to her attack sent said boy careening out the nearest wall and crashing into the tree a dozen plus paces from the building.

"Sorry, who doesn't have raw strength again?" Servass asked sarcastically, "I didn't hear you the first time."

"Enough of your stupidity," Aylin ordered as she straightened and put her hands on her hips. "Kaltrina-Rū, they're here for Isha, aren't they?"

"Correct," Kaltrina answered, looking at their teacher. "They need your help Alexis Göbelázár-Rū."

"They called for me by name?" Alexis asked, frowning as he moved towards Kaltrina. "no nicknames or insults?"

"The female did," Kaltrina replied with a careless shrug. "Even mentioned something about 'Dia-puār." Kaltrina was not a small man, all the same he was forced to jump out of the shack-entrance when Alex burst into a sprint. Kaltrina watched the man race towards the village, a golden-glow over taking his meaty legs. It wasn't long before the three children were giving chase, each aided in the mad-rush with the elegant glow of white-crystals and glowing dust. "So reckless," he sighed as he followed the team down the steps of the hill and into the village, it wasn't a long walk to the center of the village. When he arrived the village's three doctors and Aylin were all standing in a circle around the injured dragons, their palms all facing each other where a bolt of white lightning connected each of them. Their voices were whispering, words to soft and foreign for anyone to make out, and their eyes were glowing a bright pristine white. In the circle were ten individuals, each suffering from lethal injuries. Alexis was nearby, propping up a young mage no older than twelve or thirteen, his armor was heavily damaged and he was still crying.

"Please, you have to talk clearly," Alexis was patting the boy's shoulder, clearly at a loss with the crying child. "I don't understand what you're saying, you're stuttering too much." Without warning Servass stooped to the boy's level, grabbed his shoulder, pulled him back and left a giant red handprint of the teenager's face. Kaltrina cringed with the echo of the slap, knowing that it must've hurt the stone-faced boy more than it did the teenager.

"How dare you!" the teenager blubbered out, fat tears still rolling down his dark cheeks.

"Since when did the honorable Caelestis cry like newborn babes?" Servass questioned. Kaltrina sighed with the blunt question, admittedly he hadn't noticed that the crying boy was a part of one of the big families of Azurlyn. From this distance he could only see the boy's warm rosewood skin, his dragon-helmet was covering the top half of his head and the morning mist prevented any other family-markings to be seen.

"Caelestis-Rū, I need you to calm down and explain your mission to me," Alexis patted the boy's shoulder and smiled gently at him.

"We… Nanaibek-Rū asked us to form a team, we-we were to protect Souma Village just on the other side of the mountains." The boy whipped at his cheeks with his arms, cringing when one of the scales flexed and scraped his chin. "uh-um… Big sister brought me along, she said it would be beneficial to have a teleporter on this kind of mission. I'm not physically strong or very experienced but… I'm the best at the teleportation spells, even compared to my elders. My family head agreed to releasing me on such an important mission and my teacher said it would be good experience for me too. So Nanaibek-Rū allowed me to go on this mission."

"What were the mission details?" Behruz asked, his eyes were still clued on his female classmate. He wasn't standing too far away from the purple haired girl, his body posture was relaxed but the serious look in his eyes and the lack of a smile on his face said he was ready to catch her should she feint.

"Um we were to protect Souma Village and if not possible, we were to retreat all residents into our forest." Caelestis explained as he half-coughed and half-gasped in his attempt to stifle the urge to cry as he had been upon arrival to the soldier village. "However… before they got to the village they were caught in a pincher-attack."

"A pincher-formation? Between who?" Alexis asked seriously, his face morphing into a strange frown.

"Trégaron and Gaiglen," the boy answered. "Big sister had previously sent me and Albena-Rū's team to head towards Flintlyn City on our Trégaron-Mountain Boarder to secure a secondary escape route but... halfway there I sensed something wrong." The boy pulled up a scale on his left wrist, revealing a broken looking golden four-leaf clover. "When I saw this I knew Elder sister was in danger...so I teleported to her location. I arrived just in time to shield her from a three-way scorpion attack. But... she was already heavily injured." He tucked his scale back down, hiding the golden four-leaf clover perfectly and cradling that wrist close to his heart. "She gave me instructions to teleport all of us to this location for back up but... I can only teleport those who are living."

There are only ten people here, Kaltrina thought, looking back at the medics in their healing circle. By now the dragons had been separated from their charges and were floating just over their individual mages. Out of everyone in the healing circle, he could only see one female amongst them and even after so much time in the healing circle she still did not look good. Her short marron-red locks were smoldering still and the red stripes spanning from her brows to down her cheeks could either by a still bleeding wound or tattooed family-marks. Regardless, her pale skin seemed translucent in the healing circle; paler then any human should ever be.

"How many were actually in your team?" Kaltrina asked seriously, he knew his Nanaibek would never send so many people out for one mission; not for something as simple as protecting a village.

"Each of the four Karys have one Koalvar, one Toarr and three Arryder," Caelestis answered. "As the lowest ranking on the team, I was a part of the last team as a last-minute addition. I was meant to keep record of every step in the journey and provide emergency retreat if need-be."

"So there were a total of forty-four dragons on this mission," Alexis murmured. "We've never sent out so many dragons for a mission like this."

"Albena-Rū's team should be in Flintlyn City by now," Caelestis continued. "I still haven't felt anything different in their auras yet so they must be safe."

"What do you mean?" Kaltrina asked, frowning at the boy.

"All Caelestis can detect those who are in their same team," the boy answered. "each of my team members have given me one of their scales for that purpose but... again I can only detect the aura of those living."

"Who were you to protect?" Servass demanded the answer, his lips tugging slightly down as his eyes pinched into a squint towards the young Caelestis-boy.

"The Kūnnene Family," Caelestis answered.

"Koon-nai-ne?" Behruz questioned

"Koon-New-ney," Alexis sighed, his shoulders slumping. "We need to work on your pronunciation."

"not again!" the boy whined loudly

"Why would you need to protect them?" Servass asked, his frown deepening. "They are the children of mother-earth, they don't need our aid."

"Who *are* the Kūnnene?" Behruz asked

"They're a family in Trégaron, one of the ancient survivors from before the meteorite," Servass answered blandly. "They're incredibly powerful but also seriously underrated. No one takes them seriously because they're by far too gentle in nature."

"They're gentle alright," Kaltrina scoffed, "Right up till you hurt someone they love. Then you better pray for mercy." Alexis sighed and stood on his feet, he moved away from the young Caelestis and approached the healing circle. "Alexis? What are you doing?"

"Hey golden-clover! Guess you're not so lucky now are you?" Alexis asked, stuffing his hands in his pockets and staring at one of the men further back in the circle. He had hair like black wool, skin like mud, torn up brown and dull green tunic and slacks, even the dragon curled up on his belly looked like a ball of emerald nettles. Kaltrina frown thoughtfully, he knew that tradition demanded one female per fifty-males whenever dragons were to leave the forest. If the redhead he had been staring at wasn't female, then the young man near the back of the healing-circle was female.

"Elder sister's name is Balam Lalendzela Mayfield!" the Caelestis barked at him, clearly insulted with Alexis's nickname for the woman. Kaltrina pinched his brow, he was starting to hate not being able to tell the difference in genders of the Ancient House Holds. Alexis waved him off as he continued to watch for movement from his friend. The female-dragon coughed wetly, her face scrunching up in pain before one eye cracked open. Smirking to himself, Alexis watched as she struggled to raise a hand in his direction; then he burst out into laughter as she flipped him off.

"Fair, fair," Alexis chuckled warmly, his sun-kissed face crinkling into an amused smile he usually reserved for his students. "I suppose you want me to take command of this mission?" the woman curled all her fingers loosely, leaving her ring and middle fingers to tap against her thumb twice. "tch, one problem: I'm in charge of three kits. I can't join you on this mission." The woman breathed heavily for a moment, as if struggling to remain conscious, then—ever so slowly—she ran all of her fingers across her thumb; pinky to pointer, then the thumb ran gently across from pointer to pinky, and repeated twice over.

"I am not taking them with me," Alexis hissed. "They're ten for crying out loud!"

"Two are from ancient households and the third is on par with most Toarr," Kaltrina countered.

"I said no damn it!" Alexis barked, "They've only had two-years of dragon-training! They're not ready!"

"We can do it," Behruz smiled in his teacher's direction. "We have our dragon-armors and we spar with you daily. Aylin even managed to nick one of your scales yesterday! We can work with them!"

"The only problem is that *we* can't work together," Servass countered, crossing his arms and frowning thoughtfully. "They sent forty-four dragons to protect Suomi Village and only ten made it here for emergency treatment. That means that thirty-six of our strongest dragons were killed *before* they even got to the location."

"No it doesn't," Caelestis corrected quickly, "Elder sister is acting lead, she split each Karys into different directions specifically for this purpose. There was Mayfield-Rū, Albena-Rū, Arabella-Rū, and Sherborne-Rū."

"Each leader was from a prominent family?" Alexis questioned, *is everyone on this team from an honored house?* He looked carefully at each team member before him; four Belfour's, one Silvanus, one Alvarado, one Arabella, one Ethelstone. *Wait,* he looked back at the Ethelstone. The man's previously long plum hair was burnt short close to his ears, several other burns were located along his legs and left shoulder. Ethelstones were renowned geniuses, how did their mission fail so brilliantly with one on their team?

"Who else was on your team and where did they go?" Alexis looked back at the young Caelestinus. The boy seemed to cringe under the weight of his eyes; as if he's never been addressed by a superior without his name being spoken.

"Albena-Rū went straight to Flintlyn Village. Arabella-Rū went to Suomi Village. And Sherborne-Rū went to check up on secure exits back into the forest through the mountains. Elder sister went to check the boarder of Trégaron and meet up with both the border-patrol and another team that needed aid retreating." Caelestis pointed at the heavily injured people in the healing-circle, one person coughed as he pushed himself up and then stumbled out of the circle. He wasn't perfectly healed but he was good enough to recover on his own, he didn't need to be in the emergency healing-circle anymore.

"Koalvar Alaverado-Rū?" Alexis called, confused at seeing the young midnight-haired man slump into the quick arms of another person. "Danaz!" Alexis hurried over to his previous classmate, crouching for the man as he was propped up by another villager.

"That's Danaz-Rū to you, you damn bastard," the man coughed, squinting pink eyes up at Alexis. "What the hell are you doing in Asharan? You finally get kicked out?"

"I came here to train my students," Alexis answered, ignoring the insult with practiced ease. "As Nanaibek-Rū instructed me two years ago."

"Seriously? Since when did you—" Danaz cut himself off, his pink eyes having caught sight of the only children in the village. "you got stuck with some brats alright. Damn, I almost pity you."

"They're not as bad as they appear," Alexis smiled.

"You have no idea who they are do you?"

"Of course I do," Alexis's smile didn't drop. "Behruz Eld, eighty-seventh heir. Servass of Asharan, our most promising someday-Karys. And Aylin Aiello-Sarai."

"…still an idiot," Danaz grunted. "I'm impressed the Aiello's let you take her out of the city. They're notoriously picky about their dragon-selections. Only one in every five generations, right girl?"

"Correct," Aylin agreed distractedly, "Now die quietly." Behruz snickered with the dismissal of the man, it wasn't every day that Aylin completely disregarded a person's existence.

"I'm not that weak!" Danaz barked before turning to his classmate. "How'd you convince those stingy-bastard elders to let her go? Heirs aren't usually permitted to be dragons."

"They didn't exactly have a choice in the matter," Alexis snickered to himself. "The boys messed up in class and she lost her temper so the three of them got in a fight and half the academy was destroyed."

"That wasn't my fault! He started it!" the boys snapped together, pointing at each other.

"I swear to the creator if you idiots make me lose concentration, you're *dead*!" Aylin snarled angerly, four locks of hair came undone from her spell and curled about her face in a warning manner. The boys yelped in unison and quickly hid behind Kaltrina, using the grown man as a shield despite the fact that he would abandon them to Aylin's wrath in a heartbeat.

"...ah, now I get why you were sent to teach them," Danaz smirked. "They're as bad as you used to be."

"So what was your mission?" Alexis asked, none-to-smoothly changing the subject.

"We were to collect intel on some stolen dragons," Danaz's face pinched as he glared down at the earth, his teeth grinding together. "It was a trap. Gehill was waiting to ambush us at the supposed to be village. I barely managed to get my team out of there in time but... we came across Trégaron border patrol. We got caught in their little feud and-and—"

"I understand," Alexis placed a hand on his old classmate's shoulder. "How many of your teammates made it here?"

"Yusuwe Arabella," Danaz's shoulder's slumped. "The others are border patrol and Mayfeild-Rū's second in command."

"Where is the rest of Mayfeild-Rū's team?" Alexis asked, his face pinching into a frown.

"I asked her and she split everyone up," Danaz shrugged. "I guess she thought the two of them were good enough back up."

"No," they looked up as Yusuwe stumbled through the barrier of the healers. He tripped over his own feet and crashed into Alexis's arms, coughing he turned to face his commander. "Figures we're the only ones to survive," Yusuwe coughed and rubbed at his golden-cat eyes. A tiny purple and pink lizard flitted across the air, like a floating leaf, till it landed on his knees; purring and chirping like a wounded bird. Yusuwe sighed as he reached out and stroked his baby-dragon's hornless head, cringing as his nails flicked a few dead scales off. "Golden-clover, the smart ass that she is, sent the rest of her team both north and south to report back to the other Karys. They should be updated by now. I don't know what they're thinking but the ones heading to Flintlyn should be making preparations for a fast evacuation of Suomi Village."

"What about Suomi Village?" Danaz asked, turning towards the young Caelestis-boy as he approached cautiously. "Weren't you supposed to protect it?"

"We were supposed to hide them from Trégaron's scouts but that might not be possible anymore." Caelestis corrected softly, seemingly shrinking in his gray-blue armor.

"I told you this mission was going to end in flames." Yusuwe commented offhandedly.

"You say that every time we leave the forest," Danaz scoffed at him.

"And I'm usually right."

"No, you just deem everything to be a failure before you even get out of bed!"

"Alright enough you two," Alexis sighed. "Since golden-clover is confident that the others are well enough to lend aid to us, I will take up lead of this mission."

"What about your students?" Yusuwe asked, "They don't even have dragons yet."

"Says who?" Behruz asked as he pressed two fingers to his lips and gave a shrill whistle that echoed through the air like the haunting ring of church bells. Servass sighed but clapped his hands in four rhythmic concussions. Two answering squeaks cried out somewhere high overhead, making the residents of Asharan snicker and chuckle while the new combers looked about in confusion.

"Aylin-Rū, please step out of the magic circle." One of the doctors called out, "only three left, we can take care of the others from here." Alexis perked at the information and looked about the healing-circle. He found many others sitting about the circle edge with their dragon-armors in their laps but he didn't see his old friend. Looking again at the healing-circle he found Balam still trying to recover inside it, thick dark lines were growing beneath her eyes; her dragon was curled up into a little emerald-clover-leaf ball on her belly.

"But—"

"Now young lady," one of the doctors ordered. "you'll be leaving soon and you'll be needing your strength for the mission." Behruz yelped cheerfully as he saw something in the fog and began waving his arms about wildly. Servass scoffed at him and moved away, giving his teammate a disgusted look while he was at it.

"Yes sir." Aylin sighed as she moved with the other doctors, waiting till they were all lined up in a perfect triangle before she circled her arms around herself and bringing them together in front of herself; letting the two magics of the two other doctors merge between her tiny palms before slowly releasing the magics and stepping back.

"Very good," the head doctor bobbed his head, a smile on his face. "You didn't mess up this time." No one noticed when Behruz caught a flaming missile and crashed into one of the stone buildings of Asharan. All the villagers started talking about plans and equipment they could give to the children for safe travels, after all it was unwise to leave young ones alone on the border of three warring countries.

"Great now you smell worse," Servass drawled as he moved further away from his teammates.

"I knew you'd be a great medic," another doctor snickered as Servass held out his arm and a swirl of water traveled around his body before settling on his shoulder. A gentle three shades of blue serpent curled around his shoulders, harboring six legs, four unreasonably long wings and a head as smooth and hornless as a garden snake.

"She'll be a great aid in the future," the other doctor smiled in agreement. Aylin blushed brightly, ringing her hands together as she smiled at the ground, her long purple locks slipping over her shoulders to hide her face.

"How is Balam Mayfield doing?" Alexis asked as he rose to his feet, quickly double checking that Yusuwe was stable enough to support himself before totally releasing the man He looked up to see an excited ball of orange and red bound around the village center, seemingly looking for something. "Behruz! Your dragon!" Alexis called and waved a dismissive hand at his student, the box of glittering scales perked with the name and then spiraled about in search of Behruz. Many villagers shooed the sparking-not-quite-a-flame lizard away from their feet and towards the broken house where Behruz remained sprawled.

"disgusting," Servass commented as Behruz waved a hand in the air before flopping gracelessly back on the cobble stones.

"Amaru," Aylin giggled, drawing the sunset-scaled lizard's attention, "over there boy." She pointed and 'Amaru'—the flaming box of scales that he was—took off like a rocket towards his human.

"Commander Mayfield is suffering from magic-over use," the head doctor replied as Alexis stopped near him. "her dragon shows signs of partial merging. I'd say that if Caelestinus-Rū hadn't arrived when he did then Mayfield-Rū most likely would've subcommand to the Great Breath." Everyone present stilled, Aylin wrapping both hands over her mouth to stifle her gasp just as a dark shadow appeared at her feet. Amaru chittered at the dark shadow, moving to charge it only to hide behind a rock when the shadow snarled angerly at him. Servass straightened from where he was crouched beside the village well; his dragon straightening her spin to continue its look of nobility. Behruz pulled himself out of the house, one hand pressed to his forehead to keep his scarlet-scaled lizard from climbing over his face. The other adults slowly backed away from the magic circle, the weakened soldiers tugging their own dragons closer to their chests and giving the woman a disgusted look.

"There's no way she would've actually done that," Alexis hissed at him, angry that the doctor would even mention something like that. "She would never make the same mistake as her brother!"

"Perhaps… the children should remain here," one of the villager's suggested, others quickly agreed with him.

"Our dragons are gone," another villager whispered

"We cannot protect them any better,"

"Entering a warfront without armor is suicide."

"Sending children with a half-awakened one is worse."

"Will protect the border if we leave?"

"Judging by the amount of damage she and her dragon have withstood, she may not have realized what was happening." One of the other doctors countered, bringing the whispering of concern back down as everyone turned to listen. "The Mayfield's have always been an emotional bunch, it's possible that she started the process subconsciously."

"Go," Balam opened her eyes, her breath still heavy and her eyes expressing her exhaustion. "They… they're waiting… we… we pro-promised…"

"Elder sister don't talk!" the Caelestinus-boy called out, rushing to the edge of the healing-triangle only to be held back by Kaltrina. "Save your strength! I'll gather the other Karys so a meeting can be held and we can figure everything out!"

"Three kits," Balam smiled at Caelestinus before turning back towards Alexis, "We can… we can pro-protect them. There… there are for-forty o-others… d-dragons… we-we can—"

"Alright, alright, you win," Alexis sighed heavily, rubbing the back of his neck. "Just stop talking." Balam chuckled weakly, "Caelestinus-Rū! What's your name?"

"Huh?" the boy looked up at Alexis in bewilderment, his masked head tilting to the side curiously.

"Are you deaf? I asked for your name." Alexis grouched, feeling irritable with the loss of the argument.

"Oh… its um…Neilior," the boy answered slowly, as if he was expecting a negative response from Alexis.

"I meant your dragon name kid, not your family name." Alexis sighed, "you clearly need practice introducing yourself with your dragon name. seriously."

"Oh! Um it's just that… no one ever asks me for my name," Neilior informed him. "Everyone usually calls me Caelestinus-Rū or kid or brat or stripes or—"

"I get it, your dragon name, what is it?" Alexis rubbed at his face, already predicting that this mission was going to be a long one.

"um, well Elder sister calls me 'Jiane'." Neilior smiled shyly as he scratched the back of his neck.

"Alright, then that's what we'll address you as." Alexis bobbed his head as he turned to look at his three students. "As for you three, I'll have to think of something quickly…" he stared at his three students, Aylin was cradling her black dragon in her arms and smiling shyly at it. Servass was standing with his arms crossed, seemingly unhindered with his dragon's weight on his shoulder. Behruz was struggling to pull himself out of the hole he made in someone's house, no one appeared to care that his own fiery-dragon was sitting his feet looking like a good puppy.

"How about various versions of your own name?" Yusuwe asked, "you're well known and a successful Dragon with few losses. If they have a version of your name no doubt they'll walk a similar path as you."

"Hmm," Alexis sighed and frowned at his three students. "Alright… then, this is what you three will go by from now on."

Chapter 2

The storm raged along the aspen forest, making every branch and leaf shutter with explosions of golden light and poisoned swords. Flashes of white light made jade armor glint amongst the merciless crystal spears and glass dust that filled the forest like raining meteorites. Spiraling pillars of golden and scarlet sparks spurred into motion great flames that ate steal and flesh alike; unhindered by the heavy down pour of a storm. Geysers arose from sodden earth and the rain fell with pin-point accuracy; no soldiers were missed in the melee of elemental weapons. The army of Trégaron, the military might of the eastern valleys, raced in their jade armor and silver tunics. The knot work display of leaves, vines and their favored flower crawled across their every surface; from their leathers to their flowing tunics. Great emerald banners fluttered in the storm wind, displaying the ten petal cheery blossom with all the pride of a rising nation.

"Mū: Hūtan Fermo Musùhku!" Seven soldier's braced their hands against a white-barked tree, an elaborate expanse of glowing jade light and emerald flames burst into ancient inscriptions and sigils. The forest groaned as it was brought to life, leaves twittered, branches twisted, trunks bent and bowed towards the sources of elemental magic. The crystals protruding from the sodden earth pulsed with the source of a new magic; alerting their creator to the impending danger.

"Cūrrā," a gentle and soft voice emitted from the crystals, like the voice of a slowly waking child.

"Cūrrā," a golden sword flashed, reflecting the light of the white crystal and emphasizing its gentle voice to its allies.

"Cūrrā," the sparks spiraled into a tornado, a massive pillar of not-quite-flame arose, consuming the soldiers in jade armor.

"Cūrrā," an azure serpent slashed out like twirling wind, creating a vortex of boiling water.

"Cūrrā," a silver and blue scaled soldier tilted his broken dragon-mask towards the crystal dangling from his wrist. Without consideration of the soldier's at his feet, he clapped his hands and spread them out wide. A dark teal vortex opened up beneath the feet of the soldiers, sending each one through with terrified screams. High overhead, too high for mercy to still their hearts, the soldiers plummeted through the rainstorm only to be impaled by the very trees they called home. Pulling off five dozen glowing teal-scales the soldier whispered under breath, his chapped lips twisting and rolling through words none could translate.

"There! a Caelestinus!" the gray-blue soldier glanced back at the jade-encased soldier's charging him, rapier blades held in each hand and simple seal-arrays swirling along their silver blades. Scoffing the young serpentine-soldier spread his arms out wide to either side and fell backwards off the branch he had been crouching on. A dark teal oval spiraled like a vortex below him, it did not consume him before a Trégaron arrow pierced his unprotected belly; the location where his scales had previously been removed. Crying out in pain, the serpentine-soldier wrapped his thin claws around the arrow, curling up into a ball just as his portal consumed his being. The Trégaron soldier's cursed as the portal disappeared and their target's remaining scales vanishing with him.

"Catch the others!" one soldier barked, "They're dragons! We can't afford to waste this moment!"

"Šyma Cūrrā," the sparking whirlwind pulsed thrice before diving into the earth and sending a shockwave of power throughout the forest. Then, several dozen feet wide, a platform of soil and stone arose with the force of a volcanic eruption. A dozen elders clung together as their scarlet-scaled protector sat in the center of the platform and concentrated on their flight. Their platform burst from the stretching branches of the forest and barreled like a shooting star into the storm overhead. Just when the elders believed that they couldn't breech the storm, they watched as the dark clouds parted and they burst out into clear open air. Before them the storm once raging above them now seemed like a misty lake beneath their earthen boat and the sky over head was a kaleidoscope of stars too beautiful to describe.

"Are we safe?" one of the elders asked, looking about for threats.

"Where are the children?" another asked, clasping the hand of their lover as close as they could. Suddenly the dark mist-like surface rippled apart into a vertex that released a great watery-dragon before merging closed once more. Upon its smooth back the survivors of Suomi Village sat, single file, staring in awe at the vision bestowed to them. It wasn't long before the elders called out to their children, relief flooding them at the sight of their cherished children ridding the back of a watery winged serpent.

"Maor! Barak!" everyone watched as another earthen platform burst from the clouds, quickly followed by four more dragons carved from stone and leaves alike. Upon the earthen platform a bulky-golden-scaled soldier stood, his snarling mask twisting further as he spied the two young children supporting more survivors of Suomi Village. "Where is Eirian?" behind him a teal vertex opened and out came a crashing body of gray and teal, blood spewing out of the young soldier's belly as he cried out upon landing. "Jiane!" The golden-soldier twisted but he wasn't able to move without losing control of his platform, several other dragon-soldiers rushed to the young boy's aid instead; each leaping from their previous serpentine ride.

"Damn," the young soldier coughed, his claws wrapping around his belly as his comrades supported his body.

"Tracer arrow," one soldier murmured as he stuck his thick claws into the four-points of the arrow hole. Any recoil from the younger soldier was firmly ignored and the other two elder dragons firmly pinned the teenager in place.

"Brace yourself," another ordered as he wrapped his own claws around the thick shaft.

"Hurry," the third hissed, "He'll bleed out at this rate."

"If shock doesn't get me first," the young soldier grunted out. The others chuckled at him, each agreeing that a joke equaled long life. One-soldier cut the four-pronged arrow free of the teen's flesh with his claws. One-soldier ripped out the arrow out quickly, cringing back only when a splatter of blood hit his mask. three-soldiers kept the young soldier pinned so the wound wouldn't get worse as the teen thrashed. One-soldier quickly crushed his dull-claws over the wound and began whispering under breath, too feint for anyone to hear the ancient words.

"Behruz! Barak! Hurry to Flintlyn City! I'll join you shortly!" the two boys rolled towards each other, the dragon coiling around the earthen platform to create a beautiful scaled dome; the survivors safe within. The golden-scaled dragon then brought forth seven golden swords and sent them spiraling into the bottom of the boy's earthen platform. With the aid of his magic, the two boys were sent flying at high speed towards their destination; a circular sphere of white cloud left behind as evidence of their passing. Two of the four dragons glowed before giving chase to the orb, a trail of white cloud left in their wake.

"Where is Aylin?" the golden-scaled solder asked as he looked about, "She should be here!"

"The girl was charged with the children," one of the others ridding another dragon informed them.

"We gave her a clear path," another added

"Trégaron sent many soldiers today, perhaps they sent more?" a pink-scaled solder questioned, one clawed palm pressed to her side.

"Are you kidding? That kid is fast!" one of the others waved a dismissive hand. "she outran all of us, she could outrun a few tree rats!"

"But she had a six-dozen children with her," one of the others pipped up, "none know flight magic!"

"No matter her burden, she shouldn't be this late," the golden dragon retorted, looking about worriedly. Aylin was his strongest student, his most versatile and intelligent. She is the one with the most promise of a dragon's future.

"Ziya! Go!" the young dragon coughed and hacked, "She's in trouble!" he lifted a clawed hand and revealed one of his scales glowing bright white, "She's bleeding!" he coughed, sickly and with a wave of blood cascading down his chin. The white-glowing scale flared close to Ziya, creating a dark green portal that quickly swallowed him; transporting him to his student's side.

"Again," the gray-scaled solder coughed, sweeping a handout before them and creating a large swirling vertex of dark ocean green. The flying-reptiles roared as they swirled together, catching those with Jiane as they all barreled through the portal and the platform the golden-soldier created shattered apart.

"Stupid boy!" one of the commanders barked as they appeared over Flintlyn City, a horrible looking wreckage of stone and sodden earth left an ugly trail towards the mountain village. The young gray and blue scaled solder was caught easily by his commander, coughing as his wound spilt more blood. The other soldier's twisted in the air, their own magics rolling forth, forming a platform for their landing as they fell gracelessly into the city. Flintlyn City bore tall towering walls around their mountain city, the dragon's platform burst into millions of colorful flower petals as they entered the city and landed in the closest city-square.

"We need a medic!" One of the solder's cried out, his voice cracking with desperation as the teenager in his arms spat out a mouth full of scarlet liquid. Many people scattered at first, crying out in terror and believing their lives were about to end but once they realized that it was soldier-dragons in the city they calmed down quickly. Residents of Flintlyn City hurried forward, those with medicine or healing magics moving forward with whispers on their lips and glowing rune-seals in their hands.

"Neilior!" One of the young child-dragons cry was followed by a whiplash of water propelling both of the young children towards their wounded comrades.

"Behruz," the gray and blue scaled solder coughed as one of the mages created a seven layered healing rune-seal-array with the help of two others. "Se-servass... you... you're d-dragons now."

"Save your strength," Servass demanded, his voice hard and unwavering.

"You... you stand together," Neilior coughed, thrashing suddenly as something with the rune-seal-array went wrong.

"Neilior!" Behruz went to leap towards his comrade but Servass quickly held him back as their elders converged on the teenager in gray-blue armor.

"We need clean water!" one of the medics ordered, pulling one hand back and forcing out black blood. "They used White Snakeroot!"

"The closest well is fifteen minutes away!" a villager informed them, clinging tightly to an old friend from Suomi Village.

"Hold on!" Servass ordered as he scrambled a few steps away. He stopped, near the edge of the village road, and spread his arms out to either side. Before him a simple ring of sky blue twirled into existence, from it bubbles and snowflakes arose from barely legible runes from ancient times. Servass whispered under breath, his armor shook and shuttered before flinging off one scale from its spine. The large scale twirled through the air before settling into the ancient looking seal-array; growing seven times its original size. The dark navy scale rolled back and forth till a brace of ice arose from the glowing seal-array. Servass whispered something, low and ominous sounding, and in answer the air converged on the basin; its great torrents condensing till unorganized blobs of water began forming.

"Finished," Servass commented, turning on the ball of his foot and smiling towards his elders. "it's done!" he had no time to appreciate anyone's praise, nor see any allies' faces before he was surrounded in dark winds and angry thunder clasps. A flutter of teal from the corner of his eye, he twisted to see what it was but instead found himself falling through empty air. Barely a moment later, he spotted a flurry of sparks quickly followed by Behruz's terrified screams. Sighing, Servass understood what happened; their teammate must've used the last ounces of his power to send them to the battle front.

If that was true then... Neilior was probably dead.

Ω Ω Ω

The storm raged along the aspen forest, making every branch and leaf shutter with explosions of golden light and poisoned swords. Flashes of white light made jade armor glint amongst the merciless crystal spears and glass dust that filled the forest like raining meteorites. Spiraling pillars of golden and scarlet sparks spurred into motion great flames that ate steal and flesh alike; unhindered by the heavy down pour of a storm. Geysers arose from sodden earth and the rain fell with pin-point accuracy; no soldiers were missed in the melee of elemental weapons. The army of Trégaron, the military might of the eastern valleys, raced in their jade armor and silver tunics. The knot work display of leaves, vines and their favored flower crawled across their every surface; from their leathers to their flowing tunics. Great emerald banners fluttered in the storm wind, displaying the ten petal cheery blossom with all the pride of a rising nation.

"Mū: Hūtan Fermo Musùhku!" seven soldier's braced their hands against a white-barked tree, an elaborate expanse of glowing jade light and emerald flames burst into ancient inscriptions and sigils. The forest groaned as it was brought to life, leaves twittered, branches twisted, trunks bent and bowed towards the sources of elemental magic. The crystals protruding from the sodden earth pulsed with the source of a new magic; alerting their creator to the impending danger. The crystals re-laid the message, whispering gently to every alley. Then the maker gathered those left to them and created a great white sphere, without further prompt they took through the air. The aspen forest seemed to grow and reach towards the white sphere, thick branches and quick roots stretching out to entrap them. But the white sphere could not be caught, not by the likes of an aspen forest.

The soldiers of Trégaron cursed as they gave chase, several dozen mages relaying messages to their kinsmen, giving directions to their comrades. Finally, after many minutes of barging through branches and trunks, the spiraling ball of white light burst from the nightmarish aspen forest—and straight into the range Trégaron's army. The army of Trégaron, the military might of the eastern valleys, stood proudly in their jade armor and emerald tunics. The knotwork display of leaves, vines and their favored flower crawled their every surface, from their leathers to their flowing tunics. Great emerald banners fluttered in the storm wind, displaying the ten petal cheery blossom with all the pride of a rising nation. Several times the soring ball of light neared the earthen surface, barely evading the attacks of several mage-solders. Eventually the glowing orbit couldn't remain out of reach, soon enough it began barreling through the banners, horses and men alike. Dozens of solders tried to stop the white-orb, mages band together to cage it, it was all for not. The orb soon enough took to the sky, leaving behind a divot in the muddy terrain and a small stuffed animal.

"Tirta: Göksu Jian!" a mage dressed in bright layered tunics of jade and black shouted, lines and wisps of jade light surrounded him. A great watery hand arose from amongst the soldiers, growing with the rain that filled it ever stronger. Without care the watery palm struck down on the white orbit, electing startled cries as the orb crashed into the surface of the muddy-valley. The wet land reacted like a commit in the ocean, dosing all in thick mud and heavy stones; a furious roar of a monster shook the air. The soldiers charged the white orb, watching the light dim as the source weakened. The sound of crying children crept louder and louder as the soldier's neared the dimming orb. One soldier whispered a spell, coating his hand in thick mud that quickly hardened into a thick stone spike. He leaped into the crater and his fist crashed through the white-glowing shield, he ignored the deep gorges in his hand as his spike shattered upon impact. But his goal was achieved.

Inside the orb a great cry, like a hundred spirits wailing in despair, arose with a near deafening ring. He swatted blindly inside the orb, pushing his arm further in, his teeth grinding together as the pressure of the orb tightened on his limb. There, cloth brushed against his fingertips. He took a deep breath, made eye contact with another soldier-mage and shoved all his weight into the hole, pushing his meaty-hand even further inside. Then, accompanied with a cry of despair, he wrapped his fingers around another's limb and pulled. His fellow soldiers acted quickly, they each chanted their own spells and crashed against the orb repeatedly, ignoring how their earthen-spells rebounded and cut deeply into their fists and feet. Two mages scrambled to his side, whispering enchantments that aided with their strength. Finally he was able to rip the being inside the orb out, a young female child with hair like storm clouds and eyes of purest copper. She was dressed in a ragged orange tunic, dark pants and a bloody leather apron. The soldier didn't even think about his next action, he followed with his orders—in one smooth movement he drew out his dagger.

"Aem!" The child screamed as she crashed into the surface of the muddy-crater, orange-eyes wide in terror, one hand outstretched towards him as if that would be enough to stop him. He brought the dagger down and threw away his humanity. "Saùf Na!" the earth roared with her cry. He had no time to register what happened before his world blackened and he left the world of the living; the last thing he saw was his dagger caught by a glittering fragment of white-glass. The soldiers scrambled back, the mages quickly chanting spells that pushed them all further away from the impact sight. Their comrade was left behind, a spear of magma reaching out of the creator to puncture the soldier too brave for the fight. The white orb pulsed, the girl scrambled back into the orb, sobbing in relief with the new safety. The earth shuttered and rolled as the glittering white orb shattered apart, sending great walls of earth flying through the air to crash into the soldiers and mages. Many mages tried to protect themselves but none of them could compare to the power of the being inside the orb.

"Tirta: Göksu Jian!" four soldier-mages cried out in unity, using the storm to their advantage to form four towering fists of water. They commanded the water to crash into the creator but the gathered water did nothing more than shatter as the solder-mage's blood coated their comrades. Soldiers cried out in despair as three of the mages were bent back words, long white-glass spears logged into their necks and buried into the mud behind them.

"Terra: Telum Sai!" the mud at the fourth soldier-mage's feet shifted and rolled but his spell failed as claws tore through the straps of his armor and buried into his ribcage. The soldiers turned back to their magician, eyes wide and mouths open in shock at the creature who stood above the solder-mage's corpse. The night storm hid the creature's body well, making it appear as if it were a shadowy monster that walked on two legs but its glowing white eyes could not be hidden by the fury of the storm. Like a blur of shadows, hidden even from the flashing of lightning, the monster raced forward with merciless onyx claws and angry moonstone eyes. Before long the monster was once more standing at the edge of the crater where many small human children huddled together with tears in their eyes and whimpers on their lips. Without the white orb protecting them, the soldiers could see clearly the occupants of the white-orb; the young lives cowering in the crater did nothing to the soldiers staring down on them. The children, several dozen between the ages two and twelve, bore hair of every silver shade and bewitching orange wolf eyes. They were dressed in dark tunics and dresses with thick leather aprons strapped tightly around their waists; the typical robes of blacksmiths.

The solder's of Trégaron steeled their hearts and charged the creator. The creature snarled furiously and lunged with glittering white-glass coating its every scale and claw.

It wasn't long before the battlefield was littered in floral banners and Trégaron soldier-corpses. The surviving soldiers trembled in exhaustion and fear, their given task interrupted by their worst possible imagination. The single figure stood crouching before the group of village children, still stained in soldier's blood and the ashes of their home. The shadowy-monster shifted, looking back at the whimpering children. Overhead a flash of lightning lit up the sky and for a moment it engulfed the monster in blinding blue-white. The protector of the children was small and thin, its armor thick black scales interspaced with steal spikes. Its face was hidden behind a mask of scales and whimsical feathers. Its paws wrapped in thick black gauntlets with claws too long to believe, its legs and arms protected by layered scales and small spikes. Even its neck gleamed with the haunting glow of scaled chain mail. Everything about this monster was shades of black, from the feathers hinting about its face, to the spikes on its back, to the tip of its razor tail, to the gleaming claws of its paws. Everything was onyx, coating the monster in an air that promised death's approach with every glance of its moonlit eyes.

"Die monster!" One of the soldiers bellowed as he rushed forward, saber held high overhead. The sword was long and thin, its silver handle with the maple leave guard shined in the lightning eerily. The wide silver loop on the end of the handle jingled, the cord attached to it danced mockingly; alerting all to its hidden partner. The strange creature twisted like a pendulum, dashing forward with its dagger tail weaving threatening back and forth. The man gasped as the creature's clawed hand slipped through his armor and belly like a knife in warm butter; then watched helplessly as its tail sent glittering white spears at three mages. The man coughed wetly, his sabre tumbled into the wet soil as his thick fingers buried themselves into the creature's shoulders.

From behind the dying man two of his comrades burst forward, sabers held at the ready and aiming for the kill, both engulfed in the bright glow of their magics of scarlet and gold. The creature didn't look at them as it twisted like a pendulum, swinging its body onto the dying soldier and using him as a shield against the first attack. The monster snarled disdainfully at the two soldiers and with a flick of its wrist, sent the soldier clinging to it crippling apart. Ripping the dead man apart came easily to the monster, sending each half of the soldier into his comrades with enough force and power to send them crashing into the thick mud. While they were distracted the creature swiped its fore-paws towards the ground, creating a glittering-white spear. Clinging to the spear the creature spiraled, ending two soldier-mages quickly, before shooting itself into the sky. Twirling amongst the harsh storm currents, the creature released its magical white-glass and watched as the soldiers below crumbled lifelessly.

"Ahi: Ignatius Salamandra!" One soldier stepped forward, his hands blooming green glowing runes to create several simple seals in the air. The rains surround the soldier flared to life with blinding crimson flames, all too soon the man himself was surrounded in the flaming face of a summoned fire lizard. The soldier smirked, proud his control over the fire element was strong enough to summon one of the great fire salamanders of old. Looking about he saw that more soldiers were nearing him, finding comfort in his rare fire magic. Unfortunately he didn't see any other strong mages, there were plenty such people littering the earth in great pools of scarlet but none who were living or well enough to lend him aid. Snarling the young man waved a hand towards the monster still floating in the air, furious as he realized that the creature had targeted the strong mages first before slaughtering the soldiers.

"Aid me in this battle! Secure my victory!!" he felt the shadowy-monster glare down on him, observing him with disinterest, knowing all too well that his vulnerable body beneath the silver armor. It would not take much for the creature to disembowel him as it had done to several of his comrades.

"Fool," the creature murmured its voice soft like that of a child, a very young child at that. "Watch your step and you live another fortnight." The soaring monster spread its lithe arms to either side, allowing its own white magic to roll forth like the suffocating waves of the ocean. Complex three dimensional rune-seal-arrays bloomed to life around the monster and all too soon the soldier's flames were being smothered by great torrents of blistering storm winds. The summoned salamander howled in agony, bellowing out one last breath of fire in an attempt to comply with the wish of its summoner. The village children wailed in hysteria at the stream of fire rushed them, intending to swallow them whole. In a second too fast for the human eye to follow, the strange guardian was before the children, arms braced before it as the fire crashed against its ancient scales and white glowing shards.

"Got ya!" From either side of the bellowing flame, two more soldiers burst forward with glowing avarian sabres held ready for a beheading. "Die!!" the fire Salamander disappeared in steam and curses, prompting a smirk from the monster. The monster whispered to the flames and all too soon allowed them to engulf its forelimbs. The two men's gleaming blades neared the monster, voices screaming in assured victory.

"Fools." The monster murmured as it stood once more, the flames now brilliant white and attached to its arms. "Learn from your mistakes!" The monster flung its arms and the flames leaped from it to the charging men. The mage screamed shrilly, tears bursting forth from his eyes as he watched his comrades shatter into ashes. The monster shifted a foot and in a second it was before the man, its claws ripping through unprotected flesh without restraint or mercy. That was that. The army it stumbled upon were either corpses in the mud or fleeing as far away as they could. The shadowy-monster turned away from the dying mage, intending to return to the skies with the children but its retreat was stopped short by the sound of a falling tree. The sound of snapping branches, the groaning of the trunk, followed by the heavy crash of a tree crashing into thick soil—was not followed by rolling earth. Moonlit-eyes squinted slightly, the black-scaled monster turned towards the sound…there on the edge of the battlefield, more Trégaron troops were marching forward. Had the soldiers of Trégaron remained in their forests then the battle between shadowy-monster and forest-soldiers would've been vastly different. But out here, amongst the muddy valley and awful thunderstorm, the soldiers of Trégaron stood out like a lone fire in the night.

"Shall they never learn?" the monster asked itself, watching the soldiers continue charging, their magicians soon chanting, their healers soon splitting, their commanders soon pausing. Sighing in remorse, the shadow-monster propelled itself high in the air and spun, calling forth the storm's currents and power. Brightly lit runes were scribbled hurriedly around it, ancient seals and magic circles swirled into life around the monster. Brilliant onyx scales bloomed to life beneath the light of the ancient white-glowing seal-arrays, revealing the monster's almost human form. With the appearance of its mostly human body, the great tail and even larger wings it harbored spared little comfort to the soldier's approaching it. The mages whispered their enchantments, surrounding themselves in glowing seal-arrays and gathering the storm rains towards themselves.

"FIRE!!" Bursts of watery-arrows from the magicians were interspaced with poisoned arrows from archers. However, none met their target as the currents of the storm bent to the monsters will. The soldiers of Trégaron cried out in surprise and agony as the watery-arrows were absorbed and the normal-arrows were propelled back to their previous masters. Floating high over the bloody battlefield the monster stood solemnly, head bowed in regret as it watched the medics scramble to lend aid. The healers were soon crying hysterically as lovers were lost and siblings breathed their last. Another wave of soldiers neared from the western side. The monster turned away from the decimated platoon, knowing all too well that the sound of wailing and agony were soon going to chill the already frigid winds of the unforgivable storm.

Summoning more wind to its side, the monster bust to the front of the next group rushing towards the children. The soldier's hollered in surprise, horses and men alike scrambled back from the monster coated in scales with claws dripping red. Too fast for them the monster was rushing through their ranks, its claws racking through ribs and throats of those with rank displayed over their hearts. Before its claws could sink into the flesh and armor of a horseback commander, a figure in palest jade jumped forward, arms spread wide and a prayer whispered through the storm. The monster froze, staring at the woman as her medic tunic was stained with her crimson blood. The monster pulled its thin paw back, and the woman reached up for her neck and face, where long slashes ran down the side of her face and slipped along the side of her thin neck. Her long two-tone hair was released to surround her in the haunting waves of a forgotten spirit.

"SAFFRON!!" The commander screamed, his eyes widening to stare at the back of the woman who saved his life. The monster stepped back, watching the woman collapse against the cold muddy ground while the man hurried down from his horse to cradle the woman with ember and onyx locks. "Saffron! Saffron! Wake up damn it!" The man bellowed out, his hands shaking the woman's shoulders. "Saffron!" The woman's eyes opened weakly, her smile small and sad as she raised a hand to brush back the tears of her lover.

"Child of embers and leaves, make your choice." The monster ordered coldly. The commander and woman looked at the monster, acceptance filling them as they realized that they were at the monster's mercy. "To retreat and live or go forth and fall. The choice is yours, child of embers and leaves." The lightning flashed again, lighting up the face of the monster and revealing its glowing pearl eyes. The commander looked down at his lover, then at the slaughter behind the monster. He could not see his end goal beyond the piles of upturned earth and twisted corpse of his comrades. He tightened his hold on Saffron before pulling her into his arms and rising to his feet. He nodded stiffly at the monster and quickly climbed his horse, a look at his second in command reassured him that there wouldn't be any disagreements with the order.

"Birds of the trees retreat!!" The second in command bellowed, rising in his stirrups to wave the white flag of retreat. The commander quickly tore a part of Saffron's medic top off and pressed it against her throat, where more blood pored. The cry of retreat, the sound of a hundred singing birds, warmed the monster's heart as the men lowered their sabres and proceeded to gather their wounded and dead.

"Child of dragons," the commander hesitated, his face twisting into a strange expression of regret and acceptance. "Thank you." The monster tilted its head to the side curiously, as if not understanding his words. The commander pulled on his stirrups, turning his horse away from the monster, but not before the monster raised a paw and three small white glass-shards pierced the leather in his hands. The commander looked back at the monster but it was already spreading its wings out as far as it could, its glowing white eyes gentle and kind looking despite the blood on its claws. A child's wail pierced the roaring storm and the shadowy-monster was suddenly soaring through the blistering winds, great scaly wings spread out to either side, flapping at blinding speeds and propelling the 'dragon child' back to the children it was to protect.

One group of Trégaron soldiers chose to avoid the monster and attack the children it rescued. Before the blade of the first soldier could reach the closest child, the monster was crashing into the mud before them and blocking the attack with its raised left arm. The avarian sabre crashed into the scaled arm, creating sparks from the blade and a splatter of blood to coat it. The monster cried out in pain, not used to its scales giving way beneath the thrust of a sword. The great wings it bore glowed white as they shrunk, the disjointed scales rushing to coat the limbs of the monster, glowing green wherever it touched the being's skin.

"Heh, so you *are* human!" The soldier smirked, adding his weight down on the handle of his weapon to cut the rest of the way through the thick scales. The scales settled once more, the wings small scale-less bones dangling limply from the monster's shoulders. One white eye squinted through the rain at the soldier above, bracing its bloody arm with the glow of white magic while the other claw buried deep into the muddy soil. Its knees gave way, its wounded arm trembling against the weight of the soldier who only cackled at the monster's obvious pain.

"Let's see if you look like one!" The man ripped his sword out of the monster's arm, raising it high overhead. The new scales rushed to cover the injury; the monster had no intentions of bleeding any further than it already did. White magic surrounded the wounded limb, mixing with the gentle green of the glowing scales beneath the coat of blood. With its right hand the monster let its claws burst into bright golden sparks, a twist of thin fingers reformed the sparks into a long thin dagger. The man laughed as he brought down his sword, eyes wide in enjoyment and mouth split with deranged laughter. The monster thrust its new blade forward, ignoring the blood that splattered its feathered mask and the disbelieving expression of the Trégaron soldier now frozen above.

"You aren't worthy of my claws." The monster snarled, twisting the blade in the soldier's side between the metallic plates and through the leather clasps. He coughed wetly, his blood filling his mouth and dripping past his chin. The monster's blade shattered, the bright golden dust entering the man through his wound and proceeded to rip him apart from the inside. Several archers tried to take advantage of the distracted monster but their arrows were returned to them without effort from the monster. The magicians summoned water and roots to destroy and capture but the waters burst into steam and the roots were sent a blaze. In a perfect ring around the crater, a thick band of magma twisted through the stone. All around the sodden earth heated, great rivers of boiling earth erupted. Solid stone liquified, rain mystified, roots burned, soldiers became ashes. The single eldest child trembled and sobbed uncontrollably, her thick calloused palms buried into the mud.

"Avani," the monster whispered, soft and sad sounding. "calm yourself, all is well. Do not stain your hands. Not for me." Golden dust filtered out of the soldier seeking their death and the man fell backwards, collapsing into the ring of magma while at the same time the golden dust that ripped him apart returned to its master's claws.

"But," the girl sobbed, her body shacking as tears rolled down her round face. "you're hurt! You hurt yourself to protect us! That's more then what any of us have ever thought anyone would ever do for us!"

"We're children of earth but… ultimately we're just monsters." One of the older kids agreed, his arms tightening around the baby in his arms. "there's no reason for you to go so far for us. After all, the gods cursed us."

"Perhaps the gods cursed you but not all of them," the monster replied, rising to its feet unsteadily. "After all, Mother Earth is a goddess and she welcomed you with open arms, did she not?"

"But all we can do is hurt other people!" one of others whimpered

"That's not true," the monster's voice was gentle, like an elder sibling smiling in amusement at their younger counter part. "The Earth is a great bringer of life, without her aid humans could not live. The fact that Mother Earth willingly gives all to protect you, *that* is what speaks louder than any curse could ever hope. You are not cursed, you are *blessed*." Once the monster was sure its wound was healed, it rose to its head and glared out at the soldiers who circled them like prowling wolves. Another circle of white magical runes bloomed to life before the children and with a flick of the monster's wrist, a wave of magma towered over the prowling soldiers. The men wailed as they were turned to ashes, their comrades howling like banshees as they all scattered.

"Damn demon!" a commander snarled furiously from his horse, seemingly unafraid as he glared into the monster's moonstone eyes through the haze of hot air. "Just die already!" He shot his own arrow but it was returned to him, embedding its hooked four points deep into his shoulder.

"I am a child of dragons, not demons." The monster informed the commander briskly. "Retreat or die. The choice is yours." The soldiers surrounded the monster and its charges, arrows notched, swords held ready, seal-arrays glowing eerily in the thunderstorm but none dared to test the strength of the lava-river rolling like ocean waves. The monster remained passive and unconcerned, surrounded with children slowly growing the courage it took for them to stand beside their guardian. The younger children whimpered in their mass of bodies, coated in thick mud as they pressed ever more into the wall of stone that surrounded their impact zone.

"Heh, so commander Elwood retreated because of that sorry excuse?" The commander snarled, his hand wrapping tightly into his bloody shoulder, "the dragons died out centuries ago! You're just a child playing dress up!" His archers readied themselves but their arms shook and their aim remained unfocused. The soldiers stepped back, voices low with whispers and faces contorted into fear. Even the magicians hesitated in creating more magical runes and circles, their faces paling as recognition filled them with terror. Dragons... the most powerful and feared of all creations. None could defy the rulers of their realm but then again, Dragons have not been seen for many centuries.

"A child?" The monster questioned slowly, "true. I am but a decade past the first flowers. But no, I do not lie about the blood in my veins nor the land from which I hail." The monster tilted its head at him, making the commander bristle with the impression of the child-dragon smirking at him. "Doubt my word? Confirm with my master if it pleases you." He could sense the mockery in their voice, a feeling of belittling filled the air between them. The mere fact that a child—even one dressed up in metal scales and claws, with powerful white-shard magic— could even do so much damage to his battalion was laughable. No doubt he would be ridiculed for a loss in a fight with a *child*.

"Tch, I'll kill him right after I slaughter you!" The commander bellowed furiously. "Men! Ready!"

"Really? I'm right here." The commander coughed as a glittering golden blade pierced his protective armor as if it weren't there. Coughing up blood, the wounded Trégaron commander struggled to twist his head back to look at his murder, the fearsome face of a snarling golden dragon glared back at him with eyes of purest ruby.

"Master, you're late." The child-dragon observed calmly, a shift in the scales about its throat and the voice came out clearer, more feminine sounding.

"My apologies Eirian," The grown dragon leaped away from the dying man and his horse, flipping through the hot air to land before his wounded student. Crouching on all fours, looking like a leopard ready to hunt, his thick tail rising above him to snap its pinches threateningly. The eldest child pulled her hands out of the earth, slumping back into the ready arms of another villager; sweat rolled down her tiered but relieved face.

"We're saved," the boy who caught her whispered, kissing her brow and hugging her tightly. Ziya glanced back at the children, watching as the circle of magma cooled into rippled black stone.

"Perhaps I shouldn't have left you to take so many children yourself," Ziya observed calmly, turning back to the army slowly testing the new stone. "A young girl like you was bound to face trouble with so much weight to carry."

"The boys wouldn't have fared any better with Sinann's fist." 'Eirian' retorted dryly, a shrill scream sounded far to their left and she moved to look in that direction. She watched as the rain shifted into spears and ended a dozen archers, several swords men were trying to protect their mages but failed quite spectacularly. Servass sored through the sky with his four wings, circling his opponents ominously; he let a loud curse echo through the air before diving and shattering the platoon. Another bout of screams to her other side produced a swirl of embers and sparks, making soldiers and magicians scream as they were swallowed hole in the incomplete flame.

"The day the two of them communicate without insults is the day of Armageddon," Eirian sighed in disappointment as her fire-happy teammate emerged from his sparks just long enough to give an angry curse back at his teammate.

"Come now Eirian, don't jinx my health like that," Ziya chided. He shifted to draw attention to the side of the commander, watching the man bleed over his jittery horse. One of the soldiers leaped quickly upon the mare and tugged urgently at its reins, pulling away from the dragons with a terrified cry of retreat. Those not slain by water, nor engulfed in embers, scrambled together for retreat; blood coating them and tears staining their dark eyes.

"Barak, Maor get down here and help me." Eirian ordered with a heavy sigh. "Harm not the fleeing for they hold more mind than those who fight." The embers and water needles stilled, quickly they both converged on themselves only to shatter once more; leaving behind a scarlet and navy child-dragons in their once place. The scarlet child-dragon appeared in a mass of muscles, his eyes glowing angry jade amongst his golden and orange sparking mask. His short square wings tucked tightly to give room for his thick muscled arms and legs with their claws stained scarlet. His overly muscled tail continued sparked with not yet quelled fury, still flipping back forth with embers and sparks. The navy child-dragon was much smaller compared to his scarlet counterpart. Slender and lean, looking like rope and scales amongst the rain shower surrounding them. His own elegant wings dragged in the mud, trailing after him like a too long cloak. His tail swished and swirled in the mud, pulling water out to surround the surface in clear and clean liquid that kept the navy child-dragon clean amongst the slippery soil.

"Eirian your hurt!" The scarlet child-dragon shouted in a panic, noticing the blood the black child-dragon's left arm. "Damn it! Hold on I'm coming down!" The boy moved to leap into the crater, only to slip in the mud and end up tumbling down into the crater left behind from Eirian's earlier landing. His sparks bloomed around him impressively but quickly died off as a thick coat of mud covered him from brow to tail tip.

"It's because you were too slow to protect her Barak." The navy child-dragon drawled coldly as he gracefully floated down to the same level as his team. The water surrounding him like a floating pedestal to keep him from getting mud on his pristine navy-scaled armor. "Perhaps you need more practice with that ember spell..." he observed his teammate as the boy scrambled about in the mud and pooling water, struggling to get his feet under himself.

"Shut it water boy!" Barak bellowed furiously as he succeed in getting his feet under himself and glared at the other boy. "Why didn't you make the water shield her?! Can't you do that?!" he lunged at Maor, fist pulled back, sparks blooming to life along his knuckles.

"ENOUGH!" Eirian bellowed, reaching out to slap clawed palms on their chests. "We're not here to bicker! Our job is to protect the villagers! Thanks to your inability to work as a team said village was destroyed and the people scattered!!" The children's master chuckled and shook his head in amusement. Leaving the scolding to his female student the dragon-man turned and crouched in front of the terrified children.

"Worry not little ones, your parents are well and safe." He suppressed his aura and dismissed his claws, allowing them to bust into golden light and reform his dagger that floated back into its sheath sitting on his lower back. He raised his barren tanned hands towards the children and tried to show the village children that he meant them no harm. "We are children of the dragon, third team of eastern side, hailing from the great forest of Aeoman." The children whimpered and sniffed, distrustful of the man who looked like a golden monster ready to devour them. Still one of them reached forward, touching his calloused palm tenderly, as if afraid of being reprimanded. When he only chuckled at them, lowering himself even further into the mud, the children saw the symbol etched upon his armored chest. A circle within a five point star, within an eight point star, within a twelve point star. It was the crest of dragons, created when twelve of the strongest ancient households had retreated during the great war of blood with the aid of eight of the holy dragons. The children murmured, their voices sounding in relief with the truth of the man's words declared proudly on his breast plate.

"Ziya-Isha!!" The man jumped at the annoyed voice of his student. "Scold them for once! You're the teacher not me!"

"But Eirian, you scold them plenty well." Ziya tried to placate the girl, turning back towards her with raised hands. "They already look plenty nullified." The boys did, their heads bowed and their shoulders slumped, pouting and glaring at the mud and rain that surrounded them.

"ISHA!!" Eirian screeched, making the man cringe at the volume.

"Okay, okay." Ziya rose to his feet slowly, his hands raising higher in surrender, as if trying to placate an angry cat. Eirian stepped aside and waved her bloody arm towards the sullen boys. Ziya chuckled as he carefully walked around the girl to approach his other students, once before them he tried to look down on them in disappointment. The boys' relaxed stances said he wasn't successful, there were times he wondered if the boys even cared for his words.

"Now listen boys, you don't like having Eirian screaming at you do you?" The two boys shook their heads at him. "Good, neither do I."

"Ziya-Isha!" Eirian groaned, "Don't make *me* the bad guy!" Ziya ignored her and simply slapped both palms on each of the boy's shoulders.

"So for the sake of my sanity, I beg you, quite making her scream." He sounded so traumatized that the two boys looked at each other, looked at their female teammate and returned their understanding gazes back to their teacher.

"We understand Isha." The boys said together, both turning wiry eyes towards their now glaring teammate.

"You lot are hopeless." Eirian growled in irritation.

"M-Mrs.?" Eirian turned towards the soft voice of one of the children, her whole aura changing from hostile to comforting. One of the children hesitantly approached her, keeping one eye on the strange males. "Y-your wound... Dose it hurt?" Eirian blinked in bewilderment before looking down at her wounded left arm, as if she forgot about it.

"My injury is fine Harlan," Eirian tilted her head towards the boy, "Wanna know a secret?" the young boy nodded enthusiastically, the other children leaning in close to hear as well. "I'm a—"

"Eirian! Your arm is still bleeding!" Behruz shouted, seemingly remembering about the blood on her arm. Eirian sighed and rose to her feet, petting Harlan's head carefully, she turned back to her teammates.

"My injury is well enough," Eirian said dismissively. "We should get going, we don't want the rest of Trégaron's forces to reach us."

"Eirian, come here," Ziya ordered holding his hand out for Eirian to place her arm in it. When she did so, he inspected the damaged scales thoughtfully before sighing heavily. "no matter what happens next, don't interfere in any fights. Rely on your shields, understand?"

"Yes Isha," Eirian nodded at him, pulling her arm back to her side.

"Ziya-Isha, how do you know she doesn't need medical attention?" Barak asked, tilting his red and orange head to the side curiously

"Because Eirian is a healer first and foremost," Ziya drawled. "It'd be foolish if she couldn't tend to her own injuries."

"Why do you think I wasn't worried about her?" Maor asked, staring dully at his teammate. "How do you forget her bloodline so easily?"

"Shut up!" Barak ordered loudly, "I'm aloud to care if she gets hurt!"

"You don't care when Maor gets hurt," Ziya pointed out

"Ziya-Isha have you ever seen water-boy bleed?" Barak asked, "it'd be the end of the world if he got hurt over a minor fight like this one!" he ignored the glare and threatening fist of his teammate spectacularly. It was only by the grace of the children tugging at Eirian's arm, tail and wing that prevented the girl from hitting Barak.

"Barak, you started crying halfway through the fight." Maor said in a tone of annoyance, "Eirian nearly got her arm chopped off, lost her wings, had her first kills today and her eyes are still dry."

"Hey! We all got our first kills! It's okay to cry when someone dies!"

"Boys, spare me, please," Ziya begged while he watched Eirian rise her left arm up to inspect the damage. She was pleased to note that it was nothing more than a very long scratch.

"Ryū, you did great," Eirian murmured gently, her silver-orbs gentling into mercury pools as the dragon hummed with the sound of a purring lion.

"Um Mrs.?" Eirian looked down on the children she barely managed to save in time. Again the oldest girl was addressing her, looking exhausted compared to the boy who supported her. "What's a 'Ziyaisha'?" Eirian couldn't help but chuckle at the girl, crouching in the mud Eirian addressed all the children that slowly surrounded her.

"'Ziya' is my teacher's name. 'Isha' is his rank." Eirian explained patently, smiling as the children's eyes lit up in wonder. "It means master or teacher. That's why I say 'Ziya-Isha'."

"Um..." One of the boys murmured, his brows pinching as his dark eyes drifted to the older girl's sleeves unable to look at her reptilian face. "Are... Uh, wh-when... Um, when are we going to-to see uh, our-our p-p-par-parents?"

"Soon little one," Eirian smiled reassuringly at him, "Very soon." Eirian stood and counted the number of heads she managed to spare, much to her relief all she chose to bring with were still at her side. Being the most versatile of her teammates, and the one with the capability to adapt to any number of situations, most of the village's children had been entrusted to Eirian; a number that rested will into a few dozen souls. "We need to get out of this valley, to do that we need to reach those hills over there." she pointed in the direction of the towering earthen domes that were hidden by the darkness of the storm. "There is a village north-east of us called Flintlyn, Trégaron soldiers can't touch you there because it would only damage their own resources."

"Will our parents be there?" another girl asked, frightened and confused with the chaos that befell her home.

"It was agreed to take all the villagers to Flintlyn should your village fall," Eirian explained. "This was the backup location we were to regather should protecting the village itself fall though." She patted the little girl's head, ignoring the painful cries of her teammates when Ziya managed to violently subdue them. "I have faith that my teammates succeeded in retreating the rest of the villagers to Flintlyn City. Especially since we're already halfway to the village. We'll be able to see its gates by dawn tomorrow." One of the children tugged at Eirian's sleeve, looking fitfully at her wounded arm. Eirian patted the child's head, smiling as she pulled her hand back and whispered gently under breath. A small rune-seal-array appeared in her right palm, the inscriptions too small and foreign for the children to decipher but its intent clear when the scratch disappeared beneath its warm teal light. Now knowing that Eirian was well and no longer in danger of infection, the children relaxed in her presence; only to stiffen when one of the male dragons neared.

Chapter 3

T rue to Eirian's words, the children were delivered to Flintlyn City as the light of dawn bathed the cold gray mountain side. Flintlyn City was carved into one of the lesser mountains of Baīlāy Mountain Range, a great towering seven tier village of stone and earthen flags with a winding sloped road leading to its towering gates. Halfway up Eirian stopped walking, urging the children to move ahead of herself. The children did so, slow and reluctant, trudging their feet through the cold dirt and shivering in the early morning misty air. Still they left her, with her teammates at her side, and walked towards their source of safety. Eirian remained behind, spreading her hands out to either side of herself as her teammates formed a triangle around her. Bracing their empty palms in her direction, they each summoned their own magics, creating a whirl wind that surrounded Eirian. The children stopped approaching the village, turning back to watch as the male dragon's gave Eirian a portion of their magic. As a loud bell began ringing in Flintlyn City, the whirl wind surrounding Eirian shattered apart, revealing the ten year old in her thick black armor. Frowning thoughtfully one of the girls, Avani, stooped into the cold gray dirt of the road and pressed her swollen hands into the dirt. Closing her eyes, she concentrated on where her guards were and asked the earth to tell her what they were saying.

"*This isn't good*," the blue-dragon said

"*Ziya-Isha that looks bad!*" the red-dragon whimpered, "*like really bad! Can that even be healed?*"

"*She won't be able to fly with us but otherwise Ryū is technically operational*," Ziya answered. "*We'll need to figure out a different way of transportation…*"

"*It'll be okay Barak*," her voice sounded soft and comforting, like she wasn't worried at all. "*you can just carry me home.*"

"*The idiot isn't that strong*," the blue dragon drawled. "*He can barely keep himself in the air.*"

"*Shut up water boy!*" Avani lost concentration as dozens of names began filling the air, twisting around she found her mother, accompanied by dozens of other adults, come charging down the gray road. Between her and the rushing adults, the other children were also kneeled into the dirt, hands buried into the gray dust of the road; a few were even crying. as she looked about at the others, Avani realized that she wasn't the only one curious about what the dragons were doing and so they listened in on the conversation. looking down the road she saw the dragons were examining Eirian's back carefully. Her once discreetly hidden raven wings were now skeleton remains, held together with some black thread; a sad reminder of the shadowy beauty she once walked with.

"Avani!" the other children realized that their parents were coming and they each moved, their minds working at different speeds to register the information given to them. Before she knew it, Avani was racing up the path with all the other kids, crying out in joy as her mother caught her. All around them, dozens of names were called out. The misty mountain air filled with the sound of mother's crying as they cradled their children, father's spinning their only kin through the air, grandparents collapsing with their last family tangled in their arms.

Everything was joyous, their family, their village, was finally reunited and whole once more.

The dragon children remained at the base of the path, observing the villager's they saved. It had been tricky, with Eirian doing most of the work, but they were able to protect the lives of the villagers. Although Suomi village was lost, the people themselves survived and that was worth more than any reword for the children of dragons. As they watched the villagers rejoice, they noticed something strange sprouting from the village. It looked like a great pine, except its bark was red like blood, its leaves glowed white, and its branches spread out over the village like a protective dome.

"Ziya-Isha, what is that?" Eirian asked, looking up at her teacher in confusion.

"Jiane got hurt while retreating," Ziya answered, "he must be too weak to continue home."

"Not if I have anything to say," Eirian put her hands on her hips and glared up at her teacher. "Why didn't you tell me Jiane got hurt? I would've used—"

"Your flight spell can only last for so long Eirian and you were already exhausted as it was," Ziya returned the girl's glare. "Even now, you can't even put up an illusion spell to cover your own wings. Even if you have some strength left, is it truly enough to save him? Flintlyn City has some wonderful healers, if they can't heal him how can you?"

"You're not even giving me a chance!" Eirian shouted at him, anger turned her silver-orbs into cold acid-etched glass shards.

"You can only run to him, your wings won't work, how can you get to him before he passes?" Ziya asked her, "That Blekking-tree only sprouts when one is on the brink of death; which is why only *we* can see it but no one else can. Our dragons are telling us he only has a few minutes left. There is *nothing* you can do Eirian."

"Ziya-Isha, what if I carried her to the village?" Barak asked, flinching back when the two snarling masks of his teammate and commander turned to him. "My wings are good and I can carry her. My magic is still good too, I only need a little burst to increase my speed and we can be there in a few seconds."

"Barak, you're a genius!" Eirian started seriously and then threw her arms into the air and tackled her teammate. "It's settled, Ziya-Isha we're going to save Jiane! You distract everyone else!"

"Now wait a—"

"Barak hurry!" Eirian ordered as she wrapped her arms around his neck and dangled from across his back.

"Right, Right!" Barak coughed as he tucked Eirian's arms off his neck and bent to stabilize her added weight, then spread his wings out to either side.

"Don't crash," Servass advised as his two teammates took flight.

"Shut up!" Barak ordered loudly as he tilted in the air dangerously. As promised Barak used another spell that elongated his wings to twice their previous size, appearing as feathered wings made from sparks.

"Ziya-Isha," Maor turned towards his teacher, his narrowed eyes pinched behind his mask. "Our mission was to protect Soumi village. Will we not be paid for the destruction of the village?"

"Who knows?" Ziya questioned himself as he stared at the people on the incline road, "We shall see." Ziya walked forward with all the confidence of a war general, it didn't take long for the survivors to notice him. The survivors glanced back at the village where Eirian and Barak crashed with a spectacular display of fireworks, before moving to meet with Ziya and Maor.

"Thank you, children of dragons," together the villagers bowed, those who were able kneeled into the muddy soil with their wrists crossed overhead, others could only twist their spines so far before falling over. Many of the elders settled for pressing their right fist into their heart and bowing their heads with smiles on their wrinkled faces.

"There is no need to kneel, please rise," Ziya said, sounding exasperated and embarrassed. "We have failed our given task. To protect the village was our primary goal. As Suomi village has fallen there is no need for you to pay us the amount we have agreed on." Maor made a strangled sound, bewildered about his teacher offering the villagers a chance to back out of the agreement.

"But you spared the lives of my brother and grand-nephew and for that Flintlyn City is forever in your doubt." From the crowd a man with an old metal cane stepped forward, a young black haired boy at his side and a slightly younger looking man on his other. "I am the leader of Flintlyn City, thank you much, Dragon-children, for sparing my only family."

"It had been agreed upon that should the village be un-savable that all residences be retreated to Flintlyn City," Ziya replied kindly. "This was the course to be taken, should we fail our primary objective."

"Perhaps but Flintlyn City is a mining and forging City." The old man retorted, bobbing his almost-bald head thoughtfully. "We specialize in the formation of metals and minerals. Although I cannot give you the gold as payment for the failure of your primary task, I *can* give you something else for succeeding in the secondary task. Especially since no one had passed during the retreat."

"Well," Ziya hesitated, his glowing scarlet eyes turning towards the gray skies thoughtfully. "I know our stock on Thulium is low, do you mine any of that?"

"…my apologies sir but what would dragon-children like yourselves ever want with something so useless?" the village elder asked, looking bewildered. "It has no value in metal works, medicine or even in spell casting. It is the most useless of all minerals in existence, even gardeners cannot use it for their plants."

"Uh? Well I don't know what my cousin dose with the stuff I just know that he's agitated about our stock being low." Ziya shrugged, not caring whether or not he could actually get the mineral. "It was just a thought on my part. Since he lives with me, it's hard to get him to shut up about the stock supplies shortages and I know that the lack of Thulium is one of the biggest things he rants about."

"I see," the village elder shrugged carelessly. "I will see if we have any of that mineral. If we do I will send it to the remnants of Suomi village. If we do not have the mineral, what can I get for you in return?"

"Huh? Oh don't worry about delivering it to us! We'll send a convoy to you in a week's time to see if you have any or not. If you don't have Thulium then don't worry about it. I'm sure the convoy will have a different mineral in mind to exchange for the lack of Thulium." Ziya shrugged. "Honestly I shouldn't have suggested it, no doubt Nanaibek-Rū will most likely be displeased with my suggestion."

"I will see what we can't gather for the envoy," the old man bowed again, a fond smile on his lips as he shook his head ruefully. "Fly safe, children of dragons." On cue Flintlyn City lit up with golden light, the tree that once towered over it shimmered before bursting into millions of white petals and scattering on the wind. The children cheered, recognizing the pristine light easily, and began explaining excitedly that Eirian had done something. Ziya hummed in approval as Barak went tearing through the air in a display of swirling sparks and embers; making a b-line straight for his two other teammates. Soon after three dragons roared to life and tore through the air in a spectacular display of glittering lights and leaves. One dragon, great like an ancient oak, wingless like a serpent, with eight diamond claws and a temple of twelve swirling horns, spun through the air before moving down towards the path. The villagers watched, lost in amazement, as the view of two young children ridding its back passed them by. The girl had long curly amethyst hair pulled back in a high pony-tail, her tunic was simple navy and silver, her skin a gentle olive. She sat, eyes down cast and smile gentle, with one hand pressed to the boy's chest, the other combing through his wild snow-white locks. The boy was laying with his head in the girl's lap. He was dressed in silver and pastel-blue silk, eyes closed and strange white stripes curling across his face. There was a small hand-sized blood stain on his left hip, just barely hidden beneath his wide sleeve.

They knew, instantly, that the two were Eirian and Jiane; the dragons who risked everything for them.

The villagers laughed and giggled at the sight, tears of joy and regret streaming down their faces; finally the white dragon the children who road it swirled to a landing at the base of the path, looking up at the remaining dragons expectantly. Maor, Barak and their teacher Ziya each hurried down the road, Barak waving excitedly and jabbering loudly at his teammate, Maor, the entire way down.

"Will we see them again Aunty?" a little girl asked looking up at the middle aged woman, her weight braced by a thick cane.

"Someday sweetheart, someday," The woman smiled in answer, patting a thick meaty hand on the girl's dark ringlets. A great echoing cry, a roar of unnamed beasts, shattered the tranquil gray skies; all the villagers jumped and flinched with the startling cry as fear gripped their hearts once more. They watched as the dragon children took to the air with a great white wall of light enveloped them and soon enough the fully grown dragon took to the air after them. The dragon-boys hooped and hollered, laughter echoing around them as they spun in circles around their elder-dragon. Ziya soon spread his own golden wings and took flight himself, looking like a tiny golden dragon darting back and forth through the sky as if playing with the giant creature of light and snow.

"Aunty," the little girl with dark curls called, her voice quivering in fear. "She can't fly..."

"What do you mean child?" the woman looked down on her niece, confusion soon replaced with worry as she watched the tears drip down the young child's face.

"Lady Dragon protected us, she gave her arm and her wings. Now she can't fly," the little girl looked up at her elder, misery contorting her young face. "What if she can't ever heal? What if she'll never fly again? Dragons shouldn't be land creatures. They're a part of the sky, so what if she'll never fly?! What if she'll never fly again because of us?!"

"Shhh, little one, don't cry," one of the older girls murmured, stooping to her knees in the mud, her thick hands wrapping around the young child's shoulders. "You heard Ziya-Rū, the armor will repair itself upon return to their homelands. She'll be able to fly again someday and when that day comes, surly she'll come to see us again."

"Okay," the little girl sniffed, looking again to the gray skies, not surprised that her savors were long gone from her vision. As the villagers trickled back into Flintlyn City, a young messenger came rushing out, a scroll in hand as he raced with pink cheeks and a panicked air.

"Master Koujin! Master Koujin!"

"What is it?" the old leader of the village asked, his wrinkled face twisting into a frown.

"A message from the seers!" the young boy shouted as the crowd parted for him, curious about his frantic desperation to reach the village elder. "They wish to know the names of those who saved the Kūnnene family!"

"Why would they wish to know that?" another old man asked, his withered face twisted in confusion. "Can they not look into other worlds for such things?"

"The seers—" the boy skidded to a stop, nearly falling on his rear on the slick path to Flintlyn City. "They said it's a matter of war!" the boy thrust the scroll out to Koujin, the leader of Flintlyn City. He took the scroll quickly, ignoring the boy as he double over, bracing his calloused palms on his dirty knees as he panted heavily.

"This isn't good," Koujin murmured as he read the scroll.

"Master Koujin," one of the mothers murmured, her hands tugging her three children between her and her husband. "Is it really war?"

"We have two years to prepare," Koujin said as he rolled up the scroll and looked about at the villagers seeking refuge in his home. "Forgive me, children of ash and stone, but we will need your battle skills in order to survive the coming war."

"We turned our backs on the way of the blade when we left Emlyn decades ago," one of the men protested.

"We cannot withstand the slaughter of another war!"

"Please Master Koujin, we're begging you!" a young couple clutched at each other, tears in their eyes.

"Please don't make us go to war!"

"We won't survive!"

"We're only eighty-seven people!"

"We won't survive that kind of battle!"

"We'll be decimated!"

"I can't burry another child!"

"Be still my brothers and sisters!" Koujin bellowed, silencing the protests and whimpers quickly. "You've hidden from Tregaron for sixty years. within that time frame your numbers have very nearly tripled. You retreated from the military city of Tregaron, Emlyn city, at the price of dozens of your kin but your children survived! Survived long enough to bare children of their own. Now all this was done because the seers told you to retreat! Emlyn city did not care for you before, nor do they now! I promised you all refuge and I intend to keep my word!"

"How can you protect us if you declare war!" a woman shouted, clutching at her youngest child with both arms, her body shaking in terror.

"I did not declare war! The seers told you to flee sixty years ago to spare your children from annihilation and survive you children did!" Koujin reminded the villagers. "Listen to them once more. They did not declare war with the intention of using you like swords and arrows, nor do I intend to do the same. The war that will come will shake the seven kingdoms and taint our forest crimson!"

"The forest of Tregaron or our mountain trees?" someone else asked, voice full of fury and sorrow, breaking with the sharp crack of fear. Sighing Koujin unraveled the scroll and withheld it before himself, reading off the lines written to him in strict confidence; at least the part that concerned the Kūnnene family.

"The first flower blooms with the sun and moon shinning bright,
Bring with it a dozen Summers of peace and love.
Then earth shall render the eternal gleaming,
Günayang shall pass the twins of parallel bridge.
The earth shall bless the second born,
So sacred be the sapphires.
Then five stars a line to greet the four elements,
Princess of stars shall fall anew.
The sacrifice of city in lights too great,
The souls wander through the onyx skies
Then a dozen ashes be brave in soiled lands
Ten demons of creation arise,
The first of mist will curse the domains with
Weapons of hate forged in nation's ancient.
Then ashes bring dragon eternal,
Brimstone obeys great mother's bone."

"The only flower that blooms within the light of the sun and moon, is Goddess Sytra's first flower of creation: the Anhua flower!" one of the parents declared, his square face twisted into a look of confusion.

Koujin lowered the parchment to stare seriously at the people gathered before him, hoping they understood the seer's intentions.

"Mama, what does he mean?" a young boy asked, looking up at his parents curiously.

"The children of ashes and stone," the woman started, tears in her bright eyes. "Have fallen to the hands of leaves and branches. There are no more soldiers of our family left. Emlyn city was sure to make that a fact."

"But the Anhua flower bloomed ten years ago," an old woman murmured. "The time of peace has ended. The seer's vision has come too late."

"Bring with it, a decade of summer sun," Koujin repeated. "It's been ten years since the first flower of creation last bloomed. Now the earth shall—"

"The prophecy brother," Koujin's slightly younger brother called out, "Doesn't it say something about ashes?" confused Koujin went back to the scroll and reread a portion of the letter again.

"Then a dozen ashes be brave in soiled lands," Koujin read aloud then froze, his eyes widening as he reread the line again and again. *"Then five stars a line to greet the four elements, Princess of stars shall fall anew. The sacrifice of city in lights too great, the souls wander through the onyx skies. Then a dozen ashes be brave in soiled lands, Ten demons of creation arise. The first of mist will curse the domains with weapons of hate forged in nation's ancient. Then ashes bring dragons eternal, brimstone obeys great mother's bone."*

"Soon a dozen children, ten of our youngest, will be born." Koujin turned to his baby brother, regret on his face and sorrow spreading tears in his orange eyes. "These ten children shall be raised in our old ways. To fight, to wage war, to survive against the worst of odds. These ten shall be our soldiers. We will cherish them but we *must* prepare them. For when the time of the blood-wars reaches us once more, we must be ready to battle the seven kingdoms."

"But what about the five stars?" one of the younger children asked, looking curiously at his village leader. "What about the dragons eternal?"

"Many years ago children used to be named after the stars," an elder murmured gently. "In honor of the gods who forged our world anew."

"…no one in our land has ever been able to bare such a high number of children since the blood war." Koujin answered, bowing his head in shame. "Our own family can't bear any more than the twins that we all ways have born. I'm afraid… 'the five stars' are in reference to the five children who gave their very lives to call forth the guardian dragons. They were the reason why the ancient ones were able to survive for as long as they have, even though the price was seclusion."

"What do you mean?" one of the teens asked, his face scrunching up in confusion.

"Are you saying… the seers saw a vision where Aeoman Forest falls and the ancient ones will be sold to the greedy?" One of the mothers asked, looking up anxiously. "Are you saying that another blood war is coming?"

"The last one lasted centuries," another elder commented with a heavy sigh. "Will these wars ever end?"

"Then who will protect the dragon children?" another little girl asked curiously.

"No one love, no one," the girl's aunt murmured gently.

"But… they protected us," the girl replied, confused with the answer. "Shouldn't we return the gift they gave us?"

"You're much too sweet." The old aunt murmured, biting back tears as she smiled at the young girl. Koujin pointed at a line in the letter to his brother, frowning at the phrase thoughtfully.

"Does this mean?" the younger couldn't continue, horror etching his face as he stared.

"Yes," Koujin murmured mournfully. "Princess Sitareh is going to die… in the city of lights."

"Then, the seer's request for the dragon-children's names?"

"Yes, they wish to save their princess."

"Do you think they'll succeed?" the younger asked softly. "We don't even know when the next blood war will begin…"

"Perharps, it'll happen when our dozen are born," Koujin said thoughtfully. "I'm more worried about this line about *ten demons of creation* arising."

"Could it be symbolism?" the younger brother asked hopefully, "Everyone knows the ten demons of creation are just a myth. They don't actually exist…right?"

"A seer is rarely wrong," Koujin pointed at the seal at the bottom of the paper. "Rarer still is the princess of foresight."

"…to see one's own death," he shook his head mournfully. "What an awful fate."

Chapter 4

Two years later: at the 'Mountain union' between four countries of Aeoman.

They had been asked to go to the northern curve of the Baīlāy Mountain Range, or more specifically to reach the base of the most northern Mountain. The curved valley sitting between two great mountains bore great cliff faces as pale as fresh snow, the soil was pale like white sand. The vegetation was not so different from the moon kissed stone and soil that bathed the Great Baīlāy Mountain Range. The trees grew with pealing white bark, revealing thick gray rings beneath, their leaves were as dark as white jade could be and they bore fruit the color of a golden dusk. The group arrived at the foot of a mountain and began climbing the sheer white-washed marble walls to arrive at 'Seer's Valley'. It was an experience none of the three preteens were going to forget. Dressed in their battle armor of foreboding dragons, Barak and Maor raced each other to reach the valley before the other. Eirian and Ziya remained behind, hiding their tracks and pretending that they weren't about to discover the valley of seers.

"I'm still worried Ziya-isha," Eirian murmured, her brow wrinkling as they continued up the steep incline that required more crawling and less walking. "For what reason did they ask for our aid and why now of all times? They survived centuries without our aid or anyone else's influence for that matter, what changed?"

"We will find out when we arrive," Ziya replied patently, as he had said such words a dozen times before to the racing boys ahead of them. "As it is, we must keep an eye out. To betray their trust with accidental exposure will not bode well for them nor our home."

"Yes Ziya-isha," Eirian sighed heavily. "have I said I hate this place?"

"Since we stepped foot here," Ziya chuckled

"Children of the forest, you've arrived!" both master and student looked up to where their teammates were supposed to be arguing, discovering only a plump woman holding both boys beneath her arms in headlocks neither could escape; much to the boy's frustration. The three appeared to be leaning over an edge, judging by the tilt of their bodies, to peer down on Ziya and Eirian. The woman had her long white locks pulled back into a high and tight bun, a fond blush stained her round cheeks as she smiled down on them. "Master Chanitri has been awaiting your arrival most anxiously! Hurry up now! The scouts will arrive soon!" hoping that the woman wasn't speaking of an enemy scouting team, Eirian and Ziya both picked up their pace and hurried to reach the top of the steep cliff face. When the woman started looking about frantically, nibbling on her bottom lip, Ziya cursed under breath. Murmuring a chant he used a gentle glowing seal array to glide up the cliff face as if he were scatting on ice, snatching up Eirian while he neared the top. The woman sighed in relief when they both landed at her side, hurrying the team in dragon scales further away from the white-marble cliff side. Eirian and Ziya both looked back just in time for a scent of embers and ashes to waft up the cliff side, signaling the arrival of an unwanted mage-scout.

"Too close, too close," the woman chanted as she hurried away, a horrified flush tinted her round features. "Point three seconds longer and all be lost." Eirian and Ziya glanced at each other, their own beating hearts thumping loudly in their ears. They decided not to ask the strange woman any questions as they hurried after her, smirking in amusement as neither Barak nor Maor could use their voices as the woman's hands was firmly clamped over the boy's masked-mouths. The team walked through a valley with white-washed soil, no grass or moss covering the earth nor bark of the trees now surrounding them. It was not until after the group crossed a bridge over a trickling river that the woman decided to release the boys. Both Barak and Maor stopped walking, taking in deep breaths while the woman continued across the bridge, not caring if they followed or not. Neither boy could chance a word before Eirian and Ziya were hurrying past, trying to keep up with the woman looking like a literal peach but much faster than either expected.

"That house over there is where all our cloth comes from," the woman said suddenly, waving at set of three wooden buildings closely built together but not indicating which was which. "It has access to the glowing cave worms who live in the underground lake below us. The worms eat the minerals in the steam vents and spin the silk thread they use to catch the minerals. We use these silken threads to create our clothes, which is why they are so white and clean looking."

"...you don't ever have to wash them?" Barak asked as he hurried to catch up.

"No, it takes great levels of effort to get the silk dirty. Even playing in mud and our clothes need only a good shake to return to cleanliness again." The woman answered patently. "The trees are our primary food source, they're the Marnthe berries and the only trees that grow in the Baīlāy Mountain Range with eatable fruit."

"I see," Ziya murmured as he glanced at a set of trees with several people beneath their eves, harvesting the next batch of ready fruits. "Are these trees the reason behind your ability to remain here in this valley without being discovered for so long?"

"There are many secrets that are behind our ability to remain undetected by the greedy and wicked." The woman replied, "Many more I can neither speak of nor know all of." Ziya said nothing to the answer and continued to follow her with his students at his side. They passed several types of large hefty birds with a beautiful display of colorful feathers and a few other meaty animals that roamed about. Once they caught a break in the orchard, the team discovered a great white marble wall; they had finally crossed the valley to reach the other great cliff face. The surface of the cliff face was interspaced with large towering sectors of square buildings mingled with decorative paths and smooth slopped roofs. The white-marble buildings were carved from the cliff face, great and towering they took the height of three floors just to house two sectors.

"…whoa," Barak whispered, his voice barely a whisper, his bright sky blue eyes comically wide at the sight.

"Where is everyone?" Maor asked but no one answered, everyone looked about but saw no other 'seers' in the orchard and no one on the steps leading to the white-washed village.

"These are our homes and learning place," The woman murmured as she kept walking. "The work force, something everyone participates in, even the princesses, is our orchard." Again the woman's speed surprised the group as they struggled to keep up with her swift steps, unable to truly stop and appreciate the rare opportunity presented to them. They hurried, trying to look around at all the pale hues of white hair and shimmering robes, even the woven baskets they used to carry things were woven from the white branches of the trees in the valley. They approached a great twisting stone staircase, sprawling up like diamonds up the cliff face, guarded by two male statues. The statues garb consisted of a tunic that ended halfway down to their knees, held in place with a sash decorated with constellation embroidery. Their pants were wide like a skirt, their feet bare and exposed to the warm sun-kissed stone of the cliff face. Their tunics had long billowing sleeves, elegant embroidery lined them from shoulder to wrist in great swirls and spirals. Their thick hoods were wide, shadowing their faces from the mountain sun and its reflection, revealing only the gemstone rings representing their eyes; sapphire and amethyst. Held out before themselves with both hands, were long thin staffs of snow white, etched in hypnotic swirls and tipped with white-bone-arrows. The team did not wish to know where these bone-blades were carved nor did the children wish to find out.

"Astra, you're nearly late," the man to the right grumbled, his voice low and steady, his violet eyes thin and unwavering from his staff.

"Holly shit!" Barak screamed

"They're alive?! / They're people?!" Eirian and Maor yelped simultaneously.

"Point three seconds and all be lost," the man on the left murmured just as softly. Ziya discreetly tucked his claws behind himself, hiding the fact that he had very nearly beheaded the should've-been-a-statue males when the children screamed.

"Point three seconds and all is safe," the woman, Astra, answered them in kind. She breezed past the guards, ignoring their statue still bodies as she hurried up the white stone steps. The team glanced at each other but hurried forwards, wiry of the guardsmen but continued after Astra when neither male moved. They followed the woman up the five flights of intermixed stairs, each set interrupted by a building-entrance or pathway that spiraled off to another building. Eventually they reached the highest stone building, the final flight of stairs, and continued down the white-marble path to enter a building decorated with thousands of constellations. Inside the building was swarmed with more white clouds of cloth, tables and armors carved from thick white wood. The small doorways into various rooms, some with multiple beds, others looking like very large closets, the largest room they past appeared to be a kitchen. Everything in the kitchen seemed to be carved from the white marble of the cliff face, more tools appeared to be carved from bones, the exception of which appeared to be pots hanging over the hearths and fire pits; all made from blackened silver.

"Hurry now," Astra ordered as she left Barak behind to gawk at the massive kitchen, "point three seconds, point three seconds!" not having a clue as to what the woman was chittering about, Barak glanced back at the kitchen full of bustling bodies before chasing after his teammates and guild.

"Where are you taking us?" Eirian asked, growing wiry of chasing the woman.

"To center hall," Astra answered. "Must hurry now. Much longer and life sealed."

"If we must hurry shouldn't we run?" Ziya asked, his fingertips already glowing with the need to write a seal-array.

"No." Astra answered firmly. "Run creates panic. Panic creates fear. Fear creates fate. Fate creates destiny. Destiny is unshakable." The glow from Ziya's fingertips faded, and turned to share an uneasy look with Eirian, already guessing that something vital was the purpose for their being brought to the seer's valley. "Many Aisling are there," Astra said suddenly, as if trying to fill the empty air with the sound of her voice. "To gather and die or gather to live is fate you must decide."

"What do you mean?" Eirian asked, "Why were we brought here?" as they hurried along they passed an open room, glancing inside Eirian very nearly tripped over her own feet. For one brief moment in time, she found herself staring at a child—not much older than herself—taking a blade to her wrist; a shallow blind-glaze in her autumn eyes and a dopy, sad smile on her round face. Eirian hadn't taken two steps past the doorway before another seer entered the room, just a pace slower than herself, and screamed in agony as the child's blood arced out of her wrist. As they hurried along, Astra pausing only a brief second to grab Eirian's wrist and jerking the child after herself, Eirian watched as several others from the kitchens hurried into the room.

"*You* must decide," Astra answered as they turned a corner, her voice soft and sad. Twenty feet or so further down the hall, were pair of great white doors with beautifully crafted figures crawling across the surface. "To let one live then all shall fall, to let all live then one shall fall. Whose fate is what you must decide." The woman stopped, her large meaty-hands pressing against the doors, her face pinking with the effort to move them. From the other side the sound of voices, cheerful and bright, laughter and giggling, sounded through the thick white marble doors.

"P-p-p-point," Astra grunted, "Th-th-threeeeee," she huffed, "Sssssssse—"

"MOVE!" Astra barely managed to leap to the side before Barak was flying through the air, his foot colliding with the white doors in a show of brute force and a spiral of golden embers. The doors crashed open, silencing all on the other side. Barak collapsed in the entrance way, flat on his back, trying hard not to cry about his maybe-broken foot. Astra strolled into the room with all the dignity of a queen, acting as if Barak didn't just slam the doors open and possibly hurt himself.

"Point three seconds and all is well." Astra said as she walked away from the group, Ziya remained behind with his students, his glowing eyes glued to the scene beyond the door. With what happened along their way to the room, he became uneasy and distrustful of the seers they were too meet. It wasn't normal to just let a child die while everyone else was celebrating and having a good time. They were seers for crying out loud, how did they not know about the suicidal child three rooms down from them?

"Idiot," Eirian grumbled as she stooped with Maor to lift Barak, one arm over each of their shoulders. "You're gonna have to suffer until I get the time to heal it." Barak's armor whimpered pitifully in his place. "I am *not* going to heal you with a thousand eyes on me. The—"

"Five hundred, thirty-seven," a voice from further inside the room called out, making the team turn towards the occupancy in confusion. The room they saw, the center hall as Astra called it, was easily the largest room that they've ever seen. It was easily three stories tall and possibly just as long, the room was filled with low tables all filled with hundreds of people who sat on pillows. From the high ceiling was a great network of thread and beads interspaced together, using the candlelight from the tables and the sunlight from the windows to the far left, the ceiling appeared to be a white glittering abyss of endless depths. At the furthest end from the entrance was a table sitting vertical compared to the others, curved gently for the seven individuals who could view everyone in the chamber. At the very center sat a man dressed in the same robes as Astra, decorated only with a simple golden band across his brow. The simple golden loop held a simple white stone embed in its center. The people sitting at the other tables were all shoulder to shoulder, some even sitting in another's lap as they all shared the low sitting tables. Everyone inside the giant chamber were all the same color of white as their robes; no one had a single splash of color outside of a food stain or the hue of their eyes. Eirian was the first to notice that their eyes ranged from blue, silver, purple, green, red and every shade in between.

"I'm sorry?" Ziya questioned, not understanding the statement amongst the silence of the occupancy.

"Five hundred, thirty-seven people, child of fate." The man elaborated, patting the hand of the woman who sat beside him, the same crown on his brow was mimicked on her own. "Not a thousand people, just five hundred thirty-seven." Ziya glanced at Eirian, alarm in his scarlet eyes. Eirian felt just as uneasy as her teacher. They were several dozen yards away from the man, an easy acker or two between them, and yet the old man still heard her soft whisper.

"I am glad you have all arrived, point three seconds to spare, as well." The man said as he stood from the table, his face splitting into a gentle smile as he waved them in. "Come, sit with me and my family. I promise to tell you all." Ziya glanced at his students, they each looked wiry but curious, with a sigh he stepped forward. This was a mission after all, they were tasked to meet with the fortune tellers in 'Seer Valley' and receive more details about their mission from the fortune tellers. As they walked down the center of the hall, the children huddled together even closer than they needed to help Barak walk, the air filled with gentle whispers and hushed voices. Out of curiosity Eirian glanced at a group of children as she passed them, the most outstanding one was the tiny six year old staring open mouthed with wide wolf eyes.

"Pretty," one of the older girls murmured, receiving several hummed agreements from the others. Sharing a confused look with her teammates, the children kept walking till they reached the front of the vast room. Stopping just before the man and his long curved table, the group glanced at each other before looking more pointedly at him. Upon closer look the man was easily middle aged, his silver-green eyes shown beautifully, his white robes appearing new and well used at the same time. the woman at his side had long flowing star-white hair, wide baby blue eyes stared curiously at the group, her face was smooth and round, implying her young age. the two adults stepped away from the table and moved together to approach the dragon-children. At the table were four young girls, the eldest appearing to be fourteen and the youngest easily four. The family looked no different than everyone else in the room: white from head to two, round faced, various shades of blue eyes and shorter than even Barak.

"Welcome, children of the forest." The man greeted them, holding a handout to Ziya expectantly, "We expect great things from each of you." Ziya reluctantly shook the man's hand, refusing to give the man anything more than his pointer finger so his claws wouldn't rip the man's hand open. "My name is Chanitri, I'm the family head of the Aisling family." He offered his hand to Eirian but the preteen merely wiggled her fingers over Barak's arm, which was braced over her shoulders, and the man seemed to understand. Chanitri bobbed his head and looked at the two boys but neither made a move to shake his hand either. Shrugging carelessly, Chanitri patted his wife's hand and smiled at her, as if sharing a funny secret together. "The Aisling family are the seers who sent the request for aid," Chanitri turned his attention back to Ziya, his smile still present. "Thank you for arriving to meet with us. These are all of our people!" the residents around them cheered loudly, a few words were slurred from a few adults, but most of the voices were clear.

"This is my bride, Citlali," the man said, smiling at his wife in adoration. His reword was a blinding smile from his blushing wife, her baby blue eyes dancing like sunlight on water.

"My beloved groom," Citlali cooed at him, leaning in close so their shoulders touched and their fingers entangled together. The second youngest stuck a finger close to her mouth and made a gagging noise as she turned away from the table.

"Seren, not at the table," the eldest ordered, looking disapprovingly on the girl across from her.

"Ah, My apologies, children of the forest," Citlali gasped, her fond smile never wavering. "This is my beloved, Chanitri, and these are our daughters: Csilla, Sitora, Seren and Izar." She turned and swept an arm out at their daughters. Chanitri leaned in close to his wife and whispered something in her ear; earning himself a pleased giggle.

The eldest, Csilla, had pastel white-gold locks trailing down to her waist. Only her sideburns were bound in white cloth to frame her childish-round face. Her glacier-blue eyes were permanently narrowed, as if she detested the world and wished her glare could burn it all to ashes. Her brow was braced with a thin golden band, the center of which was full of five white stones, the center was long and oval while the two circles on either side were much smaller than the other two on the further ends.

Beside Csilla was Sitora who wore the same crown as her elder sister. Sitora had wide bright lavender eyes, her pale cheeks were flushed as her smile has yet to drop. The young girl had silver-gold locks as compared to her sister and mother, a strand wrapped about her head to keep the freer locks from going wild and the silver-gold mane that trailed down her back was bound by a similar braid.

Seren's hair was by far the darkest of gold as her crown seemed to disappear amongst her locks perfectly. Seren's golden strands were parted into four sections, each section was bound at her shoulders with white cloth. Her eyes were the palest of her family as she stared ahead with silver orbs that over exaggerated her emotionless mask; she appeared blind at first but her eyes kept moving whenever the little one in her lap moved.

In Seren's lap sat the squirmy toddler Izar. Unlike her elder sisters and parents, Izar had luscious full waves of platinum locks, the top half of which was pulled back from her round face and pinned with two thin sticks tipped with beads of white marble. Izar wore the same crown as her elder sisters, but unlike them she bore the darkest blue eyes; her large orbits appearing black amongst all the pale light of her skin and hair. There was no question in the four girl's relation to each other and there was no question in who their parents were, they each held the same nose and cheeks, their brows appearing long since costumed to the crowns they wore.

"...Sis-ill-a, Sea-ree, Sea-ren, is-are?" Ziya questioned slowly, pronouncing the words slowly just in case.

"C-la, and Ee-Z-are," Csilla corrected with a bland expression, sitting closest to the group and to her father's furthest right.

"Sigh-ra," the second youngest corrected, smiling at the youngest in her lap as the four year old clambered for their mother's cup.

"Why is 'Izar' the only one different?" Eirian asked out of curiosity. The youngest perked at the table, her platinum gold head popping up and her big blue eyes looked about in bewilderment.

"We ran out of 'S' names," Citlali giggled. "Anyways, the one we are entrusting to you has yet to arrive..." she turned to look at her husband who only sighed and shrugged helplessly, his small smile denoting his clueless of the mentioned individual. "Ah, well, she'll be here shortly." Citlali waved a dismissive hand, her smile brightening at the group. "Why don't you join us for dinner?" Appearing from a side door, far to the group's right, was a rushing team of four, carrying a large table with platters and bowls. The couple backed several paces as servants brought a fully equipped table before the team. The large white table was soon showered in a white cloth and was just as quickly accompanied by several other people hurrying forward with practiced grace to set the table with food and drink. Several others gently set about pillows on the floor for the group to sit upon. One of them even set a small bowl out for Barak to set his foot outstretched; a small curved pot of ice near the far left of the table. Maor and Eirian huffed as they struggled to put their teammate at the furthest end, Maor held no mercy as he purposefully dropped Barak's foot straight into the ice bowl. To his teammates Barak appeared to be torn from crying in pain and crying in relief, no doubt he looked really awkward to everyone else.

"If I am not mistaken, Ziya-Isha, I believe Nanaibek-Rū gave you a talisman to activate upon arrival, yes?" Chanitri questioned, as he helped his wife to sit on the other side of the table. Although Chanitri had questioned Ziya, it appeared as if it were a rhetorical question; its answer obvious when the middle aged man took a slow drink from a cup with a content smile. Ziya lifted a hand, a glowing seal array appearing in his palm that quickly produced a small wooden plank. The plank was hexagonal in shape and barely larger than Ziya's palm, the black etching on its surface was of the same proud crest that was etched upon Ziya's golden chest plate: a circle within a five point star, within an eight-point star, within a twelve-point star.

"Ahiris." Ziya murmured, in answer the crest burst into flame and from its surface the flaming figure of a willowy male arose, head bowed as if in shame.

"Ziya, I have received a distressing message from the children of foresight. When you arrive at Seer Valley, do not hesitate to reveal your true selves." The message ended, the willowy flaming figure retreated back within the shell of the talisman, and Ziya looked at his students. The three were oddly silent, the only clue to their apprehension were their shaking hands and their legs trembling in preparation to flee. It was such an odd demand from their Military Leader. All their lives the children had been brought up to understand that once they leave the safety of the forest, their true faces must never be seen. To reveal their true faces to anyone while outside of the forest could endanger their families and in turn the people who might be housing the 'lost ones'. Ziya understood that there were instances where one's true identity was required to be shown while outside of the forest but honestly those instances were encroaching on protective barriers of fellow 'dragon-children'. This was no such time and it worried even him that he too was ordered to reveal his true face to these recluses who held no loyalty to anyone but themselves.

"Test," Eirian gasped, her shoulders leveled, and fluttering wings twittered no more. Her voice was so soft, Ziya almost didn't hear her. As it was, his own scarlet eyes widened in bewilderment when the twelve year old leaped to her feet and took several paces back.

"Aditimre." Eirian's whole body erupted into shadows and flame, contorted and disfigured, the pillar of magic slowly bleached white like moon light. The shadows faded, the flames softened, feathers of white light surrounded Eirian and her true *human* face was revealed for all to see. Eirian had hair like ocean waves at midnight, cascading down her back to whisper against her thighs, the top half was pulled back with a high ribbon of lavender, revealing her face for all to see. Her eyes were the color of dark Amethyst, highlighted with specks of lavender and periwinkle stripes; a single stripe of gold shown in the bottom of each iris. Beneath her left eye, curving with the brush of her long dark lashes, were two distinctive black marks commonly mistaken for moles; they were truly Eirian's birth marks. Her round childish face was framed by two forelocks bound in thick scripted gold bands, the gentle waves of deep purple ended just below her bust. Her armor had retreated, disappearing beneath the tablecloth, leaving Eirian bare in her own traditional wraps. Eirian's shirt was square collared with a sharp 'V' incision just below her collar bone, her sleeves wide and bell shaped ending just shy of her elbows; revealing her thick black arm bands. Her legs were sheathed in thick brown leather with protective knee-braces shinning silver in the hall's light. She wore a cloth wrap that surrounded her body in lose folds, looking like a sleeveless gown four sizes too large.

Both Barak and Maor moved to follow their teammate but when Barak grunted on his way to his feet, Maor mercilessly kicked his arm out from under him and made the scarlet-scaled teenager crash into the white marbled floor. Eirian glared at Maor but he simply shrugged at her and raised his own hands to either side of himself.

Maor's power surrounded him in a show of bubbles, reflected light and glittering white mist. A flash of something dark darted from Maor's twirling power to scurry beneath the table Ziya still sat at. From the depths of the twirling light a young boy with short navy curls, sleepy ocean-blue eyes and ghostly white skin stepped out. He looked so much like a spirit of the sea that for a moment many children were lost in their own imaginations of playful water spirits. He was dressed in a simple layered tunic in shades of blue and green; which only highlighted his other worldly appearance.

"Thank you children for trusting us," Chanitri said, straightening in his seat to regard the children seriously. "As seers of the worlds, we can afford trust in very few individuals. That being said, we needed to be sure you four were who you said you were." Chanitri looked pointedly at Ziya, annoyed acceptance twisting his weathered face. "Even though we know not your true names, we are still honored you children of fate have come to lend aid." Ziya ignored the glare of his students with practice ease, knowing and still distrusting of the seers, Ziya remained with his golden scales still encasing his body.

"What's that supposed to mean?" Barak asked, as he pushed himself up.

"How do you know that our current appearances aren't another appearance-spell?" Maor asked, his ocean-blue eyes narrowed in calculation.

"The number of people who can perform layered appearance spells remain in less than the point of a percentage." Chanitri answered him.

"Besides that all those individuals are not currently living." Citlali continued, her smile gentle. "The first to show such skills has yet to be born, still residing in his mother's womb even now. He'll not show such skill for another decade or so." The children didn't know how to feel about that, the knowledge that a potential threat could appear with the face of a friend but the heart of an enemy was more alarming then an alley with the face of an enemy but the heart of a friend.

"Our dragon names are Ziya, Eirian, Maor and Barak." Ziya introduced everyone in accordance to their sitting placement. "How can we—"

"Maor means light, to whom do you lead?" Csilla asked suddenly, the cup she was going to drink from set before herself somberly. There was a strange glow to her eyes, like violet stripes, and her face had smoothed as if she were asleep. Citlali hurried to her feet and clambered the four simple steps that separated their table from everyone else's; she hurried to place her palm on Csilla's forehead. She turned long enough to frown at her husband before moving on to her next child.

"...my team?" Maor answered hesitantly, only to be elbowed by both simultaneously. "hey, I have," he grumbled defensively, not seeing Ziya's scarlet eyes narrow at the princess.

"Once in a blue moon doesn't count," Eirian whispered back, her smile neatly hidden behind her tea-cup. It seemed strange to Eirian that Citlali was merely pressing a hand to each of the girl's foreheads, as if she was checking their temperatures.

"Especially when we're still in forest," Barak whispered, referring to the last time Maor led them on a mission.

"To where?" Csilla asked, ignoring the small banter between the children. Citlali looked up from her task of checking Izar's temperature to look back at Csilla, she bit her lip worriedly and looked down at her husband but the man wasn't face her to see her look of worry.

"...safety?" Barak scoffed and Eirian rolled her eyes, Ziya tried to ignore Citlali's facial expressions.

"Barak means blessing but it also means lightning. Whose message do you bring?" Csilla asked, turning the questions towards the boy with a maybe-broken foot. Citlali sighed and took her place between her daughters, looking back and forth between her cup, Csilla, and Seren.

"No idea." Barak answered honestly, Maor elbowed him and he silently returned the favor.

"'Eir' means mercy, 'an' means heaven. Just what makes you the 'divine mercy'?"

"There's no divine mercy in her," Barak whispered to his teammate, only to cringe as Ziya's tail collided with the back of his head.

"Who says I'm divine?" Eirian questioned the teenager patiently, ignoring her teammates with practiced ease.

"Either you are divine or you are cursed, you must chose." Ziya clapped his cup against the table harshly, drawing attention towards himself instantly. He tried hard to ignore how Citlali flinched harshly with the sound of his cup and the way Chanitri reached towards his leg didn't go unnoticed either.

"My name is Ziya. I lead this team. And her name is Eirian not Eiraan."

"Ziya means light, you have taken this meaning a bit too far." Csilla retorted without hesitance, earning snickering from Barak.

"Not my fault," Ziya grumbled, his dragon armor agreeing with a low warning rumble of its own. The teenager turned towards the children again, her glassy-eyes covered in thin violet-lines seemed to lock on Eirian.

"Eran the watchful one. So young one, when will you interfere? When the world is ashes or when all is lost?"

"Eirian, Ear-ree-ann." Ziya hissed in answer, the girl was about to respond when her father interrupted her.

"Enough Csilla." the teenager closed her eyes and turned away, her father sighed heavily as he pinched his brow. "I beg your forgiveness dragon-children. Csilla has a pertinent for understanding names and the fates tied to them."

"But she kept saying the wrong name," Barak whispered to Maor, completely confused with the answer of the tiered looking man. However, before any other explanation could take formation, Sitora straightened in her seat with a big smile and glassy-eyes.

"Sister!" Sitora called, "Your hair is down today! It looks good!" the guests stared at the girl beside Csilla in utter bewilderment, their faces scrunched up in confusion. No one else has entered the hall and all others have remained silent while the group interacted with the head of the household.

"Our eldest, our princess, is here," Citlali murmured as she rose to her feet, her husband soon joining her. "Perhaps it is best for you to hide your faces once more. This one holds little trust for others, even less than our eldest seer." She moved past her youngest daughters to stand between the right-entrance and the dragon-children's table.

"Zephaniah," Eirian and Maor murmured, their voices soft and gentle in the quite room. Like a reversal of their revealing, the children's magic swirled around them; distorting their figures in brilliant colors before curling apart into blackened mists. From beneath the table two dark forms darted back into the dark shadows of the children, making the depths of black smoke billow before dissipating to reveal the two returned dragon children. The air filled with rumbling, emitting from the two children standing tall and proud amongst the light and giggles of the Aisling family. To the far right wall, the wooden doors opened once more, no one but the curious eyes of the dragon-children dared to look at the late arrival; not even Chanitri dared to lift his eyes from his cup.

The woman who entered the great hall bore all the regality of an empress, her steps small and soundless, the trailing of her cloak barely whispering against the cold white marble of the stone. Out of everyone in the hall, this woman did not appear the same as the others in the Aisling family tree. Where the others were short and plump, this woman was as thin as a rail; she was just as short as everyone else but she was much thinner. Her lithe figure belied her height and as she strode past her relatives, she appeared so much taller than those who bowed respectively to her. She was dressed in a multitude of layers, the most prominent being the thick outer tunic that wrapped about her frame like a cloak, flaring out from her waste with graceful twirls to end at her bare feet. Knee long white curls surrounded her, looking like the kisses of a morning mist, her bangs were pulled atop her head in a tangle of curls and pins. Despite all of her elegance, there was one flaw that seemed to hamper her seemingly other worldly beauty: the marks upon her face. Hundreds of thousands of dots, needle-point small, encompassed the young woman's face. Flowing down the bridge of her nose were seven small suns. The inside of her eyes, beside the tear ducts, were small hollow moons; as if the crescents were painted there to catch her every teardrop. The fine black dots on her face were formed to create the outline of several flowers, each with seven petals and filled with thirteen rows of dots converging into the center of the flower. From beneath her skirts and her bellowing sleeves, they could see more fine dots of tattoos upon her bare feet and bony hands; hinting that more tattoos littered her body from beneath the expanse of layered white silk.

"Daraytac," Eirian murmured, her pearl colored eyes rolling across the woman's revealed skin. Upon second look, one could see that the dots upon the woman's face were truly the shape of a flower weed known as: Daraytac. The Daraytac was a white seven petal weed that grew regardless of the water consistency or the dryness of the soil; it could even grow in the frigid snow of the southern Silver Plains or the vast sands of Dubol.

"Dragon child," the woman drawled, her voice cold enough to mimic an artic wind.

"…how many flowers do you bear?" Eirian murmured, sounding sad to her teammates who knew her but cold to the family who didn't. She could count three flowers on the woman's brow, one on each cheek and a very small flower on her chin. The flowers on the woman's forehead curved to follow the circle of a crown, disappearing beneath the woman's waves of white-gold. The black lines of the woman's face filtered down beneath the high and tight collar of her tunic, reappearing again on her thin fingers and calloused feet.

"How many pressure points are there?" the woman asked, her narrowed ice-blue eyes turning towards Eirian as if she couldn't be bothered with the young girl playing dress up. "You ask many questions child but none come with answers for your wound."

"My body is unharmed," Eirian retorted, irritated with the assumption that she was physically inferior to her teammates. The woman hummed, sliding her icy-gaze to the table where her family remained unmoved.

"These are your guardsmen," Citlali said as she stepped forward, wrapping her hands around her daughter's bony fingers. "They will take you—" The young woman slid her hands out of Citlali's and moved to take her place beside her siblings, just as silent and still as when she first entered the room. Citlali took in a deep steadying breath, turned away from her daughters and quietly took her seat beside her husband.

"This is Setareh Aisiling," Chanitri introduced the tattooed woman while he took his wife's hand. "She is our most powerful seer, our family heiress and is sixteen this year." Citlali quietly set her head against his shoulder and closed her eyes, pretending to fall asleep despite the shaking of her hands.

"Sea-tar-ree?" Ziya questioned, receiving an approving nod from the tattooed woman in question.

"She's *sixteen*?" Barak whispered to Maor, "She looks *thirty-something*." Maor hummed in agreement, staring at the table the sisters were sitting at so he wouldn't be caught staring at the eldest daughter.

"I can hear you," Setareh murmured, starring at the boys from over the rim of her teacup; suddenly the boy's tea-cups were very interesting.

"If you don't mind me being rude," Ziya spoke up, turning his gaze towards Citlali. "Your eldest daughter appears to be the only teenager here."

"I'm fourteen," Csilla murmured.

"…your eldest two daughters appear to be the only teenagers here." Ziya corrected himself with a roll of his eyes.

"…That is true," Chanitri confirmed while his wife remained still. "once the family heir becomes the family head, there will be no children born for the next ten to twenty years. Once the next family heir is born, others in the family tree may give birth as well. The status of one's parents does not indicate who will give birth first as Fate decides who is worthy of giving birth to the heir, not the blood line."

"How do you manage to keep the couples under control?" Ziya asked, his voice sounding in bewilderment. "Aren't accidents prone to happen?"

"Perhaps for you that is such a thing," Chanitri agreed with a heavy sigh. "As for my people's birthing rate… I'm afraid there is no controlling it on our end. The births who arrive and the deaths who follow are done in accordance to the goddess's will. This is how the Aisling are able to keep our family powers within our own family tree. There will be no stealing from our family during this time frame of infertility."

"That's not to say that occasionally we get someone who wants to join our family tree," Csilla mumbled, rolling her eyes towards the decorative roof.

"It is during this fertile time that our family returns to our lands here in the Crescent Valley." Citlali continued with practiced ease. "This is why we've been here for the past eighteen years and why we feared your arrival down to the milli-seconds."

"That reminds me, Lady Citlali, what was so important about the 'point three seconds' that Mrs. Astra was going on about?" Eirian asked, curious and polite as she addressed the matriarch of the Aisiling family. If it was possible the quietness of the family became even more so, prompting Barak to turn and look about at the rows of white-washed peopled behind him.

"Point three seconds," Citlali murmured, her eyes glistening in unshed tears as she stared down on the tabletop. "That was the time frame in which the passing scouts would've seen a pebble tumble from the cliff face that you and your master had climbed."

"Do you understand child of fate?" Chanitri asked, his dark sapphire eyes clouded over as he stared sorrowfully down into his cup. "Point three seconds and a *pebble*. That's all it would take for our family to be discovered and slaughtered." That was a scary thought indeed. The mere fact that Ziya had managed to act *point three seconds* in time to spare hundreds of people and that it would've been less than a second to destroy them all— all over the fact of a single rock no larger than a pinky nail.

"Point three seconds," Eirian murmured turning to look at Barak.

"Yeah I totally knew that!" Barak laughed nervously, "That's why I kicked the door down!"

"…you kicked it open, not down." Maor corrected his teammate. "Besides that, I'm sure you didn't understand the significance of the point three seconds and only thought that Mrs. Astra was simply struggling with the door. Hence why you decided to kick it open."

"Hey!"

"You weren't hoping to impress some pretty girl beyond the door at all?" Ziya asked mischievously. "I'm impressed, that's the first act of maturity you've shown since you graduated."

"Uh…yeah… sure," Barak sank into his seat, not looking at his teammates. The distinctive sound of teenage girls giggling somewhere behind them sounded, and Barak's blush was very nearly burning through his own mask. His teammates gave him unimpressed looks, each knowing the true reasons behind his actions: to impress girls.

"It'll be unwise to leave for the next three days," Setareh murmured, her soft voice garnering the attention of everyone present. "It'll be best for us to rest here while the scouts continue to bypass us."

"When will the scouts stop searching for us?" Chanitri asked

"The seekers of greed will never stop searching for us," Setareh answered calmly.

"Dear," Citlali murmured as she moved to stand up again.

"Three days from now is the highest, most opportune time to leave the valley." Setareh answered as she rose to her feet and turned away from her family. "A second sooner and all will be lost."

"Dear where are you going? You haven't touched your food," Citlali questioned, rising to her feet and moving to follow her eldest daughter.

"I am not hungry," Setareh answered as she left the hall, no one daring to follow her.

"Sister?" Sitora questioned after the doors closed, looking about in innocent confusion. "Will you return soon?"

"No dear," Citlali sighed as she moved towards her second youngest and gently shook the girl's shoulder. "Wake up Sitora, it's time to go."

"Uh-huh? Mama?" Sitora blinked, her eyes seemingly focusing on the strangers before looking up at her mother. "Mama, where did sister go? She looked so pretty today, is she finally going to marry?"

"Don't be stupid," Csilla ordered as she rose to her feet, "You know Setareh will never marry."

"Uh? But I clearly saw big sister off to marry! She looked so pretty too!" Sitora declared, glaring at Csilla with all the anger of a twelve year old.

"That was not this world Sitora," Seren murmured as she too rose to her feet. "You saw an image from another world. That Setareh is not *our* Setareh."

"Don't scold me Seren! Sitora had all the marks! And the same memories! She even told me that Mama is gonna have another baby!" the room very nearly exploded with whispers, the dragon-children each glancing at each other as everyone very nearly lost their minds.

"It was another world love," Citlali murmured, brushing a hand against her youngest's brow. "You know Izar is the last to be born in this fertile time. Another heir will not be born for another decade." The matriarch lifted the tiny toddler out of Seren's lap and gently took Sitora's hand to guild the girl out of the room, the golden haired girl complaining about what she saw verses what her mother had seen the entire way.

"That would be the draw back to our powers," Chanitri murmured as his wife and younger daughters left the room. "Seren is skilled with her visions but she is not able to control them."

"This is not the first time she's gotten lost in a vision?" Ziya questioned, watching Csilla carefully. The teenager was standing aside, watching the servants gather the large curved table and hurry it away. One of the other young preteens of the family hurried up the steps to Csilla, gabbing the princess's attention quickly and whispering away in her ear.

"All of our daughters have awakened the ability to world-see, which is why they all have seals." Citlali explained, "For Csilla and Seren, the crowns are good enough to keep their powers sealed for the exception of life-arks. We placed the seal-crown on Izar as a precaution, we don't know when or if she'll awaken the dimensional-viewing skill. However, Sitora and Setareh are both different. As we have learned with Setareh, no amount of seal-arrays will keep the power from Sitora, all we can do is pray the visions don't drive her insane."

"That's possible?" Eirian questioned, surprise tilting her voice.

"It's rare but yes." Chanitri agreed, heaving a heavy sigh before he continued. "When a seer's power becomes too much, they become confused, unable to determine which world they are seeing is the world they are living. They become lost in the visions, unable to find their way home."

"And when a vision is bad," Csilla continued, her face a mask of indifference, "the seer can be forever lost in the agony and sorrow of the death lands."

"What—" Maor was interrupted by Chanitri

"By death land we do not mean the cursed land of Nyxena, we mean the visions will continuously reveal only the death of those closest to the seer. Such as lovers, children, parents, siblings, friends. The death lands for a seer is the visions of humanity's death and not just one world's annihilation but all the parallel-worlds of existence as well."

"Such sorrow can drive even a saint mad with grief," Csilla murmured. "Setareh is one who holds such a fate and unfortunately the seals we tattooed upon her skin and etched into her clothes and jewelry are not strong enough to keep back the visions of death any longer."

"This is why we have asked for Azurelyn's aid," Chanitri said, looking pointedly at Ziya. "Please save my daughter, before she falls into the clutches of Death." Ziya glanced at his students, wondering what was on their minds as they stared back at him. Glancing down at the wooden cup in his hand, Ziya took in a deep breath, trying to ignore the weight settling in his belly.

"We are children of the dragons, third team of eastern side, hailing from the great forest of Aeoman." Ziya said as he fisted his left hand and set his open palm over it, bowing his head briefly to the leader of the Aisling family. "We accept this mission." Eirian couldn't help but feel a great weight settle over her shoulders, a feeling of dread twisting like snakes in her belly. She set her cup down on the table and shuffled her weight so that she could lean her scaled arm against Maor's.

"Just how are we supposed to save your princess?" Barak asked, waving one hand in the air childishly. "Where are we taking her?"

"Home," Maor answered, eyes narrowed thoughtfully behind his mask. "We're taking 'Kaur' home, to Azurlyn."

"That didn't take long," Ziya sighed

"Wait, does this mean she's going to become a resident of our forest?!" Barak asked loudly.

"Should you succeed in saving my daughter," Chanitri smiled fondly down on Barak, amusement in his blue eyes. "Then our entire family shall move south to join your home."

Chapter 5

They were given a room with a great view of Seer Valley, the setting sun painted the white marble cliff-faces in beautiful hues of pink and orange. The far off cliff face that bordered Aeoman's great forest seemed like a distant memory, a barely discernable smudge amongst the rolling pink clouds of the mountains at twilight. Eirian remained outside on the balcony, staring out at the distant wall were her home sat waiting for her. The valley that fed the near six hundred people was little more than half a mile wide and nearly two miles long. No matter where anyone stood at beyond the valley, they would not be able to see the village carved in the cliff-face. Even now, when the movement of shadows and reflected light should give them away the most, there was arising mist and a lowering of clouds that prevented view of this hidden notch. Far to the left edge of valley, she could see a twisted knotwork of a tree standing alone and barren of life. She tapped at her temple and Ryū blinked twice before focusing on the tree, revealing a glittering burst of water that produced a thick mist. The tree must be sitting atop the waterfall, no doubt it was the reason the water could even find an exit.

"Eirian?" Maor's voice brought Eirian out of her thoughts, prompting her to turn back and look at her masked teammate. "You're quitter than usual. What's wrong?" his mask was parted, revealing his partial three-shades of blue scaled face staring back at her.

"We can't just cross the gorge and go home, can we?" Eirian asked in return, turning her moonstone eyes back to the distant haze of a wall. Why did the gorge have to be so wide? It took them eight days to travel from one side to the other and now they must find a different rout home.

"The lake below sees many scouts dressed in Gehill's sigil of three mountains." Maor answered, his eyes not straying from Eirian's glowing orbs. "What path should we take?"

"We can't cross the gorge without alerting Gehill's soldiers," both students turned to look back at Ziya who approached with a slow calm gate, as if unconcerned with the struggle that was about to befall them. "We'll have to head south-east, towards Ashan. The civilian lands will be much safer for us to travel through. Especially since Gehill is trying to figure out how to breach the mountain range."

"Do you think they'll succeed this year?" Eirian asked, her voice softened with her worry. "They try so hard to breach our lands, do you think they'll finally succeed? It's been eleven years since their last attempt."

"Have more faith in your comrades Eirian," Ziya chuckled, patting her scaled head affectionately. "The border patrol won't let them get too close without a fight. You know that."

"They didn't do so great two years ago," She reminded him

"hey now, they all have new protocells to follow. Each boarder team has a teleporter and healer now." Ziya chuckled, "Thanks to your efforts, there wasn't a single dragon lost that day."

"Where's Barak?" Maor asked, looking inside the room. "Seriously?" from the balcony they could see the dining table, which was full of yellow fruits and variously cooked meats. Barak was sitting at the center, his back turned to them, his mask split in half to encompass his neck and forehead, the large fruits they saw on the trees were interspaced with large forks full of meats all disappearing into Barak's face.

"...did the Eld family forget to teach this one manners?" Eirian hissed as she spun on her heal, rushing into their room. "Barak! Slow down before you choke!"

"Ehm? Gha!" Barak yelped as Eirian's palm collided with the back of his head, "OW! E-kin!"

"That's not how you eat Barak! Show your manners!"

"But I'm hungry!"

"I don't care! Don't be a pig!"

"There's never a dull moment around with them," Ziya chuckled as he turned to follow Eirian into the room. "Well let's eat and hit the sack, we need to rest up if we want to leave in top condition on day three."

"Ziya-Isha," Maor called, making the tall golden-scaled man hesitate at the entrance. "Will... will we succeed in this mission? Isn't everything too odd? Nothing matches up... nothing makes sense..."

"You're thinking too much," Ziya chuckled, flipping his mask closed so he could pat Maor's head roughly. "Don't you have more faith in your teacher? What about your teammates? We all know Eirian is stronger than she looks."

"Except when her family gets involved," Maor grunted. His reply was answered by Ziya's quick fingers wrapping around a leather clasp and pulling making Maor squeak and reach towards the hand trying to lift him into the air. "Ziya-Isha! Stop it! That hurts!" while Ziya couldn't actually grab Maor's ear, he settled for hooking his fingers beneath the mask and lifting the boy to his tip-toes.

"Everyone in the world wears masks Maor," Ziya sighed heavily. "Some of us wear more than others. Eirian simply has to wear chains to go with her mask, that's all. When she's with us, she's the freest that she'll ever be. We are the ones who get to see the most of her heart, even if it's not all of it. Doesn't that make you content? To know that we are the ones who see the most of her true face, even if it is only a little bit?" Ziya left Maor on the balcony, not waiting for an answer from his student as he encaged the other two in light banter and laughter. Maor glanced back out at the gorge, his shoulders slumping as he listened to Barak whine to Ziya about Eirian's scolding and Ziya simply laughed everything off like it wasn't a problem; only to be scolded by said female.

The clouds are getting thicker, like the water in the air is trying to make a protective bubble around us. Maor thought as he stared out at the orange and red twilight clouds. *Eirian REALLY doesn't like this, Ziya-Isha doesn't like this either. Can they sense something wrong, like I can?*

"Maor?" Eirian called out from inside, "Hey we're making plans, what you think of this one?" Maor turned around and entered the building, approaching the small table of the lounge, staring at the map of Ashan with their beloved mountains taking up the entire western border. "Isha says we should head east, meet here at a small merchant village named Lesart with our informant for the documents we'll need to travel through Ashan unhindered. Then we'll travel south-east some more, passing these villages and towns on the way to here, Niyatara city."

"Uuuuh, Eirian, I don't mean to sound like a party-pooper, but like, isn't that a bad idea?" Barak asked from his place at the dining table, pausing in his shoving food down his throat to look back at his team. "Niyatara City is like huge, like really huge, like it was almost made the capital of Ashan because it's so huge."

"Barak, that's the exact reason why we need to go there." Eirian glared at him, irritation in her voice as she explained. "From Niyatara we can take a ship and follow the river upstream and into the forest lands."

"Why can't we just cross the gorge?" Barak asked, "We can fly can't we?" stupid, rhetorical question with a very obvious answer: of course they could.

"Yes but Kaur can't," Maor grouched at him. "Plus there's the patrols and Gehill's scouts to worry about. Idiot."

"If it was just us and no extra baggage, like say another human being, then you would have a point Barak and we could travel through the border." Ziya said from his seat, still hunched over his knees and grinning beneath his mask at his more excitable student. "However, Kaur is not used to ten percent oxygen usage. She will suffocate at the altitude we'll need to be at to pass over the mountains."

"So one of us can't carry her?" Barak asked curiously, "We can fly at low altitudes too…"

"Yes but too low will alert Gehill Scouts," Maor countered. "They'll discover that our weakness is the sky, they'll develop something, somehow, to travel through the air and then our border patrols won't be as effective."

"*If* Gehill scouts see us," Barak retorted with a pointed look at his teammate.

"Stop being difficult Barak," Eirian ordered. "If we go with your plan, despite how reasonable it is, it puts too much risk on the others of the forest. Based on the location of our departure, the roots of Gehill's scouts, Kaur's survival necessities…" Eirian drew a finger across the map, frowning thoughtfully as she redid her calculations three times before sitting back in her chair. "If we get caught by Gehill scouts, then the village in our forest to be attacked first would be Asharan the secluded." Everyone was silent as they stared at Eirian, Maor was the most noticeably still of the three males. Asharan was not a very large village, home to a few dozen, but every resident was a soldier of war so few bothered to near them. Asharan was also Maor's home village and their training village off and on for the past two years.

"We would never know if they got attacked," Maor frowned at the village Eirian pointed at on the map. "We must not draw attention to anyone in our forest. If that means we must travel through civilian lands to protect our homeland then so be it. We shouldn't even be forced to have this discussion."

"Asharan is the village of disgraced soldiers," Barak huffed. "Who would be stupid enough to take on a village of *soldiers*?"

"Barak," Maor said as calmly as he could. "We are not drawing attention to *anyone* in our home forest. Just because you want to go back to your mother's skirts, doesn't mean you have to put the rest of the nation in jeopardy."

"At least I have a mother!" Barak snapped back at him. "I'm not some murder clinging to a shadow hoping to see a glimpse of my past!"

"Barak!" Ziya shouted, but his scolding came too late. Maor was before Barak, one fist wrapped into the tangle of scales on Barak's chest, ignoring the whimpering of his own armor. The dragon armor wasn't designed to do battle with its own, it was designed to protect its wearer. As such the armors were at war with themselves, unable to decide what to do: attack its brother or abandon its child?

"Stop this at once!" Ziya shouted but was unheard as Barak's scales lit up with copper sparks, Maor's hand trembled as blood began to seep around his fingers.

"Bastard!" Barak shouted, his clawed hands lighting up with sparks to slam down on Maor's left arm, his legs kicking out at his teammate. "Put me down damn it!" Ziya went to stop them, halfway out of his seat already, when he saw that Eirian was already there. She stood between Barak and Maor, one hand pressed against Maor's arm, her attention turned and focused entirely on her navy-scaled teammate.

"Maor, calm down." Eirian instructed, her voice soft and gentle. "He didn't mean it as crude as it came out. He meant you should be looking towards your future, not your past."

"He still—" Maor cut himself off, his arm trembling with the weight of Barak's body and the hot sparks now dancing across his palm. "He...he—!"

"I know Maor, don't let it bother you. You're better than your past, you had no control over your birth." Eirian murmured, her voice soothing the tensions between her teammates. Maor lowered Barak, his teeth grinding together hard enough to squeak.

"I won't forgive you," Maor declared

"Like I want your forgiveness," Barak growled. "I'm going to bed." Barak left and Eirian guided Maor back to the table to discuss more their travel path; hoping to distract the boy. Ziya remained in his seat, wondering how to calm the storm before him.

Worst timing ever, Ziya thought with a heavy sigh.

Ω Ω Ω

Barak and Maor didn't speak for the first day, remaining silent and not acknowledging the other's presence. One day of this was enough to make Ziya snap under the silent pressure of his students. Knowing that the fight between the boys was a particularly nasty as it bruised both boys in sensitive, still raw, wounds in their hearts, Ziya would ordinarily give the boys a week to calm down. However they were on a mission and that was a time frame they could not afford to lose. So, without anyone's knowledge nor acceptance of his actions, and even better with no one there to scold him for it, Ziya devised his cruelest plan yet to get the boys back on speaking terms. This was how Maor and Barak woke up chained to a cold wall somewhere deep in the earthen bedrock of the Aisling's home.

"Ug, what happened?" Barak's voice wheezed and his words slurred as he awoke in the dark dry cell.

"You're awake," Maor drawled, staring at his teammate from his side. "About time."

"Huh?" Barak stared sleepily at Maor for all of two seconds before his memory came back. "Damn it! ZIYA-ISHA!!" commence the flaying feet made of sparks, "Get back here you painted up serpent! I'm gonna kick your false-gold ass straight to the sun!"

"Quite kicking," Maor grunted, unable to protect himself from the thrashing sparks of his teammate's magic because his hands were bound over head. "Damn it Barak! I said quite kicking! You're setting me on fire!"

"Then roast quietly!" Barak shouted, only to freeze as a bubble of water surrounded his head.

"You should try drowning first!" Maor ordered. "For the love of mercy! Don't you remember what Ziya-Isha said before he knocked us out? We have to work together to save Eirian!" Barak glared at Maor, who only glared back, neither moving to put out his flames or remove the bubble of water. "Remember what Isha said?"

"Since you two idiots can't work together you can stay here!" Ziya declared, pointing at them in exasperation. "Eirian and I will go take out the scouts, block their entrance point and then take Kaur home without you two idiots interfering!"

"Eirian will end up fighting *Gehill soldiers*," Maor hissed, struggling to relax with his hands bound over his head. "You know what they do to female dragons." The water bubble started to steam, Barak's fury growing with enough heat to turn his scales into glittering sparks of orange and yellow. "She will never be our 'Eirian' ever again. She won't even be a dragon anymore." With that Maor lifted the water bubble from Barak's head and used that same water to douse his own body, cooling it from Barak's waves of heat. "We need to find Eirian, let Ziya-Isha battle Gehill, but Eirian cannot fight the people who murdered her own parents."

"Tch, you don't have to remind me Maor," Barak growled. "I know… once Gehill figures out how to beat someone, they'll not stop until that family line is gone forever."

"Then let's go get our teammate back." Maor ordered, "We can't waste time here waiting any longer!" Barak said nothing, his bright sky blue eyes brightened with an eerie light, a single golden stripe blooming like a crescent moon to surround his pupil. A rune appeared between his palms, a whisper left his lips, and a wave of sparks appeared to surround the chains. The sparks swirled faster and faster till they had more heat and the metal started to turn color; on cue a bolt of water spiraled into the glowing chains.

"Physics one-oh-one: Super-heated metals never react well with sudden cold." Barak smirked as he landed on his feet, his hands set out before himself.

"I'd be more impressed if you got the cuffs off," Maor drawled. "Let's go, no time to waste." Maor turned towards the door, walking away without thinking twice about it.

"Oh yeah, come here water-boy, I'll get the cuffs off ya!" Barak retorted, one hand encased in sparks raised threatening.

"This door is reinforced with runes." Maor grumbled, one hand pressed against its wooden surface and his eyes closed in concentration. "Damn Ziya-Isha isn't going to be making this easy for us... Barak st—whoa!!" Maor leaped away as a great ball of spiraling sparks crashed into the door. "No you idiot!" Maor cried out in despair as the runes bloomed to life in brilliant golden scriptures.

"Shut up Maor! I'll just blast them off the door!"

"Stop before it's too late!" Maor shouted as he scrambled away from the door that now creaked and groaned ominously. "Seriously Barak! STOP!!" but it was too late, the runes exploded, the door shattered and in rushed a wall of water to fast for Maor to stop. Maor had been half across the room, reaching out to Barak with wide eyes and a panicked cry so when the wall of water came it was Maor who cushioned Barak when the water collided with them. Barak barely had the time to see that it was Maor behind him, pinned to the stone wall, before the water moved on its own. Barak coughed, the air in his lungs replaced with water as he crashed into a different wall, his arm burning like fire ants eating away at his flesh. Through the haze of rushing water he could see the current surrounding Maor like a protective embrace, like a mother cradling her child for the first time.

'Damn it,' Barak thought, trying to fight off the darkness from encroaching his vision. '*That bastard teacher! He must've used a dry seal array on the door to keep the water out of our cell. He knew what the water would do to Maor, damn it!*' Barak cringed as he struggled against the pressure of water. The water thrashed, pinning Barak in place against the cold stone wall. The current shifted before him, a stipe of white amongst the darkness, was it just his imagination or did he see the face of a serpent? The water twirling around Maor protectively snarled like a rapid beast. The sound so strong it rumbled in his chest and pounded in Barak's mind like the echoing howls of an Inugami.

'*Don't play with me, damn it!*' Barak thought, anger seizing his heart. '*I am a child of flame!*' It was a struggle to bring his hands together, even harder still were the runes he needed to push back the water. But he could, of course he could, he was a child of fire—the element that started all of creation. Water was merely a steppingstone for Barak, fire was his friend, his shield, his sword, his way of life and his someday eternity. He could not, *would not*, drown because water was as clingy as a stalker to his teammate.

I am child of fire! Descendent of the sun and stars! Come forth my kin, Shani Livazar!

The ancient rune from his home spread to life before him, burning so brightly the water screamed as great bellowing clouds of mist separated water from stone, air and flesh. Barak let out a scream, bracing himself against the stone as the ancient inscription pulsed brighter, making the water recoil. He dashed towards his friend, ignoring the howl of water and the ominous hissing of sparks and mist battling for superiority. A large bubble remained around Maor, small enough to make the navy-scaled boy curl into himself like a child. Skidding to a halt before his teammate, Barak faced the wall of water, panting heavily in the hot air space he was able to create with the extreme temperature of his sparks and embers. the ancient rune he was taught remained the size of his palm, emitting a brilliant circle of sparks and embers that circled the rune protectively.

"Back off stalker!" Barak shouted, glaring at the wall of water beyond his fiery seal array. "Maor isn't interested in being one of your damn sprits!" the watery-wall bobbed back and forth, searching for a weak point in the defense but Barak's control over his family spell extended only to this one spell. Shani Livazar, a spell designed to push back darkness and 'suffocation' with the warmth of the Eld family's sprits. All those who came to live in the Eld family before Barak were essentially lending Barak their power for the sake of survival. The water shifted back and forth, like a pool-floaty in a strong ocean current, searching for a way around the warmth of generations of fire-descendants.

"I said: BACK OFF!!" The seal array pulsed, the empty space between the rock wall and the wall of water filled with sparks and embers alike, pushing back the water with a force of a hundred explosions. The water wailed in despair, the moisture of the room disappeared, replaced with a dry heat that mimicked the core of a volcano. Still Barak remained standing before his unconscious teammate, glaring furiously at the water beyond his rune. He ground his teeth, his body trembling with exhaustion of using the spell for so long but he couldn't end the spell just yet. Letting the seal array push the water out the entrance, Barak turned to look back at his teammate. Maor was curled up in a tiny ball, looking like a baby in his little ball of water; like an infant waiting to be born.

"And you call me the child," Barak murmured as he crouched before the ball of water. "Come on Maor, it's time to save Eirian. If we don't, the only one who accepts us is going to disappear forever." He set one palm against the water-bubble's surface, a gentle teal seal array between his glowing palm and the bubble. Maor shifted, curling up further, looking more and more like a child still inside its mother's womb. Sighing heavily Barak shifted his body around to cradle the bubble-encased-Maor, another teal glowing seal array coating his other palm as he carefully lifted the bubble from the floor of the cell.

"I can't belief this," Barak grumbled as he turned slowly, his ancient rune still active as he approached the exit. "I am Behruz, eighty-seventh in line, will my ancestors please lend me aid."

More sparks and embers surround Barak, sprouting from air and the course of his magic seeping out of his body to saturate the air. The sparks formed the hour-glass figure of a woman, created entirely from twirling sparks and glowing embers the woman glanced back at him before marching forward as if she were leaving for a battle. Barak quickly followed behind the spark-figure, curious about her appearance but not daring to speak, afraid the spirit would abandon him instead of aiding him. The figure placed a palm in the air of the entrance, the water beyond it screeched horribly, the figure glanced back once before moving forward. Barak hurried forward, keeping half an eye on the glowing inscriptions slowly blooming to life around him but most of his attention on the ember female figure. He hurried out of the room, his eyes widening as a weight settled on his shoulders, his lungs emptying of air, his fingers and toes numbing at the sight presented to him. They appeared to be in a giant stone bowl, filled to the brim with enough water to drawn a village or two. There wasn't any plant life that he could see, just great towering pillars of rocks with strange white glowing algae on them. Taking a deep breath, Barak stepped forward, glad when a rune appeared beneath his feet, the three rune seal array's surrounding his back and sides remaining strong against the pressure of the water.

"Whoa," Barak said in awe, his bright blue eyes wide in surprise. The ember figure remained before him, unhindered with the water baring down on them, seeking an entrance in the waves of heat emitting from Barak and the woman. He watched as the currents in the water twisted and parted, creating brief images of serpents and monsters in the dark watery depths.

So the water is going to fight for Maor, Barak thought, his glowing fingers twisting against the runes that allowed him to carry the water encased Maor. He wanted to shatter the bubble around Maor, to wrap his arms tightly around his comrade and use as much fire power as he had to launch both of them out of the deep watery-grave but he knew that would do more damage than good. Maor was sensitive to large bodies of water, the bubble encasing him right now was a defense mechanism against that problem. Except it also created a problem for Barak. As Barak's body naturally ran at unnaturally high temperature, coming in contact with water usually resulted in a hot steam bath. This was why Barak had to practice with specific water transfer rune-seal-arrays incase things like this happened. In fact, everyone on their team was efficient with this method of transportation except for Maor, he needed only to think and the water would do what he wanted it to do.

It still wants him, Barak looked down at his teammate, unconscious and curled up like an infant, unaware and unsuspecting of the danger he was in. *Damn it, Ziya-Isha went too far this time. The water could've seriously taken Maor away forever this time!*

"*Kundze Adaryu iškart sustok tai, Illi Voster nav.*" To say Barak was surprised to hear the ember woman speak would be an understatement, to hear her speak a language he couldn't understand even more so. He watched as the water bobbed and weaved, a snarling face pushed against the waves of heat emitting from the orange-glowing runes. A gurgling growl emitted from the body of water, so different from the thunderous voice of the ember-figure.

"*Tebūnie*," the ember-figure raised a hand, pulled close to the opposite shoulder, and slashed it forward like a blade. A great ark of fire erupted from the ember-figure's limb, cutting through the water and electing a shrill scream. "*Bērns nāc*," the figure murmured as she arched her body and dove through the open air created by the flaming whip she used to push the water back. Barak cursed under breath as he adjusted his legs to the sudden elevation and pushed himself forward after the woman, watching her use great arcs and shields of pure flame to push the water away from them.

I wish I could do that, Barak thought, *I wish I could use flames and not sparks.* He continued moving up, noticing that every inch that gave way to hot air left behind a pocket of steam behind him. The water was quick to close the gap behind Barak, eager to find the weakness in power of embers and the ember-woman's excessive heat. The light overhead, indicating the way out, grew ever larger as they drew closer and closer to the surface.

"*Bērns steigā*," the ember-woman called out, sending out another blistering blade of flame, breaking the surface of the water. The air that assaulted Barak's nose was like sweet honey and bitter autumn leaves that filled him with comfort and familiarity. His sigh of relief relaxed him and for a moment he forgot that he was fleeing water that currently remained obsessed with his teammate. That was his mistake.

"Ghaaa!!" Barak let out a scream of pain, his right calf flaring with a burn that was greater than anything he's ever felt, greater than the Acacia tree's acidic sap. As an Eld family member fire doesn't burn him, doesn't even put a scratch on his clothes, so he's never understood the feeling of being burned. However, the blade of water that succeeded in entering his bubble of hot air, slicing through his lower leg, felt much the same as the horrible sensation of the Acacia tree's sap. Eirian had once described the tree's horrible sap as a feeling of being set on fire, as if everything was slowly—*agonizingly* slowly—melting away. Barak hadn't ever been burned before so he went to an Acacia Tree and cut into it deeply, pulling out its sap and setting it in his palm. It took about thirty seconds before he understood what Eirian was talking about and he regretted every second of it. He wasn't able to use his hand for two months and received daily scolds from his mother who mercilessly undid the wrapping, medicine application and rewrapping.

This sensation the water created was a hundred times worse than the Acacia Tree's sap.

"*BĒRNS!*" the ember woman cried out, "*NĒ!*" she twisted in the air over the water's surface and dived back in to surround Barak in an orb of blistering hot coals and fire. "*Kundze Adaryu, tu cĕx kā!*" the water howled in agony, bursting into steam as the ember-woman shattered her body to surround Barak and Maor protectively. He wondered what the ember woman was saying, so furious and angry, he could only feel her rage with the water that slash so deeply into his leg. He had no time to adjust his hold on Maor before the fire around him twisted and gathered, shooting out with enough power and speed to launch him and Maor out of the watery-depths. Upon contact with the earth, the bubble surrounding Maor burst, reforming as a protective mist-blanket that coated Barak as well; cooling his glowing skin from the intense heat of the ember-woman. Coughing hoarsely Barak struggled to sit up, the cool mist weighing him down like a thick blanket of snow. As he did he watched as the water's surface bulged and bubbled, like a geyser ready to explode. A great flame burst out and circled the water, setting the various stones a flame as if they were candles. Once the circle was complete the ball of flame reformed into the ember woman, floating high overhead with an air of outrage surrounding her flaming figure. A scream tore through the air as the water burst upward, sparkling like a thousand diamonds as it raced to meet the ember-woman at the edge of the flaming circle.

"*Eum vicis!*" The water cried out, taking on the form of a young woman with long bellowing hair and a face morphed into panic and desperation.

"*NĒ!*" the two women clashed, struggling hand and hand, forming hot steam that muffed their cries of pain. "*Nox zrēck ito!*"

"*Nē! Niekada!*" the two figures continued to struggle, huge clouds of white steam bellowed around them, filling their space with blistering hot air. Barak watched as five of the flaming stones pulsed before sending out great towering geysers of flame. Before the water-lady could react, the flames were piercing through her body, ripping it apart from the waist down and sending her tumbling back into the pool with a cry of pain on her lips. He watched, hypnotized, as tears gathered in her eyes, desperation twisted her round face, her one hand outstretched to the ember-woman. It was like watching a woman fall from a cliff side while her baby sister watched her fall to her death.

"*Fili mi!*" the watery woman cried out, her round face turning to look at Barak and Maor, despair contorting her face as she shattered against the surface of the pool.

"*Ita sit,*" the ember woman murmured, lowering herself from her height to touch down on the flaming stones. "*Bērns bene?*" The ember woman turned to face Barak, her whole body sinking down onto the stone surrounding the flaming rock candles. It looked like it was how she was going to regenerate, the fire was restoring her previous strength.

"I," Barak hesitated a moment, unsure if he should continue or not, "I… I don't understand…" the woman tilted her head to the side, seemingly considering his words as if she could understand him just fine. The woman kneeled on the stone and patted gently at her knees, pointing with her other hand at his injured leg. Frowning, Barak pulled his leg to the side, revealing the deep ugly slash in the flesh of his calf. The woman stared at Barak for a moment, as if confused before reaching forward to touch his leg. "OW!" Barak yelped, pressing his hands into his thigh to keep his leg in place even though his body naturally jerked away from the source of pain. The woman flinched back, jerking away from him as if she had been harmed by touching him and not the other way around.

"*Malus*," the woman whimpered, pulling herself back from Barak, "*Egoment malus*." He didn't understand what she was saying but he got the feeling that it wasn't anything good, as if she was murmuring condolences.

"Who... who are you?" Barak asked, staring at the faceless woman created from embers. The figure turned to him, stiff and cooling, wiry and tense; then she relaxed. Her ember body morphing back into the flames of the stones as she stood and retreated to the stone edge of the pool.

"*Darahi*," the woman murmured, pressing one palm to her chest. "*Ego Darahi Rinnsólahi, dea lumen spe.*"

"That's... a really long name," Barak replied, giving the woman a look of bewilderment which only earned him amused giggles. "Can I ... can I call you 'Darahi'?"

"*Jā,*" the woman nodded, sinking into the flames of the rocks.

"Can I," Barak hesitated, not sure if he should or shouldn't go through with his request. "Can I call on you again?!" the flaming woman seemed to brighten, her flames filling the place with so much light that Barak had to squint to see the woman in her sea of flams.

"*Jā! Iznāk dea lumen spe, Darahi Rinnsólahi!*"

"Mrs. Darahi! I'll make sure to call on you again!" Barak shouted, watching the woman disappear into a ring of fire; amused giggles and feminine laughter was his only answer. Seeing that the imminent threat to Maor and himself was gone, Barak looked about himself for the first time, confusion filling him at the sight presented. They appeared to be in a very large cave, several dwarf trees with glowing leaves and speckled trunks sat around the curves of the large space. The pool itself was very large, nearly an entire acker all the way around, and surrounded by (now) burning limestone rocks as big as his head and baring deep gouges in the shapes of ancient runes of the likes he's never seen. Barak looked at the stone beneath himself and saw more pale limestone, a thick layer of dirt lined the edge where he sat before seeping into the tall glowing grass that coated the floor of the place. A soft melody filled the air, like a mother's lullaby to her newborn, and from the nearby tree three glowing Blue jays took to the air. He watched as they flitted through the dark empty space overhead playfully before turning to fly further away. Just beyond Maor, the stone surrounding the large pool and the path that sprouted from it, was an ancient run down temple. Its scarlet roof was drooping and broken, sweeping out from the flat top like sweeping brush strokes of a painting. Moss and flowers grew along its cracked walls and broken roof, its pillars encircled with ivy and roses, its deck splintered and broken with rout.

What is this place? Barak thought as he looked about. All of the plant life were glowing, as if sunlight filled their every vane, seeping up from the earth like glittering life giving liquid sunlight. *What do I do now?* Barak asked himself as he sat up, carefully placing a hand over his injury while he looked down at Maor worriedly. It appeared that the separation of water from his person took a heavier toll than usual, it was the only thing that explained why Maor hadn't woken up yet. The sound of shattering glass and a raised voice sounded from the temple, drawing Barak's attention long enough to see a flash of white light.

"Eirian?" Barak whispered, frowning in confusion. Moving carefully, Barak rose to his feet and with a wince accompanying every step, forcefully moved himself towards the ancient broken temple. He had to stop several times just to breathe, pushing back the pain in his leg so he could continue towards his maybe-teammate.

"I don't care!" he recognized that voice as clearly as he recognized the sun and stars, that was Eirian and she was *not* happy. "I will..."

there was more soft murmurs, a voice gentle like whispering breezes, to gentle for him to make the words out. Barak stumbled closer, wondering who was talking and what the point of the conversation was. He's never heard Eirian get so angry at someone that she'd surround herself with her magic and scream at the top of her voice. Scolding Maor and himself sure; throw a giant glowing bolder at Ziya, no problem. But to shout with her magic active around her? He's never seen that happen. Eirian was a quiet fury, either her magic lashed out under tightly controlled spells or her words tore down your pride with all the ferocity of angry lioness.

"I will protect…" Eirian's voice retorted loudly, as if she was insulted with the other person's words. More gentle whispers, more soft murmurs and then he heard it: *price*. What did that mean? Did Eirian have to pay for something? Did Ziya skip out on another payment? What price was Eirian being so fussy with? "Yes!" he moved to take a step up to the porch, he could see her inside the temple. Eirian stood with her back to him, glowing like a ghost in the darkness of the room, standing furiously with all the white flames of an enraged sky goddess. "A thousand times yes! A million lifetimes, a trillion worlds, for all of eternity my answer stands! I will—"

"Eirian?" his teammate snapped around, her brilliant amethyst eyes wide and glowing. "What—"

"Barak!" Eirian gasped, before charging him. "You're hurt!" She stopped in front of him, violet and purple sleeves flying about like storm winds, her wild waves of midnight purple were released from her ribbon to float about like wisps of smoke. To Barak she had achieved another level of beauty he couldn't adjust too fast enough, the after-glow of her magic still surrounding her as if she were an angel sent from above. "How did this happen?" Eirian asked, as she kneeled to examine the gash on his leg. "Where is your dragon? Why aren't you in uniform? This wouldn't have happened if you were in uniform!" the barrage of questions startled Barak from hypnosis, he twisted his leg to look at the deep gash; seeing it again and cringing back from the rivers of scarlet running down his leg.

"Huh? Oh, uh, yeah—"

"Don't 'oh yeah' me, mister!" Eirian snapped, glaring up at him. "Where the hell have you been?! Ziya is out looking for you! Where's Maor?!" Her hands lit up, glowing runes appearing in both palms as she gently set them on either side of the long deep gap in his leg. A large white circle surrounded his calf, much like a giant circular bead, trendless of white thread bounced back and forth between his injury and the edges of the giant white-glass-bead. Barak sighed in relief when the pain disappeared from his leg, his mind clearing with the perfect cool touch of Eirian's aura surrounding his injury. "Barak! Answer me!"

"Huh? Oh, uh, Maor's over there," Barak pointed over his shoulder, watching her glance around him. "Ziya-isha trapped us behind a seal-array that prevented water from reaching Maor. Maor tried to stop me from knocking the door down but I didn't listen..." Eirian remained silent for a moment, thinking about his words and focusing on Barak's leg before she spoke. Once the injury was gone, blood left behind to dry on its own, Eirian stood and faced Barak with a dull expression.

"You're an idiot, you know that?" Eirian asked, not expecting an answer from her teammate. "Did it occur to you that Maor had figured out what Ziya-Isha had done and was going to release the runes so that the water wouldn't overload his aura system and knock him out?" Barak's pout turned into an expression of embarrassment, now understanding why Maor was shouting at him to stop with his attack on the door. Eirian sighed and shook her head, mumbling about how he needs to think before he acts so accidents like this wouldn't happen. Stepping down from the porch of the broken temple, Eirian stopped and turned back to look inside the temple.

"As for you princess," Eirian hissed, her face morphing into determination and her voice cooling into ice. "My answer stands till the end of time." She turned away, walking down the path towards the burning stones that surrounded a large pool of crystalline water. Barak turned to look back into the building, wondering which of the princess's was speaking to Eirian but his sight was only greeted with darkness.

Chapter 6

"Barak! Hurry up! I'll need your help!" Eirian demanded, drawing Barak back from the temple.

"Ah, right, okay, I'm coming!" Barak shouted as he turned and hurried after his teammate, "Wait up Eirian! Why do you have to walk so fast?!"

"Why do you have to walk so slow?" Eirian asked in return, smiling as Barak caught up to her. Barak laughed, glad that for once on this mission she could smile and joke again. She's been stiff since the whole affair at the center hall occurred and even when they left for seer valley, she hadn't been acting like normal. They reached Maor just as he was groaning, his face scrunched up in delirious pain. Frowning Eirian kneeled on the stone beside Maor, more familiar runes forming in her palms as she set her hands on either side of his face; easing his pain within a single moment.

"This isn't right," Eirian murmured, moving one hand to settle it on Maor's chest; her frown deepened. "This isn't an injury due to an over loaded Aura system. This an impact injury."

"Impact injury?" Barak asked, dumbfounded by the statement.

"Yeah," Eirian murmured, distracted with the injury. "A great force knocked into him, he must've hit his head on a blunt surface like a wall. Judging by the bruising on his chest...a large body of water crashed into him with the intent to kill..." Eirian looked at Maor's face, noticing the sweat gathering on his near translucent face. "But... it's never tried to kill him before..." Barak remained silent, head bowed and fists clenched as he recalled what happened in the cell. Maor was trying to warn him, trying to stop him from acting rashly again and when he failed to listen to Maor, the other boy moved behind him to protect him from the assault of the water. It was Barak the water was trying to kill, not Maor. Maor was trying to protect Barak by taking the brunt of the force, making sure that the receiving end of the water's force and the unmovable stone wall was landed all onto *him*.

"...it must've been overly eager," Barak started slowly. "You know how it gets with members of Riveroak, I can only imagine how much worse it must be for a half breed."

"Maor isn't a part of the Riveroak family any more than me and you are," Eirian huffed at him. "Nanaibek-Rū checked that when Maor arrived in the forest, remember?"

"No because if *you* recall, we weren't even toddlers yet." Barak grumbled at her. "Everyone is checked to see which family household they need to go reside in upon entrance to the forest. Maor was hardly a few days old when he arrived. With no blood contacts in Azurlyn he and his guard were sent to Asharan village, because they couldn't be trusted."

"That's not why they were sent to Asharan and you know it." Eirian glared at Barak. "That's enough, whatever feud is between you two needs to end. From now on, act like a team or so help me Barak, when we get home, I *will* request a team reassignment."

"But Eirian!"

"No buts Barak!" Eirian snapped at him, "I'm sick and tired of you always poking at Maor's sours! We're a team and there's no 'I' in team!" Eirian snapped away from Barak, returning her hands to Maor's head injury, fighting back the urge to hiss and snarl at Barak like she wanted to. "We're not talking about this anymore. Just do me a favor and grow up. I am not dealing with children for the next week, got that?" Eirian didn't wait for Barak's answer, she raised both hands and ran her fingers across her thumbs in quick succession; distinctive snaps sounded with the last being the loudest. Glittering white fragments of magic bloomed to life around Eirian, settling around Maor they quickly lifted him into the air. Eirian rose to her feet and turned around, never facing Barak, and marched with Maor at her side towards the broken temple.

Barak remained silent, waiting several moments with fists at his side, before turning around and walking behind Eirian. Inside the temple Eirian glanced back at Barak once before sending out four glittering arrows. The four arrows split to either side of the room, bursting down the sliding doors and barreling down the halls. Eirian closed her eyes and concentrated, she knew from walking down the halls with the princess that it was nothing more than a glorified maze of stone and dead ends. Seconds ticked by till minutes began to pass and then Eirian finally found the way out, opening her eyes she marched forward unafraid. Not thinking twice about it, Eirian raised one leg forward and crushed it against the far wall, knocking down the screen with enough force to shutter the temple.

"Come," Eirian ordered, marching forward with furiously glowing amethyst eyes. The path was long, dark and winding, a maze of stone corridors intermixed with old paper sliding doors. By the time they reached the long awaited exit, raised voices were rolling down the halls towards them. Eirian reached the end of the hall and smashed the door open, a scowl on her face and fury making her white shards of magic pulse and sharpen.

"Ah! Eirian!" Ziya turned away from one of the elder Aislings, his hands raised peacefully towards the shorter woman, "I've been looking for you!" Eirian's answer was a frustrated scream and the firing of a white square bullet of magic straight at her teacher. The Aisling-woman took two steps back and smirked as Ziya grunted behind the force of the attack.

"Serves you right," The woman huffed, turning on her heal and marching away. "Hurry now! Sitareh says it's time!"

"What? But!" the woman was gone before Barak could finish speaking.

"Let's go," Eirian ordered, moving forward without a sound. "Ziya-Isha! I can't believe you!"

"Oh come on, it's not the first time!" Ziya whined as he carefully pulled himself out of the stone wall where he landed. That's when he saw Maor was unconscious and being transported by Eirian's white crystalline magic fragments. "…what happened?" Ziya asked as he hurried forward, taking up a place beside Barak. "Maor shouldn't have had any problem releasing those rune-seal-arrays!"

Barak said nothing, glancing at his teacher only to stare sullenly at his feet. Sighing, Ziya continued walking, guessing about what happened by Barak's expression and reluctance to speak. Once again his attempt at getting them to work together failed miserably; they were both too strong headed. Thankfully, their only necessities were the realignment of their dragons which took only thirty seconds to complete. The tiny magical armors chirped and chatted together in the team's given room, not far from the maze of hallways that led to the cell the boys had been trapped in. Ziya watched as Eirian greeted her armor with all the love of a mother's favorite child. Barak and his armor had a staring contest before the elusive scarlet lizard darted away, seemingly laughing at Barak as he shouted curses and gave chase. Maor carefully plopped himself into one of the chairs by the dining table, weight braced on his elbows that buried deep into his knees, one hand tangled into his short navy waves.

"Maor, good to see you amongst the living again," Ziya joked as he approached the young boy.

"Don't joke about that Ziya-Isha," Eirian ordered, a pout on her face as her surprisingly black dragon wrapped itself around her shoulders and started purring like a pleased cat. "Ryū," Eirian smiled in exasperation at her living armor, "We're to be leaving *now*." Ryū cracked open a pearl-eye and pouted at Eirian, with a heavy disappointed sigh he stood up and shook his body. Eirian closed her eyes and allowed her magic to surround them in brilliant glowing white shards, so bright that Ziya had to look away while Maor covered his eyes with a pained groan.

"Thank you Ryū," Eirian spoke, her voice muffled into a soft murmur. "Ready?" her armor rumbled, its scales shuffling all across her body.

"Get back here you blasted pyro-lizard monster from hell!" Barak screeched as he barreled across the room.

"Amaru," Eirian giggled. The glittering scarlet lizard perked at Eirian's voice, chittering like excited birds as it swirled into an ark and dashed quickly to the scaled young girl awaiting it with an outstretched arm. Barak cursed as he skidded to a stop but still crashed into a low table and tumbled to the stone floor with a pained curse echoing through the air around him.

"Hah," Maor smirked at his teammate, "Serves you right."

"Maor, be nice," Eirian scolded him, pulling her outstretched arm close to look Amaru in the eye. "Amaru, we need you to be nice today. We need to hurry out of here to protect our charge, okay?" the little dragon tilted its wide square head to the side, its smooth scales rippling like embers down its body as it chittered back. "Please Amaru, we need to hurry." The baby dragon straightened, shuffled its paws, wagged its long thick tail, and then darted forward, its forked tongue arching out to swipe across Eirian's masked face. "Ghaa! Amaru!" the creature seemed to cackled mischievously as it flew away, flapping its wide box wings and circled the room to crash face first into Barak's upper back.

"OW! Damn it!" Barak cried out, stumbling forward to catch himself but had no time before Ziya was before him. The boy cried out as a golden scaled foot snapped out with all the force of a storm, sending Barak across the room, over the table and out the doors leading to the balcony. Eirian sent out an extra burst of power, sending Barak over the edge and into the open air over the orchards below. With an explosion of power and appearing like a scarlet flaming super nova, Amaru burst into sparks and embers; flaring out like a thousand baby suns breathing for the first time.

"DAMN IT ZIYA-ISHA!" Barak cried out as he fell from the place his armor snapped around him, landing gracelessly into the soft soil of the orchard.

"Always so dramatic," Eirian sighed, placing a clawed hand on her hip.

"Eirian... you launched him out a window." Maor grumbled, looking up at the girl through his fingers.

"I did not," Eirian turned back to him. "I kicked him off the balcony before he could destroy it. He and Amaru are so different that their magics literally explode every time they merge. They're like bickering siblings who can't get along to save their own lives."

"Well... he is twelve," Ziya shrugged. "Maybe he'll grow out of it."

"Don't count on it Ziya-isha," Eirian huffed impatiently. "Maor, you're still cradling your head. Are your migraines back or is it the landing?"

"Uh... both?" Maor grumbled, pulling back from his hand to squint at Eirian with an expression of exhaustion. Huffing Eirian walked over and leaned forward, placing a gently glowing white palm along his navy temple while Ziya disappeared to rummage in the bathroom cupboard. Ziya quickly found a small bottle of medicine, a small picture of someone's head with needles being pounded into it on the front. Hovering the bottle in his hand while a small seal-array bloomed in his palm, Ziya was pleased to note that the medicine contained all the ingredients to help reduce a headache.

"That's all I can do for now Maor, take the medicine from Ziya-isha." Eirian ordered as she pulled back from her teammate while Ziya hurried back to them with a glass of water. He never knew how Eirian always knew when he carried medicine but he figured it had something to do with her strange observation skills. "We should hurry, so put on Tanith as soon as you swallow the pills."

Maor grunted in acknowledgement as he took the small bottle from Ziya and read the instructions, or at least tried to guess the meaning of the pictures. Tanith, Maor's dragon armor, shifted its six delicate paws impatiently, its rigged bone-spiked spine straightening to lift its torso from the coil it formed on the table, its smooth armored spiked tail sweeping around to wrap around itself with a nervous tick, its four wings fluttering at its side excitedly. Tanith, compared to Amaru, was very small. Her scales were all shades of blue, clean and sharp, changing from harmless silk on her face to wicked daggers along her neck and spine. Even her brows bore two blades of sapphire bone that curved regally back from her face like a crown. Her body was made for swirling through ocean currents, spiraling out of geysers, and coiling around great ships. Thin and tiny, hardly any wider than three of Ziya's fingers but as long as Eirian's hole arm. By contrast Amaru was as stout as Ziya's boot, looking more like dozens of tiny scaled squares smashed together and painted in shades of red and orange. His face was square, hornless, with too-wide too-yellow eyes and teeth too small to look like threats; Eirian knew better as she's had to sow-up Barak's bite marks multiple times. Amaru's limbs were thick coils of muscle, even his tail resembled a battering ram with its thick mass and sharp scales.

"Make sure you drink plenty of water while we travel," Ziya ordered as he crossed his arms and frowned thoughtfully. "It's possible the mountain range isn't good for you. We should hurry to deliver Kaur so we can ask the Riveroak if they have a medicine for you to use outside of the forest."

"Ziya-isha, I thought the Riveroak were mutes?" Eirian questioned, turning from a platter of fruits on the table, one black scale lifted on her back hip.

"They are but they also leave the forest on a regular basis." Ziya shrugged as if he didn't care one way or the other. "They might have a remedy for those mages who are more bound to water than others." Eirian shrugged and dislodged the thick scale from her hip. Whispering to it under breath, Eirian let her magic form a seal-array on the underside of the scale before gently hovering the magical white light over the fruit dish. Each of the fruit shimmered before bursting into dust, filtering up like spindles into the scale until nothing but the bowl was left. Eirian bobbed her head, kissed the scale and returned it to its place on her hip. she lifted two more scales and repeated the processes: one for meats and one for vegetables.

"I'm not diseased," Maor grumbled as he rose to his feet stiffly. "Tanith, come." The watery-serpent wasted no time in springing forward, blobs of water surrounding her to reflect light like a beautiful kaleidoscope of color. Like shattering sapphires and ice clusters, Tanith parted to envelop Maor in steal scales and leather clasps that held her body around Maor tightly. Any gaps of her joints were pointedly covered by leather straps or metallic buckles; all signs of the unity between Maor and Tanith.

"Why is it that out of everyone, only Eirian looks like a real serpent lady?" Ziya asked, his answer was Eirian flipping the wooden table around to crash it into his head. The grown man groaned beneath the shattered remains of the dining table, not daring to move incase Eirian wanted to throw something else at him.

"I'm a dragoness!" Eirian screeched, red faced and furious with the question of her teacher. However, he was correct. Out of everyone on their team, Eirian was the only who appeared like a full blooded human-serpent-hybrid, the only one who didn't look like a human in scaled armor. Her dragon, so dark and ominous, curled around her body so perfectly that she had no need for clasps or leather straps to keep her dragon in place. He simply wrapped around her body like a second skin, his face melding perfectly over her own, his eyes slipping over her own like protective bubbles of glass. She truly did look intimidating in her swath of black scales, her feet large forked claws, her tail a thin pendulum of a blade, her wings neatly tucked like folded fans, her hands sharp feline claws, her face long and thin with many blades curling about her face in elegant feathers. A true dragon of the night, as black as a starless night, as dangerous as death's scythe: regal, strong, foreboding, *dangerous*, these were all words used to describe the young girl in her armor.

"Let's go! She's waiting!" And her temperament matches. Eirian stalked away, snarling furiously as she marched out of the room and down the hall. Maor looked at his teacher with sleepy eyes before abandoning the man beneath the wooden table, ignoring his whining about cruel students and unfair fates. Outside, Maor and Eirian met with a maid, she was shorter than the others, chubby, platinum white hair pulled back into a high and tight bun, deep storm-purple eyes, and her hard round face accented her battle hardened aura. The woman blinked slowly at them, as if not expecting them to leave their room before she reached them. Then she gave a stiff smile and snapped on the ball of her foot, explaining sharply that she was to guild them to the staircase. The walk with the seemingly young woman was silent and awkward to the young preteens, who kept looking at each other and the few curious children following them uneasily. The halls were long, twisting, slipping through large rooms and windowless corridors, a haunting maze of gold white stone and bright pale sunlight. Finally reaching the top of the courtyard to the staircase, Eirian and Maor both saw Setareh standing before the first steps, silently staring out at the gorge before her. Her tattoos made her thin face appear even colder than before, her icy blue eyes appeared lifeless and haunted at the same time. She looked like a mournful star-child, unable to see past the devastation of the human wars presented to her like quilt of regret.

"Setareh," the young woman murmured, bowing at the waste. "It is time."

"I said three days," Setareh retorted, not looking away from the white-washed valley. "It's been thirty-two hours."

"Your father has deemed it necessary to leave now."

"It is too soon," Setareh murmured, her brows pinched together and her lips twisted down. It was strange to see that passive, uncaring mask shift into a look of displeasure; especially since she showed no previous signs of emotion. The young woman glanced up through her shallow white hair, stormy eyes narrowed warningly.

"Setareh, your father knows best." The maid murmured. "We have survived for as long as we have do to his leadership." Setareh glanced at the maid, remaining silent as she stared coolly down on the young woman. Setareh's sharp blue eyes glinted with violet lines and her seal-array tattoos glowed a faint scarlet.

"Careful there Yildiz, your plans may erupt in flames." Setareh murmured, her voice stern, her eyes narrowing further, her nose flattening while her lips twisted again; an expression of disgust. "You failed once before, you will do so again. Do not test fate's patience."

"Setareh should obey her father's commands," 'Yildiz' replied patently, her own deep purple eyes glinting with the glow of violet outlines. "Though fate evades him, destiny still whispers to him."

"Do not test *my* patience Yildiz," Setareh retorted as she began to descend the stairs, all the regality and elegance of an empress surrounding her once more. "I have told you before and will tell you once more: The vision you seek is not the fate of this world. *Give up* before Xolotl visits."

"I'll keep your words in mind, Setareh." Yildiz replied, though there was no discernable tone with her words there was something that set Eirian on edge as she passed the short plump woman. Maor glanced back at the young woman, watching her face smooth over into a neutral expression as her eyes cooled to amethyst coins.

"Kaur," Eirian called out as she descended the second flight down, "What was that about?"

"Yildiz is perusing father," Setareh answered blandly. "Once his marriage to mother was cemented she sought to be his mistress, which isn't uncommon in our family and occasionally its encouraged. Usually an heir doesn't birth the next heir, in fact it's fairly rare for an heir to come with child and if the previous heir dose come with child they are the last of the family to give birth. Father married mother knowing that he may never have a child of his own."

"Okay," Eirian said as she paused to watch Maor leap from one level down to her own so he could stand at her side. "So who was the heir before you?"

"My mother." Setareh answered blandly. "It is because of this, and that of my abilities, that many in the family are discontent. An heir does not give birth to another heir."

"But your father said that the birth of the heir isn't something you, as a whole family, can control." Maor interjected, "So how can your family be discontent if the birth of the heir isn't something your parents can control?"

"In order for an heir to give birth, they must give up their life for the birth of their child." Setareh answered flatly. "This is how the family has always been. This is all they've ever known." She stopped to look up at the children, staring up at them with eyes too blue, too sad, too mournful, to belong to a sixteen year old girl. "Now do you understand? My sisters and I are not the norm. This is why father has made the choice that he has made." Though Setareh spoke matter of fatly, as if she were stating a math problem, there was a tinge of *something* in Setareh's voice that Eirian couldn't name. They continued walking down, the end of the diamond-shaped staircase nearing them with every step. Eirian paused when she heard a loud shout, looking out at the valley, examining the orchard and the animals ambling about aimlessly, she found Barak struggling out of the hole he made upon landing. She knew it took time to go from their room to the top of the stairs, their descent of the stairs and their bickering set aside, Barak should've been able to pull himself out of the earth already.

"That idiot," Maor grunted, bland and unsurprised with Barak's struggle out of the earth. "How'd he get stuck so deep he couldn't climb out on his own?"

"I kicked him off the balcony." Eirian reminded Maor with a dull voice.

"Oh yeah," Maor blinked slowly, looking back out at Barak as he succeeded in pulling himself out with Ziya's help and started racing towards them. "Still an idiot." Maor shrugged and meandered down the stairs, ignoring Eirian's disappointed sigh as she followed him in exasperation. Setareh stepped off the last of the stairs, walking past the two guards as if they were statues, and approached the rushing Barak.

"Kaur! I just realized something!" Barak shouted as he raced towards her, his hazel eyes wide and his one hand waving about franticly overhead. He skidded to a stop, franticly waving both arms to stop himself in time to not crash into Setareh as she stopped walking as well. "If there are no are no child births after the heir's sixteenth birthday and twenty years had passed between your mom's sixteenth year and

120

your birth, then doesn't that mean your mom is REALLY old?!" For a moment the sixteen year old stared at Barak as if he lost his mind. Both brows were tilted slightly up, as if she couldn't raise just the one brow, and her face had smoothed and gentled out as she stared. No more narrowed, hawk-faced, empress staring down on the world with ice-berg neutrality. Instead a truly surprised teenager was staring at Barak as if she never considered such a thing before, she just accepted her reality without question.

"...That's rude," the guard to the left drawled, unimpressed with the loud question.

"Is it truly unusual for a thirty-six year old to give birth?" the right guard questioned, genuinely curious.

"Don't say that to her face," Setareh answered at last, her 'empress-mask' returning full force. "We should go before the next platoon sweeps by." Setareh turned her full attention towards Ziya, who was grinning cheekily at his other two students who had decided to walk down with Setareh instead of leaping off a balcony like their teacher. Seemingly understanding that Ziya had chosen to leap from the balcony to reach the ground level, Setareh blinked slowly and began the walk away. Eirian gave Barak an unamused look as she past him, rolling her eyes heaven word before she followed Setareh through the orchard. Instead of going to the cliff edge where their team had climbed up, Setareh headed for the far left side of the orchard where the cliff face curved sharply through the valley.

"Princess, where are you going?" Eirian asked as she hurried to walk beside the teenager. "Shouldn't we leave the same way we arrived?"

"No," Setareh answered. "The scouts have found evidence of humans in the lower canyon valley. To avoid them best would be to head to the edge of the canyon and the edge of the mountain range."

"How long will that take?" Ziya asked, "Shouldn't we hurry to get you to Azurlyn?"

"It'll take twenty minutes to reach the valley edge and three days to reach the mountain range edge." Setareh answered, she continued forward, never looking back at her guards. As they walked, the children looked about at the various workers climbing up the large white-barked trees. The large white trees harbored thick sturdy limbs strong enough to hold two or three of the workers, their bright yellow fruit wiggled back and forth as the workers brushed them gently before moving on. Barak was the shortest in the team but he was also physically strongest, standing at four feet even and most of the workers were Barak's height or shorter. It was similar to looking at a bunch of apples and squares with legs clamber up ladders and crawl over tree branches. The Aisling family weren't a 'pudgy' type of family tree, more like 'stocky' as their family had long since adapted to sowing, climbing stairs and plucking fruit. Setareh seemed the only one standing out amongst the crowd, a little taller than everyone else in her family tree and by far the thinnest.

"Setareh, where are you taking us?" Ziya asked as the orchard trees began to thin out, revealing a tall white stone wall. Setareh didn't glance back as she lifted her skirts and sped up, forcing her guardsmen to race after her as the surrounding trees gave way to boulders of white and gray stones. Setareh hurried up to a sprawling white tree with vast branches drooping low to the white-sandy ground, leafless and barren it stood as tall as any proud tree would.

"Hurry," Setareh ordered as she swept low to the sandy surface and slipped beneath the trunk of the tree, disappearing beneath the earth surface without a whisper. Eirian was the first to dive in after Setareh, she didn't even hesitate to swing around the trunk and barrel into the hole headfirst. Maor hesitated just long enough for Barak to clumsily slide into the hole, then with a shared look with Ziya, he headed in after his teammates. Ziya quickly slapped his hands against the sandy surface of the ground, erasing their footprints before following his students underground. Underneath the tree was a great circle, six rooms splintered off the wide center, five of the rooms splintered off into darkness and the last appeared to be a very small kitchen.

"There's no running water here and it can get smoky on occasion but otherwise it's a good home to live in." Setareh said, continuing to chip away at some vegetables as if she hadn't just been running away from her guardsmen. "Maisoror and I used to come here when I was young. There are powerful spells here that she taught me. No one can see nor hear us. All we have to do is make sure no one follows us here." Eirian moved towards the center of the underground space, the center was a small hearth about three feet in diameter, protected by a high earthen shelf that doubled as a small table. The three children took their seats, staring in awe at the intricate wooden bowls with their beautiful artwork and matching utensils. Ziya grunted as he tried to stand only to find himself hunched over and bracing himself on his knees.

"It's very cramped in here," Ziya grunted as he tried to look about.

"What are you talking about Ziya-Isha?" Eirian turned to look back at him and discovered the man struggling to get down on his knees. "Oh," she cringed as he fell, jostling several items and making the dragon-armors whimper in sympathy for their elder who moaned in pain.

"It might be best for you to go to your room now." Setareh suggested as she waved a hand towards the room left of the entrance. Ziya remained laying on his belly, using his arms to pull himself towards the indicated room and gracelessly tumbled inside. He yelped loudly, apparently there was a steep ledge between the entrance and the floor leading down to his rooms.

"Setareh? If you don't mind me asking, how did this place come about?" Maor asked as he looked about, resisting the tug from Tanith to go towards the furthest room.

"You seem much more relaxed now Setareh," Barak commented, green eyes blinking slowly at Setareh.

"Yes, only Maisoror and I know of this place so I don't need to worry about politics here." Setareh answered as she set three bowls down by the hearth, took a seat beside Eirian and across from Maor. "Maisoror taught me everything I know, including how to build this cavity."

"I'll say it's quite spacious over here," Ziya commented from the entrance to his room. He set his arms on the earthen floor and leaned forward, completely relaxed in the entrance to 'his room'. "I can sprawl out and everything. It's wonderful and the bed in here is perfect!"

"Ziya-Isha!" Eirian gasped, "Ekhi is gone!" Ziya's yellow and orange scaled face grinned wolfishly back at his students, his brilliant scarlet eyes dancing in mischief. If he had a choice in the manner his dragon would still be on his person, but there was a special little treat that Eki was currently enjoying. The abandonment of his person forced him to rely on his appearance spell before he returned to his student's side.

"Yes, she's currently enjoying the small magma pool down here." Ziya shrugged carelessly, scarlet eyes glittering as he turned his attention towards Setareh. "Kaur, you've yet to take a look at me."

"In all of the worlds of creation, only fifteen present of them are worlds were I see your face." Setareh replied calmly, "twelve of them, I die immediately after words."

"I'm that hot?" Ziya snickered out, smile wide enough to reveal gleaming golden daggers

"You're that terrifying." Setareh corrected, much to Barak's endless amount of amusement.

"Now I know why you're facing Maor's ugly-ass!" Barak laughed loudly, Maor's response was to encase his teammate's head in a bubble of water.

"Kaur, May I ask what you mean about the percentage of worlds?" Eirian asked, ignoring Barak's flaying about and Maor's struggle to keep the water-orb from bursting.

"Hmm... let me put it this way," Setareh ran her fingers over the edge of the hearth and from it sprung up thousands of glowing specks of dust. The bubble encasing Barak's head disappearing with Maor's distraction and the shorter boy didn't seem to mind as he was just as distracted by the glittering dots floating in empty dark space above the hearth. "If I were to talk about the worlds in terms of percentages, then one-percent would represent one-hundred worlds. For the Aisling family, our entire world sensory perceptions gets overrun by common occurrences in ninety to ninety-nine percent. Seventy-five to eighty-nine percent commonalities are usually occurring in the form of sound. fifty to seventy-four percent is typically impressions and feelings. Thirty-five to fifty percent of commonalities is nothing more than discovery of intentions and so on. Fifteen to thirty-four percent requires our utmost patience and concentration, predictions made this way are less likely to happen then when they appear before us naturally. Anything less than fourteen percent is something we typically can't sense and even if we do get an impression of a world like that, it's difficult decrypt much less understand."

"And even if you can sense something with a twenty-percent commonality, your prediction can be in accurate because of its low possibility?" Ziya asked, "With so many other words to see and hear, there is no grantee that what happens in a twenty-percent commonality will happen in this world. Correct?"

"Correct." Setareh bobbed her head and waved her hand, the glowing specs of light very nearly vanished, leaving behind only a dozen or so lights. "Many Aislings cannot see nor hear anything less than fifteen-percent-commonality. So we base most of predictions from grand mass of commonalities. Therefore only the occasions where a ninety-five to a ninety-nine present commonality are permitted to be released to the desert nomads."

"you trade your visions for resources?" Barak asked, receiving a stiff node from the princess in answer.

"Then... Kaur Can I ask you a question?" Maor asked, "What's the chance of success for this mission?"

"You do not want that answer." Setareh answered without hesitation.

"Yes I do."

"No you do not." Setareh sighed heavily, her narrow face morphing into a look of exhaustion. "In eighty-five percent of the worlds were I tell you the answer, ninety-eight percent of them you regret asking and eventually die an early death."

"...your information is that accurate?" Ziya asked, surprised with the information. Setareh nodded sharply, staring out at the glittering example of worlds. "...Your sister mentioned your wedding at last night's dinner. What did she mean by that?"

"...anyways," Setareh waved a hand, distracting the children with the twirling of lights and glitter. "The rules of the Aisling family are simple. An heir does not give birth to another heir and when they do give birth, it typically marks the next dry spell. We can see an individual's death, their life-partner, their child, major life arks, the remaining time they have in our current world, the amount of time they share with their life-partners, cross-roads or the results of choices and most individual fates. Ninety-nine percent of Aisling sees these things as numbers above one's heads. What Aislings cannot see nor hear nor predict is anything that happens in our own lives in this current reality... or in any other reality."

"What do you mean?" Barak asked

"Aislings are not capable of seeing past our death-days," Setareh replied with a careless shrug. "Plus in all the words we see we can only see or hear from worlds that do not have our physical presence. For example." She waved a hand and the thousands glittering lights vanished completely. "This half of the worlds I do not exist. These are the worlds were I die in mother's womb or died at a young age or were I was simply not conceived at all. Ordinarily these are the worlds I should not be able to look into and see their percentages of success and failures but... I can."

"...why?" Barak asked curiously

"...your seals," Eirian murmured. "but I thought they were to protect you?"

"you're not entirely incorrect," Setareh sighed. "In the worlds that I don't exist, you all live long happy lives and my family continue in their safe-haven undisturbed for another millennia. The Aisling family never contacts Azurlyn and the dragons never come-across the Aislings."

"...but your visions—" Ziya started then stopped with a harsh curse, his scarlet eyes widening in horror.

"Yes, my seals were tattooed into my body by many seers as such I am able to see all other worlds and make predictions but they all share one commonality." Setareh closed her eyes, her body slumping as the glittering worlds turned into stark scarlet, a few even disappearing in black smoke or gray dust. "I see the worlds in which I am fated to die, the worlds where I exist, where I live...and were I will certainly *die*."

"So you literally watch yourself die hundreds of times?" Barak asked, staring at the worlds with a growing sense of pity. "That's messed up."

"Thousands," Maor corrected though admittedly everyone ignored him.

"I assure you it was all accidental. No one knew that the magic of several people would remain in the seals themselves; which brought about this anomaly." Setareh smiled mirthlessly, "after all, something as simple as a blink can change the course of history."

"What?" Maor asked in bewilderment, thrown for a loop with the information.

"A blink can change history." Setareh smiled at Maor, amusement dancing in her baby-blues. "The Aisling family believe that one chance, one word, one look, one step can change anyone's fate. Turn left or right? Look up or down? Say yes or no? Meet at dusk or dawn? Remain silent or speak up? Interrupt or remain silent? Step forward or step back? Look ahead or look away? Pretend to be unafraid or submit to terror. These are all things that change fates. So our saying is that 'a blink can change history'."

"So let me get this straight," Ziya straightened against his perch, his scarlet eyes clued to Setareh's platinum locks. "You albinos can't see your own joys, can't watch current events, can't see the full picture half the time, and can't escape your given fates?"

"Correct," Setareh agreed. "An Aisling must accept our death-days in order to become seers. Those who do not accept their fates live twice shortened lives."

"What do you mean?" Eirian asked, a foreboding sense of horror creeped along her spine, making her dread Setareh's following words.

"The Aisling family typically awaken our power of foresight when our bodies change into adult hood, so about twelve to fourteen is when we see our first vision." Setareh answered, not looking at anyone. "Our fist vision is always about our own deaths. We can never see the when, who, where; only the *how*. Accepting our deaths is the first step any seer must perform."

"What if you don't accept your deaths," Barak asked, "What if you choose to change your death-day?"

"Then the seer in question will not live long enough to see the next generation." Setareh said firmly, "As I said, they will live twice shortened lives."

"What does that mean?" Barak persisted.

"The girl in that room," Eirian murmured, "just past the kitchens…"

"Little Astaraea," Setareh's face morphed into a sad acceptive smile, "Accepting our death-days is the only way for us to survive. She could not accept hers."

Chapter 7

"Children, I think it's time for you to go to bed." Ziya ordered suddenly, his voice hard and booking no room for arguments, "We have to get up early tomorrow."

"Yes Ziya-Isha," children's voices were sullen and soft, their minds distracted with the information given to them. Ziya slipped back beneath the lift, the children moved into their own rooms. Setareh smiled as each of the children gave startled shouts before erupting in barely stifled giggles. She knew without having to look that each of the dragons had freed themselves from their respective partners and barreled into their own little pools. Reaching beneath the hearth-counter, Setareh grabbed a long thin piece of cloth and smoothly wrapped it around her eyes. With both experience from her world and the very helpful visions of another, Setareh carefully moved herself away from the hearth; blindfold never moving. She climbed into the entrance to Ziya's 'room' and followed the path to the stairs leading even further down into the surface of the earth. It was only when the children's laughter faded completely and the heat began to suffocate her, that Setareh stopped walking.

"...I'm assuming you came down here to answer my questions—"

"Because it has a ninety-five percent commonality." Setareh interrupted. "Yes you are correct."

"So, since you know what I want to ask. Just tell me the answers."

"Maisoror means 'eldest sister'. A world told me that 'Kaur' means princess is this correct?"

"Correct." Ziya bobbed his head

"Maisoror is from a reflection-world. You save her life and in return she led the Hammurabi into the forest. Maisoror visits me often, though I last saw her the day before your arrival. She asked me for names. No father does not know of Maisoror and I'd rather he not know about her. Seventy-nine percent says father dies of a heart attack after learning of the news. Mother may or may not know of Maisoror, I have not seen nor heard of worlds where mother had a reaction of discovering Maisoror and she's never questioned Maisoror's existence. The seven family elders are responsible for the tattoos on my body. The sage of Dubol is the one who created and presented the seal-array to my father. Do not seek revenge on the sage of Dubol. You *will* die. In the forty-five thousand worlds that I live in, four hundred-fifty-nine point eighteen worlds I die."

"…math is not my friend…"

"…say there are one million worlds," Setareh rolled her eyes, knowing he couldn't see them beneath her blindfold. "I exist in half of them. Of that half that I exist, I die by my sixteenth year."

"…alright, how many of them do you survive in?" Ziya asked, "Like past this year."

"I survive in only forty-five worlds. That's point zero-forty-five percent against ninety-nine point zero-fifty-five percent. Which is the greater number?"

"The ninety-nine," Ziya answered with a careless shrug. "So the possibility of you dyeing is ninety-nine percent. That means there's still that one percent—"

"I die in ninety-nine *point fifty-five* percent," Setareh corrected. "I survive in only forty-five worlds and of those worlds I do not live long. I marry and then there are three outcomes: the child dies, I die, we both die."

"To let one live then all shall fall, to let all live then one shall fall," Ziya quoted the old servant, Astra, from the previous day. "You're the one who must fall... for what? Your kinsmen?"

"It is my fate," Setareh sighed. "It does not matter if I leave seer valley this year or fifty-years from now. If the Aisling family is to leave, *I must pay the price of safe passage.*"

"Why dose the Aisling family need to leave seer valley? You could just remain—"

"We cannot remain any longer," Setareh's voice cracked, a mixture of distress and resolve shook the heated air of the underground room. "Gehill is close to discovering us and soon Dubol will crumble into war. The mountain range is no longer a safe place to hide."

"...and Gehill is not kind to its females."

"Nor any female of any land." Setareh replied. "However, procreation in Gehill is not the problem. If Gehill finds my family, they will slaughter everyone."

"But your family is one of the ancients, one of the families protected by the gods, a holy family with the greatest form of divine protection—"

"The Aisling family will be *slaughtered* because they will resist Gehill's demand of dimensional-war-fair."

"That doesn't mean they'll slaughter *everyone*." Ziya hissed at her. "Gehill is known for its male-dominance, they could spare the younger children. Train the males for loyalty to Gehill while keeping the female's subservient. Your family wouldn't be slaugh—"

"But dimensional-viewing is an *eventuality*. One of them would discover Gehill's sins and betray them. This will happen and when it does, no one of the 'holly family Aisling' will be left alive." Setareh hissed, growing tiered with the repetition. "Besides that, Aislings awaken their foresight between the ages of twelve and fourteen. The first vision is of our death, a death we must accept in order to survive. Gehill will not understand that."

"They'll reject and in turn…"

"The seer will also reject their death." Setareh nodded her head in agreement, glad the man was catching on.

"But you said they'd get trapped in their own minds, that they'll die when their bodies give up—"

"The first stages are the visions of loved ones dyeing *pointlessly*. Within a few days they will no longer be able to tell the difference between a vision and the world they live in. Besides, without an elder to guild them they will never understand the difference between a certainty and a plausibility. Gehill won't understand what the seer was going through and there for, kill the seer. Which honestly is a mercy so early on," Setareh shrugged, having full knowledge of the drawbacks of her powers has made her less empathetic to the internal struggle her relatives face on a daily basis. "Even if they spared all the children under the age of five tomorrow, within the following four years of the eldest's twelve birthday, all previously spared Aisling-children *will. Be. Dead*. Either because they saw a dimension that revealed Gehill's crimes against the Aislings or because they rejected their death and were killed by Gehill."

"So… what you said about remaining in Seer Valley for another millennia…"

"That was an occurrence based on my *stillborn-self*."

"…you mean if you were never born," Ziya cut himself off, unable to continue the sentence. A cruel reminder of his own past and internal-battle all 'ancient' ones must confront at some point in their life; the battle dictating the reason of their birth.

"Had my mother birthed a dead child, the Aisling family would be safe for another millennia however…" Setareh took a deep breath, stealing her nerves and trying to ignore the trembling in her hands. "That is not *this* world's fortune…I am alive and my living-self brings with it great hardships and many trials. Not just for my family nor just your team. My existence brings with it a shifting of the nations. Every human on our Aeoman Continent will be tested."

"…tested for what?"

"The right to live." Setareh turned her head towards Ziya but the vision that unraveled before her was not the one in which her body stood. Before her was a man, dressed in lose pants and a three-sizes too large sweater, his short locks resembled black-emerald leaves and his eyes were frightening wolf-gold. He was well built, a thick bulky frame used to carrying heavy boxes but there was a distinctive way his body slouched, the way his muscles coiled beneath the cotton-sweater; he was a life-long soldier. She watched with tears gathering in her eyes, as her vision shifted from the slouching man with sad-orange-gold eyes, to the photo behind him. It was of the man, dressed in white robes and smiling brightly, in his arms was a woman with an abundance of white-ocean waves, her thin angular face was coated in a rare white foundation and her thin ocean eyes were dancing with joyful tears.

"*Daddy!*" she watched a tiny child come racing into the vision, tackling the man's leg and giggling shrilly as he jostled with her weight. "*Daddy! Guess what! I saw Aunty today!*" the man chuckled and patted the child's faintly green but mostly white curls. "*Aunty says I'll see mommy soon!*"

"*Don't gloat too much,*" the man smiled as he kneeled before his child, a sadness contorting his golden eyes despite the smile on his face. "*I'll get jealous.*" The child giggled then, suddenly, they turned. She couldn't see the child's face, nor tell the child's gender, but she knew-in that moment-that the child was of Aisling blood.

"...*mommy?*"

"Three by three by three by three, the fates decide this world. Starting first with the three fates birth." The man turned towards her, as if seeing her for the first time, and she thought for a moment that something broke inside him. She was helpless to keep the vision before herself, it spiraled away like swirling mists, and once more she found herself in the darkness she knew she lived in.

"In the morning we leave for Lesart," Ziya informed her calmly, appearing to not hear her words at all. "We will make contact and contain some documents that will allow us passage through the Civilian lands. It'll be a long journey through Ashan but this is safest for both you and us."

"Then the path has been set." Setareh turned on her heal and began her slow walk back to the main cervices. "I pray your divine powers bring us fortune, for we will need it on this trip."

"I thought the Aislings saw the fates of all those around them?" Ziya asked, attempting to joke with the young teenager.

"Point zero one percent," Setareh murmured. "point zero one percent is where all of us have survived... your team, my family, my child, our nation, the ancients, the three fates...I pray we are that point one percent..." *what a lovely world that one is...* Setareh didn't make it to her own room, beside the kitchen, she was distracted with the glitter of light from one of the other rooms. Frowning she moved towards the room, walking down its smooth slop till she reached the very end. A great circle greeted her, several clusters of diamonds protruded around the top of the room giving everything an eerie white glow. There was a young girl sitting on a large white crystal, staring up at an old map Setareh had carved into the stone years ago.

"So, you're Eirian," she greeted the young girl passively, she closed her eyes and tugged her blindfold back down over eyes just as the girl turned to look at her.

"I guess my appearance spell is pointless if you're wearing a blindfold," Eirian commented, Setareh shrugged in indifference.

"I do believe the others are sleeping, why aren't you?"

"I was just thinking that your map doesn't look like the one back home," Eirian answered. "The spelling of the nations is wrong, the locations of features are wrong too."

"What do you mean the spelling is wrong?" Setareh asked, "I carved that myself."

"Well for starters, Trégaron is supposed to have a dash over the 'e'." Eirian answered, "The dash turns the 'trey' into 'tri'. This is in reference to their three great rivers. Urmër is supposed to have two dots over their 'e', it makes it makes it sound stronger as well. The 'i' in Nyxnia is silent so it should have a silent dash above it. Gehill should be spelt G-A-I not G-A-Y. Gehill should have two 'l's in it. The way the Baīlāy Mountain Range curves is wrong, it curves down here, not up here. The Aisiling family village sits on this Mountain side, not this northern one." Eirian continued to point out the inconsistencies and Setareh listened, slowly making the edits with her own glowing fingertips and Eirian's gentle guidance. "There's a forbidden sea-side in Trégaron's southern border called 'Devil's Horns Bay', people often go missing there. it's shaped similar to a spiral but it floods easily so no one really knows what it truly looks like. Malbril is basically a bunch of marble pillars with dome houses sitting on their sides. Did you know that at high tide all the houses crawl towards the top of the pillars to avoid the flying sword fish? And at low tide they have this monstrous little sea-urchin that looks like sea-snail in hibernation but it has a hive-mind and their favorite food is human flesh. Thank the gods they can't climb well!"

"If that's true then why do the villagers in Malbril ever go down their mountains during low tide?" Setareh asked as she carefully carved out the 'pillars' of Malbril.

"Oh that's easy, they're basically hunter-gathers. Without the abandoned sea-life they can't sustain their village very well. There's also the fact that smugglers try to hide in their pillars and end up stranded so they usually make out pretty good when they climb down. But at the same time, they can't stray too far from their mountains, otherwise when high-tide comes back they end up devoured by the serpent school."

"Serpent school?"

"it's basically a sea lizard that dies from dehydration really easily and it travels in a pack of a few hundred, hence why they're called 'serpent school'."

"You're very knowledgeable about the other kingdoms," Setareh chuckled and shook her head

"I have to be," Eirian answered, "I'm training to be a dragon. One day I'll be sent out to find our missing kinsmen. In order to find them, I have to know the terrain. It'd be really sad if I fell into a pit in Gehill and died because I couldn't figure out that the damp rocks were because of an underground river."

"I can see why that'd be a problem," Setareh smiled to herself. "I noticed you haven't said anything about Dubol yet, why is that?"

"That's because it's not necessary to correct it," Eirian answered. "Dubol is a giant waste land of sand and human-eating-monsters, so there are no distinctive landmarks or specific land-formations. The only human civilizations in it are long the ocean coast and the three spreading out from Clearway that lead to Drogo and Aljana. Everything else is sand dunes and monsters, there's no possibility of civilization living anywhere else then along the coast."

"how do the people survive there?"

"they fish in the ocean," Eirian chuckled. "They're lucky to have a protective reef 12 miles out from their coast. It's the only thing that's protecting them from the rest of the monsters in the ocean. Urmër suffers from monstrous attacks all the time; they have no form of ocean-protection. some monsters appear to be serpents that isolate whole islands. Others devour whole ships and there are some with tentacles that crush whole armadas just to devour the survivors.

"Note to self: don't visit the ocean." Setareh grumbled. "Any other horrifying creatures I should know about?"

"Most live in Nyxnìa," Eirian answered simply. "Thankfully there are no known humans living in that region. As far as anyone knows it's a nation of monsters."

"Isn't Nyxnìa the land of the damned?"

"Yeah. According to legend, when the gods were done creating life they took all the creatures that weren't so pretty and banished them to Nyxnìa. To make sure they could never escape they sent their war god to stomp the monsters into the core of the earth. Except the war-god wasn't heavy enough to reach the core and Mother Earth was very mad that he dared to step on her. She removed his foot as punishment and made it the dome that protects the very monsters he tried to stomp out of existence."

"That was nice of her," Setareh commented dryly

"Not really," Eirian snickered. "Mother Earth is the bringer of life and Death. She decides if we're to live or die *by the masses*. For someone else to make the choice in her stead *really* makes her mad. That's why the War God is missing a leg. She made damn sure the other gods didn't forget who's in charge of the balance."

"Any other frightening tails you want to tell me?"

"Have you heard about the tail of the five siblings?" Eirian asked, seemingly excited in an instant. "it's my favorite!"

"Tell away," Setareh didn't need to give Eirian any encouragement, the preteen was already excitedly chittering away.

"The blood wars happened four centuries ago right? Well it all started after a great asteroid landed on our continent and turned everything black for five centuries! The survivors actually managed to cultivate the earth again and their populations grew with the expanse of food resources. Then one day the survivors met and for whatever reason they didn't like each other and battle broke out between them. Each survivor grew their numbers till they formed families and then multiple families formed alliances to create Tribes. At some point many tribes gathered together to create villages and when alliances formed between villages a nation was formed. The nations grew as they forcefully overtook land, resources, villages and tribes. When the nations could no longer grow, they started selecting people with special skills to fight in their wars. That's how the blood-wars began. Everyone was fighting to find someone with a special skill to fight in the war. The men were of course trained for battle and the women were of course restrained in the bases, forced to breed for more occupants with their special powers. During all this time, centuries passed and there remained as one consecutive trend: no one dared to pass through the asteroid's landing sight. All anyone knew was that the asteroid brought poison and the land it carved out was saturated with the sickly gas.

In Trégaron's twelfth-year, one of the generals discovered a family with five children. The parents were powerful, erasing over half of the general's army before they fell. The five siblings were caught but they refused to fight in the war, even after being beaten brutally the siblings refused to join the war. It was only when the general threatened to sell their sister to the highest bidder that the brothers finally caved to the general's demand. They told the general that they had the power to purify all forms of poison, no matter what was infected. The general asked if they could purify the land that the asteroid had contaminated and the brothers said that they could. The general and his army marched, the children caged along the way. But when they reached the valley edge, where Trégaron ended and the waste-lands began, the brothers asked for their sister to join them in purifying the land for it would take all five of them to do so. The general refused and stated that the girl would be sold to the highest bidder; this way if the boys failed then their bloodline would continue. Furious the boys refused to comply and fought against the general and his remaining army; once she was back at their side, nothing could stop them. No one knows what happened first, all anyone knows is the end result.

The children managed to create a vast forest that fed off the poison of the asteroid that in turned purified the soil and waters still remaining. The earth rumbled and roared with their power, forcing up great towers of hot marble and boiling crystals from their creation and with the sacrifice of their lives, five ancient dragons ascended into our world. With the spirits of the siblings, the dragons parted from the once poisonous land and searched for those like the children. That night, no matter the distance between them, those with the blood of ancients heard a cry and left their homes and disappeared from existence. No one knows how the people were chosen, many left behind siblings, cousins, and other elders. So no one knows why these people suddenly disappeared for no apparent reason. Some say it was because their magic was stronger than their kinsmen, some say it was because the dragons found them first, others say that it could have a deeper meaning; a meaning that resonated with souls."

"but... not all those of ancient bloodlines were able to flee the blood-wars," Setareh sat back from the wall, her hands in her lap as she stared through more visions containing the truths of Eirian's words. "Many ancient-ones were left behind... like my family..."

"It's thought that those left behind were not able to leave." Eirian explained patiently, "it's possible they were chained down or knocked unconscious or simply too injured to move towards the dragons calling them. That's why we decedents are tasked to find our kinsmen and bring them back home, where they'll be safe."

Chapter 8

By morning the boys were ready to eat, they both clambered their way into the common area and slumped against the warm hearth with only coals inside. Having already foreseen their morning reluctance, Setareh had prepared a blindfold for their eventual awakening. Eirian helped her with breakfast, mostly so the blonde wouldn't burn or cut herself. Ziya sleepily leaned against the entrance way to his room, smiling as Barak struggled to wake himself up and Maor pretended to be awake by sipping on water; only problem was that they were both leaning dangerously close together. It wouldn't be long before each of their armors came out, Amaru instantly started a fight with Tanith; who did not appreciate having her tail snapped at. The resulting fight was quite amusing to watch, the two rolling, flying, barking, hissing and clambering all over everything was just enough noise to wake Eki. Eki was not a morning dragon, she did *not* appreciate being woken up by two younger dragons fighting. As such she came barreling out of Ziya's room, using him as a launching pad, and proceeded to blind everyone but Ziya and Setareh; the forming having ducked his head down to avoid the bursting sun that was his dragon.

Upside: the boys were awake and cursing the other for Eki's brilliance

Downside: Ryū was wrapping himself around Eirian as she sank to the floor, apparently trying to heal the damage to her eyes by Eki's light-explosion.

"Eki-Rū, please do not blind the children, they are not at fault." Setareh moved into the main room and kneeled beside the hearth, carefully sliding a bowl of steaming mush towards Ziya as she did so.

"If we were in enemy territory you boys would've been dead a long time ago," Ziya commented as Eki literally sat on Amaru and glared Tanith down. Which was another amusing sight as Amaru was promptly squashed undeath the queen Eki and Tanith looked like a scolded princess.

"But Ziya-Isha!" the boys whined

"Shut up and eat your food," Eirian ordered as she set both of their bowls down in front of them. "We need to leave by the next hour, otherwise the next platoon will discover us."

"I don't know how they haven't," Maor grumbled, "I have a waterfall in my room."

"Of course you do," Setareh agreed easily. "you're a water-mage. It would be best if a small portion of the underground river near my home fed through your room and exited on this side of the cliff-face. This way we have an exit and a strong armor against intruders."

"So what happens to the water that exits this place?" Barak asked, "I mean, it has to go somewhere, right?"

"I'm fairly sure nature has found a way," Setareh answered calmly, "There have been no visions where it became a problem." Of course it became a problem later, when Ziya had been forced to dive out of the waterfall with the rising sun and beat the scouting team below into bloody spears across the white stone of the valley. Once he was sure Gehill's scouts had been handled he gave the signal to his students, who each used Maor's skill to escape out the waterfall. Setareh was seated next to Eirian, who created a bridge for them to pass through the forest quickly and without stopping, Maor stood at the front, using his magic to bend the water in the plants to allow them passage without injury. Barak stood at their back, using his own ember spells to propel them across the bridge without stopping for a breath.

"See?" Barak asked loudly as they fled Seer Valley, "I told you it wouldn't be a problem!"

Ω Ω Ω

They were to meet with Ziya at the bottom of the mountain, Eirian and Setareh patient and calm beside the stream while Maor fished and Barak found firewood. There was village not too far away from them, barely a few hour's hike, they knew it was the place where their informant was but without Ziya to guild them they had no way of knowing who that was. Eirian used their high noon sun to her advantage and called fourth five crystals from the earth, each pointed slightly further away from each other. Eirian whispered a strange word under breath and an image appeared in the space between the crystals, it looked similar to a map except it showed where the earth rose and fell.

"What is Asharan like?" Setareh asked as Eirian started twitching her fingers over the image, expanding the section they were in; their location marked by a strange three-dimensional diamond.

"It's all pretty flat, until you get to the other side of the valley where it becomes rolling hills and rivers." Eirian answered, "the southern section looks quite similar to Trégaron like that, except that instead of all the plants being painted in neon colors, everything's pretty plain looking. The grass and leaves are similar shades of green, most tree barks are brown, same with bush limbs. The grass turns this weird gold-brown in autumn and they get snow in winter though admittedly it's not very thick. Just deep enough to numb your toes."

142

"The animals though, those things are bizarre!" Barak called as he removed himself from the forest-edge and walk towards them with both arms and tail full of wood they could burn. "They're all kinds of colors! Mom once took me to meet her relatives over there and we saw this giant dear that was blue and green and its horns were gold with silver stripes and—"

"That's a stag not a dear," Maor called out from the river side, sliding another fish out of the river and into his hovering orb.

"No it wasn't!" Barak shouted at him, "It's horns went straight up! And they spiraled! And its blue-green eyes were as big as your head!" here Barak dropped his arm load and gestured to his left palm the actual size of the eye; seemingly snickering at Eirian and Setareh as if passing along a secret.

"Sure it was," Maor drawled in distraction, "you were still a kit back then so it properly looked ten times bigger than it actually was."

"Quite being reasonable!" Barak ordered loudly

"What's a kit?" Setareh asked

"It's what we call our young ones," Eirian answered as the boys went straight into argumentative mode. "We usually call kids who aren't in the academy yet 'kits', meaning their too young to be leaving home just yet. We all enter the academy when we're five, so kits are typically those under the age of five."

"Dose everyone in your home attend the dragon-academy?"

"Oh no, everyone attends the same school until they're ten, then we chose if we want to be dragons or if we want to remain in the village. When we're twenty we can leave the village to the capital or nearby village but typically if you're not a dragon you can't leave the forest. If you do, your magic has to be sealed to protect the rest of the forest and you'll be branded so that our village knows if something happened to you. If you get kidnapped, seriously injured or dead, each scenario has a specific color-code to the inventory back home and a dragon-team will be assembled accordingly."

"Branded?" Setareh asked, "That sounds painful." Her response made Eirian chuckle as she tilted the map every so way, her fingers still twittering away over it, various lines appearing, changing color and bursting apart.

"Our branding is just a magical stone placed next to our hearts," Eirian elaborated. "No one can steal it without actually killing the person its inside. It also prevents it from being altered or confused with something else. Since it feeds on the very magic its suppressing, it doesn't ever lose power. It also records what's happening, since the heart is basically an open book to our emotions and current mental status. It can tell apart between emotional pain and physical pain, which tells the keepers back home if you need to be rescued or healed. It also works as a tracking devise so we can always find you no matter where you go."

"...you're very well informed," Setareh commented as Eirian sat back from the map and seemed to glare at it.

"My mother originally left the forest," Eirian explained. "a few years later she met and married dad. He was a Gehill soldier though so they struggled pretty hard to escape Gehill's clutches. Since mom's magic was sealed she couldn't help much but she could enhance their running speed and take away exhaustion. It was one of the few talents left to those who leave to the forest; just to ensure their safety. My parents got really close to the mountain boarder, they were by-passing Nyxnìa when they were caught by Gehill's trackers. Then there were the monsters who wanted an easy meal... my parents didn't get very far after that."

"You talk like you weren't there," Setareh murmured.

"In a sense I wasn't," Eirian agreed. "I was a year when I watched them die. Mom taught me a spell that allowed me to hide in plain sight and not ever get hurt. I surrounded myself in these crystals," she stopped and patted the nearest crystal fondly. "It was the east way to make sure

I wouldn't get hurt and because I was in my crystal I was influenced by the earth's magic and there for had no need to eat or drink. My parents carried me with them all the way to the edge…"

"Sorry," Setareh murmured, "you don't have to tell me. I was being nosy."

"it's okay," Eirian shrugged, "the boarder team apparently saw a white light and went to investigate. They found me in my crystal, with mom and dad on either side of me. Everyone else though… were ashes and bones; even the monsters who came to eat. Grandfather doesn't know how I survived but he thinks mom died trying to save me. He says if she wasn't burdened with me she would've made it to the edge and been able to use her magic again."

"he blames you for her death?" Setareh asked in surprise. Eirian tilted her head towards Setareh, the seer could envision the younger girl smiling at her; as if it didn't matter anymore.

"Eirian!" both girls looked at the boys, Barak baking a fish in his hands and holding it out to Eirian expectantly. "I cooked it for you! eat up!"

"No," Eirian replied, her voice tinged in disgust. "I'll eat when we get to the village."

"How far away is Isha?" Maor asked, marching himself out of the river with a near overflowing orb of fish at his side.

"About an hour," Eirian answered as she zoomed out on the map and showed them the golden diamond representing their teacher. "See, this is why I told you guys to carry my crystals. I can't find you if you don't wear them."

"Eirian! I told you already I lost it!" Barak whined loudly

"Where? Amongst that junk you call food?!" Eirian asked, pushing away the fish with a sound of disgust

"I wouldn't be surprised if he lost it in his room," Maor commented. "That's a black hole if there ever was one."

"Excuse you! at least I don't sleep in a pond!"

"No everything is just charred beyond recognition! And it's not a pond!"

"Both of you shut up!" Eirian ordered, throwing a crystalline bowl at the fish Maor caught and bracing it on the ground with three spikes. "Maor, Isha is coming, go greet him and cover any tracks that might be ours. Barak, shut up and cook our food."

"But Eirian!" Barak's whine was met with a board of crystal thrown at his face.

Eirian turned away from her teammates and started moving her map again, finding various paths to the village and possible escape routes while she was at it. Setareh remained quite at her side, listening to Eirian explain certain landmarks and the routs they would need to use for safety measures. When Ziya finally arrived, his armor was unusually sparkling clean, as if he had just washed it and Maor looked like wanted to be sick. Eki parted so Ziya could scarf down some burnt fish-fillets and observe Eirian's map at the same time. Setareh kept her eyes closed and turned away from Ziya precautionary, she did not want to die from fright. Once Ziya's energy was restored and Maor had relieved himself of his lunch, they were ready to go. Setareh sat back and waited till Eirian told her to remove her blindfold. What was presented to her was the sight of bland and plane. Each child had dark caramel skin, bright leaf-green hair, amber eyes and simple dark merchant clothes that bore a strange silver symbol on their left shoulders. It consisted of five dots in a strange 'w' shape, accompanied by two serpents twirling around a pillar bearing two gently curving crescents.

"Why do you look different Ziya-Rū?" Setareh asked as she looked at the leader curiously. It was true, instead of green hair like his charges, Ziya's hair was long and pale blue; looking like ribbons of clear topaz. Even his eyes were brilliant slivers of garnet, more red then orange.

"Ah... well, everyone has their secrets," Ziya dodged the question with a nervous laugh. "my image-recreation spell isn't nearly as strong as others my rank and this is kind of all I can really do for myself."

"Any other questions Kaur?" Eirian asked, looking young and boyish. Across her face was a strange assortment of white freckles looking mashed together constellations; her only unique feature. Even her curly dull jade hair was left short, barely even touching her shoulders and forming cute ringlets all around her face.

"Can't she look into another world for the answers she wants?" Barak asked, blinking his even larger than usual amber eyes at his younger counterpart. Were Eirian appeared more boyish, Barak appeared more feminine. He bore long pale green hair half pulled up into a high ponytail, the thick belt around his middle made his waste look small and made the cloth around his bust and waste flare out; making him appear to have feminine curves.

"How much you wanna bet that, that's really exhausting?" Eirian asked in return, giving her teammate a dull look.

"The five dots are thought to be the five siblings who gave their lives for the forest," Maor sighed as Eirian and Barak slipped into a debate about Setareh's strengths and weaknesses. His hair was shoulder length and pinned back on the top of his head, a beautiful display of dark jade ringlets surrounded his heart-shaped angelic face. His previously ocean-blue orbs were now sharp looking amber coins, accompanied with golden dots. "Other legends says the 'w' is the end of a whip of the War-God who lost it in his fight with Mother Earth. The serpent is a weaker decedent of the dragons who saved our ancestors from extinction; so they're very highly regarded in our forest. The infinity swirl the serpent makes is called the 'Ouroboros', it symbolizes life and death; meaning we live to find our kinsmen and we'll die protecting them. The staff indicates our will to fight should we be forced and the crescent moons represent the great scales of old; also known as the balance the dragons struggle to keep."

"Maor, you studied well," Ziya smiled and patted the boy's green curls affectionately. "you forgot the crescent moon is a symbol of the Autumn Triad. Which is also in reverence to Mother Earth's Scales that she uses to keep the balance of our world."

"The scales are in reference to the horoscope libra," Setareh commented offhandedly, "They usually appear in the first days of Autumn, when the hours of day and night are equal. As the first sign of the autumn triad, it is also the cardinal sigh; often referenced as the air sign. When this sign appears there is no work to be done in the fields. What needs to be done then is discussion, plans and ideas that'll carry the lives throughout the harsh winter coming. However, I do not see libra scales in your crest, that looks more like the Aries symbol."

"…not to self: don't argue with someone who has the power to see through dimensions." Ziya snickered to himself. "I'll keep that in mind in my next lesson Setareh-Kaur. For now though, we'd better change your appearance."

"I don't know any such spells," Setareh replied.

"I thought you could look into other worlds," Barak looked at her in confusion.

"Me looking into other worlds has nothing to do with my learning speed." Setareh gave him an exasperated look. "Yes I can find myself a teacher but that doesn't mean I'll learn or understand the concept of something in seconds. I still have the learning processes of all other humans."

"I'll just do the spell," Ziya sighed, "Thankfully I'm better at disguising others then myself." Ziya stepped forward and placed his hands on either side of Setareh's shoulders, making sure to keep a respectful distance between her body and his hands. "Close your eyes, I don't want you to go blind for this." Setareh did so and felt the moment

Ziya's magic started to surround her body. It felt warm and comforting, like the first time she met Maisoror. That was a day when they had put the very first tattoo on her back, big and black and burning like artic ice. Maisoror had appeared and placed her hands on her tattoo, warming the flesh hardening with the winter storm tattooed into her back.

"You can open your eyes now," Eirian's voice was soft and gentle, like that of a young boy teasing a sibling. Setareh did so, she felt no different than before and when she turned to look at the children in confusion it was Eirian who produced a large mirror for Setareh. Now Setareh had dark chocolate skin, an assortment of white freckles dancing across her nose and cheeks, full large lips painted a dark red that matched her equally large and bewitching scarlet eyes. even her hair, as long as she was tall and all snow white waves, was now as pink as a cherry blossom and straight like a needle. She had bangs that brushed just across her eyebrows and the rest of her hair was pulled up high into a braided bun braced with two golden butterflies, leaving only one long tail to cascade down her shoulder; various golden ornaments stationed here and there along its length. Even her clothes changed, no longer was she dressed in her family's traditional white garb. She now wore a golden corset decorated with white embroidery of flowers and leaves. Her sleeves were just long enough to match the very edge of her corset and cascaded down her caramel arms in a beautiful display of floral embroidery. She wore a thick leather jacket that buttoned along her belly, leaving her amble bust on display in all of its golden brilliance. Its sleeves were slit along her arms, giving her ample movement should she need it, and only reaching to her elbows. The collar ran high up her neck, covering the golden choker she wore from all sides but the front. When she turned to look at her back, she saw that the black leather jacket extended along her back as well, a separate piece of long black leather sowed somewhere along her shoulders. Sitting in the center of her back was the same strange crest her guards wore displayed in beautiful golden embroidery.

"Pink hair is four times more common than green and about twice as common as blue hair," Ziya smiled as Setareh twisted every which way in Eirian's mirror, trying to see every aspect of her new appearance. "Since my eyes appear red I thought it would be best to give you the same eyes, and Eirian has white freckles because she can't get rid of them no matter what she does; so I gave you the same thing. I thought it would be a nice contrast if I gave you the same skin tone as Maor."

"Why do I need to look like you?" Setareh asked, feeling confused.

"Oh, sorry, It's kind of tradition at this point," Ziya snickered to himself as Eirian produced two more mirrors for Setareh's viewing benefit. "You see whenever I'm forced to take the children with me outside of the forest, I have us all take on this basic appearance. I pretend to be their elder cousin taking them along for the ride and they usually keep themselves out of trouble. But this way we can incorporate you into our typical showcase. You can pretend to be the heiress of our family and you're just out here to learn the trade."

"…did you chose this task because I *am* an heiress?" Setareh asked, giving her eldest guild a bland look. "Do you believe I can't act any other way?"

"I didn't say that!" Ziya tried to correct himself

"But that's how it came out." Eirian agreed with Setareh easily.

"Don't side with her!"

"Too late Ziya-Isha," Barak commented, "Those two already bonded."

"We usually act like merchants in training and Ziya is our teacher," Maor said, turning to the princess. "Now that you're with us, we'll have to pretend that you're the inheritor to our family. This way it'll give us an excuse to keep at least two of us with you at all times. No one should be getting any funny ideas when all of us are with you."

"Alright, I understand." Setareh nodded her head in acceptance. "I do have one more question though: why do you boys look like girls and why dose Eirian look like a boy?"

"Oh that? Well… we tried our best to transform into the opposite gender, but it doesn't always work out," Barak chuckled as he scratched the back of his head. "We usually end up making people confused on our gender which, I guess, isn't entirely a bad thing."

"speaking of which, I apologize Setareh-Kaur," Ziya smiled nervously at her. "There really wasn't anything I could do about your… assets. In that aspect I'm much the same as Eirian. She can't tame her curls when she does an image-illusion spell so she just changes their color and length. There's also the draw back that for whatever reason her clan-marks don't ever disappear so she scatters their light across her face; giving herself the appearance of white freckles."

Setareh blinked slowly at them, tilting her head to the side she looked at Eirian. In a moment too fast for her to stop, the disguised Eirian before her slipped away to reveal a different Eirian. This one looked the same as the disguised one she knew but there was a huge difference. Her Eirian had hundreds of little white dots spanning across her face in beautiful and integrate constellations. This Eirian had two simple looking white dots on her left cheek and they were producing quite the dazzling flame; it reached up into the air like a great phoenix's flaming feathers.

"I see," Setareh commented, the vision spiraling out of view. "Did you already plan new names for us?"

"Yes," Ziya agreed. "I am Zhismat, Z-I-mat."

"Zivân, Z-i-van." Eirian introduced herself

"Zola," Maor yawned, "Zo-lah"

"Zorion, Zo-re-on!" Barak laughed, his amber eyes brightening into orange sap.

"Then… My name should be," Setareh stopped speaking, her vision over lapsing with others, each with only one commonality: her giving aid to others. "Zaneo," Setareh smiled to herself "Zaneo Ryūmasha."

"Huh?! How'd you know the surname we were using?!" Barak asked loudly, Setareh raised an eyebrow at him.

"Seriously?" Eirian commented in disbelieve

"Oh yea," Barak chuckled, blushing under the disbelieving looks of his teammates. "Well, since we all know each other's names now, we should get used to saying them!"

"You only need to remember Zaneo," Setareh commented. "Your names aren't so hard to remember, especially since their commonality is ninety-eight percent."

"We understand," The children commented together. With that they all walked through the forest to Lesart village, the walk was a remarkable one to Setareh who had never seen so much green in all of her life. All of her visions were of people dying in black scorched lands or bloodied halls or amongst a fogy abbeys with no sense of direction. She had not seen so much display of life since Maisoror had shown her a fraction of her own world and the hope she had for their family. Setareh genially did wish to see the dragon children's home, Maisoror painted such a brilliant and beautiful picture for her, but she also knew the possibility of seeing the great forest was not high.

Ω Ω Ω

Maya Gériunathi was a young Arryder who was a part of Gehill's scouting team, the fifth division. She had planned to keep every discovery to herself and she had been doing a beautiful job of it, until the third division showed up. Why didn't they climb the cliff next to their waterfall-base-camp? She discovered some insects that *really* liked human flesh, none of her teammates had wanted to double check her discovery; they trusted her too much. Why hadn't they tried to go through the entire valley? No other team had made it past their waterfall-pool and they weren't about to test their luck. Why did she beat the shit out of third-division's swordsman? She assumed they sent him to kill her but do it his lacking swordsmanship she played with him for an hour or two before blinding him and throwing him at his commander.

Maya Gériunathi was a half breed of the Bray family in Gehill and the Kaminski family of Gaiglen, not that her father had a choice in the matter of her existence. Her father had been a captured scout, they targeted him *specifically* for her mother's mate and her government got what they wanted on the first try. They had originally planned to force her father into getting her mother and aunts pregnant until one of them produced a child with both bloodlines in their veins but they got lucky with her mother's first born. Her father had done his job and was killed for it, after all he wasn't needed anymore.

Her government had been struggling with creating super-soldiers for centuries now. They were overjoyed with her existence but that only made her existence all the more damnable. Her mother had just barely managed to keep custody of her, at least until she was of age to join the academy. She had been enrolled into Sthenosge—amusingly pronounced as 'the nose'—for the specific purpose that out of the three academies in Gehill, Sthenosge was the most respected; even their Gaiabek had to be respectful of their principle. It was the only insurance she had about not being bred off the second she started her period. Thankfully her academy principle and their Gaiabek weren't on the best of terms and when graduation came, her teammates ended up being the very same people who protected her throughout the years of learning. They were the same as her, rejects of their mothers, the pride of their families, the hope of their nation; two ancient house-holds ran in each of their veins.

But when that monster burst out of that waterfall… their powers of old did nothing to protect them. She had been further down the river, collecting eatable berries and hunting for fish eggs. She heard the screams but what she heard above all of the screams from third-division were her teammates demand: Sheridan. It meant search but the rule that they created with that name felt like a thousand teeth ripping into her heart. Sheridan, to chase after the hidden one; the one fleeing with the distraction.

She slipped away in her mother's powers, hidden from sight and sound, no light nor shadow touched her, matter barely restrained her. Then it was her father's power that bloomed through her veins, threatening to lift her mother's power. But she kept it in check, the power in her veins would obey no one but *her*. Magic felt like fire in her legs, fueling them with a power that aided her every leap and step; the world blurred around her, leaving only the orange light as a target to chase.

When she did catch up with the inhabitants of the orange light, she became afraid. Maya was a lone, no teammates to trick, no allies to call, no secrets to hide. She remained hidden behind a thick trunk, listening to the children and their gentle bantering, pretending for a moment that she was back in school with her friends and everyone she knew was still living. She didn't know when she started crying, just that she was and she was quite with every tear that fell. She knew the moment the golden monster appeared, she felt his approach like an added weight with every step he took towards her. The location she was hidden in, was just far enough to keep the children in sight but far enough away they'd never notice her. So she pulled herself out of her pity party and smiled as the monster slipped his sword through her ribcage. When he stopped, just shy of her lung, she smiled at him.

"Thank you," she said, ignoring the blood that drippled past her lips and down her chin. "now... I'm safe... I... I won't be bred... l-like... cattle..." she leaned against the tree, breathing hard. A rustling of branches nearby alerted her and the golden monster, a young baby dragon painted in three shades of blue stepped out.

"Ah Ziya-Isha, i—oh creation," the voice was light and soft, typical of a young boy who hadn't hit puberty yet. She chuckled weakly at the thought, who knew dragons raised their young outside of the forest? "isha, Eirian is nearby! We can save—"

"Don't," her voice was weak, like her darkening vision. "I... I want... to-to die."

"What about your family? Don't you have someone waiting for you?" the boy asked, stepping forward, his voice hard with disapproval.

"no," she answered, smiling bitterly as the golden monster ripped out his sword and kneeled before her. "They're... all gone... no-no one left..." the golden dragon placed his sword between them, bracing his hands and his weight on the hilt while he pressed his forehead against his wrists.

"Please forgive me... lost one." The golden dragon pleaded, his voice hoarse and broken sounding.

"Don't... cry..." keeping herself awake was getting difficult. "I... I... want...th-thissss." Maybe now she could look her father in the eye and say she tried her best to make him proud. Her mother used to tell her that he used to always apologize to her, regretting and crying over what Gehill was forcing her mother to do. It was the reason why her mother had killed her father, so that Maya's successful birth wouldn't be repeated with anyone else ever again.

Chapter 9

The village of Lesart was small, fed by a nearby man-made river just big enough for a rowboat and nothing else. There were of course fish and other sources of water-life but they weren't to be eaten, the life in the river was essential for clean water. There weren't many buildings taller than two stories, the only four story building was a giant clock tower made out of a strange white stone. Their contact hadn't been in the village, he was out with a few hunters gathering some supplies for the coming winter. The team found their inn, Serpent's nest, and settled in for a long wait. Setareh remained close to Eirian and often times was able to convince the girl to let her go outside and explore. It had been the first time she was able to walk amongst other people without anyone bowing, staring, whispering; here she could disappear amongst the masses and still be herself. It was fascinating. She felt free, content to watch the people sow seeds into the clear waters of the rice fields. More than one farmer asked if she wanted to try but she was much to afraid of making a mess of things. When she got caught staring at a cook, the kind grandmother asked if she wanted to help. After setting the pan on fire and nearly catching the whole house on fire too, Setareh thought it would be best if she didn't attempt such things again. The villagers of Lesart were kind, gentle, patient, and forgave her for every wrong she committed.

"I wonder about the life she lived," one villager whispered, watching Setareh try to stir a dish in a frying pan without flinging it everywhere. "To have never seen people sow seeds, nor cook, or seen our gardens or fruits... some of her questions are truly confusing. How can someone not know what a pen or paper is? And our churros and our croquette, it's like she's never eaten with her hands before."

"I heard she came from the north," another whispered, smiling gently as she set her fruits out on display. "Perhaps she's never been in such a warm place. We all know paper dose not last well in the cold." She had no response for their foods, the strange pinkette truly seemed to treat every dish and drink as if she's never seen such dishes before. Zaneo was even found staring in utter awe at some of their animals, like their farm animals, but the animals that seemed to capture her attention were the birds. As if she had spent a lifetime watching them from a distance and was thrilled to have one within reaching distance. The pinkette even froze when a bird decided she was a great perch, admittedly though the first time a bird landed on her the pinkette very nearly had a panic attack.

"Fair enough," the other conceded, twisting partially to press a kiss to the woman's temple before walking into the back of their little store. Eirian and Maor had been nearby, half watching Setareh in the restaurant kitchen and half listening to the couple in the stall next to them.

"Do they really not have paper in the mountains?" Maor asked under breath, turning to look at Eirian curiously.

"She's a princess who wasn't even supposed to be born," Eirian reminded him gently. "I wouldn't be surprised if they kept her locked up in a room somewhere. I mean, do you remember how everyone acted when she entered the dining hall a while back? Everyone went tombstone quiet and just *stared*, like they've never seen her before or worse, they were *scared* of her."

"I'm bringing to feel less and less inclined in bringing her clan to our forest," Maor grumbled, "The Caelestis family is vain enough. Can't we just keep Setareh-Rū and leave the rest of them alone?"

"You know we can't." Eirian chided, "And its Zaneo now, remember?"

"Right, Right," Maor shrugged carelessly.

Ω Ω Ω

He coughed and hacked, his body burning as his magic buried into the earth and ripped out the power it needed to repair his injuries. There were always draw backs to being an inheritor of two ancient households, near unbearable pain was one of them. As a child of both Gaiglen's Eckerra family and Gehill's Barlow family, many people believed that Kunero Gériunathi had only inherited his mother's 'innate understanding'; a trait she inherited from her father. It wasn't until the plaque nearly twelve years ago that everyone understood that he had inherited his father's 'longevity' as well. With his survival that day, he ceased being a 'Barlow' and inherited the name 'Gériunathi'. A ridiculous name that meant 'Earth is with us', only those with two-ancient powers in their veins inherited the name; although most viewed it as a burden. many of his superiors hinted that they were merely awaiting for the day he revealed his Barlow-inheritance: the strange ability of matter ingestion. That strange power was only partially connected to his mother, her diet directly influenced the speed of her brain's neurons. He showed no such tendencies and no bottomless-stomach like the rest of the Barlow family-members. It was believed he only inherited his mother's—and grandfather's—intelligence, and his father's longevity.

Where is everyone? Kunero blinked slowly at the sky over head, it was either still morning or early afternoon. It didn't particularly matter much, mostly because he was still killing the vegetation around him to heal his own injuries. Do to his mother's blood he won't be able to move for a little while, maybe another hour, the tree he was closest too wasn't completely dead yet; that is properly his primary source of regeneration.

"Anyone alive?" his voice cracked from lack of use, he counted to 'ten Naoska' before he accepted that no one else was living. He closed his eyes and took a quick nap, just waiting till his body too fully heal. When he opened his eyes again and his body didn't hurt anymore, he knew he was fully healed. The tree next to him didn't look nearly as dead as he was expecting, it must've had deep roots; regardless it wouldn't survive another winter. His body didn't hurt anymore but that didn't mean his muscles weren't aching from lack of movement, he groaned as he forced his body to move.

"Great, another Eckerra," Kunero looked towards the speaker and found the commander of fifth-division braced against the pool-edge. He was still bleeding, one arm missing and a hole in his side, but he was conscious. "Commander Kunero, what are you mixed with?"

"Commander Uzoma, you're also a part of the Eckerra?" Kunero asked, moving towards his fellow commander.

"My father," Uzoma commented, "mom's a Vela."

"That's an interesting combination," Kunero commented

"Heh, everyone on my team is a Gériunathi," Uzoma answered him, "Even Maya."

"I'm aware,"

"So she was right, your team did come here for her." Uzoma smiled humorlessly at Kunero. "So now what Commander of third-division? Are you going to kill me?"

"Why would I do that?"

"Because I betrayed our nation." Uzoma answered, his silver eyes were bright and his smile was growing. "you know as well as I that Eckerra are at their weakest when they are recovering. Once we find a source of healing we are unable to remove ourselves from it, least our injuries become worse."

"Or if someone damages our central regeneration system," Kunero replied calmly. "Explain what that word meant earlier. The one you were shouting while fighting that monster."

"Heh, as if I'd tell you," Uzoma snickered weakly. "Our team came up with contingencies a long time ago, you'll never figure it out."

"You seem to have forgotten that we've all went to the same school," Kunero said slowly as he searched his memories, trying to sort out the numerous times he spied on their little meetings. "Do you know why you got away with as much as you did in the academy?" he could see Uzoma frown at him, confusion filling him as his blood continued to pour into the pool. "Do you know why you four fools were placed onto the same team as Maya?" he could see the man begin to struggle to put the pieces together, but his injuries were great and he was struggling to breath.

"It's because *I* hacked the system," with that tidbit of information, Kunero shot his dagger through the commander's throat.

I better hurry, Kunero thought as he grabbed the commander and pulled him out of the pool. Now, even if their shared Eckerra blood remained strong, his fellow commander should still die from blood lose. After all, the more serious their injury, the longer it'll take to heal. Walking away Kunero waited till he found a clean patch of earth before kneeling and drawing out a three-ringed Run-seal-array. He gathered some leaves, a handful of river-mud, and a few river-stones and placed them all into the rune-seal-array. Once activated a pile of dirt gathered together to create a mush-ball with four legs and large river-stone eyes. He absolutely hated this spell, golems were not his forte and it always felt so exhausting every time he used one; still he couldn't deny a golem's usefulness.

"Hello old friend," Kunero greeted the strange looking earthen-golem. "I request aid from my kinsmen, they should not be too far away. Please find the people with this crest," he gestured to the embroidery on his tunic and the tiny golem nodded in acceptance. It quickly dashed away, leaving nothing behind but a whisper of its steps. Sighing Kunero adjusted himself to stand, only to stop as he caught sight of a brown woven basket with various berries, leaves and a rabbit in its woven embrace. He looked about himself, wondering if Maya was actually closer than he first thought but he didn't see any other signs of his comrade. Frowning in thought, Kunero pulled a small silver chain out from beneath his shirt and held up a small glass vial covered in a complicated seven-layer rune-seal-array. Beneath the layers of etchings, he could see a clump of translucent strands, something that reflected light and yet still looked like strands of spiderweb silk. In truth it was a small piece of Maya's hair, a chunk of hair he had been able to capture during a spar back when they were in the academy. He put a great deal of research into creating the vial and its seven-layer-seal-array, this vial could only be destroyed by dragon fire and only because he had no way of preventing it from breaking under that much stress. The other, simpler, runes allowed him to locate the owner of who's ever DNA was within the seal-circle; in this case Maya's hair.

"Hironīden," the whispered command made the seals glow a bright guiding white, the same white as reflected light on snow. The crystal instantly began floating and swiveled harshly to his left, he passed through the stream to the other side, he would've kept walking if he hadn't caught sight of scorched earth on the white stone of the river side. The black scorch marks were in the form of a familiar foot-size, thick black lines indicated the pattern of the soul of the boot he knew Maya wore. He knew she wore them because he was the one who made them for her, they allowed her to use both aspects of her family's bloodlines without the drawbacks of excruciating pain. He's given her many such things throughout the years but he's never indicated who he was, just explaining what the items did and how they were helpful to her. He knew she hated him but that was okay, she still wore the boots he made for her, the gloves with the inscriptions, the dagger he forged to match her invisibility power and its matching sheath that always teleported it back into its proper place. There were many things he's made for her throughout the years and she still wore them even now, it was the reason why he knew she was much stronger than she ever told their nation.

I should hurry, Kunero thought, he turned to look again in the direction of the seal-glass and saw that its glow was pulsing a bright red, its light slowly dimming with every pulse. Fear seized his heart, a red glow meant that she was injured, maybe dying. "Shit," Kunero pulled out the dagger form his back pouch, his magic swirling around his hand in a bright fog of teal. "Agekeruarc!" the runes along his dagger glowed and with a burst of power his dagger turned into a giant sword just as tall and wide as he was. He quickly jumped onto its wide blade and kneeled, keeping his right leg bent up so he could brace most of his weight on it while he used his left leg to put pressure on one side of the blade to turn it.

"Ricwazo!" a burst of power from his blade and he was sent careening through the forest, anything in his way was ripped apart. He swerved around great trees with trunks so thick and round he wondered if he was just passing around in a circle; then his pendent would turn and he followed the sharp twist at the last possible moment. The setting sun was fading, the forest darkening with every passing second; this was the time where Maya's invisibility would be at its weakest. No wonder she had been caught, she must not have noticed the set of the sun and how long the twilight in these mountains were. He hurried, urging his blade to go faster despite knowing that he could only sacrifice so much power to reach her. What if she was still fighting? What if she was outnumbered? He had to save some power to protect her.

When he found Maya, just as the last of the light was fading from the sky, he wished for a moment that he had never met her.

Ω Ω Ω

It was another dark hallway amongst all the other dark hallways, the earth that surrounded them was warm, producing a stifling heat that very nearly suffocated them. Like tradition dictates from the days after the meteorite, Gehill residents remained underground. Everything from their streets, buildings, homes, markets, military centers even their schools; everything was underground. It was the only way of living that they knew, the surface earth was still poisonous after all; even after so many centuries. It was as if the earth couldn't heal, like the meteorite was just too toxic. Still, the few times they could leave the earth was when they were moving from one hill to another. The bridges connecting the hills were elaborate and beautiful, solid stone as black as smoke and beautiful archways with banners carving out figures from old tales. They were not a people who were used to the sun but their earth was plenty poisonous so although they weren't used to the sun, they still retained their dark completions that protected them from the radiation of the sun. This unique skin tone remained strong throughout the centuries as it was those with a certain skin tone who survived the poisonous soil and continued to reproduce.

That's how it was explained to them, those with darker skin survived the radiation of the sun and the poison of the meteorite. No one was sure how the two were connected, just that they were and the survivors of the radiation and the poison produced individuals with skin just like their soil. Nothing explained their two-colored eyes and fire-bright hair, all anyone could think of was the old creation myths. How Mother Earth was creating tiny figures and used river mud to make the bodies before placing shinny crystals in their heads for eyes. These figures were very weak and fragile though and she had no way of sustaining the muddy-creatures lives; especially when the other gods came to visit her and began laughing at her creations. The little creatures she made were ugly and not at all pleasing to the eye, the other gods tried to destroy the muddy-creatures but Mother Earth was stubborn, she quickly opened up her very bowels and hide all of her little muddy creations inside. The other gods wouldn't dare to harm Mother Earth, NEVER Mother Earth.

Kunero Gériunathi was just promoted into the Gériunathi family, whose house was in the same hill as Sthenosge Academy. He could've taken the chance to go to one of the other two academies, to see what the surface of their country looks like, but he chose to go to Sthenosge Academy. He discovered rather quickly that he was shorter than others his age and appeared to receive all the darker genes compared to his classmates as well. He could melt into the shadows as easily as closing his eyes and often times that's all he had to do to hide from anyone. Their surroundings were all shades of brown and their people favored black cloth anyways, so closing his silver-blue eyes was all he needed to do to hide. He found this skill useful around the others, no one ever noticed him anyways and they always seemed to forget that he existed the second he closed his eyes. One day they received a new student, a female Gériunathi who came of age to join the academy. He would've been content to ignore her as he ignored everyone in their class but the silence of his classmates was curious. When he opened his eyes, he discovered something breath taking.

A girl just as short as him, with hair the color of crystal threads, waste long and braided back from her face in a beautiful floral design and decorated with simple golden beads. Her eyes were large and round, colored a strange ghostly blue with a ring of faintly darker blue surrounding the iris; he's never seen anyone with matching irises before. She was dressed in their uniform, black with brown stripes around her collar and sleeves, with the red bow on her chest and black ribbon on her lower back. She stood out amongst everyone with her pale coloring, so very opposite of himself; even her skin was a paler brown then what he's used to seeing.

"I am Maya Gériunathi of house Bray, nice to meet you all," her voice was sullen and soft, like the ever present heat of their earthen city. It reminded him of his mother, before she was sent away to the healing house. He felt like he'd lose his life to those ghostly blue orbs, like her smile would stop his heart, like she was the reason he was born. When she looked at him for the first time, he learned quickly that she did not feel the same. There was hatred and loathing in those ghostly hues, a bone fire that burned any who dared to glance into those beautiful ocean depths.

Ω Ω Ω

"Commander Kunero?" The voice jerked him out of his memories, his silver-blue eyes locking on the man in front of him; an old friend by the name of Nilam. "You good man?" Kunero looked down at the weight in his arms, staring dully at the white haired bloodied woman. There was a thin slit that ran from her collar bone down into her ribcage, stopping just above what should've been her lung and heart.

"I think she's dead," Nilam murmured, moving to take Maya from Kunero.

"Don't," his order was weak sounding but his old friend did so, even going so far as to step back. "How are the others?"

"Commander Uzoma is weak but he'll live," Nilam answered, "hard to say if the man will ever say a word again though. The others weren't so lucky. Were you all attacked by a monster? I don't know of any creatures that leave behind six claws like that."

"I need you to make a Terralthos home," Kunero ordered, "over there, between the pool and that oak." Nilam looked down at Maya, seeing nothing but a corpse in his friend's arms.

"you… you're not gonna try to revive the dead are you?"

"She's still living," Kunero replied, "She's just… unconscious…" Nilam sighed and shook his head. Walking away he quickly formed a perfect white-marble cone with a single square entrance right where his friend ordered him to make it. "Thank you," Kunero said as he walked past, entering the cone with a dark aura surrounding himself.

"Hey Kunero," Nilam called out but his friend didn't stop walking, "I know you love her but make sure you don't go too far." Kunero's body was being swallowed by the shadow of the cone, disappearing like the shadow he often mimicked, "she's not worth your life! She hates you! Remember that!" his friend disappeared and the entrance disappeared as the cone closed in on itself, sealing the excite perfectly.

"Don't worry about Commander Kunero," Nilam looked towards one of his other comrades, the older man smiled sadly. "After all he's heir to Sthenosge academy. Even if he performs that forbidden spell of his family, he won't die. He has too much reasonability in our city."

"He's been following her for years," Nilam replied softly, concern on his face and in his gray-green eyes. "He's been protecting her since they met twenty years ago and she doesn't even know it. I'm afraid that when he heals her... she'll only reject his efforts..."

"Reject or not, Commander Kunero will want vengeance," The elder said thoughtfully, "Let's get ourselves prepared for that. This will be our new base. We'll send scouts ahead and call for back up. How long do we have till he comes out?"

"Maybe three days?" Nilam suggested uncertainly. "I don't know how long it'll be this time. She looked pretty bad..."

$$\Omega \ \Omega \ \Omega$$

They waited in Lesart village for three days before they began to worry, it was strange for the hunters to be longer than a day. At first they thought the hunters had traveled to one of the nearby villages and stayed the night in one of them, but by the afternoon of the second day and still no word; everyone began to worry. By dawn on the third day four teams of five were sent out to the nearby villages, wondering if they had seen their missing hunters. The only ones who returned where the ones who went east, towards the villages Nashun and Lukip. It was strange that their hunters weren't found, stranger that their scouts from Mowan, Kiwui, and Chizhou never returned. It was a silent demand of the village head to keep the information to themselves, least the rest of the village fall into panic. That night they were going to send a message through the great hall, it would reach Rinnan emergency headquarters nearly instantly.

Not all plans are meant to take place and Lesart's plan to receive aid from their country's officers was never met.

An army from Gehill came charging through the mountains, setting up defensive basis to retreat and recover as they plowed through the dangerous terrain. After three days, an army of three hundred had breached the boarders of Ashan, they recuperated in the hills just above a village; a village named Lesart. They had watched as scouts had been sent out from the village, they sent out their own soldiers to apprehend said civilians. It would be best if Gehill overtook Ashan with little force, they didn't want to lose soldier's pointlessly.

Ashan was a civilian nation, they didn't have soldiers because they were perfectly protected by the elements. The dragons roamed the mountain side separating Ashan from both Gehill and Trégaron, a great cliff face isolated Dubol from everyone and Malbril was two steps away from extinction every time winter paid a visit. Ashan had no neighbors who would willing take them over for the sake of their fertile land and happy-go-lucky child-bearers. It was well known that women from Ashan could birth up to five children before any problems began occurring in pregnancies and they rarely had miscarriages. Gehill was the opposite of Ashan, one in every ten pregnancies ended successfully; *if* they were in a good year.

Commanders Kunero and Uzoma were both heavily weakened do to an encounter with a dragon but they were determined to participate in the espionage. There wasn't a scenario they didn't plan for and with the aid of four hundred solders gathering, they were ready to lay siege to the village harboring the seer princess.

Ω Ω Ω

"Setareh-Kaur, Setareh-Kaur, wake up," Eirian struggled to wake the princess, even going so far as sending Ryū to her teacher. "Setareh-Kaur!"

"Eirian what's wrong?" Ziya was already in his dragon armor, panic contorting his voice as he entered the room.

"She's having a nightmare and I can't wake her," Eirian explained quickly

"Look at her marks, it may not be a nightmare," Ziya instructed as he hurried forward and pinned Setareh's shoulder down. Her face twisted as she turned in moonlight, revealing her gently glowing seals. "This isn't right, these seals are hurting her."

"What are we going to do?" Eirian asked, "release them?"

"I don't know if we can," Ziya answered, "But we can take a closer look." Ziya quickly summoned three sets of seven swords, each set a different size then the other. Murmuring under breath, Ziya conveyed what he wanted to his swords and they began circling around Setareh's face. Seconds ticked by and the tattoos on Setareh's face only thrummed with red light, as if the pulsing light was in tune too her heartbeat; fast and irregular. "Eirian, stabilize her," Eirian gasped with the order, quickly she threw out her hands and summoned her glowing white glass shards. Her intent was to calm Setareh, slow the panic that was growing inside her, instead Eirian's Magic and Ziya's Magic merged and amplified the other's intention. With a burst of magical power, they were blinded as the seals on Setareh's face burst off to surround the room in a reflection of her face.

"What is that?" Eirian asked, rubbing at her eyes to remove the dancing black dots.

"Something I hadn't expected," Ziya answered, "it's been years since I last saw these inscriptions." All around them the shimmering red of Setareh's tattoos glowed along the walls of the inn room but this time they looked much different. This time it was an assortment of a strange symbol, a circle with a slash through the middle; hundreds of these strange symbols outlining the shapes that covered Setareh's face. "This isn't right... they're not uniform. No wonder the seals weren't working," Ziya frowned as he stared intently at the symbol.

"Ziya-Isha, why aren't you blind?" Eirian asked as blinked about, trying to clear her vision.

"Because my power is light-based, there for sudden bursts of light have no effect on me," Ziya answered.

"What's got you concerned then?" Eirian pouted as she sat on her bed, trying to blink her eyes clear and looking ridiculous while she was at it.

"This symbol is an ancient one meaning 'don't' or 'not allowed' but the lines through the center of the circles isn't uniform." Ziya explained, "there's also no indication of what the sealers were trying to limit in Setareh-Kaur's powers, which is another factor as to why it's not working the way it's meant to. The one who designed this seal forgot to place a limiter and the indication of what is not allowed. Without such things the seal will act up and not work the way the sealers intended for it to work."

"So the seal doesn't work because someone forgot to tell it what it's supposed to not allow?" Eirian asked as began rubbing at her face, "how do you forget that?!"

"Do not seek revenge on the sage of the desert," Ziya murmured, "You'll only die."

"huh?"

"It's something Setareh-Kaur said back in her cave," Ziya answered. "She said we mustn't take revenge on the sage of the desert, We'll only die."

"'Cause that's not a creepy prediction," Eirian grumbled. "How come you never taught us about the sage of the desert?"

"huh? Oh I don't know much about Dubol honestly," Ziya rubbed the back of his neck as he stared at the symbol before him. "I was going to leave that lesson to Kaltrina-Rū, it's his home country after all."

"What does the Sage of the desert have to do with Setareh-Kaur's seal?"

"The sage is the one who created the seal," Ziya answered. "That's why Setareh-Rū told me not to seek revenge on her." Eirian's response was cut off as a scream tore through the night air, the zoomed-image of Setareh's tattoo shrunk back to her face and she sat up with an expression of bewilderment. Eirian hurried to the window and leaned out, staring in horror at the flaming arrows raining down on them.

"Isha! We're under attack!" Eirian cried as she ducked back in time to avoid an arrow to her temple. "Asharan is a peaceful nation! Why would a village attack it's kinsmen?"

"This isn't the attack of residents of Asharan," Ziya said as he looked outside as well, his scarlet eyes glowing brilliantly in the reflected fire light. "Those are Soldiers of Gehill! They found a way through the mountains!"

"Ryū!" Eirian cried out and her dragon quickly wrapped around her, sparkling like a thousand glittering stars.

"I don't understand," Setareh whispered, staring out the window at the burning buildings and the people now running out of their homes. "How... how did I not..."

"Fourteen percent..." Ziya grunted as he pulled Setareh back from the window. "Aislings can't detect anything less than fourteen percent of commonality!"

"Ziya-Isha! Isha!" Barak and Maor cried out as they stumbled into the room.

"There are Gehill soldier's in the village! They're going to kill everyone at this rate!" Barak bawled. Amarau shimmered and shuttered with the assault of flaming arrows, his joints rippled along Barak's body with barely restrained entertainment of the coming fight.

"Hold on!" Setareh ordered, she ripped her hand out of Ziya's hold and crashed to her knees. "Talenter Chai Trauktis!" a great seal array burst beneath her fingertips, sending out a pulse of white magic throughout the entire village, strong enough that it very nearly knocked everyone off their feet. {*Children of Asharan, listen closely. Go to the central building. Beneath the podium there is a seal-array. Use it. Dragons will save you all.*} The seal array disappeared as fast as it appeared and Setareh jumped to her feet and dashed for the door, shoving both Barak and Maor out the door while she was at it. The spell she used was a mass-psychosis spell, basically it sent her thoughts out to those she wanted the thoughts to reach; which was everyone *but* the Gehill soldiers.

"Ziya-Rū! Can you distract the soldiers?!" Setareh asked loudly, not even looking over her shoulder as their room exploded on itself.

"For how long?" Ziya asked, "What was that spell?!" Ziya was regretting choosing the highest room in the furthest corner from the entrance, they had such a long run.

"It's an Emergency spell Maisoror taught me," Setareh answered. "It's a massive-psychosis spell! Basically I sent my thoughts out to everyone in the village and gave them direction that'll protect them!"

"Where did you send them?!" Maor asked as he summoned a whip of water to put out a fire before it ruined the hall they were rushing through.

"To the dragon-summoning seal array in the central building! Those on boarder detail will receive the summons and come here! At the same time I was able to get the villagers of Lesart to retreat in their bunker that was set up when the village was founded!"

"How did you know about the bunker and seal-array?" Barak asked only to yelp as the floor he was running on crumbled under him and he was sent to the floor directly beneath him.

"Are you serious right now?!" Setareh asked as she leaped from the floor, to the banister and back to the floor just in time to avoid following Barak. Barak ignored the jab as he defended himself against a soldier in the inn, shouts of the soldiers were followed as Maor leaped into the hole and aided his teammate. Ziya and Eirian remained close behind Setareh, careful not to make the same mistake as Barak.

"How long dose Isha have to distract the soldiers?" Eirian asked as they swerved to dash down a pair of stairs. Ziya sent out three swords and crumbled the support beams that sent a bedroom atop the soldiers attacking Barak and Maor. The boys quickly rushed towards them while they raced for the main floor of the Inn.

"Just long enough for Barak and Maor to escape to the next village over," Setareh answered, leaping over three arrows shot at her. Eirian swung midair, sending out a blade of white-glass with her foot and beheaded the two archers waiting on them. "Don't worry, he won't be playing distraction alone! You and I are going to lead the soldier's away from the village!"

"Are you insane?!" Barak shouted as he tripped and rolled across the first floor, sending out a blast of blistering embers at a soldier in the entrance of the Inn. "I'm not running from a fight!"

"Do you want this mission to succeed?!" Setareh asked as they raced out of the inn, turned and raced for the closest village exit. "Then you and Maor must go ahead and secure our exit in Niyatara city! Trust no one!"

"Ziya-Isha!" Maor shouted as they began running through the village.

"We'll trust Setareh-Kaur for now," Ziya ordered. "Boys, go!" Maor summoned a rope of water and wrapped it around Barak, ignoring his teammate's screams of defiance as he took to the air. Maor's great ocean gentle wings spread out four-times his height and began beating too fast for the human eye to trace, they were gone before Barak could let out a second scream.

"In five minutes take after them!" Setareh ordered Ziya as he splintered off to play blockade. Eirian summoned a board of white glass, the princess quickly leaped onto it while Eirian sent them both into the air. "Lady Eirian, we must be a beacon! It'll be the only way to protect the villagers!"

"A beacon? Come now at least try to challenge me!" they lit up like a newly born sun, very nearly blinding the very solders who quickly changed course and began chasing them. "They're like killer bee's!" Eirian shouted as she raced beside Setareh, "They totally forgot their primary objective just to chase us!"

"Maybe *we're* they're primary objective," Setareh retorted as they passed the village gates. *How long can we remain like this?* She feared sooner or later, they'd run out of places to run and accidentally involve another village. "Do you know where we're going?" Eirian pulled back to block what originally looked like some arrows, only to discover at the last minute that there were some explosives attached. Eirian just barely managed to make the blast part around her but her concentration had been disrupted and the board Setareh was riding shattered into dust. Setareh yelped as she was sent crashing into the ground, rolling several feet before stopping with a harsh slide into a bolder with the village name carved into its face.

"RUN!" Eirian ordered, twirling up from the ground like a tornado, white magic surrounding her like an angry whip lashing out violently. "I'll hold them off!" Setareh coughed as she scrambled back onto her feet, she looked up to search for a way out, unaware that her eyes were glowing and her seals were scarlet. She was seeing a dozen images, each overlapping the next, blurring the individuals charging her with spears and ropes.

No, Setareh thought, *not like this.* An arrow, smoking with poison and glowing with violet runes, was shot in her direction. If that arrow hit her, it would no doubt kill her. *This is... this not my death!* She felt the pulse of magic before she realized what was happening, in a moment too soon for anyone to counter she was grabbing that arrow and throwing it at a soldier. Then she was countering the sword attack and the magic whips that covered the solder were quickly shredded. She felt as if someone else was moving her body, her mind was clear like a glass platter and her body was cold with the touch of a mountain mist. Everything was tingling as if she weren't in her own body, just standing by and watching as someone else moved it. Her over lapping vision contorted and her body moved to counter each attack aimed her way, even the seals beneath her clothing were beginning to glow bright enough to burn etchings onto her silk robes.

"There! that's what we want!" one of the commanders further away was pointing at Setareh and Eirian, a big grin on his grizzly face. "Capture the dimensional-walker!" The soldiers charged without thinking at Setareh and Eirian, both now moving in near perfect reflection of the other.

"Sir?" one of the commanders began hesitantly, "What do you mean by 'dimensional-walker'?"

"There's an old legend about the Aisling family," the commander began, "They were originally a part of the great Caelestis family but one of the members had fallen in love with someone their family did not approve of. So this Caelestis-person went to the gods and said 'I will give my eyes, ears, tongue, flesh and soul for this chance to stand beside my love. Please bless our marriage.' The gods denied the Caelestis's request, saying they were already fated to marry another but the goddess of fate saw a change in her threads. She sent down one of her star-children to keep an eye on the Caelestis, hoping he wouldn't change the fate she wrote for him. It was not long after that she discovered the star-child she sent had been the one the Caelestis had fallen in love with. Furious the goddess of fate cursed them and their descendants: They shall watch all those they love, perish before them. The Goddess of Fate's star-child, however, was the heir to the goddess of fate and as such had made their own declaration: no matter where we wander nor the life we live, never shall there be a time where we will not survive by the act of our own hand!"

The commander laughed as the princess bobbed and weaved with the shadowy-monster, both looking like dancers amongst a deadly display of glowing swords, bladed whips and poisonous arrows. How were they surviving? The soldiers didn't know but they were trying anyways, anything was better than giving up.

"This is how the Aislings were able to gain the power to look through all the worlds of existence!" the commander waved both arms through the air, smiling down on the princess who dodged and weaved between his men like a ghost. Her image splintering into three different forms a few times just to avoid an attack, it was as if she had no center of gravity. Her tattoos were glowing brighter and brighter, alighting the night in brilliant dawn-scarlet. "What you're seeing is that there promise! Without her consent the fates opened their doors and forced their information through to this Dimensional-walker! A soldier is being born! One without equal! With the knowledge of a thousand generals! The strength of a thousand armadas! With the ability that would make even the war god jealous! This here is the *dimensional-walker*! The soldiers of a thousand worlds merging together just so this-*this* here Aisling can survive the fight! That's how a Dimensional-walker is born!"

"Oh shit!" the young soldier gasped, they twisted on the ball of their foot and tackled their commander.

"Atgal Ordo imber!" the monster's voice made the earth quack as it shattered to send millions of finger sized bursts of light. Two seconds and the five dozen people attacking them were suddenly bloody ribbons amongst upturned earth. Huge boulders thundered across the land scape, crushing those trying to flee the original attack. Coughing the young soldier pushed himself up to look back on his comrades, his commander scrambling up to look as well.

"I see why he's jealous," The young man grunted. "Damn, I'm really starting to hate dragons." An ear shattering roar sounded through the air, rumbling the earth and shaking thick limbs from their sturdy trunks. Turning both commander and soldier watched as a dozen dragons descended from the sky, eyes glowing furiously as they enveloped the village Lesart.

"Great, adult dragons," the young soldier turned to his commander, "now what, they're here and we're screwed!"

"Not if we get the baby dragon," the commander said thoughtfully. "Dragons are notoriously overprotective of their young. All we have to do is capture that black one with the white magic and we'll be able to retreat." The commander turned back to the team of solders rushing forward to collect their dead and wounded. "Leave them!" the commander ordered, "They died with honor! We need to complete our task!"

"But commander!" the soldier whined loudly, pointing and waving at the monsters descending on their comrades still in the village. "Dragons! Hellllooo! Big ass flaming lizards with *wings*!"

"We must capture the Aisling Princess! She is the key to our great peace!" the commander threw a fist into the air, his mismatched eyes glinting with suppressed laughter. "As our ancestors had so declared! The princess of stars is protected by the Midnight Dragon! Capture the princess and peace will flow into our land! Capture the Midnight dragon and our land will be cured! Capture both and our nation will outlive all others!" the troop threw their fists into the air and shouted in unity, then they turned and followed their commander to chase down the Aisling Princess. The soldier that spared the commander's life remained behind, watching his comrades give chase to the princess and her dragon.

"Am I the only sane person here?!" the soldier asked as he gave chase, "NO! because I'm following!"

Ω Ω Ω

"Are we safe now?" Eirian asked, bracing her hands on her knees as she panted heavily. Setareh wasn't far away, sprawled out on the ground like dead goose; all former grace gone in this moment of utter exhaustion.

"I wouldn't be lying if we weren't," Setareh answered breathlessly. "is it normal... to... not feel my toes?"

"You were... flying on... poisoned oak bark," Eirian chuckled, "I'm... not surprised..."

"Ah," Setareh gave a breathless wheeze of a chuckle, "'Pūklum dìrige mê', there are advantages and disadvantages."

"How long can you remain," Eirian stopped to gasp for breath, "on... that board?"

"How're me feet?" Setareh asked, cracking open an eye to look at Eirian.

"Bad," Eirian gasped out, staring at the swollen, pimpled, scarlet hued, appendages that appeared to be two seconds away from bursting. "You... allergic... too wood?"

"Maybe," Setareh gasped, "I ache... *everywhere*."

"I'll create... a-a hiding pl-place," Eirian said, looking about... "S-suggestions?"

"Y-you know best," Setareh waved a hand dismissively as she sat back up and tugged her layered robe back into proper place. Groaning Setareh stared down at her swollen feet, "Lady Eirian, is there water nearby?"

"There should be a river up ahead," Eirian said, her voice still hoarse and breathless sounding. "Don't move, I'll be right back."

"Can't if I wanted too," Setareh chuckled weakly. Not only was there a river, there was a gray bolder big enough to be mistaken for a house. It was tilted slightly to the side, reaching out of the earth to lean against another boulder that supported it surprisingly well for being only half of the larger boulder's size. Supported by both boulders was an ancient bonsai apple blossom, its white flowers glowing in the moonlight. Judging by the wet stone and how the roots dangled across the boulders the tree sat atop, the river rose quite a few feet during rainy season. Eirian was able to use her magic to manipulate the branches into growing and thickening, just big enough to sustain Setareh's weight without collapsing. Eirian carried Setareh to the tree and settled the princess between two thick branches, then created a simple glass plate for each of Setareh's feet and etched out a simple ice-rune-seal that would help cool the burning of the princess's feet. Eirian then climbed into her own spot, slightly lower than Setareh and closer to the entrance of the tilted to the side bolder.

"Oh," Eirian whispered, pulling and tugging at her armor until a small white crystal floated out from beneath her breast plate. "Ziya-Isha, you awake?"

"Eirian? Where are you?" Ziya's voice was calm, sounding with relieve with Eirian's apparent check in. Setareh smiled to herself and settled closer to the center of the tree, yawning sleepily as Eirian reported back to her teacher. After a debate on revealing their location, Ziya finally decided to accompany the boys to Niyatara City. Eirian was geographically intelligent but the boys weren't, they'd get lost after a

mile and end up heading in the wrong direction. Eirian would keep Ziya updated along their travels, she had the magic to both protect the princess and herself. Any injuries could be healed and should they need a place to hide, Eirian could easily locate or create a safe place.

Eirian's magic was just that versatile and her intelligence was that high; there was little she couldn't do.

Chapter 10

S he ran hurriedly through the dark forest, branches and limbs scraped at her, tearing her fine robes and tangling in her long platinum waves. She tripped and stumbled, scraping her hands and bruising her body but she stood again and ran once more. Her body ached, her lungs burned with every breath, her vision blurred in panic and exhaustion; blurring the dark forest with a deeper darkness more foreboding than anything she's seen before. Haunting howls and sharp whistles sounded too close for comfort, she turned to look back and saw moonstone eyes glowing hauntingly just behind her. The strange white-eyed creature swirled around her, brilliant glowing stardust sweeping out in an ark, protecting them from the onslaught of arrows and fire, then stooped and pulled the blonde onto its back before dashing ahead. Faster than the blonde could ever hope to be, the scaly creature rushed ahead, glittering silver dust arced around them, protecting them from other forms of magic aiming to maim. When a burst of flame came to close and the dark forest was suddenly ablaze in firelight, the blonde tightened her hold on the creature carrying her and tried to be quiet. However the onrush of fire scorching her eyes and the smell of smoke burning her nose was too much and a frightened whimper escaped her painted lips. To be fair the teen did try to be quiet but relying entirely on someone half your size to carry you amongst flaming bushes and angry soldiers was hardly a confidence booster.

The creature leaped, its tail whipping out with a crack against the grasping hands of their enemy. A whispered command and great wings opened, slapping against thick wires and beating back the darkened forms of her pursuers. One beat and her enemy was scattered, cursing her wildly as they fell from the darkened tree branches. Two beats and they were free of the trees, bursting past their snarled branches and curious occupants. Three beats and they were high in the air, the stars winking at them like laughing children; even the moon seemed to smile down on them. The teen gasped, relief flooding her body as the creature she knew flattened itself, its limbs angling together for less wind resistance. Slowly she raised her head, letting the cool night air whip her long golden locks back from her dirty face. She could see the dark forest, rolling hills and beautiful fields of her home country curve out before her, as if the world itself was just a ball. A large ball containing a countless number of lives. Lives she was responsible for sparing or sentencing; to the gods or to the demons, she's yet to decide.

"Setareh-Kaur, are you well?" the creature asked, its voice soft and feminine, like that of a young girl. She gasped, her azure eyes widening in surprise. She had forgotten her guardians, lost in her thoughts of the choice she was fated to make. She leaned down, staring at the masked face tilted towards her, eerie white eyes and all. She had forgotten, her only allies, the forest residents, the children of dragons; hired to protect her by her father. Humans they truly were, mortal in every way but their battle armor was fearsome and their magic ancient beyond compare.

"You... You can fly?!" Setareh asked loudly, surprise filling her as her arms tightened around the smaller girl even as her body sored gently on a hidden current, making her tiny body appear even more so like that of a dragon.

"We are dragon children." Eirian confirmed softly, turning her purl glowing eyes towards the horizon. "Hold tightly," she dived to the side, barely avoiding weighted ropes; the smell of poison stung her nose like acid to skin. Setareh bit her lip, trying not to make a sound as the dragoness dived, rose, spun and turned at dizzying speeds. Nearly dislodging the teenager's hold several times along the way to the meet point. Shooting straight up, far out of the reach of the enchanted arrows, the dragoness flattened out to sore on the currents; hoping that her charge's warm clothes were doing what they were made for.

"I see the town lights." Eirian murmured, "almost there, Setareh-Kaur. Just a little further."

"H-ho-How much f-further?" Setareh asked, her teeth chattering and her voice shaking. They were all signs that she needed to lower her altitude or risk Setareh getting hypothermia.

"Not long, just three or four minutes." She reassured quickly, hopping the older girl could remain strong enough until they reached the desired location. At hotel Malay they could change their appearances to match the new identities given to them from their contact in Niyatara city. Ziya was supposed to have all the paperwork handled, reassuring them that no one else would be able to interrupt their mission. Barak was supposed to secure their residence, which would allow them to recover from the long journey and change their appearances at will. Maor was supposed to secure their resources necessary for their almost over journey.

All Eirian could do was pray nothing went wrong.

"Lady Dragon do you see the city?" Setareh asked, her voice sounding startling clear for the amount of shivering she was doing.

"The city of lights lives to its name," Eirian agreed. Biting her lip in nervous apprehension, Eirian couldn't help but wonder why Setareh was suddenly so calm. "What can you see Setareh-Kaur?" Eirian shivered as something in the air shifted, she could feel her armor stiffen and tingle with an odd sensation; as if sensing something she couldn't. There were benefits to being a searer: seeing you're unborn, seeing your lover, seeing your family grow, seeing your allies, seeing your siblings, seeing your parents. There were so many positives about being able to see the future, knowing your fate, believing in something because you already know the outcome.

"A great fire envelops the city, an even greater enemy marches unhindered." Setareh answered, her voice whisper soft as her vision switched to another world. "The eight gates of the sea have been scattered. The king of oceans and seas found and bound. The child of fate and destiny forgot the path and took the place of the child of storms. So be it the first step of ruin."

And then there were the drawbacks.

Watching your child die, seeing your lover breathe their last, seeing your family scatter like leaves, seeing your allies fall, seeing your siblings fight, and helplessly watching your parents fall apart. Watching armies collide, men beg and plead for their lives, wives and mothers weep as a coffin is lowered, listening to children scream hysterically. Seeing through another's eyes as they walked through a field of corpses, identifying a pile of ash, witnessing a murder, watching a massacre or partake in a genocide.

"The balances shall tip and the tides shall turn. The destroyer of life shall awaken as the child of balance slumbers forever more. The Aisling shall fall and scatter like embers on the wind. The ancients shall be stolen. The stars shall fall and the lands fill with blood."

"Will we succeed tonight?" Eirian questioned. Her heart sank, her eyes burned, her fingers tingled and her belly twisted like a pit of snakes. That was not a prophecy she wanted to see come true. It was a riddle, she would need to wright it down and present it to her master later but for now she would have to settle for remembering it.

"Look out!" Setareh shifted her weight, making Eirian curse as they suddenly dived to the left, barely managing to escape the barrage of ropes and arrows. Cursing under breath, Eirian tried to regain control of her dragon armor, she whispered chants, summoned runes, created ancient seals and pleaded with the ancient ones. But it was all for not. Eirian could not stifle her scream as an arrow made mark on her arm, bringing with it the burn of poison. Her great amore faltered, crying out as the poison ate through its scales and scared her living flesh beneath, Setareh whimpered and all of a sudden, the prophecy made sense. In the back of Eirian's mind pieces of the puzzle were falling into place, whispers of memories surfaced and realization was like the cold touch of death's scythe.

"Hold tight!" Eirian cried over the rushing wind, tears pricked the edges of her eyes as the acidic poison ate through her skin and entered her rushing blood stream. Gritting her teeth and trying to ignore her pain, Eirian summoned her strength back to the surface. Taking in deep breathes Eirian focused again on the glowing city of Nìyatara, a port town sitting on the Naoska River bordering Aeoman forest and the defenseless Ashan. However, to Eirian's horror and Setareh's tiered sight, the 'city of lights' was bathed in fire light. Great black pillars filled the sky, screams echoed through the air and a horrible storm of glowing embers and swirling water needles appeared to be consuming the city.

"Damn," Eirian cursed as they flew over the walls of the city. The stench of flesh and burning hair filled her nose, making her stomach flip and a cold shiver crawl up her spine. All of her worst fears became reality and to think, they were told that this city was the make or break of their mission; survival here meant survival of a blessed family.

"Nation of islands have arrived," Setareh murmured distractedly. "They bring the Demon of oceans and seas. Searching for the child of storms. They hope to create a new Duinin." There was nothing more bone chilling and heart stopping then the sight of Urmër's thundering army of merciless soldiers. Urmër, the nation of islands, was well known for their blood thirsty Aibecks, robotic soldiers and fearsome mages. They were known to bring disease, discord and chaos wherever they roamed. A true nation of despair, blood, and agony. They watched helplessly as soldiers on the ground torched homes and busyness, their swords and arrows marking home on all in their way; sparing not even the babes nestled in their mother's cold embrace.

"Damn the war to hell," Eirian snarled. "Damn them all *to hell!*" Setareh said nothing as Eirian forced her armor to move continually forward, searching for that glowing figure who could only be her master. Eirian tried to remain focused, tried to see past the gathering tears, tried to focus past the throbbing pain but she was just a child. The sound of a whistle was Eirian's only warning, she dropped to the right, hoping to avoid the tangles of ropes and arrows. But her effort only landed them in a range of several mages, large swirling bubbles of water held in their palms and ready for the trap she unintelligently dropped straight into.

Setareh screamed, dropping her weight to the side, and protecting Eirian from a whip of water that would've cut her in half. At that point, Eirian decided to keep them afloat while Setareh steered them through the ambush of Urmër's merciless mages. Closing her eyes to focus on the flight and leaving Setareh to guild them was a revolting feeling that nearly made Eirian's previous breakfast revisit her mouth. Eventually though, Setareh couldn't toss her weight around to avoid the attacks and Eirian could no longer keep them in the air. One of the mages leaped from a building, fingers bright sea blue as they created runes and seals. The water from the river below leaped between them and sent Eirian and Setareh screaming to the hard stone road of the city. The girls rolled and tumbled across the cobble stones, crashing into the protective wall that kept stray children from toppling down into the river.

$$\Omega \ \Omega \ \Omega$$

She coughed and hacked, rolling onto her back to look at the burning buildings. She gave a shuttering cough and wheeze, she could feel that something was wrong, her guard was too silent. She lifted her face and looked at her guard, but all she saw was a young girl nearby. Her amethyst eyes were rimmed in dark sleepless lines, her lips were stained red from where she bit her lip too hard, her midnight-purple locks tumbled around her bruised face like a mirage of waves. Her armor laid about in broken bloody pieces, scattered like a fractured meteorite, there was nothing left to protect her. The armies were coming and they were defenseless.

"Eirian! Can you fight?!" they didn't know the girl was dead

> *"Don't take her! She's not the one you seek!!" she was helpless to stop them*

"A dragon? A female dragon?" they were going to die

> *"...Right age," they were coming for her*

"According to the boy she was born in the time of storms." She couldn't save them

> *"Don't take her! She's not the one you seek!!" she couldn't save Eirian now.*

"She could be the host we've been looking for." The demon was approaching

> *"A female dragon could give a boost to our forces," her family was burning*

"She could strengthen the army" the nations were crumbling

> *"She could win us the war..." the world was breaking*

"Don't take her! She's not the one you seek!!" she did not want this fate

> *A thick fog rolled forward, covering them in stifling pressure, a force that could seal lungs and crush souls.*

Accept the demon and she will live but her kinsmen will burn.

> *Deny the demon and she will die but her kinsmen may survive.*

"To let one live then all shall fall, to let all live then one shall fall. Whose fate is what you must decide."

"Setareh-Kaur are you well?" Eirian questioned gruffly as she rolled onto her belly, hoping that Setareh's landing had gone better than her own. But the teen had no time to answer before embers swirled around them, strong arms lifted Eirian and she yelped as a familiar uniform took shape in the embers. Looking over her savior's shoulder and through the trail of embers following them, she saw a large glop of water carrying Setareh while her other teammate raced just paces behind them. However Setareh appeared unconscious atop the bubble of water, Maor did not look pleased with being down-graded to moving bed.

"Maor! Barak!" Eirian smiled in relieve, relaxing in Barak's arms while he ran through a darkened alleyway, "What took you so long?"

"Oh you know, just passing by," Barak chuckled, his glowing eyes of jade brightening with his laughter.

"On what, the bridge of destruction?" Maor asked snappishly, his own glowing eyes of deepest amethyst sparked in annoyance in his mask of a sea-serpent.

"Is that what that sound was?" Eirian asked, referring to the bridge she and Setareh had previously landed on. "That'd explain why they're not following us!"

"You're not quite right!" suddenly their teacher was leading them, his glinting armor a stark golden light in the darkness of the alleyway. "We need to find cover, Urmër brought some not so friendly sky-mages!"

"I thought we were running from Gehill?!" Eirian asked loudly.

"As far as we can tell Gehill retreated some days ago," Maor answered. "We don't know how but Trégaron and Urmër are tag-teaming Asharan now! Urmër came across the ocean front, sending one of their freighters up the smaller Daramal river!" Maor pointed to the sky, looking up Eirian could see a shimmer of blue amongst the black smoke filling the midnight sky. "That barrier is pretty strong! Ziya-Isha couldn't break it!"

"Why hadn't I noticed it?" Eirian asked, "We never would've entered—"

"As far as I can tell no one outside of the barrier can detect it but once inside, it's impossible to escape it!" Ziya answered. "We'd have to kill the caster to escape it!"

"And it's not a very nice barrier," Maor was suddenly snickering, "Just ask Barak!"

"Shut it Water-boy!" Barak barked, "You could've warned me about the bombs up there!"

"Where's the fun in that?" Maor asked with a wicked glint in his dancing eyes. Barak gave a loud frustrated scream as they excited the alleyway, about the same time someone thought that collapsing the string of buildings they were running between was a great idea. Cursing loudly, Barak stumbled as he put Eirian on her feet and covered their left flank from a wall of flaming debris. Then Maor jerked on the bubble carrying Setareh, making her tumble through smoky air to crash into Eirian's scaled back. The teenager yelped in pain, discovering the hard way the sharpness to Eirian's scales. Eirian ignored the pained whimpering from Setareh and wrapped her hands around Setareh's legs and dashed forward, her magic swirling up and down her arms in hypnotic silver swirls. Maor, who was previously transporting Setareh, had thrown the teen at Eirian in order to block a collapsing building that would've landed on them. Ziya kept running ahead, his crimson eyes glinting as they swiveled from side to side; his golden swords appeared and disappeared as he used them to behead any archers he caught sight of.

"Arrow heart!" Ziya barked as he skidded to a stop, a swirl of golden light swept out with the strength of a battering ram; the dozen soldiers charging them screamed as they were crushed alive. Eirian swirled as she skidded across the cobble stones, spinning on her talon-feet to put Setareh between her and Ziya. The boys were quick to cover up

Setareh's sides, their magic blearing brightly before them. A swirling cosmos of embers from Barak, a boiling circle of water from Maor, a wall of glittering golden knifes from Ziya. Setareh breathed heavily as she turned towards Eirian, wondering what the girl of the team had to protect them.

"Virtus locus caeli drogo sauga," Eirian's eyes glowed a haunting white, overflowing with a power that sent shivers down Setareh's spine. It was an old *familiar* magic, but she couldn't remember *why* it felt so familiar.

"I thought Dragon's didn't need to speak spells?" Setareh asked as a beautiful white-mirror shimmered into existence all around them.

"Eirian's magic is too wild, the words help guild and center her power," Ziya answered. "Each dragon's magic reacts differently to the situation, Eirian's has a habit of lashing out violently. Thus the words guild her magic to her desire to avoid such disasters." Setareh barely had time to tighten her hands on Eirian's thin shoulders before the four types of magic swirled together and propelled them high into the air, away from the explosion of their enemy's fire and yet lower than the traps hanging in the sky. The 'children of dragons' braced themselves before their beautiful scaled dragon-armor contorted and produced dazzling wings. Their great wings beat back the waves of arrows and propelling them further through the air just above the city roofs. For a moment in time, the group was suspended in the air and nothing else seemed to matter in *that* moment. Because in that moment where gravity ceased resisting and their enemy couldn't reach them, a terrifying realization occurred to them.

Before them was the navy and black army of Urmër, their soldiers numbering so high that the city of lights were dimmed and the roads were blocked. At that moment, they could only see the chaos awaiting them. Their ominous premonition only grew as they watched a great number of blue painted priests march towards the center of the city, their center mass carrying something large, stone, and with holding enough magical power to suspect the bringing of a demon.

"Please tell me that's not what I think it is," Eirian murmured as they sored over the buildings, careful not to get entangled in the ropes suspending the numerous floating bombs overhead.

"It would appear that Urmër has brought with them their sacred demon." Setareh murmured, her voice cold and distant, as if observing a play from a great distance.

"Setareh-Kaur, can you see what they seek?" Ziya asked, glancing back at Setareh with wiry scarlet eyes.

"They seek a Duinin." Setareh answered. Ziya cursed loudly, a snarl twisting his face beneath his mask as he amplified his magic through the ring that connected them, urging their dragon-armor to fly faster. It was this formation that allowed them to travel at their utmost fastest speed but the best part was that outsiders could only see a withering serpent of old.

"Isha!" Barak called out, his voice tinged in confusion and worry. "What's a Doykin?!"

"Do-ee-NIN!" Maor corrected with a snap. "They're humans who're the tortured hosts to one of the ten demons!"

"Seriously?!" Barak asked loudly, "Why would anyone want a demon sealed into them?!"

"The hosts aren't exactly volunteering." Eirian grouched at him. Beneath his scarlet and orange mask of a scaled dragon, Barak's face paled to a ghostly hue, realization filling him like a bucket of ice-water splashing down his body.

"On the contrary, the Tripisode requires several specifications to be met before he could be sealed into a human." Setareh retorted blandly. "As the demon has yet to be removed from his box summon, it is safe to assume that he has not had his first host. He may be curious at first."

"What's that supposed to mean?!" Barak asked loudly, unable to tell if that was good information or bad information.

"All the great demons were sealed away, long before the seven kingdoms were separated *into* the seven kingdoms." Eirian huffed at him in annoyance. "We learned this in the academy!"

"He skipped classes remember?" Maor jabbed rudely.

"I only skipped the boring lectures!" Barak barked at him.

"Barak, those boring lectures are ninety-percent of where your education came from." Ziya sighed, "By ignoring them or missing them entirely, you are setting yourself up for failure." Barak decided that keeping his mouth shut would be the surest way to drop the subject.

"Dive to the right," Setareh ordered suddenly and Eirian did so without thinking. The boys scrambled to keep up, unintentionally avoiding the searching eye of a platoon of soldiers.

"Ziya-Isha! Setareh's eyes are glowing!" Barak called out, sounding unnerved with the revelation.

"Alright, diamond arrow!" Ziya ordered as he flew past Maor to fly to Eirian's right side.

"She does this Isha," Eirian called to him. "It's her power acting up through her seals." The man glanced at Setareh, noting her glazed eyes and the black tattoos on her face glowing an ominous red. He narrowed his eyes at the sight but nodded for Eirian to take the lead. He hung back as Eirian's right wing, his crimson eyes keeping a firm watch on their surroundings. It wasn't long before Eirian gave up leading and allowed Setareh to toss her weight from side to side, making them dive and spiral and swing wide or swing sharply. Either way they abandoned the northern sector of the city and laid low, undetected, in the South-eastern sector. Ziya didn't like having to bunker down so close to their enemy forces but he could understand the logic. No one ever checked just within their borders for their targets, he guessed that's why the Aisling were never caught before; they hid in plain sight splendidly.

"We'll settle here for the night," Eirian murmured as she tucked Setareh behind several boxes and wrapped a dirty cloak around the teen's shoulders. "As long as we are quite we should go undetected." As promised they were safe for three days, Maor was the only one trusted to gather food undetected. On the fourth day, while they were lifting their dragons onto their backs, Setareh awoke with a scream of 'down'. The team didn't bother questioning Setareh as their natural reaction was to flatten their bodies against the floor. Eirian tugged Setareh down beneath her just in time for the building to be sliced through, just three feet above the ground a great blade of magic sliced through Anything above the cut was turned into ashes, too the team's horror several children's screams sounded as they fell, blood coating their bodies as they fell apart in agony and ashes. The children's bones thudded around them, burying into the ashes of the building. Ziya ground his teeth together as he stared at the bones of a pair of siblings clutching at each other. Maor had to leap at Barak, covering the boy's mouth with his hand as several skeletons scattered atop them, one skull landing in the pyromancer's lap; a tear still beaded in the socket.

"Ziya-Isha," Maor whimpered, his body trembling as the last of the ashes faded in the light of dusk.

"Stupid brats!" a voice shouted, "you should've died with your friends! It would've been less painful!" Ziya snarled lowly, his dragon armor began glowing with his fury, his crimson eyes glinted as he dove out from beneath the ashes and charged their attacker. He was met with a large team of green and scarlet robed soldiers, the emblem of the ten-petal cherry blossom displayed in proud ruby on their chests.

"Shit!" the commander bellowed out, his pale eyes wide as he tried to brace himself against Ziya but he was unprepared for the man's summoning of blades. Within an instant the group of twenty soldiers were slaughtered, their blood pooling out in cruel scarlet. Still Ziya stood before the once building, body shaking as he suppressed the urge to sob.

Not even dragons would kill children.

"Dra-drraaaa," the choked voice called out, wheezing and choking the guardsman stared at Ziya in utter terror. "Da-daaadra," Ziya turned towards the man, crimson eyes glinting in fury and sorrow, tears pooling in the edges of his eyes, and approached the Trégaron soldier chocking on his own blood. "Draaaa-gu…dra-a-a-gon." Ziya's blade crashed into the man's brow, ending his painful last moments in undeserved mercy. In the soldier's palm, a small opened pendent, revealing the smiling face of a young woman. Ziya ground his teeth, fighting the tears that wanted to consume his face but he was the guardian of three children and a princess, he could not break now.

"Isha," Eirian's soft voice called out, strained and sorrowful. "We have to go, they'll be here soon."

"The children?" Ziya asked, turning to look back at his students but they already read his mind. Eirian gathered the bones of the children and surrounded them in her white crystalline magic, allowing Maor's water to soak into the ashes of the building and bring it over the skeletons left behind. Holding back a sob and with numerous blobs of water spilling from his eyes, Barak took in a shaking breath and let his embers form several runes before throwing out a blanket of flame over the bodies. What was left behind was the faces of the children killed pointlessly.

Ziya stepped forward too, murmuring gently under breath, his golden blade dragging through the ashes of their once-shelter. Together their magic surged and flowed, merging together in a single point to preserve the bodies of the children. There were five small bodies in all, each dressed in tattered robes, their hair messy from the long battle taking place in their city. To the far left of the row of children was a young girl who seemed out of place, her hair was well done in braids and flowers, her clothes layered and decorated in simple designs of leaves and vines. Beside her was a young boy, looking as if he hasn't eaten in several days, his messy hair did nothing to hide the scar above his eye and his torn sleeves did nothing to hide the hand he clasped tightly; the young out-of-place girl's hand. Then it was the siblings, still clutching fearfully at each other, a small cloth doll held between them like a whisper of safety. Sitting on the far-right side of the group was another young girl, her dress was simple stripes obscured by a large apron decorated with a heart on her chest.

"Their families can find them now," Setareh whispered to the team. "Their mothers need not wonder what happened to them."

"I wish... I wish we didn't have too..." Barak hick-upped and stuttered, "have to do this..."

"No one wishes they had to do this," Ziya murmured. "Come, we've done what we could. Now let us hide again."

"Yes Isha," Eirian murmured, her hand reaching out to each teammate and clutching them close as they each turned away from the murdered children. Setareh hung back for a moment watching the dragon-children leave before turning back to the stone-children. She whispered a soft spell, watching it inscribe itself upon the stone at the children's feet. Then she bowed and took off after Eirian before the team could get too far away.

When the sun fades, the stars still shine
When Darkness grows, the light still remains
When ashes fall, the water still flows.
May the past sleep peacefully
While the future wakes joyfully.

$$\Omega \ \Omega \ \Omega$$

The team of dragon-children ran and hid wonderfully for a day before they were cornered next to a wall. With the teamwork of both

Trégaron and Urmër, the children of dragons just grew more and more tiered with each passing day. The army was relentless, they were constantly throwing more and more men at them, regardless of how many soldiers fell at their feet. While resting behind a wall of corpses and traps, the team mimicking dragons were suddenly ambushed by a sudden down poor of acidic rain. It was only Setareh's scream that even prompted any of them out of the way in time. They knew with a look that Setareh was not screaming because of a vision, those sounded by far more terrified, but knew she was seeing something they hadn't noticed right away. Eirian retreated with Setareh, keeping her back to the girl as she used varies spells to lift different objects up and use them as shields against the summoned creatures attacking them. Ducking inside a building quickly, and slaughtering the mages who were already there, the children looked outside at their air-born attackers.

Great figures of flesh dangled from the buildings like serpents in a forest, their mouths opening wide to reveal hundreds of teeth seeking fresh blood. The creatures reared up and down, straining against their glowing seals of restraint, awful snarls and chilling growls filled the air around them. Then one limbless creature dived for the cobble stones, bouncing off the harsh cobble stones with a bark of anger. Roaring in pain the creature reared up, seemingly glaring at the gray cobble stones before swinging its tail around and bashing the stone road. Again and again the creature tried till it broke the cobble stones, revealing the fresh soil beneath the cold hard stone. Seemingly grinning in satisfaction the creature swung its tail to smash again into the softened soil. It howled in dismay as more rocks arced out of the earth to pelt it. Other creatures, mirror images of this creature closest to the dragon-children chittered and chatted, moving away as the former limbless creature. The former remained behind, smashing the earth again with its tail before joining its kin through the dark and flaming streets of the city. They noticed, in dismay and in hope that the creatures did not fly through the air, they merely acted like giant snakes, coiling through buildings and glaring down on unsuspecting pray.

"It can't go underground," Barak said, excitement sounding in his voice. "We can win this!"

"Those are desert worms," Setareh replied, panic cracked her voice and bringing tears to her eyes. "They're covered in a poisonous slim and spit acid!" Eirian cursed as she spun around, a glittering white mirror forming behind them like a shield. Ziya already had his golden swords pointed and ready for the creature but their efforts were in vain. The worm that slithered through their building, silently hunting them, smashed against the golden swords, tossing them away as if they were feathers.

With a grunt, Eirian called upon more magic to suspend her shield but the second attack came too soon and with a great thrash of the giant worm, the team of dragon-children were sent bursting outside for the other worms to feast upon. Maor grunted as he rolled across the cobble stones, summoning a whip of water he quickly lashed it around Barak and yanked him towards himself. Barak shouted in surprised relieve when the worm that once towered over him crashed into the cobble stone instead. As he raced towards Maor, Barak saw the worm lunging at his teammate. Understanding filled him quickly as he let his power bloom to life and he collided with the worm feet first, sparks showing between him and the giant worm. Then Ziya was there, pulling Barak away from the worm and then Maor was there with them and before either boy could blink they were atop a building, staring at the purple and navy sky over head.

"How do we kill them?" Barak asked loudly as he scrambled to his feet. Eirian panted from where she collapsed on the roof-top, braced by Setareh as she tangled one hand into the elaborate scales of her mask and helmet. Setareh bit her lip as she cradled Eirian in her arms but a dreadful rumbling nearby alerted her to the danger; they couldn't remain on the roof for long

"Their hides are approximately a foot thick, that's thicker than a Bullrine's hide." Setareh informed them, looking up at the boys with worried blue eyes. "The only way to defeat them is from the inside out."

"So get eaten and somehow magically rip them apart?" Barak asked in disbelief.

"...Yes," Setareh agreed, one eyebrow raised for the analogy he used.

"Yeah, no, we gotta figure something else out because I'm not getting eaten by that thing." Barak said as he pointed out at the street they left behind. For a moment all was quiet, the teammates watching in horror as a pale creature rose from the back of the building, the moonlight shining across its gleaming flesh. Turning slowly, Barak looked up at the creature behind him, his own face pale like snow beneath his dragon-mask. The creature opened its mouth and lunged, Barak yelped as his magic reflexively arcing out to defend his person. His embers burst around him protectively but seemed to do little against the giant worm attacking them.

The worm attacking jerked back, shaking its head back and forth as if it tasted something foul. Maor cursed as he leaped away from another one, only to force a large shield of water to cover him as his worm spat a stream of white acid. To the younger boy's misfortune, his water became too heavy with the taint of poison; the acid-spit cursing through the water weighed it down to the point that Maor could no longer use it. Ziya flited out from between three worms, letting the creatures launch their gapping mouths at each other instead of devouring him. Eirian and Setareh took to the sky briefly, only to land atop another building just in time to watch three worms attacking Ziya howl in pain.

"I've got it!" Ziya called, drawing his student's attention as he retreated back to Eirian. "They're not very bright! Get their attacks to land on each other!"

"Understood!" Barak and Maor moved with equal speed, barely managing to avoid teeth and acid in their attempts to get the worms to hit each other. Eirian and Setareh retreated further, their glowing eyes watchful for anymore worms and the soldiers they knew were coming. Slowly the boys were getting used to being a target, diving away at the last moment and making the worms gouging out gaping holes in each other. Eirian retreated a little further every time she spotted one of the worms rising above a second story, only to watch it enter a building. She was not about to get caught off guard by a lowly *worm*, not when she had to protect a princess.

"It seems a little too easy to kill these things," Eirian whispered to Setareh as they retreated again, Setareh's fingers tightening on Eirian's shoulders as they leaped across a street to land atop another building. To Eirian's horror she watched as the worms slowly rose once more from the earth, making the smirking boys groan as they saw the worms chitter and chatter together. "Wound them... we barely managed to wound them..." Eirian groaned as she spotted the tears in flesh of the giant worms, her heart sinking as she realized that they were not so easily killed—even by each other.

"That's because these are just the babies," Setareh replied, her voice quacked slightly as she was still not used to flying. "Barley a few days old so their teeth aren't sharp yet, the monster they grow into is by far more difficult to take out." Eirian gave Setareh a sharp look, bewilderment in her glowing eyes. She set Setareh down and moved to a part of the wall where she could see one of the worms try to burry itself into the roadside. It had pulled itself into a ball, coiled together like a snake as it chirped in irritation, its tail thudding harshly against the cobble stone. Comparing the size of the worm to the building behind it, she could see that it was easily two stories tall and just as wide.

"That's a baby?" Eirian hissed as she retreated from the edge.

"Once they hatch, the desert worms grow quickly." Setareh informed her, "I'd guess they're only four or five days." Eirian made a face behind her mask, she could not imagine having a child nearly fully grown within a few days. But then again, the animal Kingdome was as strange as the constellations, perhaps that's just how the worms adapted to survive. When she looked back at the worm, she noticed that beside it was a pile of corpses, to which it occasionally went to, to feast upon the semi-fresh flesh awaiting it. Suddenly she understood how the baby worms grew so large in just a few days, Niyatara was home to hundreds of thousands of people; not to mention the two merged armies battling their way through the massive city. If they ate the corpses as well as the living, then the worms had plenty of food and were eagerly growing larger than they properly otherwise would.

"Great what idiot brought a bunch of poisonous babies to the war front?" Eirian asked as she returned to Setareh's side. "We're in Ashan for crying out loud. What harm could these people ever be in war time?" Ashan was full of civilian families, the closest thing they had towards a military were a type of police-force that guarded merchants and travelers along their paths. Not one person in Ashan is capable of withstanding soldiers, especially not well-trained soldiers. The city of lights, Niyatara, was a fine example of just how helpless the people of Ashan truly were.

"The weak are always punished for the crimes of the wicked." The teen replied evenly, somber eyes sweeping out over the burning city. "We must move. If they have any more eggs we have to destroy them before they hatch. If we don't then the entire eastern seaboard will become a waste land like Dubol."

"We can't allow that," Eirian hissed, her voice trembling in anger and fear. "Malbril and Dubol rely heavily on the farming fields of Ashan."

Chapter II

"We can't allow that," Eirian hissed, her voice trembling in anger and fear. "Malbril and Dubol rely heavily on the farming fields of Ashan."

"So dose Aeorman forest," Setareh cut her eyes at Eirian as a thought occurred to her. "As dose every nation who depends on Ashan for sustenance." Eirian paled with realization, if Ashan fell to the desert worms then it would only be a matter of time before the rest of the world would follow suit. With a pounding heart, Eirian tightened her hold on Setareh and leaped off the building top, landing amongst the rubble and debris in the street of war. Setting Setareh down both girls took off in a dead sprint, hearts pounding and fears circling in their minds. They raced along the cobble stones, dived into broken buildings to avoid the soldiers and raced through towering flames. Still, as they watched the distant horizon become painted in blushing pink and ominous gold, they could not help but feel fear for the coming day.

Just where could they find the nest of desert worms?

"What do you know of the worms?" Eirian asked, turning to Setareh. The sixteen-year-old panted heavily as she leaned against a stone building, her face dripping sweat and her hands braced on her knees.

"Not much," Setareh admitted, her glowing eyes brightening for a moment before she closed them with a painful wince. "Just how to avoid them." Eirian briefly wondered why anyone in their right mind would want to live in the northern deserts but then again, the tribes of the north were some of the most powerful people in the nation of Aeoman. Eirian glanced at the reddening sky, watching a giant worm crash through the city with the aid of a thousand glittering sparks looking like arrows. It didn't take much imagination to see the dark form within the spiraling embers was a human one, even less imagination was needed to pin Barak as the creature of such sparks.

"Yeah... they've got to be insane," Eirian murmured to herself, still distracted with thoughts of the desert residents.

"Your teammates?" Setareh questioned, looking in confusion at Eirian. She had already assumed that the embers attacking the worm was at the mercy of Barak, Eirian's louder teammate.

"Setareh-Kaur," Eirian grinned beneath her mask, a sudden thought occurring to herself. "Water is scarce in the deserts. It's so bad that animals there have adjusted to containing water pouches in their bodies."

"...correct," Setareh agreed, frowning at Eirian in confusion.

"I don't know if all worms are like this but the ones back home don't like water." Eirian murmured, her mind flitting through information. "In fact after a rainstorm or heavy snow, it's so easy to find worms because they're withering on the surface. The desert doesn't ever get rain, they have oases and underground rivers. Either way the residents have to dig a thousand feet below the sand surface to find even an ounce of water."

"...are you saying..." Setareh straightened, wincing as an ache in her side made itself known.

"These are desert worms, they're not used to such large reserves of water residing in the soil." Eirian could feel the warmth of the rising sun and it felt like a blessing from the gods as she finally connected the dots. "The soldier's must've figured it out too, so all we have to do is go where they're the strongest." Turning her back on the rising sun Eirian walked down the cobble street, her hauntingly glowing eyes in the drawn light. Setareh remained braced against the broken wall for a moment, panting heavily. Then, she lifted the edges of her skirts and chased after the twelve-year-old girl with the eyes glowing with a century's worth of untold wisdom. Glancing back at Setareh, Eirian's magic flowed out and lifted the sixteen-year-old into the air, letting her rest while they traveled through the city.

They traveled from building to building, carefully avoiding soldiers and hunting worms; the latter of which appeared much more enthusiastic in daylight. Several times Setareh had to hide while Eirian cleared out a building or distracted a worm with a carefully constructed white-mirrors taking human form. Slowly but steadily, they made their way towards the center of the city, where a tendril of the Naoska River splintered off from the mountain to weave through the southern portion of the Ashan. Half of Niyatara city was built over the river, accenting its curves and swells beautifully. Even creating several false rivers to divert the water so that every block or two had a stream curling through it. All of the different water ways connected again just outside of the city, encouraging the stolen water to flow back to the Naoska River where it would eventually merge once more with the great ocean.

"Have you seen your teammates, lady Eirian?" Setareh asked as they waited out the heat of the day in a small Warehouse somewhere near the center of the city. They've been stuck in the city just over a week now and the children of dragons were growing wiry of being so far from home for so long.

"Trust me Kaur, seeing them is a bad thing." Eirian said calmly. She was sitting on a crate, her legs folded beneath her in a perfect 'x', the soles of her feet resting on her thighs, her hands resting on her knees, her fore-finger and thumb touching, her back straight, her eyes closed.

"Why is that?" Setareh asked, genuinely curious about the boys on Eirian's team. Eirian cracked an eye open and stared at the blonde through her snarling dragon mask, observing the curious black lines dotting across Setareh's face and her long platinum waves, the white layered robes rimmed in silver vines, leaves, flowers, and stars. When they first met Setareh looked like a daughter of the moon, refined, beautiful, elegant, and utterly merciless with her words. Now she looked like a fallen kingdom, the metaphorical saying 'name dragged through mud' now looked literal on Setareh's ragged clothes, dirty hair, muddy and bruised face. She no longer looked ethereal, no longer a daughter of the moon. She looked like a banished soul, a forgotten daughter of light, a fractured jewel of forgotten memories.

"When they're desperate, they're loud." Eirian said at last. "Their silence is a blessing."

"I see," Setareh bobbed her head, looking towards the doors as they rattled with a breeze. "…What do you think of the Aisling family?"

"You don't want that answer." Eirian replied as she closed her eyes and returned to her meditation.

"…once, long ago, I had a dream. At least at the time… I thought it was a dream." Setareh said, her voice soft as she leaned against the warehouse wall. "I was four when my powers awakened and they've only grown since then. That's why I have so many seals tattooed into my skin, why every piece of jewelry I wear has acid etched runes and seals and spells designed to suppress my power. I am the strongest seer of my family, the strongest since our founder." She stopped a moment, closing her eyes in memory and regret. She pulled her legs to her chest, wrapped her arms around them and rested her brow atop her knees.

"The night my powers awakened, I had a dream of facing a creature carved from frigid mists... I died trying to seal it away. As my body fell to the cold earth, I watched as my family left our home and entered the great forest. Then I saw that had the mist taken possession of my body, had I not resisted, I would have survived... but my family would've fallen into a sea of flame."

"...what happened after that?" Eirian asked, her voice whisper soft in the dim light of the warehouse.

"...they began the process of sealing my powers." Setareh answered, just as softly. "The normal age of awakening is twelve, I was *four*. Not only was it unusual but I had foreseen my fate and the fate of my people. That's not something an Aisling is supposed to be able to see. There are strict rules and prices we must follow and withstand in order to obtain the power of foresight. That is why everyone believes the Aisling family is protected by the gods." Her lips twisted into a hateful smile, her eyes glistening in unshed tears, a contorted chuckle escaped her throat in a sound of mockery and loathing.

"They never stopped to think that we're actually *cursed*." Setareh raised a trembling hand to her face, rubbing it harshly to push back the burn of tears. "In order to awaken our foresight, we must see our deaths... and we must *accept* our fated deaths. This is the curse of the Aisling family. Those who accept their deaths, continue seeing into dimensions but are never capable of seeing their own lives. Those who reject their deaths, lose their prophecy ability and live twice-shortened lives." Eirian closed her eyes and breathed heavily, a sick sense of foreboding twisting in her belly like a thousand snakes withering in pain.

"In the Aiello family, your power is determined by the marks on your face..." Eirian said, her face shadowed by her mask. "The more marks on your face, the higher your standing is and the more respect you have. Those with fewer marks are demined as… servants. Their task is to protect those who have more marks then everyone else."

"What's the significance of the marks?" Setareh asked curiously, whipping her runny nose on her dirty sleeve.

"They're a symbol of our powers." Eirian answered. "Grandfather says that the Meadowood family is our sister-family, its why our two families have similar powers. Our magic is reincarnated into the family and the Meadowood's are reincarnated souls." Setareh perked with the information, she's come across reincarnates in other worlds but more often than not they were just people who were susceptible to receiving visions of another dimension. They were basically really weak fortune tellers, except they couldn't tell that they were looking into another dimension; they just assumed it was a memory of a previous life. How they came across such a conclusion was bewildering to Setareh, she always thought it was rather obvious that it was another world and not a previous life. Perhaps it's because in this life she was raised by fortune tellers who already knew the truth and an elder sister who was willing to share all her secrets.

"Every Aiello has a different power they are born with and that power is reborn into the family when the user dies." Eirian continued, sounding sad with the words she knew as truth. "The marks are a symbol of how many times that power has been reborn. So the more marks the better, it's a more well-known power. The fewer marks are the more disgraceful as there is little known about them which makes them perfect guardians. It's kind of like… reincarnations except with magical elemental powers instead of souls."

"…so, fear the unknown?" Setareh asked, looking at her guardian with an expression of pity and empathy. Eirian cracked an eye open to look at Setareh for a moment, then closed the eye and hummed in agreement. "…How many marks do you have?" Setareh asked, Eirian opened her eyes and Setareh knew in that moment that Eirian had accepted her 'fate' many, many years ago.

"My power has only been reborn twice, with my life being the second." Eirian turned her attention to the roof over head, looking lost with her strange glowing eyes. "Despite being the heiress, I am the lowest ranking Servant. As soon as one of my siblings come of age, I will be tossed aside and one of them will lead the family."

"...What'll happen to you?" Setareh asked, a sick feeling swelling in her belly. Something changed with Eirian, an indiscernible sadness seemed to overwhelm her for the briefest of moments, and then she was jumping to her feet and seemingly smiling at Setareh.

"Come now Setareh-Kaur, we've rested long enough." Eirian stretched her muscles, ignoring the confused look on Setareh's face.

"...It's Sea-tar-ree," Setareh said suddenly.

"Hmm?" Eirian questioned, looking back at the teenager, one arm outstretched overhead while the other tugged on it behind her head.

"Mother named me 'Setareh', it's a diminutive of the goddess of creation; Sytra." Setareh elaborated patently. "It means star."

"...Sytra," Eirian murmured slowly, "the goddess of creation... I've heard tails of her, she started out human right?"

"Yes, she lived in the world before magic and then came the time when the two reflections of the world were to either merge or destroy each other. Goddess Sytra stood against the great destroyer and vowed to end her own life and all forms of memory of her existence, in return for merging the two reflections." Setareh explained, a fond smile slipping across her dirty face as she carefully moved onto her feet. "It is said she was only nine years old... and she chose to die for a world of people who didn't even know she excited..."

"...huh," Eirian shrugged, dropping her arms to look at Setareh carefully. "What's with that fond smile? You like the legend?"

"I believe that Goddess Sytra is more than just a silly legend." Setareh replied, looking at Eirian patently. "I believe that before the great divide and even after, Goddess Sytra did exist. After all, certain legends say that it was the goddess who originally sealed away the ten great demons. Perhaps she survived despite her own sacrifice."

"Perhaps," Eirian shrugged. "Either way Setareh-Kaur, if we don't get going *we're* not going to exist." Setareh nodded in agreement, as she walked towards Eirian for a quick exit of the building, a frown marred her angelic face.

"Ready?" Eirian questioned, turning back to the open door both girls readied themselves. "Three... two... one!" they burst out of the building and followed the other without question, rushing across the street and diving through a broken window. Just in time too, a worm came crashing down on the warehouse, crushing it to pieces and screaming shrilly as a thousand golden blades ripped its body apart from the inside out.

"Ziya-Isha?" Eirian asked as she popped her head up over the windowsill. A great blade of golden light sliced through the belly of the worm, making it scream out in pain and summoning its kin. The man dressed in gold and silver scales leaped out of the giant worm, drenched in the creature's dark blood. The man glanced at Eirian and Setareh before bobbing his head and quickly dashing away, drawing the attention of the worms while he was at it.

"...Does that mean he's desperate?" Setareh asked as she pushed herself up from the awkward position she landed in.

"No, he's conserving his energy." Eirian's eyes narrowed at the worm, watching it wiggle about before settling mournfully. "Hmm," Eirian narrowed her eyes at the creature before retreating from the window. "We should go, before the soldier's arrive..."

"Wait..." Setareh murmured, her seals glowed an ominous red, Eirian hurried to the laying princess's side, clasping her hand with her own clawed ones. "The three of five eggs sleeps eternally, hiding two of trusted fate. The whispers of mist and the song of leaves gather, before sending kin to the trusted place."

Eirian frowned but she could make guesses about the analogies. She had noticed before that there were only five worms that were hatched on the day they had been first attacked by the creatures; each hatched a day apart if their sizes were to be believed. Her master killed one on the first night and the one that crushed the warehouse would be two... perhaps the boys killed another she was unaware of. That would be three of five, leaving behind... two of fate... no she said *hiding* two of trusted fate.

That was it! Trusted fate! Eirian straightened her back to look over the windowsill, her eyes flaring white with her special power. There, a subtitle shift of the worm's flesh, a gentle glow of pre-dawn light hid further up the creature's neck.

Barak down, where's Maor? He's always been so tricky, his aura so gentle that it was easily overlooked by another's, even if that other presence was that of a young child. Closing her eyes and taking in a deep breath, Eirian focused on the aura she knew all too well. The aura that felt like gentle ocean waves, silky soft, gloriously bright, fascinatingly cool, terribly forgettable...

There, the color of summer skies, the rhythm of a lullaby, the smell of wind, the feeling of safety. Maor was just further down the worm, past its core, closer to the end... no that's not right. Oh, now she remembered, worms had to heads, one at every end. They also had five hearts and two brains. When they were severed the side with more hearts will survive and continue to grow, even growing a secondary brain and mouth but the hearts? She couldn't remember if those regrew, she didn't think so, that would make them much more difficult to kill. Either way, she had her answer. With two heads, the worm had double tagged her team, who ever gotten eaten first didn't matter because the boys ended close to the mouths, away from the stomach acid but Ziya hit the very center and quickly freed himself before the acid ruined his armor.

They're safe, Eirian let go of her breath, her back hunching in relief, her hand tightening on Setareh's pale digits. "It's time to go, we need to hide."

"Along the river of haunted home, the trial begins anew." Eirian looked down on Setareh, watching the tattoos pulse with light as her eyes brightened; there was something seriously wrong with what Setareh was seeing. "The first of three, beware the crimson mist, for the Ahriman marches ahead. The second: the trust of three ends for thy and fire scorches the moon's kiss. The third: a life of silence, always known never shown, beware the cloak of envy betrays us all." She could not forget these words, she had to remember, and the best way for of that would be to write it down. Eirian did just that accept she wasn't a particularly fast writer and so had used her magic to summon her white mirror. The mirror was as small as her palm, perfectly white and shaped like a children's sun. It glittered beautifully, recording Setareh's words quickly.

"What is that?" Setareh asked as her power retreated and she awoke to the cool shadow of a stone building.

"Setareh-Kaur, this is one of my mirrors," Eirian said as she passed it to the teen as she pushed herself up, one hand bracing against her aching head. "I designed it to record your prophecies. I should've thought of this sooner. I could've recorded the other two…"

"It's alright," Setareh said as she tucked her feet beneath herself. "How do we activate it?" Eirian reached forward and bent one of the triangles mimicking a sunbeam.

"Beware the cloak of envy betrays us all."

Eirian very nearly melted into the earth in utter shame. She didn't catch all of the prophecy like she intended, she only caught the very end of it and she had been so focused on making the mirror that she hadn't caught all of what Setareh was saying.

"…is there a way to erase this?" Setareh asked curiously.

"Huh?" Eirian straightened from her slump to look at Setareh in confusion.

"Once I have a prophecy I can recite it repeatedly," Setareh explained. "Every year I've had one distinctive prophecy… but… this year…" her eyes narrowed thoughtfully as she fiddled with the tiny white mirror, she noticed silently that the white mirror didn't reflect and didn't weigh much of anything. It was small and light, looking like a children's picture of a sun that they were supposed to color in. "I've had several more important prophecies… instead of writing them down in a diary, I could record them here."

"…what's so special about these prophecies?" Eirian asked curiously.

"They're about what happens *after* my death." Setareh answered, looking up at her guardian sorrowfully. "As you know, the Aisling family aren't permitted to see anything past their death date… somehow, these prophecies are different… they feel like warnings. But I don't know how I'm supposed to avoid them, especially since they're past my death date. But the gods… they still make me see these events… perhaps this is why." Setareh lifted the small mirror towards Eirian, "Perhaps they make me see these events, knowing I would remember them, so I would meet you some day and record them. This way, even after my death, mankind is warned." Eirian stared at Setareh for a very long moment, eyes narrowed in thought, the glow long since gone. She looked out to the worm that contained the slumbering bodies of her teammates, the flesh of the creature keeping them plenty cool in this summer sun. They must've been exhausted to be slumbering now of all times, perhaps they had been fighting throughout the night while the girls slept beneath Eirian's shields.

"Alright," Eirian bobbed her head, a wave of her hand destroyed the small sun-like mirror. "But first, some place safe."

"Second floor then," Setareh replied as she pushed herself to her feet. "We can record there."

"Deal, I'll lead the way." Using her magic quickly, Eirian determined where the stairs were and they both hurried up to the second floor. Picking the window where they could be hidden and yet still look down on the hidden boys, the two females sat in the corner. Eirian summoned her magic and set about a large oval mirror, setting it on the corner wall. She sat beside Setareh and before the large oval-mirror, staring into its depths she whispered to it to awaken and its surface glinted in sunlight before reflecting back the two sitting before it.

"…I never realized how ghastly I looked before," Eirian murmured as she stared at her dirty reflection. "Damn, Ryū looks bad…"

"You could always remove your mask and let 'Ryū' rest while we record." Setareh suggested.

"What if we're attacked?" Eirian asked with a raised eyebrow.

"I doubt anyone can sneak up on you if your magic is stronger the Ziya-Rū's," Setareh returned with a smirk. Eirian shrugged and waved a hand, dosing the large dirty room with glittering white dust that quickly faded as it filled the remaining of the building. Setareh chuckled as she turned to the mirror once more and watched in its reflection as the dragon-armor pealed itself off Eirian, revealing her young features for the world to see. To the untrained eye, Eirian was a strange creature of human and serpent, looking feminine with her dusting storm-colored scales on her cheeks but frightening with the haunting hues of poison-yellow highlighting her serpentine-features.

"Sapphire hair and jade eyes?" Setareh questioned with a raised eyebrow, "Somehow I envisioned you looking different." Truthfully she knew that Eirian had hidden her face behind a spell that disguised her entire body with that of a serpent. While she appeared physically human, there was that outer-shell of something 'unnatural' that most snakes seemed to grow accustomed to. She still retained a pair of thick meaty claws, tail and lion feet, but she bore no wings and Ryū looked like a very tiny baby shadow-lizard. He shook his head, yawned, and curled up in Eirian's lap like a baby kitten snuggling in for a long nap.

"I do," Eirian huffed at her. "No one is allowed to leave the forest looking as we truly do. In case we are captured we must not look as our kin dose and our names must be changed."

"Why?" Setareh asked, though she already understood the reasons. No one would want to rape a serpent, no one would want to fight a serpent, and no one would want to cross a serpent. In this way the 'children of dragons' ensured their safety, their family's safety and their nation's safety.

"Because names hold great power." Eirian told her patently, before waving towards the mirror with one hand and snapping her fingers with the other. "Now, speak from the first to the last."

$$\Omega \ \Omega \ \Omega$$

It was sundown by the time the last of the prophecies was recorded, leaving Setareh mentally drained and Eirian trying not to nod off in boredom. By then the soldiers of Urmër and Trégaron were gathering in thicker numbers and racing in circles around the sector the dragon-children remained silent in. Shuffling closer to Setareh as she leaned against the wall with a heavy sigh, Eirian raised her hands to the large mirror, now marred with a dozen dashes across its top. She whispered into the still air, her voice barely heard through the breeze, and the mirror glowed hauntingly as it morphed and floated towards its master. Eirian fluctuated her magic, whispering gentle encouragements and tapping her fingers to her thumbs in different but simultaneous patterns. The mirror shrank down into Eirian's offered palms and the glow faded to reveal its new shape, bringing forth a fond smile on Setareh's gentle features.

"Is that…a lotus?" Setareh asked, her voice as soft as Eirian's was previously.

"Yes," Eirian murmured, shifting just enough to show Setareh the newly shaped glass, still white and unreflective. "The lotus… a symbol of wisdom and love."

"…it is also the flower that means creation and rebirth." Setareh murmured, staring at it thoughtfully, "at least to my family." Eirian shrugged carelessly, she loved the lotus flower regardless. "How many petals are there?" Setareh asked as she leaned towards it, one tattooed finger raised as she started counting, "sixteen… hmm, that sounds about right."

"Some of those visions of yours were truly long," Eirian said with amusement dancing in her eyes. "Could you not make them any shorter?"

"No, absolutely not. Every detail must be accounted for. The name of a flower or the color of one's eyes can spare the evil one while banishing the innocent." Eirian hummed in understanding as she stiffly rose to her feet, wincing slightly as the feeling slowly ebbed back into her legs. Eagerly her baby dragon yipped and hurriedly dashed towards Eirian before expanding and opening up to swallow the preteen hole. Eirian chuckled as she forced the lotus into the air so it wouldn't be consumed by her overly eager dragon-armor.

"…I never knew dragons could become actual armor," Setareh murmured as she stiffly rose to her own feet. She watched in fascination as Eirian's newly clawed palm gently caught the white lotus, holding aloft as if it were a feather.

"Dragon? Oh~ now I understand." Eirian's eyes danced and now that Setareh had seen the girl's face (or the allowed version of it), she could finally see the amusement in the now pearl-colored irises staring back at her. "My armor doesn't have a soul, though I wish it did. The second Nanaibek of the forest created our armor, called the living armor to my people, yours often call us Dragon-children because of it."

"Living armor?" Setareh asked, her eyes widening in amazement.

"Yes, it takes a fraction of our magic to sustain it but its colors are based off of our auras and special talents." Eirian shrugged, a clear smile stretching her face beneath her black mask of a fearsome dragon. "I'm not sure why but my dragon-armor doesn't look like what my magic looks like. It's all dark and scary looking, it's a little depressing honestly." Eirian heaved a heavy disappointed sigh but Setareh just started giggling at the younger girl, amusement filling her every bone.

"Like an overprotective big brother trying to scare off bullies to his favorite sister." Setareh giggled out by way of explanation to the younger girl, a strange rumbling-purr filled the space between them, electing a giggle from Eirian.

"Did you hear that Setareh-Kaur? He's happy!" Eirian continued to giggle, her hands curling in front of her masked face as if to contain all of her amusement. "Ryū likes your description! How funny!" Setareh giggled herself before seeing that the last of the light was finally dwindling away, leaving them a quickly darkening world. "We should get to the boys, they've rested long enough." Setareh nodded before looking down at the palm sized lotus, noticing her look, Eirian looked down at the glass-flower herself.

"It should be fine; do you want to leave it here?" Eirian asked as she looked back up at Setareh, only to see that the teenager's eyes were glowing a haunting violet, nearly fully encased in lines shaped a simple looking flower.

"…hm," Setareh smiled fondly at the flower as the glow faded. "Is there a way to duplicate it?"

"…how many?" Eirian asked curiously

"Three trials, three flowers," Setareh answered simply.

"Do you want to record your latest vision?" Eirian asked cautiously, only to have the older girl close her eyes in sad acceptance.

"Some things can't be described in words."

Ω Ω Ω

Barak and Maor were not pleased to be awakened, then again no one likes their cool surroundings catching fire and threatening to suffocate them. Before Eirian or Setareh could escape the building, the lower streets were filled with Urmër and Trégaron soldiers. Hesitating on their second floor, staring worriedly down on the boys, the girls watched as the worm-corps split apart, engulfed in sparks and water-spears as the boys leaped out and started to attack. They watched as the two present generals sent out commands, they each sent out two men who hurried away to 'check the treasure'. Eirian backed away from the broken window and hurried to the other room next door, where she could lean out the window and watch the men hurry down the street.

"Sending kin to trusted place," Eirian repeated, "Setareh-Kaur—"

"I'm here, we should hurry." Setareh murmured as she looked out the window too but unlike Eirian who looked down the street, she looked straight down. Eirian did too and without saying a word, she grabbed Setareh's arm and leaped out the window, pulling the teenager with her. Setareh bit her lip hard enough to break skin in her effort to not scream, she felt only slightly foolish when Eirian swept out a white mirror and they landed softly. The soldiers that had spotted them from the street didn't have a chance to even shout before the white-mirror crashed atop them, followed by Setareh and Eirian. Eirian double checked the guard's conscious state before tugging Setareh onto her back and summoning her wings once more.

"What if someone see's us?" Setareh asked, worry tinging her voice.

"No worries," Eirian murmured, a smirk twisting her face beneath her mask. Eirian's magic flared to life around them, then before Setareh could blink they were flying down the street, the wings of her armor stretched out to whisper against the building edges. It didn't take them long to catch up to the four soldiers and when they did, Eirian quickly took to a roof, landing carefully so she wouldn't jostle the ropes attached to the floating bombs overhead. As the soldiers took turns and ducked into buildings, Eirian and Setareh followed from across the roof tops. Wherever they couldn't leap, Eirian cast off the 'invisible cloak' to create a white-glowing bridge to pass from one building to the next, then re-whispered the spell that made them disappear. More than once Setareh felt panic as one soldier or another would look in their direction but for some reason never give the warning shout. It didn't take her long to realize that they could not be seen by their enemy. When she looked at Eirian in amazement, the young girl pressed one finger to her masked face in an effort to keep all questions silent. The two soldier's they were following crossed a large bridge and ducked out of sight. Eirian frowned thoughtfully before she unfolded her wings and pulled Setareh back onto her back. Taking a deep steadying breath, because flying unnerved her, Setareh clapped her mouth shut as Eirian took flight.

They were halfway across the river when they were discovered.

"Ahi: Uriel Gwendolen!" The furious shout was accompanied by a dozen flames bursting into life around them, making Eirian gasp as she focused on steadying their descent across the stream instead of the glittering shield around them.

"Eirian," Setareh gasped, looking about in panic before her eyes landed on a young man standing on the river edge, his flaming locks of strawberry flew about his head in wild bouncing curls.

"I knew it! They're here!" the young man shouted angrily, several soldiers hurried out of the buildings lining the river edge, even more wizards readied themselves in the building windows. "Archers! Fire!"

"Albena!" Eirian shouted, her pearl eyes wide in panic. "Damn it!" Setareh barely had a moment to blink before they were falling, she clung to Eirian desperately as a scream tore out of her throat. While not a single flame, arrow, curse or glowing-chain touched them, Eirian's mysterious power flared out and disrupted the river below, summoning its great purifying touches to surround them protectively.

"Maor!" Eirian cried out, "Stolen dragon!" With a great roar the river water surged around them, protecting them from the onslaught of arrows and flames. In the distance an explosion of embers flared to life, erupting screams from where the boys once fought together before dispersing as the river bulged and Eirian's trusted companion swirled before them with a protective flourish.

"Archers! Mages!" the pink haired young man bellowed, stepping back as his face twisted into an ugly snarl.

"Albena!" Eirian shouted from the river floor but her cry went unheard as Maor swept forward with the fury of a tsunami. Setareh could do nothing more than cling to Eirian as the girl caught a current and arced back into the air. This time it was the soldiers who cried out in terror as they were sent crashing into buildings and smothered by great walls of water.

"Albena!" Maor barked, his voice cold and hard as his water swept forward and wrapped around the young man with flaming locks.

"Damn it!" the young man cursed wildly, his freckled face twisting up as he tried use his magic of fire to break the water's hold but he only succeeded in scorching his own skin. "Let me go you damn demon!" the soldier bellowed furiously, tears of pain edging his pale eyes.

"Cousin," Maor murmured gently, his voice soft as he peered into the young man's pastel blue eyes. "Have you forgotten us already?"

"What are you talking about demon?" the young man snarled, his blue eyes whipping about widely for help. His searching gaze only landed on Eirian and Setareh, who floated up to them with ghostly-white magic surrounding them.

"Only those of the Albena family have the power to see all forms of magic." Eirian murmured, her pearl eyes narrowing thoughtfully at him.

"But his eyes were not stolen," Maor murmured, "For he still bares the Albena's favored pink hair." Eirian nodded in agreement, confusing the young man further. His freckled nose twitched as he sniffed, fighting off the urge to cry with the pain of his burned arms. He did not appear to be very old, barely a few years older than themselves, his face still bore his previous baby-fat.

"A descendent," Eirian murmured. "A child held back before they could escape during the great retreat."

"A survivor of the purge?" Maor questioned, "But… all of us were retreated by the Adirura."

"Not all could escape the clutches of war," Eirian replied. "Perhaps his ancestor was a captive concubine like many others."

"Hey!" the young man bellowed furiously, "I didn't insult your relatives!"

"Ah, hit the nail on the head again Eirian," Maor drawled lazily.

"Go die ya'damn demon!" The young man snarled angrily. "I am Carter Tindall! Prince of Tregaron!"

"Tri, it's pronounced as tri, not trey!" Maor corrected with an air of annoyance.

"Yeah but what rank are you?" Eirian drawled with a tone of boredom. Her answer was a disdainful look and a glare of insult; as if he were insulted with her question. "Are you in the teens or twenties? I'm not aware of the emperor of Trégaron having any children in the thirties yet, not innless that's changed in the past three years."

"Plenty of time for new wives, concubines and mistresses," Maor snorted with a disinterested look at Eirian, who only shrugged carelessly at him. "Last we checked he already had fifteen wives and thirty concubines."

"And heaven knows how many mistresses." Eirian quipped, smirking as she was given a furious blue-eyed glare.

"Lady Eirian," Setareh whispered, her eyes a strange glowing violent, nearly overrun with the violet lines.

"Right, Maor, I'll leave him to you."

"Him?" Maor questioned, his voice hitching in confusion and bewilderment. His glowing amethyst eyes snapped back to Carter, wide- bewildered eyes, ignoring the embarrassed glare of the young man. "Aren't Albena's female?"

"Typically," Eirian mumbled as she adjusted Setareh's hold on her shoulder and pulled Setareh onto her back. "It's rare but sometimes a boy can use their magic."

Chapter 12

"What are you talking about?" Carter questioned, growing confused. "Hey! Where are you going?!"

"There is an eighty-nine percent possibility of a fifth," Setareh murmured. "He was sent ahead after they crossed the river." Carter jerked with the declaration, his eyes widening in horror. "Forty-three point zero seven percent of two others accompanying him."

"You're an Aisling!" Carter's voice sounded with a crack of terror and realization, no wonder they couldn't outrun the group. "Why are you helping them hermit?!"

"We are leaving to stop this war," Eirian said as she tilted her head towards Setareh, who blindly held onto the smaller girl as her glowing eyes continued to reveal other worlds. "Enough people have suffered for you ignorance." With that the girls took off through the air, hunting down the men who had previously escaped their sight thanks to a particularly lost boy.

"Well then," Maor smirked to himself as he lowered the boy to the cobble stones and took a seat on the wall of the river. "Should I start from the beginning or do you want to ask the questions?" The young man glared at Maor, his blue eyes snapping around in search of help but only saw his comrades unconscious and soaked in the river water still surrounding them like a cage.

Maor just smirked knowingly at the teenager.

Further away, soaring through the streets with growing anxiety, Setareh and Eirian urged the magical armor forward with their rushing hearts and glowing eyes. Spotting the group of three men, realization dawned on Eirian quickly that the Albena-boy was originally a part of the four-man team sent to find the 'treasure'.

"Go ahead!" one of the soldiers shouted as he surrounded himself with glowing runes of teal, summoning forth a half-formed army of muddy humanoid creatures. "Terra: Harlow Aran!"

"Seriously?" Eirian murmured, "Idiot." Without mercy, crystalline white fragments appeared around Eirian and Setareh before blurring in beautiful stripes of light that shattered the muddy-humanoids.

"What?!" the soldier shouted, horrified that his spell couldn't stop the glowing advisory, "Terra: Kunryū!" his voice echoed out desperately, the runes around him pulsed with a more foreboding color of deeper navy. Eirian's pearl eyes glinted angrily behind her mask, her white mirrors shifted and twirled like sparks as they surrounded her like a drill. The soldier smirked to himself, the cobble stones and earth underfoot shifted and moved up to create a great gapping mouth of a monster long since dead; a creature with scales and sharp teeth, eager to devour all in its wake.

"Idiot," Eirian murmured, her white eyes glowing hauntingly in her black snarling mask. "You shouldn't summon what you can't control."

"Just die ya' ugly demon!" The soldier bellowed, only to freeze as a glittering white light appeared to his right side. With growing horror, his brown eyes turned to see the masked child and her charge fly past him, one wing extended with six silver claws. He could barely register the pain in his side or the waves of blood spilling from his now shredded arm. All he could see was the glowing white-haired maiden riding the back of a black dragon with haunting white-eyes. He crashed to his knees, oblivious to the monstrous creature turning towards him with an angry growl. He looked down at his missing arm then at the blood pooling around him, hazy and blurry eyes tried to look up at his summon but the muddy-creature howled and lunged at him. He smiled bitterly as he was consumed by his own summon, what a cruel twist of spells.

One hit from a stranger and his own summon turned against him.

"...the soldier remains silent," Setareh murmured as they left the man behind to be devoured.

"Serves him right for summoning an earthen-spirit." Eirian murmured, "Only the Mayfield may receive their aid." Setareh said nothing as they caught up once more to the soldiers, this time the remaining two from Trégaron stood side by side, their faces twisted in fury.

"Terra: Hayden Knox!"

"Tirta: Winslow Lamar!"

The two men's voice cried out in righteous unity, their runes and seals appearing around them in neon green and shy jade. The cobble stones broke apart before liquefying into foreboding umber. Great waves of somber earth arose around the two men, protecting them from whatever attack Eirian may throw their way. The buildings on either side of the street liquefied, moving like waves, ebbing and flowing to mimic the rise of a tidal wave that'd swallow the girl's hole. The two forms of magic merged to create a great hill with weeping waves of mud spewing out from two holes like sorrowful eyes overflowing with misery. A splash of water reached up and slap pointlessly at the girls, making Setareh cringe with the scent of rout burying deep into her nose.

Eirian shook herself, a low growl of disapproval rumbled from her chest when she saw that the liquid revealed its sticky marron substance.

It took only for a moment for Eirian to realize that the sticky substance was mimicking blood, containing its rancid smell and haunting thickness. While the men smirked for their efforts, Eirian remained unmoved. These spells were good practice against young mages and soldiers or stronger opponents like her teammates. She didn't know what Ziya would've done if placed in her shoes but she knew he would've been able to get out of it, as nothing appeared to trap the man dressed in golden dragon scales. Barak would've panic with the abundance of 'blood' surrounding him and Maor would've been helpless with the mud tainting the rivers, making them useless for his style of combat.

But Eirian was not her teammates.

Eirian's white mirrors glowed hauntingly before dashing forward, looking like white sparks and shattering drills as they barreled through the Trégaron's forest spells. The waters returned to the river, where they overflowed the stone walls and glowed with purified magic. The earth returned back to its natural state, crumbling around the two soldiers who slumped to the ground in growing crimson pools. Merciless were Eirian's arrows of white light and cruel was the war that ended the two men with sorrowful hearts and tears in their eyes.

"I don't want to know that spell, do I?" Setareh asked, her voice quivered with the words and her fingers tightened on Eirian's shoulders.

"No." was Eirian's simple response. Again they shot through the offensive spells, leaving behind a gaping hole in the mound of earth from one of the mages. Setareh squinted her eyes, a frown twisting her angelic face. She knew they were moving, at impeccable speeds that should've had her clutching at Eirian for dear life; and yet she wasn't. Instead she remained sitting on Eirian's back as if she were on horseback, the wind pushing into her face was just as gentle as a horse's gallop. The brief realization made her wonder if perhaps Eirian was making an effort with her current comfort though she knew no such effort was made that haunting morning when they had been caught unawares at the foothills of Ashan and crescent mountains. They caught up with the last soldier just as he ducked around a corner, two other soldiers shouted in warning as they readied their weapons before themselves.

"Simple soldiers," Setareh murmured, her sight activating to show her the past of the men before her. "No magic here." Yet, with the fall of her last words, the spears lit up with magical inscriptions, Eirian shouted in surprise; barely managing to right herself in time to use her wings to deflect the surprise attack aimed at them.

"No magic huh?!" Eirian barked as she landed on the cobble stone street, Setareh slipping from her back to crumble onto the street. "Setareh-Kaur?" Eirian looked down on Setareh, her glowing eyes widening as she watched blood spill past Setareh's nose and the dumbfounded expression on her tattooed face.

"Hah!" One of the soldiers laughed, lunging forward to cut Eirian. Seeing his attack from the corner of her eye, she swept one wing at him dismissively but watched in horror as her armor's wings were batted aside and her dragon let out a terrible shrike. As the man's swing turned full scale, Setareh coughed a mouthful of blood onto the white swaths of her dress with a look of bewilderment. The magical armor ripped itself from Eirian to entangle itself around the spear with another cry of pain, crumbling back into its weak hatchling state paces away. The man cursed as his spear was ripped from his palms, still wrapped around the tiny dragon-hatchling, he quickly reached into his back pouch for extra weapons.

"Take this!" The man twirled his daggers in his hands, aiming another swipe that would cut deep into Eirian's chest. The only thing he didn't take account on, was Eirian's freely wondering magic. With a clash of sparks, glowing runes and white mirror fractures, the soldier and Eirian remained in a dead lock inches apart. It was pure instinct to react with braced arms, Eirian adjusted her feet for a stronger balance while she resisted the power of the ominous glowing blades.

"I understand now," Eirian murmured, her clan marks glittered to life. The two small dots beneath her left eye sparked and glittered like white flames threatening to come to life. Setareh coughed weakly, her body trembling as she braced herself with her weak arms, her thin-tattooed fingers tangling in her bloodied skirts soaking in the crimson splashed cobblestones. "Angra-ore." The soldier smirked at Eirian, his dark eyes glinting in triumph in her revealed face. There had been no time for her to hide herself before her dragon released her and no time to whisper the spell before the man was crashing down on her with new blades. Her true self, unmasked and without shield was revealed to his black abyss eyes and cruel smile.

"Of course, there's plenty of bloody-souls in Urmër." the soldier retorted smugly, using another name for the cursed minerals of his homeland. Eirian ground her teeth together, Angra-ore was a mineral that was formed by the corpse of humans—*hundreds* of humans—who were all burned alive and brimming with resentment. Another way for Angra-ore to be forged is naturally, over the span of centuries, where the land is soaked in the blood of *thousands*. The more blood or corpses left behind, the stronger the Angra-ore.

"Ee....eera...eeree...ree...aaannn." Setareh wheezed weakly, her sight doubling as she trembled, struggling to keep herself upright in her suddenly weakened state.

"If you give up now, I'm sure the Uraibek will be happy to take you as his concubine." The navy-coated soldier smirked at Eirian, believing he won the battle the moment she used magic and he relied on the cursed blades.

"I'm *twelve*," Eirian stressed her age with a look of disgust.

"So?" The solder retorted, as if her age was something trivial. "Uraibek won't take tattoo-girl over there, her face is too fucked up for him. But I would be reworded with her, so I don't mind having a tattooed woman in my bed." Setareh shivered as she felt the man's eyes slide towards her, her body weakening further as the blade wavered against Eirian's glass-incased arms.

"Setareh-Kaur!" Eirian called, her voice tinging in panic as she took a step back but remained focused on the soldier struggling against her glass shields.

"To bad you can't keep this up girly!" The soldier cackled at her, grinning widely at the sight of her trembling arms. "Angra-ore deprives one of magical abilities. Sooner or later, you'll run out of strength to use!" Setareh coughed and collapsed against the cobble stones, unable to keep herself up any longer. "See? Your friend already accepted her fate. Soon, you'll accept that you too belong *beneath men*." Like a flip had been switched, the white fragments surrounding Eirian and Setareh froze, as if time had stopped around them. The man blinked, frowning as he saw that the white fragments became motionless, even the one beneath his humming cursed blade stopped trembling.

"Tell me, child of mists, where is your friend?" Eirian asked, her voice whisper soft and empty of all emotion. The soldier's brows pinched in confusion, one of the white mirror-fragments glinted and as his eyes snapped up to look at it, he saw the dark vague form with a strange spike reaching high into the air. Without warning, the white fragments glinted and once more converged on the soldier before he could react to the attack. Deep gashes carved into his flesh, spilling out his organs and inner fluids. The man tilted back with the force of the fragments, his slowly darkening mind reeled as his blurry sight landed on his once companion. His comrade remained motionless, his eyes open and his body perfectly still, his back straight and his face empty of emotion but the blood pooling at his feet was unmistakable. Sprouting from the man's head was a long thin pole, glowing ominous white even around the soldier's cranium and burying itself into the cobble stones at his feet.

His comrade had died long before he could even deliver the first strike.

"d-d-d-d-d-d-d-d-d," his stuttering went unanswered as his eyes swiveled towards the young girl standing at his knees, face as passive as a Venice mask.

"You should respect your betters, *boy*." Eirian drawled coldly, with her words brought forth the glittering white of her magic, rising to hide her human-face beneath her serpentine-mask. She summoned her assortment of white fragments and pulled them back to herself, distorting her image into that of a human-lizard-hybrid colored in shades of black and silver. Spinning on her heal, Eirian took the necessary steps to kneel beside the unconscious form of Setareh. Sighing heavily, Eirian held out her hand and the Angra-ore blades shattered as they were ripped apart into particles of dust. Curling her fingers and whispering an ancient word under breath, the Angra-ore was purified and the captured magic turned into green glowing liquid that pooled into a small glass bottle.

"Angra-Ore dose more than sap magical abilities," Eirian murmured as she gently splattered the eerie glowing liquid over Setareh. "It steals life forces too. That's why you're so weak, Setareh-Kaur. Your family has always been standing on the border of in-between, so the ore has always had the greatest effect on you." Suddenly Setareh started coughing, wheezing breathlessly as she clutched at her chest. Her breaths were short and desperate, her lungs burning and her eyes hazy, as if she just awoke from being beneath water for too long.

"Careful Setareh-Kaur," Eirian murmured as she dispersed the glass bottle and scattered the last of the strange liquid over the teenager's body. "It'll take you time to recover what you lost. Angra-ore isn't something to be trifled with."

"Ee-ee—"

"Shhh, Setareh-Kaur. All is well." Eirian murmured, smiling gently at the weakened teenager. "I took back what they stole and returned it to you. However you still lost a great deal of strength, so you need to rest now." Weakly Setareh nodded, her eyes closing once more.

Eirian nodded to herself, using her magic to surround them in a thick glittering white mist. She lifted Setareh from the ground, lifted Ryū from his entanglement with the Angra-ore-spear and walked into the nearest building. Finding a room on the third floor, Eirian carefully lowered Setareh to the bed, covered her with a filthy blanket and left the teenager.

Of course the blonde wasn't alone, Eirian performed a spell that created a living reflection of herself, a copy of her person that required none of the necessities of living. The reflection would protect Setareh while Eirian herself hunted down the last soldier. The only problem with the reflection spell was that Eirian wasn't able to hold up the spell that contorted her facial features. She would have to drop her serpent-mask in order to protect Setareh. Nodding in silent agreement to her reflection, she watched as the mirrored-creature took a seat on a desk at Setareh's feet. Eirian decided she could take the risk, it wouldn't take much to destroy anyone who saw her face for too long. Eirian had the distinctive impression the soldiers were leading them away from the 'treasure'. Lifting her weak dragon into her arms, Eirian walked out of the room, using her magic to make her steps silent and set undetectable traps behind for her reflection. She floated down the stairs, her feet glowing as she touched down on the ground floor and remained silent as she continued to leave the building.

Eirian glanced at the corpses she left behind, ordinarily she would be tasked with reducing their bodies to ashes and ensuring their souls went to the afterlife but she felt no such obligation this time around. The soldier she gutted disgusted her the most but that was nothing compared to the memories she had seen from the other man's mind. She had wanted to know why these two were left behind with Angra-ore and so had pierced the other man's head with one of her magical fragments but the information she received from the fragment was none that she had ever wanted to know. Words could not describe her fury and disgust for the men with blackened hearts and bloodied hands. So for their crimes against humanity, and their unspeakable actions, she left their bodies to rout and their souls to wonder in misery.

Eirian stared at the shimmery dark figures of the men's souls, looking about confused and bewildered, their silver eyes glossy and hazy. There was nothing she could do about the darkness in their hearts and she felt no desire to free them from it. So she turned away from the tormented souls of the soldiers and walked silently away from the building and the corpses. Using her magic she followed the magical traces of the man who tried to rush away from her with the aid of his magic. He should've known that such tactics were easily traceable and would only lead to his own demise. Sighing in aggravation as the night drawled on, Eirian calmly followed the magic-footprints, her arms cradling her whimpering dragon-armor. It wasn't until she reached three blocks away from Setareh that she stopped walking, wondering just where the man was going as he was leading her away from the heart of the city.

"Tirta: Dayū!" She watched passively the river to her left shot up a geyser that then rained down on her a thousand needles. Her body was ripped apart and her blood spilled across the cobble stones, leaving her helpless to the attack of the last Urmër soldiers.

"Alright! Nice hit Mūir!" The soldier she was tracking shouted from the safety of another building. The priest in question pulled himself out of the river with a victorious grin. Using old runes he pulled himself to the surface and walked quickly to the river edge before he lost control of the spell. His robes of sapphire and gold rippled and draped with every hurried step he took towards the building the soldier was hiding in.

"Tīamat, I thought you said the enemy was strong?" the priest questioned as he hurried towards the young soldier. "That was too easy!"

"Was it?" both men froze at the sound of her voice, their eyes widening as they realized that Eirian had not died with the simple attack. "Maor does it better." Eirian was sitting on one of the crates in the building, looking bored as she petted the scaly head of her dragon armor, staring passively at the two men with cold lilac eyes.

"Hello, I am Eirian of the forest." She was bored with this traditional response, the purpose of having to introduce herself when she wasn't in uniform was annoying to say the least. These two men wouldn't even live long enough to see dawn and yet she had to tell them who *she* was. "I would like to know what you did with the Desert Worm's Nest." The two were stunned silent for a moment before her words sank in, then the soldier yelped shrilly (like a girl if she were to be honest with herself) before flinging a dagger at her blindly as he tried to scrabble out the window he was previously braced in.

"Run!" the priest, Mūir, shouted desperately as he snatched the soldier out of the window and let him tumble to the ground at his feet. Ryū lifted his head and let out a sharp bark, his reflexive power sending the dagger back out the window and into Mūir's shoulder. The priest shouted in pain, stumbling back as the dagger logged itself deep into his shoulder joint.

"Brother!" Tīamat, the soldier, shouted, panic twisting his face. The priest winced as he stumbled away from the building, tripping over his own feet he landed on the cobblestone road. "Stay away!" the soldier shouted desperately, moving to crouch protectively in front of the priest with a short sword held before himself. "I'll tell you what you want!" Eirian's magic floated around her like glowing dust, the window's gap lengthened to the ground as the white dust ate away at the bottom portion of the window, creating a large doorway instead of a window.

"I am looking for the desert worm's nest," Eirian drawled as she let her magic swirl around her, lifting her into the air to float gracefully towards the new doorway. "Do not bother to tell me it is outside the city. If that was the case your priests would not need to bring the demon of oceans to the city center."

"Don't Tīamat!" Mūir shouted, panic twisting his face as he pushed himself up onto his knees. "Don't betray the Uraibek for her!"

"She's a kid," Tīamat's voice cracked, his arms trembling with the weight of his sword. "What could she do against the Uraibek?" it was a question with an obvious answer but she did feel insulted with the 'kid' remark, so she answered with a tone of voice belying her irritation.

"I'm a dragoness," Eirian drawled, "There is plenty I can do against your army."

"Yeah we've noticed!" Tīamat barked at her, suddenly angry. "Why do you think we made a pact with Tregaron? We didn't want to agree to their terms but you guys didn't give us much choice!"

"its 'tri', *tri*, not 'trey'," Eirian corrected in annoyance.

"Tīamat!" Mūir called angrily, "Lets retreat! The others will be here soon!"

"Oh really?" Eirian questioned with a raised eyebrow. "I am of ancient times and ways, the magic I hold is as great as the forest I reside and my knowledge as fast as the great ocean. Do not underestimate me for my age. Now tell me what I want to know."

"Tīamat!" Mūir cried out, his eyes swiveling around them, searching for an enemy that wasn't the child standing before them.

"Where is the nest?" Eirian asked again, her patience running thin.

"City center," Tīamat answered quickly

"The demon is in city center." Eirian narrowed her eyes at him, she could hear the raised voices of the soldiers and their pounding feet that drew them closer and closer to their location.

"Correct," Mūir answered, his voice sharp like the crack of whip. "Now leave you cursed demon!"

"There! I found the Elishri!" A distant voice shouted, making the two siblings cringe as they had been spotted by their allies. Eirian stared passively at them for a moment, before smirking, making Tīamat cringe as he expected to be killed and Mūir to cry out in anguish as he expected his brother to die. The approaching soldiers, now aware that the brothers were under attack, let out shouts of dismay but their voices went unheard. Eirian's power burst out like a bomb around her, destroying the building she was still standing in and knocking the brothers unconscious. As they had given her what she wanted, and had not lied about it, she allowed her magic to protect them from the explosive spell she used. What happened to the approaching soldier's she didn't care, whether or not they remained conscious or perished was none of her concern. Not caring what the other soldier's thought, Eirian summoned up her magic to lift her into the air, taking on form of a great arrow. Before any of them grew enough strength to attack her, Eirian disappeared into the smoke filled sky, her glittering white magic disappearing like mist at dawn.

She created a small glass mirror, peering through it to spy on the slumbering princess before noting that the teenager was still safe and sound. Nodding her head patently, Eirian sent out three glowing white mirrors to search the burning city, hoping they'll discover her teammates before they discover enemies. Drifting back down to the building tops, careful not to jostle the thick ropes of the floating bombs and with her sightless-spell extra strong, she returned to the building she hid the princess. Stepping through the first-floor window, Eirian quickly went into the hall where one of her mini-mirrors discovered something useful.

Stopping halfway down the hall, Eirian pressed one glowing palm to the smooth surface of the simple hall mirror, smirking to herself as it connected with one of her mirrors overhead. Without hesitance she stepped through the mirror and reappeared through one of her own mirrors overhead in the hall of the third floor. Opening her eyes she stepped forward, unconcerned with the glittering crystals coating the hall and rooms of the apartment room. She entered the back-right room, her eyes sliding towards her small chunk of glittering crystals sitting on the doorframe before walking soundlessly inside. She murmured her mask-spell as she walked to the bed, her double shattering apart only to reform around Eirian as her serpentine-figure. She quickly checked Setareh's pulse and temperature before moving towards the surprisingly-undamaged window. She tapped a nail along the window frame and her magic quickly carved out ancient runes and inscriptions that would hide her physical appearance. As she counted 'ten-Nauseas', she took a seat in the window frame, waiting for the little intruder to attack.

"H-H-H-Hello," the soft feminine voice stuttered out, it was only the child's age that spared the girl from being attacked. Eirian turned her attention away from the cold black-stained sky over the city and looked towards the entrance of the room. Hiding half-heartedly behind the door was a dirty little girl with choppy fuscia locks hanging limply around the girl's freckled round face and partially obscuring her eyes. Her simple dress of yellow and white was dirty with ash and mud, stained with blood and soot, torn in places where blades and hooks had nearly ended her young life. With how many days had passed and with the cruelty of the Urmër-soldier's, Eirian was sure that there were no children left of the city. It confused her greatly that there was in fact a child still remaining.

"Hello," She answered simply. "Neon," Eirian hummed thoughtfully as the magical light of her mirror dust floated closer to the girl, revealing her unnaturally bright yellow eyes. Eirian narrowed her eyes at the young girl, she hadn't flinched back with the appearance of light and her eyes lacked a pupil. This girl was *blind*.

"Um," the girl was confused with Eirian's greeting but chose to ignore it, her round face pinching in uncertainty. "I... I'm Xiadani... Backus..."

"Zai-daw-nee... Baw-k-us?" Eirian asked with a raised eyebrow

"Sigh-a-daw-knee!" the girl corrected with a sharp snap to her voice, as if she wasn't used to having to correct the people around her. Eirian hummed in acknowledgement, introducing herself quickly before looking back out the window, her eyes narrowing as a group of soldiers went racing past. Her mirrors still hadn't returned so her teammates were either hiding splendidly or they were captured, which wasn't realistically possible.

"Um... dragon-lady... how come..." Eirian turned her attention towards Xiadani, staring into her eerie-golden eyes. "...why... c-c-can I... s-s-see... you?" the girl was shrinking behind the door again, losing confidence as she spoke to the older girl.

"What do you mean?" Eirian asked, frowning at the little girl. Her confusion stemmed from the fact that she had her serpent-mask on and even if she didn't speak that spell, the little girl was blind; she shouldn't be able to see Eirian at all.

"Uh-um... u-u-usury e-everyone l-looks like colors, different shades of colors bu-bu-but y-y-you... I... I can *see you*. Like... every detail... your hair, your eyes, your clothes... normally everyone is just blobs of color... so..." Xiadani looked up at Eirian, confused and afraid but determined to get her answers. "So how come I can see you so *clearly?*"

"Ah, I see," Eirian smiled fondly at Xiadani. "You must also be a descendent of Albena. I am glad to find you before our enemy." So, that explained how the girl survived. Xiadani's natural power of aura detection and magical-awareness spared her life from traps, soldiers, and spells alike. No wonder she survived for so long in the battlefield despite being 'blind'.

"What do you mean?" Xiadani asked her, a little bit of confidence growing in her as her back straightened and her blind-eyes seemed to lock unmistakably on Eirian.

"How much of your history do you know?" Eirian asked instead

"Lots," Xiadani shrugged. "Mommy told me lots about Aeoman's history and our family history."

"Uh-huh," Eirian stared dully at the little girl. "So… how many children do you know?"

"N-not many," Xiadani grumbled, shrinking behind the door again. "Papa says it's too dangerous for me to go outside, that's why I always stayed in my room with mommy."

"So… this is the first time you've ever been outside?"

"Uh-huh," Xiadani nodded, looking up at Eirian through her choppy bangs again. "Daddy told mommy and me to run but then those monsters came and I hid and mommy led them away but now I can't find mommy…" Eirian sighed heavily, she could already tell the woman's fate. The Albena family weren't physically strong but their power of sight wasn't to be trifled with. It wasn't likely that the woman was still living, she was properly eaten by one of the worms, like many others of this city.

"If you're not too scared of me, I can promise you someplace safe." Eirian told the little girl. "It is far from the fires of this city and far from those who would want to hurt you. There is a place where many others are just like you and have the same eyes as you, they will welcome you with open arms. You will never be locked away again and can play with many others your age."

"What about mommy and daddy?" Xiadani asked, hope in her voice.

"…I will not promise anything," Eirian answered slowly. "If they are found, they may join you in that safe place but if not, then you must go to this place with me. Understand?"

"Will mommy and daddy find me?"

"…properly," Eirian shrugged, "your mother should feel the pull of your magic leaving the city and follow you to the safe place. As for your father… I doubt he still lives."

"But if he is… could he find mommy and me?" Xiadani asked, her lips trembling as tears gathered in her eyes. Eirian sighed heavily, her shoulder's slumping.

"I don't know," she answered at last. "Anything is possible."

Ω Ω Ω

Setareh, princess of seers, awoke with a drowsy mind and heavy body. For once her dreams were nonexistent, leaving nothing but the impression of darkness and emptiness swallowing her heart. How many years had it been since she last dreamed of nothing? How long since her last moment of clarity? How long since sleep last comforted her instead of terrified her? Soft whispers sounded and she turned her face towards the whispery voices, wondering who could be with her. A great abyss of neon colors greeted her sight, along with several figures of glowing pastel. The brightest one, glorious teal and gold, stood closest to her. Beside it a figure of pure moonlight stepped forward, she couldn't see who the figure was but she could sense a great sadness from it. Like a deep well made of tears and regret, slowly consuming the figure of moonlight. Gently the glowing figure reached out a small pale hand and touched her cheek, silent tears dripping from its moonlight-face.

"May the Trinity arise anew. For now the Erebus awakens and so the Fay sleeps once more." She felt the tears roll down her cheeks, images of indescribable sorrow swarmed her mind, bringing forth her own tears. Never had her vision been so heart breaking as the images bestowed to her by this strange glowing figure.

"Forgive me my friend," the white figure murmured. "Your task is not yet complete, stay strong… Julie…" the teal figure reached forward and pulled the gentle moonlight figure away, holding them close and accepting the quiet sobs. She wanted to move, to reach out to that strange moonlight figure, to embrace them and whisper reassurances but she couldn't move. The more her tears flowed, the more blurred her surroundings became and slowly the quiet sobbing was pushed away for hurried murmurs. It took her mind a moment to register the new worried voices surrounding her and the anxious scarlet eyes suddenly staring down on her.

"Setareh-Kaur, are you awake now?" Ziya asked gently, his scarlet eyes calm and soft like red silk. Blinking many times, Setareh looked about herself before realizing that she was in his hands and leaning against a dirty gray wall. The bed nearby was a mess of dirty sheets, near the window Eirian was crouched with a worried face and a sobbing child in her arms, in the doorway Maor was looking at the wall at her back in confusion and Barak was crouched in the window, looking as confused as Maor.

Frowning at the boys Setareh turned to look at the wall at her back, her bright blue eyes widening at the deep scrapes in the gray plaster, highlighted by splatters of blood. Gasping, Setareh slapped her hands to her mouth before flinching away from her own palms as the taste of copper filled her mouth and something wet splashed her face. Looking down at her hands in horror she discovered deep gashes in her palms and fingers. Yet no pain came to her, so numb was her mind that she couldn't feel the ugly tears still spilling blood.

"You awoke with glowing eyes of gold," Eirian murmured from the base of the window. "You grabbed one of my mirrors and carved that onto the wall." Setareh looked up at the wall again, staring at the message with fresh tears rolling down her cheeks; her bloody palms cradled protectively into her chest.

Arise beloved Syzygy,
To destroy the Erebus for eternity
And awaken the Fay of victory.

Chapter 13

"I'm fairly sure no one wants to know the meaning of these words so let's just go." Barak said quickly, his fingers tightening on the windowsill between his feet. "Eirian, who's the kid?" his glowing eyes of jade landed on the little girl in Eirian's arms, drawing everyone's attentions temporarily to the pink haired child.

"I'm Xiadani Buckus," the girl huffed, seemingly glaring in Barak's general direction.

"A descendent of the Albena family, a blind one." Eirian murmured, her arms tightening on the girl briefly.

"I'll have a summoning that'll take her to the forest edge, away from this blood and war." Ziya murmured, a golden seal of stars and light circling into formation at his feet without a twitch of his fingers. From its golden glow an armored feline arose, opening its glowing pearl eyes it stared regally at Ziya. The feline's head sat level with Ziya's waist, his thin body was clearly built for speed, his sharp pointed ears twitched back and forth in irritation, his massive golden paws kneaded the dirty floor before wrapping his armored tail around them with a sense of disgust.

"For what purpose have you summoned me?" The feline asked, its voice surprisingly feminine sounding, shaking out its shoulders to sit straight as it gave the grown man a board look.

"I need you to take that child to safety," Ziya murmured as he kneeled before the regal creature. "Please take her to city edge, there is a sky-barrier so you can't leave the city but please protect her until I can kill the barrier-caster."

"I rely on your magic to remain in this realm." The large feline murmured, its voice low like a mountain's drawl. *"To stray too far is unwise for a sightless child."*

"To remain in a city full of desert worms is even more unwise for a sightless child," Ziya replied. The feline sniffed the air twice before sneezing with an expression of revulsion on its golden-armored face.

"To safety I'll take the sightless one but not far from you can I wander." The feline agreed, its voice a low growl. No one could tell what disgusted it more: the thought of carrying a defenseless child or encountering the desert worms.

"My mirrors act as extensions," Eirian murmured thoughtfully, her teeth nibbling on her pink lips. "Perhaps… you could take her to a safer place?"

"I will go to city edge and await the kit's arrival," the golden feline seemed to glare at Eirian through white-glowing eyes. For a moment it almost looked as if the armored summoning had more to say but instead lowered itself for the blind girl to climb aboard. Xiadani hesitated for a moment, shying away from the golden-glowing creature before hearing a gentle chirp of birds. Xiadani turned her blind eyes towards the sound and watched as a glob of white scales and violet eyes hobbled towards her with weak legs. Eirian tsked worriedly as she twisted away from Xiadani, lifting the black-baby dragon into her arms before wrapping her left arm around the pinkette again. The baby dragon stared at Xiadani expectantly for a moment, seemingly unconcerned with the

blind eyes staring back at it. Sniffing miserably, Xiadani twisted her body about to wrap her arms around Eirian, trying hard not to cry as the older girl tightened her free arm around the tiny body.

"Go on little one," Eirian murmured as she loosened her hold. "He'll keep you safe." Nodding slowly, Xiadani released Eirian and turned towards the glowing feline figure. Taking a deep breath, Xiadani flung her hands out and took slow hesitant steps towards the figure. While she could see magic, people and spells; inanimate objects were another story. The feline summoning was patent as it waited for the blind girl to reach him, touching his shoulder and back with tiny trembling hands. The feline stooped a little lower so the girl could swing her leg over his back, once she did he rose his feet carefully. Barak carefully lowered himself from the windowsill, stepping aside so the giant golden creature had plenty room to leap out without harming anyone.

"*Lay down little one. While I will protect you from soldiers and worms, windowsills are not lethal—just painful.*" The feline instructed, Xiadani stifled a snicker and wrapped one hand around her smiling lips. Leaning forward till her face was pressed against its shoulders, Xiadani wrapped her tiny arms around its neck and tightened her legs around its thin body. The feline glanced once back at Ziya, as if gouging a reaction or waiting for another order, before bounding out the window.

"Alright everyone, you ready to finish these worms?" Ziya asked, turning to look at his three students. Maor moved closer to the windowsill, his navy dragon armor answering in a low rumble. Barak couldn't hide his grin if his mask covered his eyes, as it was the hazel-eyed teen flung his arms behind his head and waited expectantly. Eirian remained crouched at the base of the window, her two teammates on either side of herself, her armor refusing to expand to wrap around her. Sighing as the tiny black dragon snuggled into her arms, Eirian understood quickly that she would have to be fighting without her armor.

"As much as I'll ever be." Eirian mumbled, petting her still weakened armor with a mournful expression. "I won't be able to fly with you Isha, Ryū is still recovering from his meeting with the Angra-ore."

"Angra-ore?" Ziya repeated, straightening with the new threat. "Did it touch you?"

"No, of course not," Eirian snapped at him, offended that he thought she would be so foolish. "Angra-ore is responsible for Setareh-Kaur's current condition." Ziya glanced back at the Setareh, watching her stare at her still bloody palms with an expression of bewilderment and fear. Sighing heavily, Ziya created a small golden glowing seal in the air and let a small ball of light fall from its surface. He tossed it at Setareh and she squeaked as she reflexively caught it with her hands, wincing as if she expected searing pain to flare through her palms. But no such pain came and she opened her eyes to stare at the golden ball of light, watching in amazement as it sat in palms, tiny little wisps of ghostly gold light brushing against her wounds with warmth. It didn't take her long to realize that the ball of light was healing the gashes, the process would be slow but she doubted she'd have a scare left when it was done.

"There's no way you had contact with the forbidden ore and not get harmed by it." Maor frowned behind is mask, drawing Setareh's attention from the golden orb to the team of dragon-children.

"I am well," Eirian hissed at him, angry that he thought her careless enough to be touched by the awful mineral. "Ryū is the one who is harmed." The baby dragon yawned sleepily, blinking silver eyes at Maor before settling again.

"Which meant that without him you could've been killed." Ziya retorted, crouching to get a better look at the baby dragon. "Remain here and protect Setareh-Kaur, Eirian, it is too dangerous for you now."

"But!"

"Without your armor you are *defenseless*, I will not have you fighting without protection."

241

"I can fight! I have my magic!"

"Do not be so vane as to think that it'll last forever." Ziya hissed, his crimson eyes glinting furiously at her. "Use too much and you will fall, just as all proud-mages fall with advanced spells."

"Ziya-Isha!"

"Aiello-sarai, do you as you've been *ordered*." Ziya snarled the words the same way a cat growled a warning, making the boys straighten in surprise and for Eirian to cringe back with an expression of betrayal on her pale face. "I will not repeat myself *Sarai*, remain with Setareh-Kaur. She will need your protection." He didn't remain to listen to her argument, he grabbed Maor and Barak as he dashed out the window and disappeared into the gray-dawn. Eirian remained at the base of the window, refusing to move as dark emotions flowed through her like raging storms and billowing flames.

Hot and cold were the fires and waves cursing through her veins, whispered taunts and snarled curses waged war in her mind. Though the old words, 'Aiello-sarai' remained rampant, the voices whispering them went from kind and manipulative to cold and hateful. The voices went racing through her mind like the memories of cold dark rooms and aching limbs. How she hated that 'honored title', a curse of who was born first was more like it. She knew Ziya was just trying to protect her, as he promised to protect their team many years ago, but it still *hurt*. He knew, better than anyone else, how much those words hurt her, how much she dreaded hearing them, how much she wished to be anything but the heiress of a family of tattooed fools.

Two more days passed before Setareh could even gain the strength to stand on her own, even before her great injury she was not physically fit so her weaker constitution never truly improved. At least not in Eirian's eyes. She knew Setareh was struggling to recover from the Angra-ore and so made no move to improve the teen's efforts at pushing her own body. Recovery from the cursed mineral was something that had to be done alone, there was only so much that Eirian herself could do for the princess. On the third day, Eirian was pleased to see that Setareh was good enough to travel, though they would have to be careful not to overexert her still weak body.

"How long have we been here, Lady Eirian?" Setareh asked as Eirian lifted all the spells she had on the building and carefully walked down the hall of the home they stole three days prior. "Seems like years now…"

"Not quite thirteen days," Eirian answered simply, her hands waving about as her crystals, glass and mirror fragments converged on her person, slowly piecing her serpentine-mask back together. "Tonight at ten, we'll have been here exactly thirteen days." Setareh stopped walking for a moment, watching as the last of Eirian's magic surrounded her in bursts of white robes over emphasizing her serpent-human body. On Eirian's shoulder Ryū looked back at Setareh, seemingly grinning at her as he chirped cheerfully. Setareh understood then that Eirian did not need Ryū to look like a serpent, she had a set amount of spells that the preteen used to disguise her physical appearance.

"…should we really be leaving this place?" Setareh asked as Eirian used one of her mirrors to look outside and down the steps of the building. "Ziya said to remain here."

"He told me to remain *with* you." Eirian replied. "After all, you would need my protection." Setareh watched as Eirian turned back to look at her with a smirk and realization dawned on her like the memory of their first night in the city.

"The nest?" Setareh frowned at Eirian in disapproval, "Why didn't you tell them when they were here?"

"Because they arrived a few moments before you awoke and freaked out on the wall." Eirian replied, rolling her eyes as she stepped back and held out a hand to Setareh. "Ready to kill an army?"

"A princess dose not kill," Setareh huffed, insulted with the question despite the smirk playing along her lips.

"You're right Setareh-Kaur, she just gets her soldiers to do it for her." Eirian grinned as Setareh placed her hand in her own. "Now what are the chances of mortal men standing against dragons?"

"Not a good one," Setareh answered, she didn't notice the glow on her face nor the shapes taking shape in her eyes as they walked out of the building. Outside was a mass of mist, fog and gray clouds obscuring the summer sun; Eirian had no doubt that Maor was all too pleased with the conditions of the day. They hurried down the flights of stairs, bursting out onto the misty cobble stone street Eirian created a large board of white glass for Setareh to ride while she raced along the cobble stones; their destination was the towering navy and crimson flags. They carefully moved through the buildings and alleyways, Eirian whispering various spells to keep them silent and invisible while they passed through more open areas. They had both noted that while the center of the city appeared to be slowly transforming more and more into main-camp for their enamines, the only ones seemingly remaining in city-center were low ranking mages.

"Not good," Eirian murmured as they reached the city center, peering over the edge of a roof to examine the mages and soldiers below. They discovered dozens of people all lined up in neat little kneeling lines. Men and women, a few children, all bound with their hands behind their backs and attached to their ankles. The most outstanding features about all of them were their bright, neon, hair; signature appearance of those from ancient households. Nearby, in a pile of bodies that had yet to be taken out to the worms, was a tall woman with skin like chocolate milk, sightless mismatched eyes of brown and gold, and hair of three tones of green. Gradient green hair was a common feature to only one family tree and Eirian knew the gentle giants would be none too pleased with the discovery of one of their own.

"Titenwood," Eirian murmured, her scaled face looking about hurriedly. A soft chirp sounded behind them and she turned around in time to see several sparrows, crows, robins and several other types of birds flitting onto the roof around Setareh and herself. Sighing heavily and with a look of regret on her face, Eirian took a step toward the dozens of birds before sweeping into a low kneel. One fist pressed to her heart, one knee buried into the hard stone roof of the building they stood on, her head bowed and her shoulders slumped.

"Forgive me Avians for I did not arrive in time," Eirian murmured. A concussion of chirping sounded: annoyed, consoling, heartbroken, she did not stop the birds from their mourning of their friend. "She must've fought and thus... was killed before I could save her." The chirping accelerated into a crescendo, escalating out of control before the birds took off for the sky, their voices ringing out in displeasure and sorrow. The roving soldiers below looked but didn't react to the swirling masses of avians; at least not before the birds swirled and dived like a thousand arrows raining down from the gods above. The soldiers howled and screamed, the tied and bound screeching in terror, eyes wide in horror as they watched the corpses shift and move beneath the assault. Before long several soldiers were stumbling away, unpleasantly retching into barrels while several civilians hurled over themselves with the bloody sight.

As was the Titanwood's tradition, their dead were devoured by their avian friends.

"Come," Eirian murmured, voice soft as she rose once more to her feet. Eirian didn't wait for a response before she started for the backside of the building, white fragments surrounding her like an aura of sorrow. Setareh glanced back at the corpse pile being demolished beneath the birds, shuttering in terror and disgust, she quickly hurried after Eirian. Neither girl spoke as they clasp hands and stepped out onto a glittering white bridge, instantly hiding from sight with nothing more than a whisper. They dashed side by side, Eirian using her magic shards to keep Setareh afloat as they rushed towards another plaza. More hostages, these ones less vibrant but still colorful compared to their previous counter parts, their eyes glowing brightly only to dim and repeat the process. Their eyes flared brightly as their magic surged forward to protect them; then their eyes dimmed as their magical power was drained away through the ropes binding them to a large stone chest.

"Monsters," Eirian hissed. "That's why they bound all those with magical power and killed anyone who stood against them." She backed away from edge, Setareh hurrying after her to the opposite edge where they both crouched down behind the wall. Eirian summoned up her white fragments and hid them both from the senses of anyone who may have been looking in their direction.

"Now what?" Setareh asked, own face pale as her trembling fingers clutched together before herself. Eirian ignored her as she made a basic map with her white shards, detailing only where they've been in thick white blocks. "Where are we going to look next?"

"The desert worm's nest couldn't be near water, the chance of destroying them is too great." Eirian murmured, smaller dust-sized fragments taking form throughout the blocks, looking like a shimmering white river.

"Maybe that's what they want?" Setareh asked, the elaborate black flowers on her face turning a dull brown-red. "If they become too much for the guards to handle, it would be easiest to handle them this way." Eirian blinked, her moonstone eyes growing wide as she sucked in a sharp breath of air, realizing just how correct Setareh was with her deduction. The hole time Eirian had not looked at the princess, choosing instead to watch as the glittering white map took shape between her outstretched palms.

"Why didn't I see it before?" Eirian hissed to herself, "Of course you're right Setareh-Kaur." She hunched herself closer to the simple map, staring at the shimmery rivers expectantly. "The city has three plazas… but only one of them is near the river! Here! The one furthest west! That's where we'll find the nest!" Setareh sighed in relief, they've spent too many days searching for a nest that should've been easily spotted by now. Setareh knew that she could've foreseen the location of the nest, she could've led them straight to it but Eirian did not ask her to use her abilities; none of the dragons did. As they traveled from rooftop to rooftop, Setareh wondered why Eirian did not ask her to locate the nest. Surly if Eirian did they could've left this city many days ago by now. It worried her that they remained for so long, none of the other worlds depicted them remaining in Niyatara City for so long.

"Lady Eirian," Setareh started, then stopped as she spotted a platinum-haired soldier rushing towards them. Eirian noticed and quickly hid then beneath the edge of a store, her glowing eyes peeking through the stone to watch the soldier rush past. "Um… why did you not ask me to use my powers to find the nest?"

"Setareh-Kaur, you were either running for your life, knocked out, freaking out on a wall, lost in a vision, or recovering from a poison." Eirian lowered herself back down to Setareh's side, giving the older teenager a dull look. "Just when in the past two weeks could I have possibly asked you to locate the poison worm nest?" Setareh blinked slowly at the question, thrown for a loop as she stared into the ghostly eyes of the preteen. Then, slowly, little by little, the memories of the past two weeks returned to her mind and she realized that Eirian was by far more observant and considerate than anyone else the seer-family have ever encountered. To stop herself from giggling, Setareh bit her lip and wrapped her hands around her mouth, curling in on her side to keep herself from losing it in this moment of hide-and-seek.

"He's gone Setareh-Kaur, we should keep moving." Eirian said, seemingly not noticing Setareh's small moment of joy.

"Yes lady Eirian." It was their luck that the buildings of the three plazas were close together, easily within jumping distance. Before the next platoon of soldiers could arrive as back up for the second plaza, Eirian and Setareh had arrived at the furthest plaza: waterway central. Many of the bridges and walkways were destroyed, leaving behind nothing but a small floating building kept in place by a dozen and half ropes. The girls shared looks, then they were leaping forward, Eirian's white-glass magic sliding into place; guiding them to their destinations. They landed on the bridge of the floating house, quickly they entered the large house-like structure. At first they were bewildered, unable to comprehend the numerous boxes that filled the house. Eirian and Setareh moved further into the house, hesitant and unsure, they stayed close together. Further into the house, towards the back where the entrance could hardly be seen, was what they were looking for. Eirian stepped forward, closer to the hundreds of eggs that glowed gently in the darkness, a beautiful gentle oceanic teal. She could see small marks here and there carved into the pieces of wood and mortar, just enough lines and symbols to tell her what they were.

"Space-expansion rune-seal-arrays... four layers... several of them on each wall," Eirian whispered. "No wonder they could travel with so many..." she stopped, staring at the mounds of gently glowing eggs. "What fools took these eggs away... they don't need this many to terrorize Ashan."

"How will we destroy all these eggs?" Setareh asked, scared to speak to loudly should an egg hatch to the sound of her voice. She looked toward a nearby pile, pausing briefly to stare at the water dripping down the wall from being exposed to two much water. There was an egg, set crooked amongst its siblings, half melted by the water slowly crawling down from the wall. Inside was filling with the water, slowly but surely, the half-formed infant left unprotected suffered a painful death no doubt.

"Maor," Eirian murmured, retreating carefully, walking backwards as there was no room to turn around. "We need to get Maor." With the power to manipulate water to his will, Maor would be able to dispose of these eggs quickly.

"Lady Eirian," she turned to look over her shoulder, Setareh was holding a small stone hut. Its windows were aglow in gentle gold light, the base a simple four-pegged pedicel of integrate and beautiful knot-work ribbons, on its roof tiles showed patches of yellow light where the roof was too thin. "What is this?" Eirian was too scared to guess. The things Urmër was capable of doing were horrifying, there were too many atrocities for her to actively acknowledge—not without losing her mind first.

"Lady Eirian," Setareh looked up, horror contorting her face and making her violet glowing eyes too large in the partial darkness. Fear gripped at her heart, she looked back—she had no time to prepare before the on rush of sound and color of something seeming ripping straight through her body. In a second the thing was gone and she was left standing in the house, breathless and terrified. She patted at her belly, sure she had been ripped apart, but no, her flesh was unharmed. The creature that charged her rolled back through the shadows, like a hunting serpent in shallow waters. Eirian and Setareh remained still as the creature slowly crawled forward once more, revealing a pale wrinkly salamander face. Its body resembled more like a shell-less centipede with each limb ending in a human palm but instead of five digits, four bird talons twitched along cold gray stone. Two large fins, thick with bone splints and orange-red poison veins, sat with spikes one either side of its thin pointed face. Sharp intelligent golden irises peered up at them, a mixture of liquid gold with stripes of predawn dots and white-sand stripes. The creature was beautiful and terrifying, its intelligence alone was sure to rival even that of the most intelligent of humans.

"I've never seen a desert worm with limbs before," Setareh whispered.

"...queens often look different from their children," Eirian whispered. "She's the desert worm queen..."

"How is she here?" Setareh's voice shook, horror and terror mixing together to tremble her voice because her body refused to crumble under the weight of the intelligent eye peering down on her.

"She's not," Eirian sighed, watching as the queen lifted herself up, six legs curling into her body protectively as she towered over them, glaring with all the rightful wrath of any mother. "That stone... is a... it's an illusion stone. We... mages use it to lead false trails... and messages." The queen lowered her head, peering into Eirian's eyes, suspicion and distrust colored like orange-gold flames. Eirian didn't divert her eyes, she stared back at the queen, trying to convey her regret and sorrow for the other creature. Slowly Eirian pushed one hand back, waving towards the stone box Setareh held. The blonde carefully stepped forward, setting the stone in Eirian's hand and stepping back, keeping her own glittering sapphire eyes on the creature. The queen shuttled back, hissing and spitting like an angry feline.

"I'm so sorry," Eirian murmured to the queen, presenting the stone temple to the creature. "It's all an illusion, you have to break this stone. Do you see it?" The queen tilted her head to the side, looking back and forth between Eirian's face and the glowing stone box in her hands. Slowly the queen turned towards a pile of eggs, gesturing it with her pointed face carefully.

"Break it," Eirian murmured, releasing the stone and letting it topple to the wooden floor of the floating house. She knew the exact moment the Desert Worm Queen could no longer see them, the queen lifted her head, two flaps of skin pulled aside as she sniffed the air of her den. The queen couldn't see them but because their transition was still intact, they could see her. The Queen looked around, gently scraping paws over the stone where her eggs once sat, sniffing the air and gently butting her nose along the cave edges.

Then, when everything seemed to settle in her mind, she let out a roar. It sounded like a hundred women screaming in agony, like a nation's worth of mothers wailing for the loss of their child. The queen bowed her head, shuttling back as tears leaked out of her golden eyes, splashing against the cold dark stone of the nest. The tears pooled and gave a gentle teal glow, remaining together as a single liquid; like glowing teal jell. The queen then thrashed, crushing her little stone hut and disappearing from the girl's sight completely.

There was no time for the girls to be relieved, they barely had a moment to look at each other before a deafening roar outside froze the blood in their veins.

"FIRE!!"

They walked straight into a trap.

Ω Ω Ω

He had to hurry, if he didn't make it in time they could lose everything. He knew from the display of fire where Barak was, the boy was having a grand time smothering the mages of Trégaron. No doubt he was still holding a grudge from two years before. Maor was being all too careful with his spells, purposefully disabling Urmër's mages and evacuating the surviving populace of Niyatara. What a sight those few survivors must be viewing, watching the Naoska river float over head while walking on the river floor must be fascinating to them. All the same, he was tasked with finding the princess and their most elusive teammate. Eirian, when she chose to be, could be the most problematic child in existence. He thought he made himself clear to her, keeping Setareh safe in the apartment, but when he returned to guild her and the princess out of the city they were gone. Of course she didn't leave any of her shards of magic behind, knowing he could use it to track her but all the same, he *needed* to find her. They finally met up with their contact and a path out of the now burning down city was created, all they had to do was get to the safe location.

The problem? Finding the girls on their team.

He knew their primary objective had been derailed for the past few days, weeks, with the need to survive, locate survivors and find a way out but they had their answers now. They needed to leave the city. The desert worm nest wasn't something they could find, whatever enchantments on it were from before the Great Retreat. Only the family heads or Aibeks could find it now. An explosion, close to Waterway Centrale, filled the dark night sky with black smoke and white glitter—that wasn't glitter that was Eirian's magic! He twisted in the air, his golden wings converging on his person as he spiraled and turned on the edge of a pin, redirecting himself with the speed of a shooting star. He made no mistakes as he tore into the plaza, ripping solder and mage apart so he could reach the girls.

Where was Eirian? He couldn't see her as he stopped to search for her. Without her dragon armor, his dragon could not locate her. The dragon-armors were instilled to recolonize each other regardless of distance or debris between them. There was also the problem that his dragon armor had not come across an undragoned-Eirian; when they met she was always dressed in her armor or holding up her image-illusion. Eirian's magical spell, Zephaniah, always coated her person so perfectly not a fraction of her aura could be detected by their skillful dragon-armors. Eirian's spell often presented him with nothing but a white glowing crystalline-human-thing. Honestly it was annoying when all he could see was white-glass floating in a semi-human formation. Her skill with the illusion-spell has only increased and it's given him a great headache over the years.

"Eirian!" his voice sounded hollow in the smoky air, the crumbling buildings gave no empathy as they wavered on their foundations. There, a sparkle of glittering white gave way in a violent explosion, shoving back debris and revealing a small prone form. He found Setareh first, she was making awful wet sounding coughs, trying to push herself up from her very awkward landing place. The princess was alive, weak and seriously hurt somewhere but she was alive and that was good. So long as she was alive, Eirian could save her.

"Setareh-Kaur!" he dashed for Setareh, lifting her up by her too thin shoulders and shaking her. "Where is Eirian?!" the princess looked about in a daze, as if she couldn't comprehend something. Then he saw it, the feint red glow to her tattoos, and the violet inscriptions in her azure eyes. Setareh wasn't living in this world, she was seeing another now. Cursing he shoved Setareh away and shoved his mask apart, parting the dragon mouth wide open to reveal his face beneath. He coughed as the scent of flesh seared his nose and the black smoke stung his eyes, he already felt filthy but he felt worse as that hot air touched his tanned skin.

"Eirian!" his voice cracked painfully in his throat, making him gag as he desperately searched for his student. A white sleeve, thin and trembling, still blood stained and soot covered, rose at his side. He looked at Setareh, staring at her violet-glowing eyes, and watched as her fingers twisted strangely. Palm up, middle finger curling in to lock beneath the thumb. A small ball of white-gold light, so small and tiny, gathered in the space of her touching digits.

"Setareh-Kaur?" he asked and in return, the princess smiled. Then she released her finger and the simple flick resulted in a power worthy of the world's terror. It shot through the air faster than anything he had ever seen and the devastation left behind was horrifying. The debris on the ground were thrashed aside, making the buildings tilt away from the street side, mages and soldiers alike cried out as they were crushed and forced away.

"Two-twenty energy is…" Setareh began to fall, her voice fading as her eyes closed, she never finished her sentence. He barely managed to catch her, cringing as her head made a sickening slap against his scaled arm. He didn't have the faintest clue what a 'two-twenty energy' was but it had to have been powerful to wreck that kind of damage. He gently set Setareh down and summoned five golden blades to surround her, a thick golden cloth cursed between the blades. Knowing she was protected, he rose to his feet and dashed in the direction of the strange white-gold ball.

He clicked his mask back shut and dashed after the destructive orb. Three blocks and through a broken house, that's how far he traveled before he found his student. The ball of light from Setareh was whipping around Eirian in a blinding white circle; slashing at anyone who neared. At first he didn't see her, blinded by the hundreds of soldiers charging the slashing orbit, then he saw it. A glitter of light, a shutter of white glitter, crystalline glass fractures floating aimlessly over its master. He watched, hopelessly as a scaled tail and wings flashed out, batting back two mages who got too close. Ryū, the dragon-armor of his student, sheathed in Eirian's white crystals, still protecting his master despite her injured state. He gave a great roar and charged, ten more golden blades bursting into life, arcing around his person like wings as he slashed and dashed erratically.

Ω Ω Ω

"These will be the children you will be teaching." His leader waved a hand at the three children, two boys and a girl. An unusual combination for a team. Typically the girls were sent to team up together and do finer tuning of their magics and battle skills. Family boys, such as the two boys before him now, were typically given special training by their families and then given a free-highway pass to outer-forest-rotations. All the same the children were young, too young to be leaving the academy. He doubted they were even eight years old, still chubby-cheeked and teary-eyed.

Why would his master instruct him to take these three on as a dragon-team?

"Give them a chance," his leader ordered calmly. "Behruz Eld, Servass of Asharan, and young Aylin Aiello-Sarai; greet your teacher children." The girl looked longing at the door and the boys just gave him dull unimpressed looks.

Ω Ω Ω

More soldiers were pouring in, more magic-users were putting him on the defensive. A powerful burst of fire forced him to spiral before Eirian and use his swords as shields, he snarled as three more mages joined in on the spell. He couldn't see past his shields, he couldn't detect any soldiers nearing them, and he certainly couldn't look back at Eirian. He couldn't, he couldn't look back at her, not now.

What if she—no, he wouldn't think about it.

He'll focus on the enemy.

He'll take out anyone who hurts his students.

Ω Ω Ω

He stealthy maneuvered into the compound, secretly delighted that he could get past the fearsome Aiello-guardsmen. He steadily moved beneath a shadowed eve and glanced down at his dragon for which direction to go before following the tiny feminine creature's silent direction. As it turns out hiding his dragon's scale in the girl's hair was a great idea. He could find her easily in this massive complex, where he would originally be lost. He swerved through the shadows, his dragon clinging tightly to his neck as he traveled as quietly as he could. Aiello's were rumored to have spells that reveal spells, like shields that undid cloaking spells or illusionary spells. That was why he had his dragon wrapped around his neck but hidden beneath his leather jacket. There, that was the house his dragon was leading him into. It looked like it belonged to a family head, he wouldn't be surprised that was the house for the family head to reside. Raised voices sounded from behind it, curious he manipulated himself towards the side fence so he could look in on the activity.

There was an old man standing on the edge of the door-light from the house, old and crippled he steeple over his cane with the weight of the world bowing his back. Beneath his bulbous moles and thousands of age-spots, there seemed to be integrate black lines, now faded from time. There was a pond just behind the man, sweeping to his left in elegant lily-pads and trickling along curved statues. From the pool four spindles of water twirled hypnotically—then they crashed violently down on something before the old man. He couldn't quite see what the target was, but he knew the old man was growing frustrated with something. Eventually the four spindles of water became eight, then twelve, then sixteen—something broke and a cry of pain chilled his heart.

"Pathetic," the old man grouched. "How can you protect our Sarai if you can't withstand the might of sixteen whips? You're useless." The old man returned the spindles back into the pond and turned away with slow wobbly steps. "Your parents died for nothing. You're an embarrassment to the family." He waited till the old man was inside and out of sight before he dared to move forward. He tried to ignore the soft rumble from his armor, the golden lizard tightened around his neck, hissing warningly and growling angrily. He reached the small thing he had witnessed the old man beating, a small round ball of white, glittering like broken glass.

"Hello?" he called out as he gently touched it, "you're safe now." His golden armor leaped out of his jacket and curled up on the small white ball. He watched as his dragon began glowing, its inner power sparking to life and beginning the process of radiating heat. Like a tiny little sun, slowly brightening with every breath it dared to take. He wondered what was inside that ball of white, why his dragon felt so compelled to protect it, why a sense of dread squeezed at at his heart like a hundred knifes.

Tear stained amethyst looked up at him from beneath a thousand layers of diamond-glass and crystal dust.

He pushed the memories away, biting his lip to keep him centered in the fight of the here and now. Two mages collapsed in exhaustion, unused to producing a flame for so long. He retracted two swords, rolling his shoulders he sent the blades careening through the air. His armor detected the whereabouts of the attacking mages, he killed the exhausted ones first then beheaded the rest. No, the last mage ducked away, bobbing and weaving like a serpent in grass, agility evading every slash and thrust of his golden swords. He snarled furiously, sounding more and more like the animal he wore with pride. He released his magic, commanding another dozen swords into existence and battling the enemies who dared to near him. He hardly listened to the voices around him, some mages, some soldiers, but eventually they were all falling. So focused on attacking his enemies, he never noticed how he steadily got further and further away from Eirian.

"*A dragon? A female dragon?*" There was still much he had to teach the children.

"*Right age,*" He had to protect them.

"*According to the boy she was born in the time of storms.*" They were entrusted TO HIM.

"*She could be the host we've been looking for.*" After what happened when they first met, he promised—PROMISED—that no one was going to hurt them ever again.

"*A female dragon could give a boost to our forces,*" They were HIS students to guide and protect.

"*She could strengthen the army.*" He'll be damned if some greedy little islanders tried to take more than they could handle.

"*She could win us the war...*" The children were *his*.

"Lady Eirian!" the familiar voice of the princess was barely heard over the growling of his armor. He turned, watching a Trégaron soldier fall from one of the buildings, twin Tao-blades shaking in his hands, his armor batter and bruised. Then Setareh, small and pale, was standing between Eirian and the soldier; all defiance and no defense. It was in this moment he realized he had gone too far, strayed too close to the mages, left his student unprotected. Setareh, once left protected in his swords, now stood defenseless above *his student*. He turned away from the team he was aiming to kill, dashing for everything he was worth back to his student.

But he knew he'd never make it in time.

Their mission was going to fail.

"SETAREH!!" Blood sprayed across gold and white glass mockingly.

Chapter 14

The princess was unharmed, the golden swords Ziya used to protect her previously unconscious form had followed her. One blade separated from the twirling golden silk, slashing out hatefully at the one who would've killed Setareh. But it wasn't just Ziya's golden blades reacting in defense. Ryū had twisted, his currently white-washed form lengthening to cover Eirian protectively, his tail arced up from the paved road, beneath Setareh's outstretched arm and plunged through the soldier's ribs. Ziya's blade buried itself hilt-deep into the man's exposed neck, missing the beheading by the thick chainmail and neck armor. The tiny orb previously protecting Eirian slashed through two pillars, sending the teetering building further away and ending the lives of those trapped inside.

"Setareh-Kaur!" Ziya shouted as he barreled between the girls, two other young soldiers, the children screeched out in terror as his swords slashed through their bodies. He regretted it, his heart broke, his magic convulsed with the ending of their life; but it had to be done. This was war.

259

"Isha," Eirian's voice was weak, a mixture of wet grass and brittle glass. She had been hurt, seriously, without her armor there to protect her as it normally would have.

"This is why you were to remain behind!" Ziya shouted as he sent his swords out in a display of light and unshakable defiance. "You're too weak without Ryū!"

"I can," she coughed, the sound chilling and sickening to the listeners, "I can fight." Setareh continued looking about, listening only to the soldiers and mages who continued to swell around them; an awful mixture of Trégaron green and Urmër navy. She watched with growing terror as the soldier's began filling the windows, porches, roofs and balconies. Eirian tried to push herself up, tried to push past the pain, tried to show she wasn't done yet. Her arms shook and her lungs burned, forcing her elbows to give under her weight and sending her crashing into Setareh's quick arms. Ziya cursed as he attacked the supports of the buildings, trying to send mayhem to the soldiers attacking them. But the whispers continued to grow, the possibilities of a female dragon filled the air with a rising hope. The more the voices grew, the more Ziya's heart sank. Urmër has always been a poor nation but to resort to a female Duinin, the most unstable of the demon hosts, was a new level of desperation.

"No!" Setareh shouted in distress, her sapphire eyes suddenly glowing with violet lines taking on a strange shape. "Don't take her! She's not the one you seek!!" but the soldiers and mages of the island nation didn't hear her, they kept approaching like a wall of earthen-dolls; too focused to see the hopelessness of their situation. Ziya kept attacking, kept pushing them back, leaping and racing across their bodies and trying not to cringe every time he slipped on blood or tripped on corpses.

"I-Isha," Eirian coughed weakly. "What happened? Where... Where are th-the boys?"

"Barak is too trusting," Ziya answered stiffly. His gleaming claws shook with barely restrained fury, his crimson stained armor shook as if the dragon it mimicked was waking for the first time. Eirian understood what her master meant. Barak had always been easily excitable, quick to trust and quicker to defend others; he always looked at the positive of everyone he met. Regardless of who they were or what their past was like.

"Hear me soldiers of islands!" Setareh shouted desperately, thin arms trembling around Eirian. "This dragon is not the child of storms! She cannot contain the demon of water!" Eirian coughed, she could feel the eyes of the men rest on them like the weight of the souls seeking freedom of the dark abyss known as death's robes. It was a feeling of oppression, desperation, and a terrified hope. A hope too other-worldly or desperate to be expressed in words clearly.

"A female dragon can save us," A solder murmured. "She can put an end to the war, we can win it!" Like a wave of the damned, the soldiers and mages of Urmër burst forward. Ziya cursed, the max number of his blades rushing out too far; he couldn't call them back without another wave slashing down on him.

"Dius Compes!" snarling like a beast, Ziya let his claws burst into golden light. The blinding gold light took the shape of glitter shaped runes and with a great roar, Ziya sent his swirling golden runes out like whips. Armor shattered beneath the touch of the whip like runes, a devastation that sent many soldiers crumbling lifelessly to the rumble-street. Ziya never noticed how, little by little, he became a little more like the armor he wore. He snarled furiously, he slashed with golden ribbons, his swords whipped like serpentine wings, his meaty-tail thrashed like a mindless beast.

"Setareh-Kaur! Take Eirian and retreat to Maor!" Ziya ordered as he sent another building crumbling apart. "I'll hold them off here!" Setareh nodded and carefully pulled Eirian onto her back, careful not to make the younger girl's broken leg any worse; Setareh started running as fast as she could. Eirian slumped against the princess's back, struggling to keep her eyes open for any attacks. Hardly a block away from Ziya, an explosion shook the foundation of the city. The road and houses shattered into large jagged chunks, releasing hot geysers of boiling river water and sending the girls crashing into broken walls and smoldering stone.

"Eirian!" Maor screamed, appearing atop a building to her left. His black claws shined hauntingly in the heat of the flames slowly consuming the city. His usually pristine navy armor was heavily damaged, sections of scales and leather were replaced by blackened skin signature of 3rd degree burns. Setareh stumbled to her feet, her back aching from the exploding geysers that sent her crashing into the shattered road. Eirian was nearby, a piece of rebar stretching out of her right side and blood dribbling down her chin.

"Lady Eirian!" Setareh cried out, headless of Maor as she struggled through the debris for the young dragon-child. Maor used the nearby water source to allow himself travel to the main road, he double checked Eirian's pulse and sighed in relief.

"Sir Maor, Where is Barak?" Setareh asked as she placed her hands on Eirian's wound.

"He's heading towards Ziya-Isha," Maor answered as he pulled water from the river and surrounded Eirian's wound. He looked at Setareh, waiting for approval before he removed his teammate from the rebar. He watched, hypnotized, as Setareh's tattoos lit up with brilliant scarlet light; her eyes widening and filling with brilliant violet glowing seals and runes. Sigils and symbols he didn't recognize, no doubt they were from ancient times, from secret scrolls surviving the great blood wars.

Truly though, he couldn't deny the beautiful shape the ancient inscriptions took—like the great and beautiful flower of creation.

"Listen closely little star," the old man smiled warmly at her, gesturing to the prone body on the operation table between them. "To stop a bleeding like this, one must apply pressure to the wound." She did so, the corpse beneath her hands felt cold even through her gloves; a horrible shiver ran up her spine. "Good, now if this one was still living we would be able to tell the level of pain by their response to the pressure on their wound. Ordinarily we would search for fast or trouble breathing, vomiting, dizziness or unconsciousness. None of these are very good symptoms but the last one, unconsciousness, is the most dangerous symptom."

"Yes sir," she felt her stomach flip beneath her lungs, the urge to revisit breakfast came ever stronger the longer her hands touched the cold and still corpse.

"Now, this injury was occurred by a rebar, so best option would be to cut the rebar so medical personal could do immanent treatment before escorting them to the hospital." He gently touched her hands and lifted them away from the wound. "You can tell by these abrasions that instead of leaving the rebar in place, the people tried to remove the girl from the item entirely. This is what caused her death through bleeding out."

"If the rebar remained, she'd still be living?"

"Provided she didn't get infection and saw a surgeon in time, then yes." He moved back over to the wound, leaving her to clasp her hands tightly before herself in the vain hope to keep her stomach settled. "I know you only applied to my course so you could prevent such deaths, that's why I'm telling you this now."

"Thank you." she murmured, taking deep breaths of the sterile air, secretly relieved that the smell of bleach calmed her fluttering insides.

"Now, then, after removing the item her saviors should've immanently applied firm pressure directly on the injury. From there, one person should've found disinfectant, one should've found clean cloth and the other person should've cleaned the wound."

$$\Omega \ \Omega \ \Omega$$

"Sir Maor, boil some water and apply it to the wound as a disinfectant." Setareh ordered sternly, her seals and eyes glowing even brighter. She didn't wait for a response before she wrapped her hands around Eirian's shoulders, instinctively Ryū wrapped himself around the princess before wrapping his claws around Eirian's middle. Then with the strength that belied her thin and tiny stature, Setareh pulled Eirian off the rebar. Eirian woke up enough to let out a horrible scream that shuttered the air and shatter the air with ripples of white-glass magic. Ryū whimpered against the assault, barely managing to protect Setareh from the unconscious attack. Maor quickly crashed his forearm into Eirian's mouth, cringing as she sank her teeth into his arm with enough force to break through Tanith's feather-like scales.

Ω Ω Ω

"Don't you know anything about aircraft?" the green haired boy asked, turning away from the book he was previously reading. *"If you're gonna be a military pilot someday you gotta know your planes!"*

"S-s-sorry," she stuttered out, fingers twisting together as she hunched her shoulders. *"I... I'm still n-new t-to this..."* the boy scoffed and rolled his golden eyes.

"Listen here rookie: The number one airplane, the world's FASTEST manned aircraft in the ENTIRE world is the Northern X-15." He ran a hand through messy jade locks, as if trying to solve a puzzle without losing his temper. *"Now, do you know what that dose to the air around it?"*

"Uh...um...no?" her voice was a shy squeak, her body curling further in on itself as the golden-glare intensified.

"It cuts the air!" the older boy growled as he put his hands on his hips and leaned over her. *"It moves so fast that the air literally breaks around it! It creates this big perfectly round white cloud the moment it breaks the sound barrier!"* before long his anger was gone and he was gesturing wildly, a smile on his face and his golden eyes glittering like newly-made golden coins.

Ω Ω Ω

Useless, Setareh thought as Maor's amethyst eyes filled with tears, he didn't want to do what he was about to but he knew there was no other way. She watched through a thousand eyes as a fist sized ball of water began boiling and steaming before colliding with Eirian's injury. The young teen arched, her scream was stifled by Maor's feathered arm but it still ripped at their hearts. *Something else. A world of magic. Something to save her.*

Ω Ω Ω

"Now you must never forget this lesson," the man set the blades out before her, unrolling the large bolt of cloth with a flourish across the hard stone floor. *"You are training to be the best assassin this country has. So YOU have to name each one of these and tell me their specifications."*

"Bu-but... I-I've never seen them..." his fist collided with her head too fast for her to block.

"Don't give me that! You're a seer of the great Aisling family! Search a world for their names!"

"...That one with the red handle is a stainless-steal dagger with an obsidian core and edge," her voice was dispassionate and cold, hopelessness consumed her heart like a plaque in the land above her. *"It's called the Kuaizhū."*

Ω Ω Ω

Useless! She had no need for such knowledge, she needed something else, something to save a life that need not end so soon. *Focus! You can do this! You've done it before! Slow down! One vision at a time! FOCUS!* She felt a gentle hand on her shoulder, warm and familiar, a comforting weight of an old friend pressing against her back.

'Breathe Siúr,' a voice from a world too far away whispered in her ear, a gentle reminder of her power. *'All visions have a purpose. Ignore none*

and you'll find the secret you need.' The old lesson repeated in her mind, calming her racing heart and clearing the jumbled, desperate search of her spiteful power. *'Breath Siúr,'* the memory whispered, *'breath, it's okay Siúr. For us, time is not. So breathe, it's okay.'*

Ω Ω Ω

"A magic blade?" her friend folded his arms, wrapping one hand around his chin. "Hmm, typically people write about great blades made of unique metals right?"

"Yeah," she whined pathetically as she slumped against her desk. "But our short-stories are supposed to be unique right? So I don't want it to be a physical, tangible thing."

"So make it a magical blade," she glared at him for the lack of help, which made him laugh. "I mean, like… use descriptions like colors or try to relate it to something intangible but everyone can relate to it."

"Like what? Mist?"

"Or like an aura," his golden eyes danced at her. "You know if you don't figure something out, I just might steal this idea from you!"

"So says the guy who published a story already!"

He just laughed, loud and booming like claps of thunder that rumbled in her chest like blooming bonfires.

Ω Ω Ω

Oh, she felt foolish. Why she couldn't put the pieces together was a thought she wouldn't dwell on. Maor's boiling water tore through the rest of the injury, contaminated blood and fragments of metal floating in the now blackened liquid. He tossed it aside, crying profusely as he readied another orb, terrified that he might have to do it again.

"Enough," her voice was soft but he stopped, relieved that he didn't have to do it again. "Keep it clean and sterol." He quickly boiled the water before centering it over the injury, he covered both entrance and exit, not daring to send the water into the injury has he did the first time. With the weight of the world's resting on her shoulders and watching through the sight of thousands of eyes mirroring her own sapphire blue, Setareh raised her hands into the air. She concentrated—*the Kuaizhū Blade—like an Aura—cuts the air!* — A magical blade made from her aura, sharp enough to cut the air, could she do that? She remembered that first vision, a world without magic where she was learning to save lives.

"Now, then, after removing the item her saviors should've immanently applied firm pressure directly on the injury. From there, one person should've found disinfectant, one should've found clean cloth and the other person should've cleaned the wound."

Setareh examined her sleeves, she knew they were beyond repairable but they were surprisingly clean with everything she knew she's been through. Perhaps they weren't sterol enough for what she needed but that was a quick fix. After all, all Aislings saw the vision of an epidemic at some point in their first year of visions. They all knew how to clean cloth. Closing her eyes and straightening her spine, Setareh set her palms facing up, her eyes closed as she focused on that immovable pond she's always had swelling inside her body. She called it forth, feeling as if her hands were plunged into a bowl of mist, hoping she could envision the cleanliness of her own sleeves.

What is she doing? Maor breathed heavily, trying hard not to place his weight on the arm stuffed into Eirian's mouth but having difficulty with his awkward balance. He tried to focus on something else, he looked about frantically, hoping that the soldiers hadn't noticed them but knowing they were closing in.

No, he didn't see a single soldier. No silver armor and green tunics. No black swords and navy robes. The soldiers of Trégaron and Urmër were nowhere to be seen, not even their priests could be spotted from his place. The sound of shredding cloth forced him to look once more at Setareh, the feeling of regret squeezing at his heart like claws. Setareh was still sitting as she had been, eyes closed in concentration, her long sleeves floating in white light above her palms. No, the sleeves were different now, they were glowing; as if the cloth itself was a source of magic.

"What are you doing?" Maor asked, his voice sounding as dry as a brittle brush; no doubt he breathed in too much hot air from all the fires. Setareh never answered, her tattoos glowed with an awful scarlet hue, as if rivers of blood flowed form the ancient seals. The sleeves fluttered in the strange white light, as if submerged in water, but he could still hear that strange sound of tearing cloth. Finally the sleeves burst apart in a show of millions of threads, each glowing like beams of starlight.

"Orbis Rahmat Naik," Setareh's voice was low, sounding with all the conviction of a hundred women answering firmly. Maor watched as the threads converged onto Eirian, entering wound and appearing on the other side spotless, then wrapping together like glowing spider webs. Eirian didn't scream, didn't thrash, didn't move nor breath for the longest time. Maor feared she died frozen but as he stared into her wide violet eyes, he saw spots of white flutter and pulse with her magic. He knew she still lived, terror and relieve a strange storm inside his body; he wanted to cry, he wanted to hug her, he wanted to kill the men who hurt her, he wanted to question Setareh but he didn't. He slowly pulled his arm back from Eirian's mouth, smiling hesitantly as Eirian continued to take deep steady breaths.

"You should be dead," Setareh murmured as she pulled her bony hands back, staring at Eirian with all the dispassion of shapeless mask. Thick scarlet hued dots crawled up her thin arms, mimicking the same flowers and lines on her face. "In the point zero three percent of worlds that you die, this is the injury that dose it."

"She's never survived from this injury?" Maor asked, the hope slowly growing like a blooming flower, suddenly withered away in the shadow of horrified terror.

"Not with this injury," Setareh answered. "However… I broke a rule in order to ensure her survival."

"Your family will suffer," Eirian wheezed, refusing to move in the position she was placed so that Setareh could tend to her.

"Their fate was sealed with my birth," Setareh replied coolly. "Now," she turned towards Maor, eyes still closed and yet expecting a prompt answer. "Why have you not followed the refugees?"

"They're already on their way to the forest." Maor answered, pulling back and rubbing at his tender arm. "Our contact is ensuring their safe return."

"Is Ejderha with him?"

"His armor?" Maor asked, confused how Setareh seemed to know the name of their informant's dragon-armor. "Yes, she had been injured in the attack but she was awake enough to recognize my armor and confirm his affiliation to the Ancients."

"Good," Setareh bobbed her head, "eighty-three point twelve percent say he was informant for Urmër." She clicked her tongue in distaste before tilting her head to the other side curiously. "Will you help us destroy the Desert Worm's Nest now?"

"I already did," Maor bobbed his head. "I felt the explosion from the ambush. The river told me Eirian's blood had been spilt so I went to her location. I didn't find you girls there but Isha was nearby so I told him you had to be somewhere close by. I found the remaining eggs and destroyed them."

"Good," Setareh nodded again, "forty-six point eighty-three percent say their destruction failed. Thirty-seven point eight say less than ten survive. The remaining fifteen point thirty-seven percent were successful annihilations."

"I hate that word," Maor grumbled as he rose his feet, whatever else he was going to say was lost in the horrible sound of a monstrous roar. The three trembled, the earth beneath their feet rolling beneath the shockwave. The boy scrambled over the rolling road, falling away as the road broke and splintered apart, flinging him away with the grace of a doll in a hurricane. Setareh quickly ripped Ryū off her back, smashing him between herself and Eirian, pulled Eirian into her arms and clasped hold of a large broken wall; using it to ride out the waves of upheaved earth and mortar.

"Maor!" Eirian's voice cracked amongst the sound of breaking stone and heated air. There was no time to worry about her wounds or tend to the damage of her armor. She had to protect her teammates. Barak was a part of a great family, one of the five noble families of Azurlyn. Their teacher was the apprentice to their Aibek, hailing from an important but minor family. Even Eirian herself was a part of the great twelve families of Azurlyn but Maor was different. He had no one standing in his corner, no one to welcome him home, no one waiting for his return, no one to call family or friend.

"SERVAS!!" he disappeared behind upheaved earth and thrashing waters, her outstretched palm highlighting his disappearance, her white-crystalline glass never reaching him. "SERRVAAAASSSS!" Setareh ground her teeth, her grip on Eirian and their perch remained strong despite the waves of magic thrashing around them. The earth hardly had a moment to stop rolling before great towering geysers took to the sky, rupturing buildings and disbanding soldier platoons with eerie ease. Setareh straightened slightly, lifting some of her weight off Eirian, and turned to look towards the sky, wondering who was approaching this time.

"We have to retreat," Setareh hissed to Eirian as Maor leaped out of a geyser. They watched as he twisted in the air, calling the jets of water to mimic him and barrel down on the city with the fury of a raging storm. "If we do not leave then the Great Breath will consume us all!" Eirian was only mildly terrified by the realization that their charge knew what the 'Great Breath' was. She looked about in search of her teacher but only saw a towering golden scaled monster standing above the buildings. The creature was built like coils of springs sheathed in great golden swords of all sizes, huge scarlet irises glared down on the city it sat in. it was only the strange golden crescent in the bottom of the scarlet irises that told Eirian *who* that giant monster was.

Her teacher, Ziya, lost all control and became one with his armor.

"SERVAS!!" Eirian cried as she looked urgently towards Maor, only to see that a new wave of Urmër soldiers set upon him like a plaque.

"Don't forget where you are," Setareh hissed, trying to stabilize Eirian, "Do not use your true names here!"

"Get out of there!!" Eirian ignored Setareh, she tried to rise, tried to look threatening before the princess, she knew she failed. "Retreat!" Her voice cracked painfully, sounding shrill and desperate in the roars of flames and screaming geysers. Servass ignored her, choosing instead to meet with a swordsman in a dead lock of claws and sparks. Even from their distance, Eirian could see the exhaustion slowly creeping up on her teammate. He's never had to fight for so long before, all his fights have ended quickly and efficiently, seemingly never breaking a sweat, always as if he had to *prove* something.

"Servass!" Eirian shouted again, amplifying her voice with magic. "Get out of there!" Servass retreated from his clash, but didn't dare near them nor lower his claws. He remained panting heavily, his shoulders rising and falling with his labored breathing. He looked exhausted, at his wits end, desperate to protect them and desperate to win.

"SERVASS!!" Eirian screamed, her hands wrapped around her injured belly, tears streaming down her cheeks and awaking her previously unconscious armor. Ryū had been clinging to Setareh and

Eirian like a lifeline, before finally being crushed between the two females in a protective embrace.

"Lady Eirian, where was that boy born?" Eirian looked back to Setareh, eyes wide and face pale. Setareh was dirty and disheveled but the haunting glow of blood-red runes sent unpleasant shivers down her spine.

"Same as me," Eirian whispered fearfully. "Year of the first flower, in the month of rain and wind." Setareh of the Aisling family turned her disturbing glowing eyes towards Eirian; the weight of thousands of eyes settled upon her like a mountain of corpses.

"Where?" Setareh asked, desperation tinging her voice. Eirian thought about her teammate, taking all of her knowledge and combing through it slowly. Servass had been brought to them by a young man who found him after a horrible hurricane appeared in the ocean. The man and Servass were the only survivors of the freak storm that appeared during a placate summer day. No one knew of any other survivors, just that the man and Servass were the only ones to reach the forest unharmed. Because no one could trust the man they had sent him to Asharan Village, a remote village full of soldier's too scarred to live beside civilians. Servass had been raised amongst thirty-soldiers of the forest and with their recommendation he was able to enter Azurlyn's Military Academy.

"The ocean," Eirian murmured slowly, frowning in concentration. "One of the smaller southern islands." What was the name? She couldn't remember. "Between... Torca and... Malbril's Volcano," *what was its name?!*

"The sea?" Setareh murmured frightfully. "He is a child of the sea?" Eirian stilled, realizing the significance of the ocean, Servass's skill, the one freak storm, the location of his home island...

"The... the rabbit keys," Eirian murmured, her eyes widening as a distant memory shimmered to the surface but she was too frightened to remember all the details; she didn't want it to be true. Setareh grabbed her by the shoulders and propped her up, staring into her amethyst eyes as seriously as any war-veteran could.

"The Rabbit Keys? The southern islands between Malbril and Torca?" Setareh asked, voice calm and gentle but her eyes full of growing panic. "Do you mean the island Caldera?"

"Ye-yes," Eirian nodded, trying desperately to push the frightful memory away; too scared to acknowledge its importance.

"...Caldera island? Are you sure? You don't mean Malbril's Calderia?" Setareh shook Eirian, panic squeezing tightly in her chest.

"Caldera," Eirian reaffirmed sternly, "Great Island Caldera! I remember-I...I..." she couldn't say it, that day from so long ago scarred her for life. The way the crowds parted for Servass as if frightened of a monster, looking at him as if any second he would explode and slaughter them all. Treating him like, like some kind of time bomb of Armageddon! She couldn't take it, she couldn't acknowledge it. That day, that day she rushed him, wrapping her tiny arms around him because she *knew*, knew on a level of souls she couldn't explain, *that* was all he ever wanted. Her sudden disobedience earned her five lashings and a nightshade berry. After that his words to her were softer, more considerate, and gentler then the words he addressed everyone else with. Every time she got hurt, he repaid the offender twice fold. He protected her, even when her own family disowned her, he took her hand and led her to a safe place.

He was anything but a monster, he was her savior.

"Caldera..." Setareh released her and slumped back, turning wide horrified eyes toward the boy fighting to protect them. "Birthplace... of the ancients..." Eirian looked at Servass, watching in fascination as the boiling river water thrashed around him like a living shield. Servass had the talent to control water in every form it has, bending it to his will and controlling it like one could control their thoughts. The power of water came naturally to him, TOO naturally, and now she understood *why*. He was a direct decedent of the ancient ones, birthed in the home of magic, the island that all true mages were born.

"A true ancient one," Eirian murmured, understanding for the first time why he was so superior to everyone else in Azurlyn. The boy quickly flitted through projectiles, his boiling geysers acting like sharp knifes as they cut through the groups of men mercilessly. Servass was like a perfect system; he calculated every move he made, determined the right amount of pressure it took to break something or propel it. That was how he had always been and his talent of calculation showed in his brutal methods of attack.

"The child of storms," Setareh murmured breathlessly. Eirian glanced at Setareh, she had heard those words before; 'Child of storms'. That was the requirement for the Water Demon to be sealed in a human—Eirian gasped as all the dots connected in her mind.

"Sev-Maor!" Eirian cried out, barely managing to correct herself in time. "Run away! Don't fight this!"

"NO!" Servass snapped, surprising the girls staring at his stiff back. "No," he repeated in a softer tone, "I can't... I can't lose... I can't..." Eirian sniffed, she knew his past, more than he realized and more than she ever wanted to know. "I swore to protect you." His claws shattered into sapphire dust, reshaping into long thin blades signature to twin naginatas. Servass adjusted his stance, one blade high another low, all his weight on the back leg to propel him in whichever direction he needs.

"Maor," Eirian called gently, "please."

"I can't lose you too," Servass replied softly, almost too soft for Eirian to hear. Further towards the center of the city, where the source of the fire started, an earth rumbling roar of a monster was quickly followed by a towering wave of embers and sparks; consuming everything in its path. Eirian knew without a doubt that the giant wave of embers was

Barak's released form, his fury and anguish echoed in the roar of the wave that consumed the living.

Barak had lost control and released everything to his fury.

"Barak," Eirian murmured, horrified that two of her teammates had fallen to the fury of their armor. A great towering beast of muscle, fire and scarlet scales arose from the flames consuming the city. Eyes like jade and emerald shields glared out furiously at the soldiers who dared to defy its solemn reign. The golden dragon looked at its bulkier brother and gave a roar of its own, alerting the scarlet youngling that it was not alone. The soldiers of Trégaron attacked the scarlet dragon, giving all they had with their silver blades and forest-spells. The soldiers of Urmër attacked the golden dragon with every spell they knew, their soulless Angra-oar blades clashing with the golden scales like bursts of lightening and sparks.

"He's fighting to protect you Eirian." Servass said, his jaw clenched tight as he restrained himself from joining his teammate in the sea of destruction. "Take Setareh-Kaur and go. You have the power to heal your wounds. Do it and get home safely." Eirian could see the feint glow to Tanith's scales, the gentle chittering of excitement and longing; even Tanith desired to join her brothers in their display of power and defiance. Eirian knew Servass wouldn't be able to keep Tanith back forever, she was his dragon after all. Ryū squirmed in her arms, chittering like an excited child, his tiny soft-skinned head swiveling back and forth between Servass and Eirian. Eirian petted Ryū gently, heart breaking as he nuzzled her hand and chittered at her; even Ryū wanted to join his kinsmen. She forgot that dragons had that tendency. Once their elder loses control, typically the younglings will follow suit.

"Maor," Eirian called as Ryū scrambled onto her shoulders and rubbed his soft head against her jaw. Her voice shook as Setareh clasped her shoulders and gently pulled her back. "Servass, look at me." Servass's answer was to release his aura, allowing his unique power to awaken and consume his surroundings. Tanith screamed shrilly as she shattered off him, quickly merging with the water and serving to protect Servass. The soldiers scattered like flies, their voices ringing loud and clear through the sudden birth of a hurricane.

"Child of storms!" Setareh hissed the words like a curse, attempting to shield Eirian with her body. "Two paths lay before him now. Duinin or death." The water dragon of Servass and the flame dragon of Barak were soon joined by the shrilly screaming dragon of Ziya, appearing as furious sun-beams her master's aura crashed around them like the hurricane now suffocating them. Ryū whimpered and quickly wrapped himself around Eirian, making sure to spare Setareh from his scales as he fitted himself around his charge.

"Lady Eirian! What is this?!" Setareh screamed shrilly, her fear filling the air like the tormented winds before them.

"Our secret," Eirian answered, clinging as tightly as she could to the princess. "The dragon's last breath..." The technique was never practiced by their people; it was something that was taught but never approved of. It was a magical spell that destroyed their enemies but it also destroyed their existence. It was a last resort suicidal move.

Her teammates were going to die and she couldn't stop them.

Setareh seemed to understand what was happening, her glowing eyes winded and she quickly lifted Eirian onto her back. Taking in a deep breath of the tempest winds, Setareh rose onto her unsteady feet and started running as fast as her short legs could move. The awakened dragons roared together, their human counter parts safely hidden as their hearts. Once their enemies were destroyed the dragons would then cover a one mile radius in their given element; destroying everything— hosts included. Eirian couldn't stop her tears as she stared at the huge terrifying creatures representing her teammates through Ryū's eyes. The dragons seemed to look down on her, eyes a glow and chests beating with the pulsing light emitting from her teammates. To Eirian, their eyes seemed to speak to her; almost calling out to her.

'*Don't go*' the one made of embers and flames seemed to plead like Barak and his poor puppy-eyes.

'*Come back, don't leave me,*' the dragon of water and wind seemed to whisper in the sullen 'I'm not pouting' way that Servass used when he didn't get his way.

'*Join us,*' the gentle voice of her master whispered.

"Ryū," Eirian murmured, knowing it was her dragon translating the soft rumblings of the awakened dragons.

"Don't think it Lady Eirian," Setareh ordered as she ran. "They're gone, lost in their anger and fury. There is nothing left of them."

"How do you know?" Eirian whispered, feeling Ryū snuggle tighter around her body. "I have the power to heal. I can bring them back..." she felt Ryū purr all around her, approving of her simple plan.

"Indeed, when everyone turned from them, you reached for them." Setareh agreed thoughtfully. "You feel responsible for them. You who knows all their secrets, all their fears, all their hopes. You who sees the end of all fates, knows theirs best of all." Setareh slowed and Eirian belatedly noticed that they had been followed by the island soldiers. Being braced against the older teen's back made seeing a little difficult but when she pushed against the seer's shoulders, giving herself the ability to examine their enemies thoroughly, Eirian saw that nothing they did could save them. The soldiers looked worse for wear but they were determined to take them back to their sick Uraibek, who undoubtedly only had plans to use them to extend his own family tree.

"Setareh-Kaur," Eirian started but was rudely interrupted.

"No Lady Eirian, I will handle it." Setareh narrowed her glowing eyes as the circle of soldiers enclosed around them. "Your fate is too rule Azurlyn without question nor doubt. You cannot die here."

"What of the fates of my family?" Eirian questioned

"The Aillows will beco—"

"Not them and you know it!" Eirian snapped, "I feel no love for those who feel no love for me."

"...their fate is death." Setareh murmured, crouching to release her hold on Eirian. "You know that."

"...but mine is life?" Eirian questioned, observing the nearest soldier thoughtfully. Setareh took in a few breaths of air, her hair rose for a moment, touched by the cursed power of foresight.

"You've made an interesting choice." Setareh answered instead. "A new world has been born and its fate has yet to be seen. The gods will watch closely with the world you've now woven."

Chapter 15

"Then stand back," Eirian ordered, nuzzling Ryū as he purred in her ear. "noctis… sudthai mea." Ryū's wings grew to tower over the girls, his body mirroring Eirian's white-magic in a beautiful display of white light.

"Capture them now!" A magician ordered hurriedly. Beside him was a large stone box covered in seashells and mollusks, its two handles were held on by six large men; their faces red with effort. The soldiers rushed the girls, their tiered faces twisted into smirks, pleased with their apparently easy win. But Eirian's magic was still growing, Ryū was still growing, the light of their spell amplifying with every second; as if a new moon was slowly blooming into existence.

"Not a chance!" Setareh slapped her palms together, "My fate is death! No road will lead elsewhere!" The magical inscriptions covering her skin flared to life with the blinding color of ruby light. "Orbis Tha Centum Ovili!" Setareh's aura was released with so much power that the soldiers were flung back from the two girls. The magicians cursed as the stone box clattered to the ground, the dragon-Servass surged towards them with its watery mouth gaping wide. The stone box rattled, large cracks appeared along its sides, releasing white mist that produced horrendous boils on the skin of the people who once held it off the ground. The six big men screamed in pain, releasing the stone box and letting it crash against the moist soil.

"Idiots!" the previous magician shouted. He thumped his staff on the ground and a thick piece of earth quickly rose to catch the box, keeping it dry from the rising water. The water-dragon roared again, its great lean body rose the water levels of the nearby rivers; the magician cursed loudly as he dived away from the box. Eirian and Setareh gasped as an indescribable force crashed atop them, making Setareh's aura submit forcefully and retreat back to the stifling suppressant seals that painted her skin. Eirian coughed and collapsed against the muddy soil, Ryū whimpering painfully in her ears, forced to watch helplessly as the wet body of Servass's dragon swirled around them protectively.

For a dragon in its last throws of defiance, it showed remarkable intelligence.

"IFE!" a deep booming voice echoed through the air, nearly defining the girls as they struggled to remain breathing in the suffocating mist. The demon sealed inside the stone box was released like an explosion, the top shattering apart as the water Servass summoned suddenly exploded from his control and converged on the stone box. In a moment too fast for Eirian to comprehend, bright tendrils surge out of the stone box, looking like the angry tentacles of a demonic octopus. The water of Servass surrounded Eirian and Setareh but didn't touch them. Great geysers awoke to shatter the earth like colliding asteroids, shattering road and building alike. Eirian couldn't even scream before the demon was free of the box, pale tendrils whispering through the gathered waves like rising fog. The image was terrifying, like witnessing a murder or awaiting the finishing blow from the grim reaper or even seeing the very ocean swallow humanity as it tried to drown the world in sapphire waves.

"*IFEEEE*!!!" The demon roared again, his power retracted, the water surrounded him in a whirlwind of roaring spheres and his pale cloud like image began to shrink. Eirian knew she should've been looking for Setareh, knew she should've been reacting to protect the teenager, knew that she had to take Setareh away from the monster that will surely consume them hole. But Eirian couldn't move. She couldn't even bring herself to care enough to turn her eyes away from the monster changing shape right before her.

"*Ife?*" The dark cloud in the water condensed and shrank, the water shattered apart, surrounding the air with floating bubbles and time seemed to stop. all she could see were silver-blue eyes staring at her in confusion. Then the demon returned to its ghostly mist, retreating to its box of cold safety. The magician closest to them had his hands slamming together, his voice ringing out in ancient words, a multitude of five-dimensional seal arrays burst around him like fireworks. Setareh screamed as several arrows buried themselves into her body, forcing her aside as weighted robes were snuggly wrapped around Eirian.

"NO!" Setareh cried out, tears streaking down her tattooed face. Eirian screamed as she was yanked towards the stone box of the demon, gasping breathlessly as she landed on her injured side. Ryū struggled to stifle her pain, the light of her magic cursed through his every scale, slowly growing stronger with the ticking seconds. But the enchantment she wanted to perform, the spell she *knew* would save her team, would never be performed soon enough. The previous magician, a strange man with no hair and cold steal-eyes, swept forward in a flourish of navy robes and a heavy oak staff thumping angrily along the cobble stones with every step.

"Stop it!" Setareh screamed as she struggled on the ground, several Urmër soldiers pinning her down. "She's not the one you seek!" one of them began mercilessly ripping out arrow after arrow. "*AILYN*!!" the mage lifted his meaty hands, great seal-arrays the color of bloodied water took shape all around him. A complicated seven layered seal-array with three small spirits at each critical point of the outer most array.

"Demon of the sea, obey me." The mage's words were as cold as his ice-berg eyes, emotionless and determined at the same time. "Here is the child of Faerie, sacrificed for catastrophe. Seal the powers of oversea, then the storms shall sleep eternally."

"NO!" Setareh's scream was heard only by the awakened dragons, who turned away from their armies of distraction with the sound of her voice. The demon's box broke once more but this time the shattered fragments formed a line to Eirian and she watched, paralyzed, as the white fog slipped out of its restraints and slithered towards her. She could hear Setareh screaming, a commotion happening with the guards, the earth trembling, the dragons howling but her eyes were focused entirely on that white fog. She tried to resist, the rope bit into her skin, but as the white smoke neared her and her panic rose to a new level; she lashed out.

In a fit of terror she tried to kick at the floating pieces, and that was her mistake. Her leg collided with the trundles of white smoke and floating stone, her damaged armor and white smoke met. Eirian screamed in agony as the mist swirled around her limb, entering her body through the broken scales and protruding bone. Ryū screeched, a horrible sound of agonized screaming children, he shook and shuttered; trying desperately to get rid of the mist. The soldiers watched, Setareh screamed, the dragons roared, still no one was prepared for the armor to shatter apart, revealing the girl hidden inside.

Long waves of violet burst to life like feathers erupting from a pillow, torn cloth of jade and sapphire revealed caramel skin. Throwing her head back as a new scream of unequaled volume and tremendous pain, revealed her young heart-shaped face, marred by two small black dots beneath her left eye. She was a little girl, maybe twelve years old. She was a child standing helplessly in a warzone.

The soldiers of Urmër felt disgusted with themselves and for their enamines for though Urmër had little morals even they kept their children-soldiers bound to their ships; away from war and bloodshed. To the soldiers of islands, the residence of the forest held no love for their beloved children and so sent them to the front lines. This was something many soldiers could not contend and began to hate the forest-dwellers with unrivaled intensity.

"Do not falter men!" the head priest of Urmër barked, silver eyes glinting in the light of his seal-arrays. "The Demon of the sea must be sealed into the child of storms! This could not be avoided!" but he didn't like it any more than they did and it was clear on his box-shaped-face; twisted in regret and sorrow. Building up strength once more, the soldiers quickly dived into their previously assigned tasks, a few even raced forward to restrain Setareh before she got free from her restrainers. The seer screamed as she was lifted from the cold cobblestone, thrashing uncontrollably she attempted to free herself so she could reach the young girl but her restrainers were strong and easily dragged her away from the bound soon-to-be-host. The priest coughed, blood splattering his teeth as he supplied the magic required for transferring the demon from the box to the bound girl. Soon other priests stepped up and offered their magic. Their seals springing forth from their offered hands transferring their magic to the head priest, sustaining him a little longer as the sealing process quickened.

"Eirian!" Setareh screamed, tears brimming in her azure eyes. Despite all her warnings, despite her plies and hints and desperate demands, the girl did not heed her word. Now, screaming in agony, tears rolling down her pastel cheeks, Setareh felt helpless watching the child fall to the demon's touch. No, that wasn't right. Eirian's fate was to rule Azurlyn for the next one-hundred years. Eirian is not to be the host to the ocean demon. Out of the hundreds of thousands of worlds, there isn't one were Eirian is taken as the host. Servass has always been the one chosen as the host, not Eirian!

"Stop this!" Setareh screamed, struggling in the tight hold of the soldiers. "She's not the child of storms!" she couldn't stop this, they weren't listening to her. Again Eirian screamed, blood splattering her lips as the white mist wound its way up her body, burning her clothes and scorching her skin. Setareh looked about, searching for someone who could save Eirian but the only one who had a chance was lost in the 'Great Breath'.

Ω Ω Ω

No, he was restrained by four Urmër-mages, their poisonous water wrapped around him in a tight black bubble. His bloodied fists pounding against the bubble edge as tears fell from his oceanic eyes. His pleading, desperate eyes turned to her, like a thousand souls begging for freedom, and it made her choice clear as day. Bobbing her head at the boy, Setareh took a deep breath, fisted her hands, closed her eyes, and prayed the gods for forgiveness of her great sin.

Ω Ω Ω

One world. One other world were Eirian was taken instead of Servass. Setareh took a deep breath, fisted her hands, closed her eyes, and prayed to the gods for forgiveness of her great sin. Defying fate was something Aislings were forbidden from doing. The consequences followed them throughout each reincarnation, appearing worse and worse with every life until eventually their very soul has been shattered beyond repair. She felt the soldiers around her stiffen, realizing she was going to do something but unsure of what she *could* do.

"Dimitte Orbis!" With a thundering crash the guards restraining Setareh were tossed away, her myriad array of gold and silver adornments shattered into dust, her complicated black tattoos disappearing to swirl around her like weapons of great destruction. Setareh opened her eyes, revealing glowing orbs of purest white, with a snarl twisting her angelic face she moved her arms, pushing her power out to surround those threatening her. The priests cursed as Setareh's power was revealed, threatening to rip the demon out of their hold and toss it back into the river where it would surly find its way back to the ocean. The demon howled in its mystical white smoke, the trendless moving from Eirian's skin to floating on currents towards Setareh, as if drawn by her power.

"NO!" the head priest bellowed, snarling disdainfully. "Someone! KILL HER!"

"It's forbidden to kill an Aisling!" one of the soldiers cried in terror, "They're protected by the gods!"

"I don't care who she is! Kill her!" the priest bellowed.

"But sir!"

"If she succeeds the demon will return to the ocean!" the priest snarled, refocusing on manipulating the demon's power into the dragon-child. "We will lose this war if she continues any further!" The hesitant soldier trembled, his eyes franticly looking between the glowing teenager and the screaming child. "I will deal with the price!" the priest shouted, barely in time as another soldier buried his blade deep into Setareh's back, letting it protrude from her belly. Setareh screamed in agony, having never before been harmed, she had no idea how to deal with the flaring pain tearing her apart. The seals that once marred her ethereal beauty struck back at the soldier before lashing about wildly, slashing and whipping like the frantic tentacles of a dying octopus. The soldiers shouted and screamed as the buildings around them sustained crippling blows, sending down contorted chunks atop their many defenseless numbers.

"Setareh-Kaur!" a distant voice cried out, full of fear and desperation. Setareh tumbled to her knees, her hands clutching at the flesh around the blade still protruding from her belly. But her task was not yet done, pushing past her pain hazed mind, pushing past the doubling sight and the cold numbness spreading from her belling to her limbs, Setareh gave one last push of *her* magic. The priests tried to focus the demon into Eirian but Setareh's magic interfered just in the nick of time. The demon howled in pain as it was ripped away from its almost-host and back into the stone box from where it came. A glittering array of five golden swords crashed around the stone box, lifting it into the air and flinging the ancient box far away.

"Damn it all," Setareh looked up, wide-eyed, at the figure standing before Eirian. A glittering white scale, small and unnoticeable at first, glowed in the dark like a beacon of hope. "Eirian! Get up!" Servass looked worse for wear, his scales tattered and torn, revealing bloody flesh and torn cloth. He was wielding two small swords in his hands, a pair he most likely stole from a Trégaron soldier. His water surrounded him in dozens of floating orbs, some bubbling in tightly restrained orbs and others blackened with a substance he could barely control. "Eirian!" Servass shouted, his violet eyes swiveling about in growing panic. "Get up!" his voice cracked, fear distorting his usually calm gaze, "I can't protect you like this!"

"I get it," Setareh coughed wetly, drawing Servass's attention. "That's her spell... the power to-to..." *reverse the great breath...* she was falling, her body weakening, her hearing fogging over and her vision darkening. *Maisoror...where... are you?*

"Setareh-Kaur!" Servass shouted, realizing just how bad the situation truly was. He hadn't noticed Setareh's condition, believing that her inheritance would protect her.

"Grab the girl quickly!" the head-priest ordered as he braced himself on his staff but when the soldiers moved to collect the now silent dragon-child, they were confronted by a bulbous ball of water. The soldiers hesitated, a moment too long as a flash of golden light struck down before the bubble. Smoke, dust and rubble arose with the impact of light, before filtering away to reveal the creature that arrived. Standing before the glob of water was a creature more demon then human, its haunting crimson eyes glowing with righteous fury through its broken mask of a snarling serpent.

"Maor! Retreat!" Ziya ordered, half his weight braced on his glowing sword, the tip of the blade buried deep into the cobblestone road where he stood. He was panting heavily, it was clear he had taken on most of the army as he was soaked in more blood then any soldier had seen before.

"What of Barak?!" Servass asked, his voice breaking as he stooped to lift Eirian from the road. His body slumped, heavily weakened with the battle and stress of prolonged magic usage. He struggled to lift her, panting heavily he resorted to using water to lift her, wrapping her over his back and using the water like one would use straps. His teammate would remain with him, he could fight if he had to but for the most part he would be burdened with Eirian's unconscious weight.

"I'm here!" the fiery-boy shouted, a burst of spiraling sparks taking shape and ripping through a wall of guards, "Maor! Over here!" Servass let his bubble disperse as he raced towards his teammate, water propelling him towards Barak with all the eager power of a rocket. "Eirian!" Barak cried out, terror cracking his voice and twisting his round revealed cheeks, tears pricked the edges of his teal-glowing eyes. Like Ziya, Barak's mask had been torn apart, barely half of it remaining on his face.

"Go now!" Ziya bellowed, "We'll heal her soon, just go!"

"R-r-r-r-right!" Barak stuttered, hurrying to cover Servass as the boy did not stop running but had slowed so his teammate could catch up. Together to two boys hurried away, tears in their eyes as they rushed with the waves of water aiding their escape as bursts of embers scorched their enamines.

"It's just one man," the priest coughed, his body trembling as several other weakened priests struggled to keep him upright. "Kill him!" the priests stumbled away, ignoring the golden-scaled monster glaring at them.

"Right!" the soldiers of Urmër charged and Ziya snarled like a rabid beast.

"You should learn to fear, the sun's dragon!" Ziya roared as he dashed to meet his enemy, his golden edged sword sparking before splitting into two, one for each hand. He moved, his armor glinting in the firelight, bursts of gold, arcs of crimson, flashes of light, splattering of scarlet. Before long the soldiers of Urmër were backing away, staring in horror at their fallen comrades but they couldn't stare for long. The golden-dragon-man was sweeping into a protective crouch over Setareh, more blades glowing before him, his shoulders rising and falling with every labored breath he took. He was exhausted, injured, and fighting on fumes. If he didn't finish his task soon, he'll die from magic overuse.

"C-can you… stand… Sea-Setar-ree?" Ziya asked with gasping breaths, his crimson eyes glinting as he looked up at his remaining enemies. Just over the platoon's heads he could see more mages rushing, some going to the head priest and others heading towards him.

"I… I'm… sorry," Setareh whispered, a sad smile on her painted lips. "I… defied fate… now… a-a… ou-and … I …wait…" he looked down on Setareh, staring into her eyes of purest white, no azure iris or onyx pupil to be seen and yet, he could tell she was looking at him. He could feel her sorrow, her regret, her physical pain and her emotional pain.

A glint of silver had him ducking low, thrusting one arm back just barely enough to roll while his foot dislodged a sword and his magic flared to twist the blade around to remove the soldier's head. He landed on the other side of Setareh, one hand curling around the handle of the sword still in her belly before yanking it out quickly and swinging it in a protective ark over her. The two blades clashed, the soldier standing above him looking pained as he bore his weight down on him, as if he wanted to abandon the mission given to him. Ziya granted the man a mercy and had his magic pull his golden sword forward and through the soldier's body. Though the young soldier would not die of his injuries, he would be in great pain until a healing mage could arrive. Ziya tried to summon another two blades but instead he was showered in golden dust while blood rushed out his mouth with a horrible sounding hack.

"Ru-run…" Setareh coughed, "it… it's okay…" it was her fate to die, of that she was sure but the vision of her death did not contain this. She remembered the soldiers and the mages and the demon of mist but… she did not remember a fire in her belly. "Go… it's… okay… this… my-my fate…"

"Setareh-Kaur, no more riddles, arise now!" Ziya barked, using his stolen sword as a cane and holding his trembling left arm out to keep his personal blades floating threatening around them. It was too much of a struggle to keep them out like this. He felt like he was a child again, struggling to keep his golden blades in existence. He couldn't attend the academy if he couldn't produce a weapon and this was the only way he knew. He needed these blades. They were his very soul now. He didn't know how to fight without them. "My task is to protect you till we reach home! Now *on your feet!*"

"I cannot," Setareh murmured. "A seer… never sees… past…th- their death day."

"I don't care about the rules you must follow! I care about completing my task!" Ziya's voice cracked as he struggled to remain standing. The strain of magic-overuse was starting to make his dragon whimper in pain. Turning his crimson eyes down to glare on Setareh but his anger fell short as he saw what was happening to the young teenager. From the very edges of her robes, glittering white sparks slowly crawled towards Setareh's body, leaving behind not ashes for the wind but stone for the fates. He watched as it crawled up her toes and legs, to join the white sparks of her lower robes and continue towards the teen's bleeding wound.

"I've known since I was young..." Setareh's voice trailed off slowly, as if she was slowly losing the battle for consciousness. "I've known... this is... how I die..." she smiled bitterly, tears dripping from her strange white eyes, a trembling hand rose; he watched helplessly as he saw that it too was turning to stone. "I wish... I could... see... her... th-the t-true... Sea..." the sparks consumed Setareh's tear-stained face and raced ever faster across her long platinum locks. The white sparks ended and what was left behind was a young, weeping woman with a sad smile and outstretched hand reaching out to someone only she could see.

High overhead, the shimmering blue shield crumbled apart in a show of blue-fire; the mage sustaining the shield had finally died. Grinding his teeth together, Ziya swung his swords about, disabling and killing anyone who lunged once more at him. He looked about for the priests but saw that they had escaped when he was making way towards Setareh. Snarling furiously Ziya summoned his swords back to his person and forced them anew at his feet. With a burst of power that stained his mask with more blood, he took to the sky. Then he flew after his students, leaving behind the stone Setareh-Kaur and ignoring the heavy weight in his chest.

Farther away from his placement in the sky, near the edge of the river leading to the ocean, a thunderous roar echoed, followed by a towering cloud of white mist. A moment of indecision, to choose between his students that he could see on the distant hill or the towering cloud in the opposite direction, and then the rolling tower of cloud was plummeting down into a center location, disappearing before he could make a choice.

As the light of dawn kissed the horizon, the roar of a demon ebbed away into the wail of a newborn babe. In horror he realized what happened: what Urmër failed to do to his student, they succeeded with another's infant. Whoever that child was, they will never know their true home nor their true name. Turning away from the horizon and angling towards the hillside, he turned his back on the demon-host-child. He hurried to his students, landing less than gracefully on the hill as he rolled before struggling to his feet. His body ached, another wave of blood spilling past his lips as he struggled to his feet. There, Servass was just cradling Eirian, his face blank as he stared into space. Behruz saw him but his muddied face of utter misery did not bring anything happy to Ziya's heart.

"Her magic..." Behruz choked on a sob, crashing to his knees and wailing loudly. "IT'S GONE! SHE'S GONE!!" while Behruz wailed, screamed, cried hysterically; Servass remained motionless, staring lifelessly out at the distant horizon. Ziya crashed to his knees beside Servass, wrapping his arms around the young boy and biting his own lip to keep from joining Behruz. It wasn't long before Behruz was crashing into them, clutching at the three of them as if they could wake him from some horrible nightmare.

But it was reality and there was nothing they could do about it.... Eirian... was gone...

$$\Omega \ \Omega \ \Omega$$

He felt the rush, the onset of nausea and disgust that followed a tilting world. His arms weakened beneath his weight and he felt himself falling down again—except gentle hands, small and cold, caught him just in time. The gentle tiny hands propped him up, allowing him to haul into what he prayed to be a bucket. After his body was done rejecting whatever was left in his stomach, he had the feeling it wasn't much, the person holding him up began to gently set him down again. A flutter of white light shuttered into his vision, making his heartbeat drop and pain pulse in his eyes.

Please, please, I'm begging you creator, he forced his eyes open, tried to focus on the image above him, *tell me I'm dead! Please! PLEASE!* Long white hair and moon kissed skin wrapped in pale white silk and gold embroidery. *PLEASE!*

"Isha?" it hurt hearing that gentle whisper, so soft and tender, sounding with the calmness of a goddess comforting wailing children. He knew in that moment, despite all the white light surrounding him, that he was still living and the person leaning over him was not the one he wanted to see most. "Isha? Do you feel better now?"

"Don't fret little Eirwen," he chuckled, trying to smile so she wouldn't be afraid. He had to remain strong for her, her and the others.

"Don't even Isha," Eirwen's voice was firm and her gentle palm felt cold like ice. "You just barely survived that poison. You've been out for three days and your injury is still open. If you move around I won't be able to keep it disinfected so it can heal correctly."

"You do know you used the wrong sentence structure, right?" he smiled at her, ignoring the green-eyed glare with practiced ease.

"We're in Flintlyn City, they found us before Trégaron could discover our hiding place." Eirwen informed him, briskly changing the subject with frightening straightforwardness. "The boys are currently with our client. Elva says that Indiana is going to be forging swords later this evening. The boys haven't decided if they want to learn sword making or not."

"It could be a valuable skill." He chuckled and then imminently cringed with the fire blooming in his chest. He forgot about the poison in his system, breathing should be fun for the next few days. He felt his dragon shift across his skin, warm comforting silk humming with worried bubbles and the sound of distant thunder. "Good morning friend," he sighed in comfort as his dragon snuggled closer around him, like a child eagerly hugging their parent during the long night.

"I'll go get the doctor. Now that you're up there's more she can do for you." Eirwen said as she rose from his side, "You are not allowed to move, twitch, speak, or do anything magic related. Your lack of energy and slow recovery is due to magic-overuse." He looked about as carefully as he could, there, he found a pitcher of water on a nearby stand. He looked again at Eirwen as she moved to open the door, he was really thirsty so maybe he could—

"Isha, *what* did I just say?" he cringed, typically she wouldn't be able to see him twitching his fingers, he must be really out of it for him to be caught so quickly. "No magic!" she swirled around so fast her appearance turned more demonic then her usual angelic. "Or do you want to die?!" he needed to divert her attention, quickly, before her glare got imprinted on the back of his eye-lids.

"Where's your dragon?" he asked, realizing only with the spoken words the problem with her dress. "*Where* is Ryū?"

"Ryū got damaged during the fight, remember?" Eirwen asked him, her glare of warning turning into a confused frown. "Master Koujin is tending to him, don't worry. Unlike the boys my Zephaniah-spell has always been perfect." Condescension rolled off her every word and pride oozed from her aura like slime on a wall. The boys weren't necessary bad at the appearance spell but it paled in comparison to the angelic grace that Eirwen walked with. The Zephaniah spell was supposed to make them look like toxic dragon-human hybrids, somehow Eirwen made herself look like an all holy dragon-human goddess.

"I'm not sure if you can call that perfect," he grumbled to himself as she moved again to leave the room.

"Isha?" Eirwen's voice was back to being gentle and kind, like a curious child seeking answers. "Who is Eirian?" he stared at her back, wondering where she heard that name, knowing he's never said it in his student's presence. "It's just... you were crying... for someone... someone named 'Eirian'..." she glanced back at him over her tiny pale shoulder, ivory danced along her silver scales like a midnight moon on the ocean surface.

"She's dead," his answer sounded bland, his voice broken with barely restrained emotion.

"Oh"